THE NAVIGATORS

DAN ALATORRE

GREAT OAK PUBLISHING
FLORIDA

THE NAVIGATORS
2ⁿᵈ edition

© This book is licensed for your personal use only. This book may not be re-sold or given away to other people. Thank you for respecting the hard work of this author. © No part of this book may be reproduced, stored in a retrieval system or transmitted by any means without the written permission of the author. Copyright © 2018 by Dan Alatorre. All rights reserved.
This book is a work of fiction. Names, characters, places and incidents are products of the author's imagination or are used fictitiously. Any resemblance to actual events or locales or persons, living or dead, is entirely coincidental.

Edited by Allison Maruska www.AllisonMaruska.com

If you enjoy this book, please stop by and say a few kind words at Amazon! 5 stars is always appreciated, too!

PRAISE FOR THE NAVIGATORS

"Dan Alatorre brilliantly weaves an exciting story of adventure, intrigue, and love. The Navigators will keep you guessing at every turn as you travel through time and evade capture right along with the characters."
Allison Maruska, author of *The Fourth Descendant*

"I never read sci-fi, time travel type books so the fact that I liked The Navigators is a true testament to how well it was written. The Navigators was riveting indeed! It was like reading a modern-day Ray Bradbury novel but funnier and wittier with snappier dialogue - an excellent job of combining fun, snappy dialogue with deeper, more meaningful conversations. This book was a fun, exciting, insightful and touching read."
Lynn Cooper, author of *Cupcake Cutie*

"An absolutely brilliant book! Dan Alatorre will keep you glued to your seat."
Lucy Brazier, author of *Secret Diary of Portergirl*

"I loved it! Really good story line and it kept the tension throughout. I couldn't wait to see the outcome and was not disappointed."
Suzanne Bowditch, author of *Elen, A Celtic Trilogy*

"It was soooooo good. I loved the characters. The way you wrapped everything up was great."
Cindy Dorminy, author of *Tuned Into You*

"Not like any time travel novel I've ever read! You don't want to miss this one!!"
D. Lindberg, Amazon review

"5 stars - Loved it! Holy cow was this book good! Action, suspense, science and humor, this book has it all. I was up way late because I HAD to find out what was going to happen next. I really really really hope there's going to be a book 2"
Debbie, Amazon review

"It's a beautiful story!! Beautiful! There is something in here, something from the spirit of Isaak Asimov and all those days when I started reading science fiction. The writing is so clean, and you kept the magic rolling all the way."
Art Jeffries, author of *The Collector*

"Dan Alatorre grabs you in chapter one and doesn't let go until the very end. You'll be glad you spent the time to read this book."
Larry Rueschhoff, author of *Surviving the Fall*

"This story had me hooked from the start, a well thought out complex storyline that has everything. Mystery, intrigue, betrayal and romance. In addition, enough danger and excitement to sink several ships!"
Anita Dawes, author of *Scarlet Ribbons*.

"This book was a mega-surprise, and not your typical time travel story. Dan Alatorre gives us a treat, complete with great writing, memorable characters, awesome suspense, and the best part is that The Navigators is completely unpredictable. Oh, and ... it's funny, too!!! My 14-year-old daughter is going to love to get her hands on this one, highly recommended."
John Darryl Winston, author of I A Initiate

OTHER BOOKS BY DAN ALATORRE

NOVELS
Double Blind *a murder mystery*
An Angel On Her Shoulder *a paranormal mystery*
Poggibonsi *a different kind of comedy romance*

ANTHOLOGIES
Dark Visions *a horror anthology*
The Box Under The Bed *a horror anthology*

FAMILY HUMOR
Savvy Stories Series *a family humor comedy*
Savvy Stories
The TERRIBLE Two's
The Long Cutie

SHORT STORIES
The Short Years
A Quick Trip To BuyMart
Night Of The Colonoscopy: A Horror Story (sort of)
Santa Maybe
A Day For Hope

CHILDREN'S BOOKS
Laguna The Lonely Mermaid
The Adventures of Pinchy Crab and Ramon D'Escargot
The Princess and the Dolphin
The Zombunny
Zombunny 2: Night Of The Scary Creatures
Zombunny 3: Quest For Battle Space

DAN ALATORRE

CONTENTS

Acknowledgements

THE NAVIGATORS

About The Author

ACKNOWLEDGMENTS

Books this fun don't happen in a vacuum, and the list of people I need to thank is almost endless, but most of you know who you are.

Allison Maruska, my friend, editor, and writing partner, who spent countless chunks of her time reading, critiquing and editing this book to make it as good as one of hers. I think we succeeded. Thanks to Joe, Nathan and Silas, too, for doing without her while she and I went over her suggestions for hours and hours (or days). My wife Michele knows the sacrifice, guys. Thanks.

Authors CJ Andrews and Larry Rueschoff, two super helpful people who gave their valuable insights along the way. You guys are the best.

J. A. Allen is an amazing writer. Jenny did the internet show Writers Off Task With Friends with me and Allison each week, and her friendship, input and attitude are always inspiring.

My amazing beta readers, blog followers, Facebook fans, and newsletter subscribers, for providing terrific help with some of the toughest questions I came across. You guys ROCK.

CHAPTER ONE

"No way." Roger shook his head and left the kitchen. "You're all crazy."

Barry jumped up from behind his desk. "Come on. A paleontology dig at a mine in central Florida is practically like going to the beach."

"Only hotter." I set my plate on the coffee table and leaned back, folding my arms.

Melissa carried her hamburger to the kitchen. "It's smellier, too. Yuck." She leaned on the counter, taking her free hand and sweeping her long brown locks behind her ear.

Riff sat in the far chair with his elbows on his knees. Even when relaxed, his massive arms looked like they were flexing. He twirled his car keys with his thick fingers. "A mine is a beach without a personality. Digging for fossils in a big open sand pit with a hot little spillway pond in the middle." He faced me. "I'm not sure that's where I want to spend my summer."

I nodded. Barry seemed oblivious to the protests, though. He made his way toward Roger, whose long, athletic frame leaned against the wall by the window.

Barry's speech would be to the apartment walls, if necessary, but Barry would get his way. He always did. His grand oratory would end up persuading the four of us. "The mines are the best place to dig. Right, Roger?"

Roger continued to eat his burger while staring out the window.

"We all know they are." Barry smiled as he looked around the room at us. "You've got the sand and the sun and the water . . . Bring a cooler and it'll be like a picnic. We'll play some tunes . . ."

I shook my head. "The mine is *nothing* like the beach. An open pit mine like you're talking about is a massively wide hole in the ground. It can present, you know, huge amounts of paleo-treasures. We all get that. But this time of year it will be a nightmare of mud from the daily thunderstorms." I glanced round the room, eyeing each of them. "The mine workers are scared of the shifting sands. And we should be, too, if we go."

I stood and eyed Roger, who continued holding up the wall. "But . . . all that rain exposes amazing amounts of artifacts." I sighed. "It's a tremendous opportunity—if you are digging in the right place. But it's definitely not the beach." I looked over at Barry. "And it's not a picnic." Then I turned back to Roger, who had remained uncharacteristically quiet this entire time. "And there won't be any pretty girls at the mine."

"Hey." Melissa swatted me from over the counter.

"Well, you know what I mean. Pretty girls that I don't know . . . that I can ogle."

"Why, Tomàs Pequant." She turned her head in mock indignance. "You're a married man."

I shrugged. "Married, not dead."

"You little Middle Eastern snake." She wagged a finger at me, flashing her brilliant smile. "I'm going to have to keep my eye on you."

Roger chuckled, finally pushing himself away from the wall. "Go ahead, it would balance things out." He strode to the kitchen and set his plate in the sink. "Peeky can't take his eyes off *you*, Missy."

She shook her head. "I know better. Peeky's a perfect gentleman."

"Well, I don't know about *perfect*." I rested an elbow on the kitchen counter. "But . . . compared to the rest of you vermin, yes." I leaned forward to Melissa. "And my beloved home country of India is not considered part of the Middle East."

Riff sat up. "Peeky's all talk." He took a swig of his beer and set it back on the coffee table. "When we go to the beach, he can't even look at girls he doesn't know. Too shy."

I pretended to bristle. "That is respect, my friend, not shyness."

Melissa patted my shoulder. "That's my boy."

"But I'm working on it, so I can be just like Roger."

"Can we get serious?" Barry moved to the middle of the room. "Let's decide."

Maybe we already *had* decided. I know I had. What better options were there? I was certain a life-changing opportunity waited for us, buried in the middle of nowhere, if only we had the nerve to go find it. But not everyone was convinced of that quite yet.

The only graduate students in the whole paleontology department doing summer session, we were talking about going big and working one of the larger mines. Everybody else was smart enough to avoid the heat and rains and search for artifacts in the fall when it is cooler—but potentially less productive.

Barry worked his magic. Under the pretense of a cookout, he lured us in. When the burgers had been eaten and the charcoal turned to ash out on the balcony, we sat in the living room and he laid out his grand plan. It was a good one.

"We'll have the place to ourselves. The erosion from the daily afternoon rains will constantly expose a new surface layer and clues to—who knows what? Woolly mammoths and great white sharks. Maybe the largest ones ever. And they'll be all ours."

Roger got up and stormed back to the window. "I don't want anything to do with digging at a mine during summer session. Not in our heat and humidity. It's brutal here. A freaking sauna would need a drink of water if it visited at this time of year." He glanced over at Barry. "Why's this such a good idea all of a sudden? Because all these amazing finds are sitting there?"

"Yes, because they're just sitting there." Barry folded his arms over his chest and put a hand to his chin. "Until the next rain, and then they are gone again."

"Which is the next day!" Riff looked at me. "Tomàs, it's such a waste of time!"

Melissa placed her empty dish in the sink and leaned on the counter, awaiting my input. Maybe I was the deciding vote.

The bigger, older, more prestigious universities in Florida demanded that their little brother pull his weight. More than his weight, usually. Being a newer school, USF had to build its reputation in the shadow of its three larger and better known siblings, and they always grabbed the best things for themselves: prestigious grants, more desirable professors, you name it.

Those schools grew their annual budgets. Ours had to combine the paleontology department with the archaeology department to keep both alive. Whether a student hunted for plant and animal fossils or the arrowheads and clay pots from an ancient civilization, diggers were diggers to the budget analysts.

THE NAVIGATORS

Barry went back to his desk and sat down in the big chair, slowly spinning around while he waited for my answer.

They were babies, this group, even though I was not so much older. But when I told them I had a wife and child back in India, I immediately gained years of perspective in their eyes.

Still, as the newest member of the group, I sometimes felt I had to tread carefully. I had only transferred to USF the prior fall, and this group— literally, the cream of the paleontology student crop— was kind enough to take me in. They were smart and ambitious, a good pairing for an exchange student from India with French roots and big dreams who could have just as easily been an outcast.

I took a deep breath. "It will be hot."

"Yes it will!" Roger folded his arms and leaned on the wall. "Seriously hot."

"*Brutally* hot. And extremely humid." I sighed. "Out there at the mine, by noon the air will hurt with each breath you take. The sun will zap your strength before you even reach the dig site. It's a terrible burden, working like that. And risky. You lose focus."

Barry seemed to weigh each word, listening for a hint at my answer.

"It is too dangerous . . ."

"Amen, brother!" Roger roared.

" . . . to not have all five of us along."

Barry grinned. "You'll do it?"

"Yeah." I nodded. "I'm in."

Roger groaned.

"Aha!" Barry jumped up. "This calls for a toast." He grabbed Melissa's arm and swung himself around, dancing. "Do we have any champagne? No? A Coke, then."

Roger glared at me. "Why?"

I shrugged. "Why not? It seems worthwhile. Barry's right. If we wait until the fall, like everybody else, we'll be picking over the same minuscule finds. That's how the department has been doing it for years. It works—but only if you want to find fossilized camel teeth and bits of whale bone."

I turned to address the room. "If you want a *real* find, something significant, you have to do what nobody else is willing to do. Stake out the rough terrain when the rains will wash through and uncover the big stuff."

Melissa pulled her hair over her shoulder and ran her fingers through it. "How is that different from any other time we dig there?"

"It's tons different." Roger walked over. "Fewer mine personnel nearby. Weaker phone signals. Flash floods. Mud slides. Lightning . . ."

"Sounds dangerous." Riff got up from the couch.

Roger nodded. "It is."

"Very dangerous," Barry agreed.

Riff smiled. "Count me in."

Melissa rolled her eyes. "You're doing it for the wrong reasons, Riff."

Riff cocked his head and glared at her. "What's the reason you're doing it, Missy?"

"Well . . ." She lowered her gaze. "I haven't said I *am* doing it."

The room fell silent. My calculations were off. We still weren't decided. All eyes were now on Melissa. Barry was in. So was Riff. And me. Roger would protest, but he wouldn't dare let us go without him, for fear that we would actually find something substantial out there in the middle of nowhere and he'd miss out. Melissa was often the lone voice of caution and reason in this male dominated clan.

She stared down at her manicure, a temporary luxury for a paleontology student.

I knew the reason somebody like Melissa hung out with these boys, though. She had become one of them. From my short time with the group, I saw she'd earned her way in through hard work. I'd seen her be a friend, co-worker, surrogate sister, and more, but she had earned their respect by getting dirty in the field. I couldn't see this happening without her being a part of it.

She sighed. "Okay, I'm in."

"Oh, for . . ." Roger put his hand to his forehead. "What is wrong with you people?"

"We want to die rich and famous, man!" Barry lifted Melissa up in his arms and swung her around wildly. Her hair drifted into his face and he closed his eyes, inhaling. "Missy's gonna help us find a tyrannosaur!"

"Put me down, you idiot." She smacked him on the head. "I'm getting dizzy. And there weren't any tyrannosaurs in Florida."

He set her down, and they held onto each other, maybe to regain their balance. She took a breath and slid her hands down his arms, lingering for a moment. He grinned at her. Then he must have remembered where he was.

"No, no tyrannosaurs in Florida! Not until we find the first one!"

The celebration was nice, but premature. The safety protocols required a minimum of five, not four. We needed Roger. But it was not my place to ruin things, so instead of stating the fact, I asked a question. "Can we go with only four?"

The jubilant room quieted again as I focused on the scowling Roger. The most physically gifted among us and a natural athlete, he seemed unlikely to let his precious Melissa venture out there without him. They were no longer an item, but we all knew he felt that she—and the rest of us, really—wanted him along if we were going to come back safely, regardless of where we were digging. Too many things could go wrong without a full team.

So we waited for his answer.

Melissa cleared her throat. "You can say 'no,' Roger . . ."

"Can I? You morons will all get killed out there if I don't go. You know that."

Barry smiled. He held all the cards and he knew it, but he wanted a solid crew—team players who were committed.

"Aw . . ." Roger shrugged. "If I'm going to be drafted, I might as well volunteer."

Cheers went up from the rest of us. Melissa leaned in to him. "You weren't being drafted, you know."

Roger scoffed. "Wasn't I?"

Barry found an old bottle of spiced rum in the back of the pantry. He poured it judiciously for his team. Normally, I wouldn't drink, but today looked like a special day. One where the regular rules didn't apply. The start of something big. Besides, traditions and rules are meant to be broken occasionally.

"A toast!" Barry held up the bottle.

We raised our assorted plastic mugs.

"To an eventful summer." He touched his mug to the others. "One that we'll never forget."

We clinked our cups and drank, then set about making our grand plans to unearth the hidden treasures that awaited us.

CHAPTER TWO

The words "Florida Mining and Minerals, Number 32" greeted us on a worn plywood sign at the conclusion of our two-hour drive. The elderly gatekeeper waved a wobbly hand at our trucks as we entered the site, barely glancing up from his newspaper.

There were no big elevators that lowered workers into deep holes here, like the coal mines in movies. We didn't wear hard hats with little lights on top. Florida mines were immensely wide and mostly flat. The sandy soil couldn't support a deep hole without falling in on itself.

We were supposed to stay in a cluster of five for safety, but we never did. Everybody had their preferred dig partner, and we usually split up in twos or threes.

Riff and Barry would pair up, allowing Barry's methodicalness to balance with Riff's eagerness to just dig and go, dig and go. Barry had a good eye.

He often unearthed a particularly interesting specimen based on clues in the surrounding soil.

The other team would usually end up being Melissa and Roger. Even though they had broken up as a couple, the two of them remained friends and usually worked well on a dig. I suspected it might be a case of "friends with benefits" but chose to look the other way. I'm sure I wasn't the only one.

Working by myself, I usually "floated," drifting between the other groups. Our instructors frowned on floating, but we all did it on occasion.

The miners turned up hundreds of acres of dirt when they extracted the valuable phosphate from a site, but their tailings–the sand and material to be discarded–created a treasure trove for paleontology students. It's hard to see a fashion model on Miami's South Beach, or a pale, potbellied Canadian tourist walking around in a Speedo swimsuit in Sarasota, and think of a woolly mammoth strolling along right next to them. But aside from a geological tick of the clock, they'd all be side by side on the beach getting a tan.

With Melissa and Roger digging on a site over the hills on the left, and Barry and Riff scouring the slopes on the right, I could float. I worked with whichever pair I wanted, or both, or go off by myself. We were never too far from each other, anyway; always within yelling distance—plus we had safety whistles in our pockets and flares on each of the All Terrain Vehicles, as required.

I took a shovel of sand and dumped it onto my sifter. The wooden frame box with the metal screen on the bottom, a large version of a kitchen colander, only allowed particles smaller than a half inch to drop through as I shook it back and forth. I could then view anything interesting, and dump the rest out.

Dig, shake, pick through it, dump it out, and start over again. Not exactly Indiana Jones.

But none of that was really a problem.

There were many dangers on a sandy dig site in the middle of nowhere. Little or no phone reception meant we had to carry heavy two-way radios. Few, if any, mining personnel were around to offer help if something went wrong, and there were no doctors within an hour's drive. Caution was supposed to be the rule of the day, because we were essentially on our own. But since we had done these things so often enough without anything bad ever happening, we allowed ourselves to think that nothing bad ever *would* happen. Safety rules became something followed more out of politeness than caution, if they were followed at all.

Manners can go out the window on a long, hot day, too. With the sun beating down, the air gets stale. It's so stuffy that even the slightest breeze can feel like a blast of air conditioning. A moment or two in the shade of a tree—which are scarce even on the perimeter of a mining site—yields a fifteen or twenty degree drop in air temperature, a godsend.

We guzzled our water and snacked on light carbs in the stifling, unrelenting heat. By noon we would be exhausted. The temporary relief of rain only allowed the heat trapped in the sand to release, sending humid waves of steam into the air. At the mines, it was always hotter after a rain than it was before. But, propped up by the possibility of discovering the elusive "big find," we'd press on.

Everybody marked their holes with simple red wire flags when we worked on flat surfaces. Digs on the side of a hill or at the water's edge were a different matter. With enough rain–and a ton of it came every afternoon in summer—everything could slide right into the water, ruining the dig spot, or worse. If it rained overnight, the flags might not even be there the next day. The loose soil couldn't hold onto any of it.

That made the dig spots on the side of the hills and slopes the most interesting—and also the most dangerous.

The intense rains constantly uncovered new goodies among the freshly extracted, loose soil—but it could be tricky working on that kind of ground. One foothold might work just fine, but the next one might not hold at all, sending an unsuspecting digger into the water with their precious fossils bouncing alongside, lost forever on the bottom of the murky silt pond. Or the poor sap might end up buried under a few tons of sand that came loose, quietly covering everything up as the sunlight disappeared in a wave of gray mud.

Digging at the water's edge or on a slope was big time *verboten* if the miners were around, but in summer supervision was nonexistent, so our digs happened on wherever the dirt looked best.

By mid-morning, I was already beat. I slogged up to the ATV to refill my water bottle. Sweat had seeped right through my first shirt, and the fresh one

I'd changed into had almost become soaked now, too. I scanned the site to gauge everyone's progress. Barry and Riff were working a side slope near the water. It was a good strategy, digging there early in the day. In the afternoon, the sun's angle would reflect off the water and be too blinding to work, even with sunglasses. Plus, the reflected light would cut through the best SPF.

Roger, shirtless, tanned and rippled, with his red handkerchief tied around his neck, worked with Melissa, who tended to stay under her ever-present umbrella. He would start out fully clothed in the traditional khaki attire–mud colored, perfect for diggers–and end up nearly naked by the end of the day. He tanned but never burned. Melissa, on the other hand, worked through a steady stream of sunscreens, hoping to not have her chosen field let the sun age her face and hands before their time. But the heat got to her, too, and her pony tail would get tied tighter, her shorts folded shorter, and her shirt tied up in a knot in front–anything to let some air through to her skin for a little reprieve from the heat.

My spot produced some interesting teeth. Sharks, camels, horses and manatees, all lumped together now by bulldozers and backhoes after having existed separately in the dirt for thousands of years. Barry and Riff, now shirtless too, seemed particularly intrigued by their hole in the hillside. I decided to go check it out.

The sand of the slope was loose. Half walking, half sliding, I made my way over to them.

"Whaddaya got, boys?"

"Peeky, you're just in time." Barry motioned to a pile of assorted small shovels. "Grab me a seven iron, would ya?"

I picked up a hand spade. "What is it?"

"Not sure. Some sort of iron ore deposit around a big bone fragment."

Sweat dripped from Riff's forehead and streamed down his back. "It's definitely metal, whatever it is. And big. But it's blocking me from what might be a mastodon jaw."

"Really? Nice!" I tried to contain my enthusiasm. That would be a great find. Lucky, too, on the first day. "Can't you tell for sure?"

"It looks like it's upside down, and it's stuck in some clay and this metal piping," Riff huffed. He tossed the spade aside and took a few deep breaths. "It's really stuck good, and it's kicking my butt."

"What kind of metal?" I asked.

"Oh, some kind of discarded construction rebar or something," Barry said. "Or a stupid washing machine or bicycle frame that some stupid moron dumped out here in a creek bed fifty stinking years ago. Who knows."

He was exhausted from the fight and it was showing in his choice of adjectives.

"You guys need a break. Let me get you some Gatorade from the ATV."

Barry nodded. "Thanks, maharaja."

"No problem," I said. "Think about breaking for lunch, soon, too."

"No way." Riff grunted, attacking the walls of the hole he had surrounded himself with. "We need

THE NAVIGATORS

to press on, old chap. Or the rain might take this away from us this afternoon."

I smiled. "Yes, we wouldn't want you to lose your antique washing machine."

He looked up at me, closing one eye to help block the sun. "Well, I know you and Prachi have been saving up for one. This was gonna be my Christmas present to you. Or Ramadan present. Whatever you guys celebrate in India."

"Bada Din," Barry said quietly.

"What? Bada bing?"

"I live here now, so I will celebrate Christmas just like you. Besides, many people in India celebrate Christmas, *old chap*." Then I started off to get the Gatorade.

Barry sighed. "Riff-Raff, you're an idiot sometimes."

"What'd I say?"

"Tomàs, hold up." Barry trotted after me.

I stopped and turned.

"Sorry about, you know, Riff." Barry hooked a thumb at the hole. "He's an idiot sometimes. He's a buddy, though; he really doesn't mean anything by it. We're all hot, so nobody's mouths or brains are working right. He's just trying to be funny."

"I know. No harm done."

"Not everybody's been around as much as some of the rest of us." Barry blinked back a bead of sweat from his eyes. "You still thinking about moving in with us and getting out of that cramped dorm room?"

"Yeah. I'm thinking about it. We're good."

"You could Skype easier with Prachi and the rest of your family back in India. Besides, it's just gotta suck being surrounded by all those freshmen."

"It's certainly something to consider."

Barry nodded. "Well, I'd love to have ya." A smile crept across his face as he squinted in the bright sunlight. "Okay, then." He made his way back to his dig site.

As I trudged off to get some drinks for the crew, I scanned the horizon to find Melissa and Roger. They were sitting under the umbrella, a few feet from their own hole. *Maybe they know enough to take a break. Good. Can't risk a heat stroke on the first day.* If we didn't find something encouraging, nobody would want to come back tomorrow anyway.

I quietly whispered a Ganesh mantra from old India under my breath, asking that the thing Riff had been digging on would turn out to be something interesting, the kind of find I'd been dreaming of.

CHAPTER THREE

"Man, this umbrella isn't getting the job done." Roger balled up his t-shirt and dragged it across his sweaty chest. "I'm burning up!"

He had already stripped down to just his shorts and boots, with a handkerchief tied around his neck. His voice bounced off the surface of the water and sand, up the hill to where I stood at the ATV. It was almost like he was using a megaphone.

"It's better than nothing." Melissa wiped her brow with her shirt sleeve.

"Yeah, maybe . . ." Roger looked at the turquoise water of the retention pond. "That's it, I'm going for it!"

He pulled off his boots and socks.

"What you doing?"

I admired his spontaneity. I cracked open a bottle of water, but the cap slipped through my sweaty fingers and fell to the ground. I squatted to retrieve it.

Roger jumped up, yanking down his shorts and underwear. "It's okay. A lot of minerals but nothing poisonous."

"Don't go in that stuff!"

He winked. "Don't worry. Just don't swallow too much." And with that he raced toward the water.

I kneeled behind the ATV, silently chuckling at Roger's antics. Melissa stood and watched him from under the umbrella as he bounded into the retention pond with a splash.

"Oh, that is so dangerous!"

The large pool was lined with small sandy areas squeezed between huge piles of dirt, with occasional cliffs rising anywhere from a few feet high to taller than a three-story building. Melissa's umbrella rested near the dig spot at the top of one small hill and the bottom of a larger one.

Roger's head popped up. He laughed. "Oh, man, does that feel good. Whew!"

"Be careful," Melissa said. "You don't know what's in there."

"*I'm* in here." He splashed around, swimming and rolling.

I shook my head, searching for the stray bottle cap. Even on a mine site, we tried to be good guests.

"But there could have been a boulder right under the surface. Or sharp lime rocks. There's all

THE NAVIGATORS

this loose, uneven ground . . . discarded equipment."

He flipped over onto his back. "Here's a piece of discarded equipment for you."

She put her hands on her hips. "Seriously, you could have gotten hurt. You . . . you could have broken your leg just now. Then the dig is over for everybody. It was stupid."

"Okay, okay, you're right." He paddled around on his back for a moment, then stood up. "So are you coming in, or what?"

Melissa stood with her mouth hanging open.

Mine, too.

Her balancing act. I had overheard her once, on the phone, joking to one of her girlfriends that Roger was an "ex": EX-tremely good looking and EX-tremely good in bed. And in the morning, she liked him to make a hasty Ex-it.

Roger. Chiseled jaw, ripped abs, smart . . . If he hadn't decided to take a degree in paleontology, he probably would've been the whole package for some other girl. Watching her look at him, swimming gracefully in the water, probably brought back memories of a lot of good times – and probably knocked her compass off course again.

"Come on in." He moved his hands over the surface. "This is exhilarating. It's liquid air conditioning. I can feel my core temperature dropping as we speak." He fell backwards, smiling and spitting water like a fountain. "Come on in, the water's fine."

She shook her head. "I can't. Someone will see."

There it was, his opening. To Roger, every word that came out of her mouth that wasn't the word "no" was almost the word "yes." Or at least "maybe." I remained crouched behind the ATV. *If I stand up now, I'll look like . . . I don't know what.*

He moved to the shallower water, then turned away from her, standing and walking, splashing the water with his hands. "Oh, wow. It feels great in here."

I watched her stare at the water, apparently weighing his offer. He was persuasive. It was hot and a swim sounded good. I held my position behind the ATV, wiping my sweaty hands on the legs of my shorts.

She bent over to remove her boots. "Someone will *see!*"

"No one will see. They're all so caught up in their own digs, they're not even looking over here." He splashed some more. "Besides, who cares if they see?"

"I care." She sat, pulling off her socks.

"Oh, this is so great." Roger let water drip from his hands as he swirled around. "You really need to get in here." Then he fell backwards with a dramatic splash.

She hunched over and glanced towards the other dig site. So did I. He was right. No one else was even aware that they were there.

Almost no one else . . .

I swallowed hard. Melissa tugged at the button on her shorts. "I'm not getting naked."

"So don't. Leave your underwear on. It's fine."

She removed her shirt and shorts, revealing her slender, curvy physique.

Good grief. I looked away, but somehow my eyes wandered back.

Half covering herself, half running, she made her way down the slope to the water's edge, her small round butt bouncing under her white panties as she ran. She eased into the pond. "Oh, this *does* feel amazing!"

"It does, doesn't it?" Roger said. "It's awesome."

She swam over to him. "Good call. I was dying up there."

He splashed around, gazing at her through her wet clothes. The water was just cool enough to cause a reaction, and I could tell he was admiring the view.

"Stop staring at me."

Roger moved toward her. "I can't help myself. You're too beautiful to not look at."

He leaned over and kissed her on the mouth, but she quickly pushed away.

"Cut it out." She glanced toward the other dig site.

"Nobody's looking. Nobody cares. Come on." He reached over and pulled her close.

He kissed her again, and this time she didn't resist. She put her hands on his shoulders but didn't push away.

As their lips parted, she looked down. "I thought you had a girlfriend."

"We broke up."

He leaned in for another kiss, but she turned her head. "When?"

"When I saw you sweating through your blouse earlier."

"Ugh, you're disgusting, Roger." She twisted out of his arms and started back to shore.

"Oh, you love it." He laughed, splashing again.

Melissa kept moving.

"No, no, come on." He chased after her. "I'm kidding. I'm not seeing anybody. You'd know if I was." He gave her his puppy dog eyes. "You always know."

She sighed. "I always did have a soft spot for a big dumb lug like you."

A grin spread over his face. "Yeah. I know."

He pulled her close again, and this time she kissed him deeply, wrapping her arms around him. They pressed hard against each other. She slid her hand down his body. "Mmm. You are just ready for action, aren't you?"

"Come on, then."

I was embarrassed to watch, but like Barry's fabled Florida T-Rex, as long as I didn't move, they couldn't see me. And if I was discovered, what would everyone think?

She kissed him again, letting her lips linger near his. Then she pulled away. "We can't do this here."

"Why not?"

"This water is gross. I don't want to get any . . . where it shouldn't go."

"Oh, come on." Roger lowered himself down into the turquoise pond. "Everybody's done it on a dig site at one time or another. Or wanted to."

"Not me." Melissa frowned. "I haven't."

He cocked his head to one side and flashed her a brilliant grin. "You haven't done it, or you haven't wanted to do it?"

"Neither. Both." She fanned herself. "I don't know."

Roger stood and glanced around, hands on his hips, his torso basking in the sun. "Really? That's like climbing up on top of the roof of the basketball stadium—the Sun Dome. Everybody does that freshman year, like a rite of passage."

"Not me."

He nodded towards the sand. "What about there on the shore, then? Nice and soft . . ."

"Oh, yeah." She made her way back toward the water's edge. "I'll get a sun burn on my front and a rug burn on my rear from the hot sand. No thanks."

"Whoa." Roger chuckled. "Talk dirty to me, baby!"

Melissa glared at him over her shoulder. "Is that what you're into now?"

I crouched down a little, begging to not be discovered. What was happening? She hadn't exclusively ruled anything out. With a few more of his dashing smiles, and a little charm, who knows?

A rumble moved through the bottoms of my feet. I felt it more than I heard it. The surface of the whole pond shimmered in little ripples.

Behind Roger, a cloud of dust curled upwards from the other dig site.

He stared into the water around him. "What was that?"

"Landslide!" Melissa shouted.

They rushed to the shore as the unmistakable sound of an emergency whistle pierced the air.

CHAPTER FOUR

A cloud of dust covered the spot where Riff and Barry had been. It cascaded all the way down the slope. A big gray mud cloud expanded through the water, too, with waves going out in all directions.

I couldn't see Barry or Riff, just waves and splashing. I ran toward the site. Barry's head popped up for a second, then submerged again.

As I got closer, he came up again, eyes wide and mouth gaping.

"Come on!" he barked at me. Then he went under again.

I ran to the water and stopped at its edge. "What's going on?"

Barry thrashed like a madman, his head breaking the surface again. "Riff is trapped!"

Then he disappeared back under the water.

I jumped in, but the water was cloudy. I felt around – nothing but mud and sand. From the surface, Barry yelled to me.

Gasping for air, I stood. Barry's face was white.

"He's right here! Come on, I can't get him out!"

I moved to Barry. He pulled on what seemed like a ball of mud. "Right here, Peeky. Grab him! Pull!"

Plunging underneath, I felt for Riff. I found Barry's hands and grabbed what he grabbed. It was an arm.

I held the arm and surfaced for air. Barry threw himself at the sludge that had piled on top of Riff, straining to move it an inch. "Keep pulling!" He groaned, clawing frantically at the mud.

Riff wasn't budging. Barry's eyes grew wild. "Pull!" He screamed. "Come on!"

It seemed hopeless. Whenever I pulled mud from Riff, more slid into its place. Every time I tried to push the dirt in one direction, my body floated in the other direction. If I tried to stand and lift, I only sunk deeper into the sticky bottom.

But I had to keep pulling on that arm. I wasn't going to just let Riff die.

Now I understood the desperate look on Barry's face. He realized we might not get Riff out. There was no life in that arm.

Under the water, I struggled. My lungs aching, I refused to give up. My head pounded. My heartbeat thumped in my chest.

THE NAVIGATORS

I pulled on the arm, straining as hard as I could. I had no more air. Red spots dotted the blackness of my closed eyes as I neared the verge of passing out.

Then the arm lifted. It practically pulled me upward.

I broke the surface to find Roger hauling a mud-covered Riff out of the water.

Melissa helped pull Riff's pale, limp body onto the sand. "Can you hear me?" She checked him quickly. "He's not breathing!" She opened his mouth and blew air into it.

After a few quick puffs, she checked his eyes. "Come on, Riff. Breathe!"

Roger worked his way up to what remained of the dig site and grabbed the field radio to alert the nearest hospital. As I gasped for breath, I thought about my earlier warning, that the closest hospital was an hour away. They would never get here in time to help.

I watched, helpless and exhausted, as one friend tried to save the life of the other. I could do nothing else. I dropped to my hands and knees, sucking in air as fast as I could.

"Come on, Riff." Melissa continued mouth to mouth resuscitation. "Come on! Breathe!"

She exhaled into Riff's mouth again.

"Come onnnn!"

Riff jerked his head to the side and coughed, spraying water across the sand.

"Oh, there we go." Melissa rolled Riff onto his side. He coughed with force.

"Tomàs!" Roger called to me. "Peeky! Get the water!"

I ran to collect the water bottles I had dropped going to the scene. Roger shouted into the handset to Shands Hospital in Gainesville. "Student crew at Central Florida Mine 31 with an injury accident. Requesting medevac. Standing by for instructions."

Medevac. A helicopter. If Riff had sustained any serious damage, that might make the difference. Good old Roger.

"Riff." Barry leaned over him. "Look at me. Can you hear me?"

Riff's eyes rolled around for a second, before gaining focus. The color returned to his cheeks.

"You're gonna be okay, Riff." Melissa patted his shoulder.

Riff bobbed his head. Then he coughed some more, spitting up mud and pond water.

I handed him one of the water bottles and splashed some water onto his face and mouth. He took a drink. "Wh . . . wha . . ."

"Take it easy," Barry said. "Go slow."

Riff nodded. He opened his mouth again. "Why . . . is Roger undressed?"

In his hurry to help, Roger hadn't bothered to stop and put on any clothes. Nobody seemed to notice until now.

"Oops!" Barry laughed. Everybody did.

"You're welcome." Roger dropped down onto the sand, exhausted.

Melissa hovered over Riff. "How do you feel?"

He propped himself up on one elbow, thinking for a moment. "Squeezed out."

"I bet," Melissa put the water bottle back to his lips.

THE NAVIGATORS

Riff took a swallow. "Thanks."

"Riff . . ." Melissa bit her lip. "You could have internal injuries. We need to get you checked out."

"Oh, what crap. I'm fine. Let me up."

Everybody yelled, "No."

I spit a few grains of sand out of my mouth. "You were practically buried alive."

"I'm okay." Riff shook his head. "I'll be fine. Where's the machine?"

Barry sighed. "We lost it, buddy."

"What do you mean?" He lifted himself on one elbow. "We worked it free. We had it out!"

Barry glanced over at the cloudy water. "It's in there."

"I bet it is. Shoot." Riff stared at the muddy pond "We had it more than halfway dug out. I was pulling on it, and it came loose." He looked around at all of us. "Next thing I knew, I was underwater."

Roger was still laying on his back catching his breath. "You almost died, and all you care about is a stupid fossil?"

"We weren't working on a fossil." Barry ran a hand over his hair, hands on hips. "It was some sort of machine."

"Some discarded junk from the miners!" Roger waved a hand. "What's the big deal?"

I glanced at him. "It wasn't junk. It was a machine of some sort. Something . . . old. Elaborate. I only saw part of it, but it sure wasn't anything the miners left behind."

"That's not important right now." Melissa put her hands on her hips. "What's important now is figuring out if Riff is okay." She turned to him.

"You tell me. How are your legs? How are your arms? Let's go through, step-by-step. Do you have any broken bones? Are you feeling any pain?"

Riff put a hand on his side and winced, but waved her off. "Stop." He sucked in a breath and squeezed his eyes closed, groaning. "I'm fine."

"See? You probably broke a rib. And I bet you're dehydrated." Melissa wiped her brow with her sleeve. "Plus, you could still go into delayed shock."

"Oh, I was shocked all right. From seeing nature boy. What gives, Roger?"

"You're still welcome." Roger flipped him off. The radio crackled. Shands hospital asked for an update.

Barry glared at Roger. "Get rid of them." Melissa's eyes flashed at him. Barry put his hands up. "Just until we get this figured out, Missy."

"He needs to get checked out by a doctor!"

I cleared my throat. "Barry, it *is* protocol . . ."

"And he will, *after* we figure out what to say." Barry rubbed his chin. "Look, we broke safety protocols. All of us. If we take him in now, we're in deep trouble. Shands will report it back to the university and Dr. Anderson will have no choice but to suspend us all."

Melissa shifted her feet. "But . . ."

"But nothing. You know I'm right. If we go in right now, we're screwed. We're suspended. No question about it. That affects all of our scholarships. Our grants." His gaze fell on me. "Exchange student status, too. Unless . . ."

"Unless what?"

"Unless we get all our stories straight right now. Then we have a way out of this."

"I don't know." Melissa's eyes darted to the others' faces.

Barry shrugged. "I don't see any other option, do you?"

"You guys broke protocol." Roger sat up. "Digging on the side of the hill like that -"

"Not just us. What were you doing, working on your sun tan?"

Roger paused, beaten. "Okay, you're right. We broke protocols. All of us." He gestured to the radio. "What do I tell them at Shands?"

"Nothing." Barry bit at his fingernail. "Wave them off. And cover up." He pulled off his T-shirt and flung it in Roger's direction.

Laying down the big radio, Roger grabbed the shirt and tied the sleeves in a knot behind his back. It covered his front but left his butt exposed like Tarzan. He held out his arms to Barry. "There. Happy?"

"Sure. How about we eclipse that moon now?"

"Whatever." Roger stared at the radio. "And feeding Shands some flimsy line won't work. They'll know something's up."

"Tell them you overreacted." Barry's eyes widened. "Better yet, explain that you were just trying to be *extra* careful. You saw something and called it in before you knew what really happened. False alarm. Then sign off. That will buy us some time." Barry eyed Melissa. "And when they eventually follow up with USF, Riff will have already been checked out by the university doctors on campus. We'll take him in ourselves. Tonight. Shands won't have an issue."

Roger remained silent for a moment, then nodded. "Okay."

He walked off, radio to his ear, to deconstruct his emergency call to the hospital.

Melissa folded her arms and stared at the horizon.

"What about the machine?" Riff stared over at the water.

I pointed, swallowing my disappointment. "It's under the landslide. In the pond."

"Is it?" Riff got up slowly and moved to the edge of the water. It was still murky. "It can't be more than a few feet under the surface, can it?"

Barry stood up and peered past Riff. The mud cloud was now a tan colored ring in a calm, gray pool.

I craned my neck for a better view. "How big was it?"

"You guys still obsessing about me?" Roger approached from behind us.

"We were talking about your imagination," Barry called over his shoulder. Then he turned to me. "The machine is right under the surface. Isn't it, Peeky?"

I stepped into the murky water again and felt around. "It's right here." I could feel the metal piping. "Right under the surface, Roger. The find of a lifetime, maybe. But we can't get it out without a little more manpower. Are you in?"

Riff waded into the water. "*I'm* in."

THE NAVIGATORS

Roger eyed the water, rubbing his chin. "How heavy do you think it is?"

"That's the strange thing." Barry rubbed his neck. "It's big, but it's not heavy. That's why we were able to work it loose."

Riff scoffed. "That, and a small landslide."

Barry and Riff's enthusiasm was contagious. I smiled. "I'm telling you, I only saw a glimpse of it, but it's unique. It's something special. I think we should try to get it out."

I clapped Riff on the back as he stared into the water that minutes ago had nearly taken his life. "Let's get it. I'm in."

Melissa went to the water's edge and placed her hands on her hips. "Well, then, why don't we just tie an ATV to it and pull it out?"

The smile barely crossed her face before Barry sprinted up the hill towards the ATVs.

CHAPTER FIVE

We didn't have time to inspect our discovery. Riff needed to go to the hospital, and the strange machine was still covered in mud. It wouldn't offer any clues until we cleaned it.

Heavy rains made the long ride back to Tampa even longer. The skies opened up and pelted us for two solid hours and the old truck's windshield wipers grunted with each swipe across the glass. Roger could barely see the road at times.

An old tarp had worked well enough to cover the machine so we could drive off the mine site without making the gatekeeper suspicious, but the moment we got up on the highway, the wind grabbed the old scrap cloth and sailed it into the weeds. In the heavy downpour, we let it go. Nobody wanted to get soaking wet again retrieving a worn out canvas. For now, the machine sat on the trailer in the parking lot of University Community Hospital with the ATVs and everything else.

THE NAVIGATORS

We checked Riff in, then the rest of us—cold, damp and muddy—took seats in the lobby. Quiet exhaustion consumed us.

While we waited for the doctors to tell us Riff was fine—hopefully—my mind focused on the strange machine. I didn't like it sitting out in the open, but I didn't want to raise a fuss either. We had a lot to learn about it.

Barry finally broke the silence. "Let's just stash it in my apartment until we can have a good look at it."

"I don't know." Roger shook his head. "It could get stolen pretty easily out of there."

"Nobody's exactly checking for it or anything, Roger." Melissa turned to Barry. "I think that's fine. We'll have . . . unobserved access to it that way."

I gazed out the window at the waning daylight. "Technically, we should take it to the department and log it in, but I guess it's a little late in the day to do that." I didn't want anybody else finding out about the machine, either. Not until we'd all had a good long look at it first.

"Let's drive past the car wash and hose it off, and then drag it up the stairs to my place." Barry leaned in. "Park it right in the living room. It'll be safe for one night. Then we can see what we want to do with it from there."

It sounded reasonable to me.

Melissa stretched out in the chair. "I'll be there first thing in the morning."

Roger nodded. "Me, too."

"Me, three." They wanted to see what the heck it was, in the light of day. I had gotten a glimpse of it before the landslide. The elaborate appearance of it, the detail in the metal. I knew it was special.

A loud, authoritative voice interrupted our plotting. "Mister . . . Picante? Thomas?" A middle-aged black man in a long white lab coat entered the waiting area and adjusted his reading glasses. "Uh, Tom . . . Tom . . . Tomàs, maybe? Pick-ant?"

I jumped up, followed by the others. "I'm Tomàs Pequant."

He raised his eyebrows at our mud stained appearance, dropping his jaw. "You are here for . . ." He scanned the chart on his clipboard. "Richard Franklin Fellings?"

"Yes." I nodded. "How is he?"

The doctor folded his arms and took a deep breath. "Well, Mr. Fellings has had quite a shock, Mr. Pequant. Can you tell me what happened?"

I hesitated. I instantly forgot the cover story we invented at the mine.

"Uh . . ."

"He fell." Melissa saved the day. "Riff – Mr. Fellings. He . . . fell."

The doctor peered over his reading glasses at her. "Mm-hmm. Must've been quite a fall. You were there, too, miss . . ."

"Oh, I'm Melissa Mills." She extended her hand. She was ready with the "You Probably Know My Father, The Next Mayor Of Tampa" card.

The doctor shook her hand.

"And, yes, I was there." Melissa motioned to the group. "We all were."

He made a few notes on his chart. "Mm-hm. Are any of you family to Mr. Fellings?"

Melissa and Roger answered simultaneously, but she replied "No" as he answered "Yes." Barry stood silent, biting his nails.

The doctor stopped writing and peered at them again. "Take a moment. Compose yourselves. Get your stories straight."

I stared at him, shocked.

"I'm an ER doctor at a hospital situated next to a large university. I'm used to talking with twentysomethings with explanations that are borderline crap."

Melissa spoke up. "Um, well, sir, we aren't family, but . . ." She read his nametag. "We are the ones who admitted him, Dr. Harper."

"We're his friends," Roger added.

"Well, I think your friend is going to be okay." The doctor scribbled on the clipboard. "Some cracked ribs, a lot of bruises and cuts, but nothing that appears too serious. Still, I'd like to keep him for observation. Twenty-four hours, just to be safe. Can you tell me how it happened? This 'fall' of his?"

"Rock climbing, sir," Roger blurted. We all stared at him. Barry bit his nail again.

"Rock climbing . . ." Dr. Harper looked us over. We were all still covered in mud. "Rock climbing in *Florida*. On one of our many mountain ranges, I suppose." He closed his clipboard and tucked it under his arm, pulling a handkerchief from his pocket to wipe the lenses of his glasses. "Okay, here's the deal. It's been a long day for me, and seeing all this mud I'm going to assume it's been a long day for all of you, too. So your buddy Cliff is going to-"

"Riff," Roger corrected, immediately grimacing as he did. We glared at him again. The idiot couldn't control himself.

"Fine, yes. Riff. Mister Fellings, the amazing Florida rock climber." He tucked the handkerchief into a pocket and placed his glasses back on his nose. "I'll tell you what. I'm not going to ask where in the very flat state of Florida you went rock climbing. I have a small daughter at home, and there would be less fantasy in one of her unicorn stories. Besides," he hooked a thumb at Barry, "I don't want to give this one a heart attack."

The doctor narrowed his eyes. "I hope you know, despite your friend's injuries, from the looks of things you were all probably very lucky today."

"Yes, we were, Dr. Harper." I nodded. "We know that. Let me make sure you have my contact information for Riff's overnight observation. Can I get you a soda?"

"I have a migraine," the doctor grumbled as I gestured to a nearby row of vending machines. "Do you know what it's like being a doctor with a migraine?"

"Uh, no sir."

"It's embarrassing, is what it is! I'm a doctor. I'm supposed to cure migraines, not get them."

I made my way to the Coke machine. Out of the corner of my eye, I could see the hushed argument the others were having about our contrived story – and our inability to remember it.

THE NAVIGATORS

But no matter. We were free and clear. Riff would get observed for twenty-four hours, and the rest of us could go home for some much needed sleep.

After we dropped our new toy off at Barry's.

* * * * *

It only took a few minutes for Roger and Barry to haul the machine up the stairs and nestle it next to the coffee table in Barry's living room. Then we said our goodnights and everybody left.

My dorm room was a short walk from Barry's place, but Melissa insisted on driving me. Her eyes looked tired. I shifted on the seat. "Long day. You okay?"

"Yeah. I'm just sleepy."

"Me, too."

We arrived at my dorm. Melissa turned and smiled. "Want me to walk you to the door?"

"No, thanks. I got it." I was achy and didn't really want to move. I put my hand on the door handle. "Good night. See you bright and early at Barry's tomorrow."

"Okay. Goodnight." Then she leaned over. "Peeky . . ."

I glanced at her.

"Thanks for not saying anything back at the mine. About me and Roger. And the swimming . . . I'm sure you could see things from the ATVs." She let out a nervous laugh. "It was bad enough we were breaking safety protocols by going off on our own, much less for . . . you know."

I lowered my head. "A gentleman doesn't notice such things . . . or comment on them if he accidentally did notice."

She glanced downward, pursing her lips. "Thanks. You're a good friend, Tomàs Pequant."

"I try."

"If it had been anybody else, I'd have died."

I pulled the handle and popped open the car door, embarrassed. Was she using a politician's trick, pretending I'd met a standard I'd obviously failed to meet? Slyly shaming me by stressing her pride in me, and making it so that I'd rather die than fail her again?

It would be a long night alone in my dorm room to think about it.

Other graduate students wouldn't lower themselves to living in a freshman dorm, but as an exchange student, I was happy to have a place to stay at all. My family didn't have money like Barry's or Melissa's. We were middle class, but that had a different meaning in India than it did here. We didn't have a TV when I was growing up. We had a car, but if you looked down, you could see the road going by through the holes in the floor. My trip here was meant to change all that, and I sacrificed a lot to make sure that it did.

I checked the time. Once again, it was too late to Skype anyone back home. They'd be at work. I started some tea to help me relax.

What things I'd seen today from this team! How lucky I was to be a part of it. I was proud of them, how they sprang into action to save Riff. Nobody hesitated for a minute.

THE NAVIGATORS

Melissa surprised me. She really took charge. Smart, beautiful and brave, she jumped right in with the resuscitation. She probably saved his life.

A moment before, she had been soaking wet, frolicking in the water—while I shamefully hid behind the ATVs and watched. Another wave of embarrassment burned my cheeks.

Put that out of your head. She is your friend.

I readied my cup and spoon, but my thoughts returned to the mine. And Roger, running over *in flagrante delicto* to save the day. I chuckled. He showed real composure. He was a naturally gifted athlete, and his strength paid off today.

My teapot whistled for me. Meanwhile, a few blocks away, I knew Barry would still be up, studying the machine.

* * * * *

He had been fascinated with its sleek, lightweight frame, and its many knobs and gauges. But tonight, by design, Barry had the machine all to himself, and he meant to make the most of it.

He stared at it for hours, standing silently in his living room. He occasionally circled it like a shark, observing every detail, taking it all into memory, only pausing to crack open a new can of Diet Coke or to use the bathroom to get rid of the prior one. Then he was back at it, mesmerized by it, and absorbing every aspect of it as if it might suddenly disappear and never return.

Its metal surface was smooth and free of corrosion of any kind—odd, for such an old machine. The piping work that made up most of its egg-shaped frame was bronze in color but completely without rust. Its underside was mostly a simple sled, just two rails, really. There were no visible nuts or bolts, or even any obvious welds. It appeared almost polished just sitting there, after getting the dirt knocked off by yesterday's rains on the drive home.

As he looked it over, he tried to decipher its many unusual features. It seemed to have some kind of self-contained, "closed" powering system, because it had no obvious opening to insert or pour a fuel of any kind. There were countless rows of metal tubing that ran under the seat. They also appeared on the surface of the large cylinder at the sled's rear, to take something very important—or dangerous—from here to there, and back again.

It had two large levers attached on each side, and a flat panel of mysterious dials that sat in front of a lone, hard metal seat. It would fit just one lucky passenger at a time. Behind him or her rested a very large and very intimidating wheel, like a turbine fan, with a hundred rectangular blades all waiting. It was probably three feet across, but located just inches from the back of the seat. The mud from the mine had held the big fan in place, but now it moved freely at the slightest touch.

The whole rig was deceptively light. At the mine, it had been laden with dirt. Now, un-muddied, two people could easily move it.

It was either very old technology, or very advanced. There was no way to tell. Glass has been around for thousands of years. Metals, form making, fans . . . nothing new there. The tubes along the underside were small and sleek, but things like that had been around for hundreds of years.

Barry was a scholar, and not just of paleontology. The fact that the machine's innovative construction gave it a futuristic aura—but that was always the leap to make when faced with something that had never been seen before. Titanium had rarely been used as a strong, lightweight support before the 1980's. By the 90's, manufacturers used it in every golf club shaft and bike frame.

The lack of numbers or letters indicated that the designer had a universal appeal in mind. Whoever used it wouldn't need to know the builder's native language to make it work, but didn't the ancient Egyptians do the same thing with their hieroglyphics? And the Mayans? Doesn't a kids' iPad game use the same approach, letting you learn as you go, never needing an instruction manual?

The dots on the dials got larger as they moved from left to right, like the volume knob on a car radio.

There were no easy answers. Every argument for one conclusion could create an equally compelling argument in the other direction.

In the end, it didn't matter.

Using the machine might have killed its inventors or allowed them to enjoy riches and a life of comfort until they died of old age. No one could know for sure.

Sometime before the morning sun peeked over his window sill, he allowed himself to shower, finally shedding all the mud he'd acquired the day before at the mine. But the questions persisted. Multiplied.

Ancient civilizations had simple electric batteries, too, and skilled metal workers, choosing to work in soft gold to praise their kings, or to use copper chisels to carve their pyramid stones. If they had focused on something else, or if they had succeeded in creating a genius work like this, and didn't tell anyone their secret, those things would just be waiting somewhere out in the sand.

* * * * *

When Roger opened the door for Melissa and me at Barry's apartment the next morning, having arrived just minutes before us, he had just one thing to say.

"He thinks he knows what it is."

CHAPTER SIX

"Come on," I teased as we entered Barry's apartment. "We're all supposed to be out doing *paleo* stuff, not tinkering with strange machines. We should be digging up important things in the Florida mud."

"But digging up an important thing in the mud is exactly what we did." Barry beamed. "This machine is significant. I'm convinced of that." He stood next to the strange bronze-colored contraption, arms folded across his chest.

Barry followed Melissa to the kitchen and grabbed a donut as she placed the box on the counter. "You're in a good mood, Missy."

"Dad's staying ahead in the polls. Looks like smooth sailing for the next few weeks."

"Nice. Daughter of the mayor. It has a ring to it. Will we have to call you 'your highness' or the First Daughter or something?"

She blushed a little. "I don't know."

"Well," Barry turned with a flourish. "I've been inspecting our new toy all night. It's not of our period."

"What do you mean?"

"Look at it." Barry gestured at the machine. "There are no circuits or computer chips, not even vacuum tube bulbs! It has all these valves, like a steam engine, or some other sort of pressure system. It's amazing. It's either from very long ago or . . ."

I eyed the big bronze egg. "Or what?"

Barry shrugged. "I don't know. It's advanced. I've never seen anything like this."

"We're stone cutters." Roger leaned on the wall and stared at the machine. "How would we know anyway?"

Barry took a bite of his donut. "I'm telling you, I look at this thing and I know." He chewed for a moment. "That's why I had Findlay check it."

"What!" Roger jumped up. "Chris Findlay? The computer geek? What's he getting involved for?"

"Why not?" Barry shrugged. "What's to fear?"

"It's *our* discovery, Barry!" Roger's face turned red. "You—you had no right to!"

"To what?" Barry cocked his head. "To get help? To seek an opinion from somebody who might know something? A minute ago, you implied that very thing!"

Melissa waved her hand. "Slow down, boys. Barry's right. We need expert eyes on this thing. People who'd know more about machines than us. Despite what Peeky saw at the mine yesterday . . ." She glanced at me out of the corner of her eye. " . . .

of the *machine*, it's not just an old washer-dryer or bicycle built for two. But," she turned back to Barry "you should have consulted us before getting anybody else involved. It's not your toy, it's our toy."

Eyes cast downward, Barry nodded. "Point taken."

She let him stew for a moment. "So? What did Findlay say?"

He grinned. "It blew his little computer geek mind. He's never seen anything like it, either."

I forced down my excitement. "How did you even get him here to look at it? It was after midnight when we left you."

"I checked to see who might be up playing Warcraft. Those computer guys never sleep. He was online, so I called him."

"And he dropped everything in the middle of the night to rush over?"

Barry nodded, munching on his donut. "Pretty much."

"What did he think it was?"

"After checking over it with me for a few hours, Findlay and I are of the same opinion." Barry wiped some sugar from the corner of his mouth and folded his arms, leaning back on his kitchen counter.

I stared at him. "Which is?"

"Well," Barry seemed to enjoy the suspense but also appeared not quite sure how to tell us. "It appears that what we have here . . . is some sort of machine for moving through what Einstein referred to as the blanket of the time space continuum."

"Oh, for . . ." Roger ran his hand over his face. "What does that mean?"

"That means it's a time machine." Melissa gazed at the machine, her voice a whisper.

Barry nodded.

There was a long silence as we sat there, perplexed and amazed, looking at the odd, oval machine in Barry's living room.

"Geez, what crap!" Roger laughed. "You had me going there for a second!"

Melissa didn't blink. "Does it work?"

"Of course it doesn't work." Roger grabbed his head. "There's no such thing as time travel. Even Einstein argued against it. This is some grad student's attempt at stupidity, or a prank, or -"

He went on, but I could see she wasn't listening. She was completely focused on Barry and his calm lack of an answer.

Against the backdrop of Roger's protests, she asked Barry again. "Does it work?"

"Maybe." A smile tugged at Barry's lips.

That stopped Roger. "What?"

"Findlay is coming over again after class today." Barry slid a hand along the oval frame. "I spent all night going over this thing, putting a reason behind every piece of technology I could see in front of me. Why *these* gauges, why *that* many knobs." He circled the machine. "The pieces started to come together in a strange pattern that I couldn't recognize. Like the four blind monks who each felt a different part of the elephant, you know?" He sat down on the edge of his desk. "I needed somebody to look at the pieces and tell me what it said to them, in their area of expertise. So I started with Findlay."

I didn't understand. "A computer science whiz?"

"Findlay's a computer engineer. He builds the things that drive the computers. I started with him, intending to go right down the line: computer science, engineering, physics, mathematics. But I got lucky. He and I started asking the same questions about what we were seeing, and after a while, there were only so many possible answers."

Melissa stood and went over to the machine, placing her hand on its bronze skin.

Barry drummed his fingers on his thighs. "It's really an amazing discovery."

"Were you both smoking crack?" Roger walked up to Barry. "A time machine? Even if it does turn out to be real, the computer geeks will steal the whole thing out from under us. Their department has all the funding, too. They'll make it their property and we'll never see it again!"

Melissa appeared unconcerned. Her eyes never left Barry's. "Do *you* think it will work?"

The smile crept back onto his face. "I do. So does Findlay."

"Then you're both crazy, Barry." Roger paced around the room. "Or high."

Melissa waved at him. "Roger, shut up for a second. Barry, give me your word: if we make this thing work, even with Findlay's help, we keep it in our department. Paleontology."

Barry folded his arms and eyed the machine. "I think Findlay's too eager to understand the technology to consider upsetting us and never seeing it again. He'll do whatever we ask."

She nodded slowly. "Okay, then." Melissa turned and dangled her car keys. "I've gotta get to class. We'll look at it tonight – all of us – and make a decision."

"About what?" I asked.

Barry answered for her, grinning. "About whether to go public with our findings, of course."

CHAPTER SEVEN

"Go public!" Roger's face turned red. He pointed at the TV in the corner. "You mean, go embarrass ourselves on television and in the press?"

Melissa tucked a strand of hair behind her ear. "It's a good idea. It would mean headlines. National attention. On *our* program for a change. That could equate to some big funding."

"Fame! Fortune!" Barry laughed.

"I don't know about this." Roger ran his hands through his hair and stared out the window. "Maybe."

"Publicity." Barry leaned on the couch. "What's wrong with that?"

I couldn't tell if Barry was playing with us or not. I certainly wasn't going to ask. Keeping my mouth shut and my excitement under control was my best bet.

Roger walked over to him. "What's wrong with publicity? Plenty. I know how your mind works. If you thought you could generate some buzz with a stunt, you'd do it. But something like this, so crazy sounding . . . it could blow up in our faces, man. Then we're embarrassed on the national stage and lose the little funding we have."

"Unless it's a real time machine that actually works," Melissa said. "Then, it's a different story."

Roger's mouth hung open.

"Which is why we need to test it first." Barry glanced around at us. "And to keep Findlay in the circle."

"Geez." Roger shook his head. "You mean keep him quiet."

"Exactly."

The scowl on Roger's face grew larger. "He never should have been in the circle in the first place. That guy Findlay is a wild card."

"Yeah." Melissa sighed. "Why didn't you call someone like Bill Cicero? Bill's discreet."

Barry's mouth opened but he didn't speak. He glanced at Melissa. "Cicero?" Then he recouped, shaking it off. "He's . . . not taking classes this summer."

"Then he's just back home in Miami." Roger threw his hands up. "That's a three-hour drive. He would've come over here for something like this."

Barry glared at him. "I made the decision."

"It wasn't your call to make!"

"Why not?" Barry said. "It's my discovery."

"What!" Roger's eyes widened. "We were all there!"

"Were we?" Barry narrowed his eyes. "I found it. I'm the one who studied the topography and

THE NAVIGATORS

determined the dig site. Riff helped me dig it up. What did you do, Roger? I mean, besides try to get with your ex?"

Roger would have punched him, but Melissa beat him to it. She slapped Barry hard across the face. It sounded like a gunshot. Barry was caught off guard and fell back on his desk before he could catch himself.

It practically made *my* ears ring. I stepped between them. "Okay, okay, that's enough."

She stood, teeth gritted, cheeks turning red. I put my hand on her arm. "Melissa..."

Still glaring at Barry, she pulled her arm away and turned in a huff, storming off toward the kitchen.

Roger lowered his voice. "Barry, you had no right."

"I did what I did." Barry rubbed his cheek. "I was right. We never would have gotten anywhere without Findlay. You know that." He glanced around. "But . . . I should have told you."

I leaned forward to catch his eye. "No, you should have *asked* us."

He nodded. "Okay. I should have asked. I got excited. It won't happen again." His eyes went to Melissa. "And I'm sorry about . . . my comment. It was rude. And stupid."

Melissa heaved a heavy sigh, righting herself. "Okay. We're decided. From now on, it's a group decision on everything. We vote before we do anything." She came into the living room and held out her hand to Barry. "Agreed?"

He took it and she helped him up. "Agreed."

"Agreed," I said. Time to reset the course and focus on the priorities.

"Fine." Roger paced around the living room. "But you're all forgetting something. We're allowed to take rocks from the mine. Bones. Little crap like that. A machine like this is definitely out of bounds. The university will lay claim to it."

"Plus, anything *over* a certain size or value, the state gets first claim on." I sighed. "Not the school."

"Or the university grabs all the good stuff first and it mysteriously disappears." Roger resumed his pacing. "The rumor was that Dr. Anderson used to back door any significant finds to the bigger state universities. Now he's the Dean of the whole department." He glanced at Barry. "Remember freshman year? Lance Montague found that big mastodon skull down in New River and it practically never saw the light of day. Anderson swooped in and made some kind of a big thing out of it, and the next thing you know, it's off to a major corporation." He looked around at us. "The paleontology department sure didn't get any credit."

"Which is why we have to keep it secret." Barry sat back down on the edge of his desk. "We study it, check it all out, and then go public once we know everything there is to know. Then they can't take it away from us. And there'll be too much publicity to cut us out."

Roger folded his arms. "Boy, you have it all figured out, don't you Barry?"

"I don't have anything figured out. I'm figuring it out right now, with you guys."

"Except for calling Findlay in." Roger leaned back on the window sill.

"Oh, will you let it drop!" Melissa shouted. "Findlay was a good call. He's a jerk, but he's a smart jerk. In fact, I can't believe he went to class instead of staying here with you and working on it now. What gives?"

Barry smirked. "He would have stayed, but he's administering an exam to a bunch of undergrads. Couldn't get out of it no matter how hard he tried, the poor schmuck."

"You played him." Roger shook his head. "You brought him in when he'd have just enough time to help you, but without enough time to figure things all the way out. You baited the hook and played him, just like you're playing all of us now."

"Who's playing you?" Barry got up. "Come on!"

Roger narrowed his eyes. "You kept the machine here, away from us. You studied it all night, and then you got Findlay involved. So are you guys partners now?"

Melissa stepped in. "You didn't, did you Barry? You're smarter than that, right?"

He looked away.

"Oh, man." Roger jumped up. "You did partner with him! What did you promise him?"

The room fell silent as we waited for an answer. Barry dropped his gaze to the floor. Wincing like it hurt to get the word out, he gave his reply. "Half."

"Half!" A vein on Roger's forehead made itself visible. "Half of what?"

"Half of the technology rights." Barry rubbed his neck. "Whether we can make it work or not."

"Half! And the rest of us share the other half?"

"That's right."

"Oh, you jerk!" Roger was steaming. He pounded his chest with his finger. "You had no right to give my share of anything."

"Yes, I did," Barry said. His voice was now more even, less emotional. "It was my find. My dig site. I'm the only reason any of us were even there!"

Melissa's cell phone rang in her pocket. She checked it. "Oh, man. It's Dean Anderson."

"So what? He calls me sometimes for updates and stuff." Barry shrugged. "Answer it."

"Wait." Roger eyed her. "He doesn't call for no reason. What could he want?"

It rang again.

I was worried. "From what Roger said, if he finds out about the machine, it's game over." I glanced at Melissa. "We'll never see it again. We're finished before we even begin."

Melissa held the phone with both hands as it rung a third time. "What do I do?"

"See what he wants," Barry said, going to her. "But don't tell him anything."

Roger joined the huddle. "Try to sound relaxed."

Melissa took a deep breath and pressed a button on her phone. "Good morning, Dr. Anderson." She held the phone away from her ear and pressed the speaker button.

"Melissa, I'm glad I caught you. Just heard the good news about your dad. It's all over the radio.

We're all pulling for him, the whole university staff."

"Yes, sir. He knows it, and he appreciates it, too—your support."

Noise permeated his words, like he called from a car. "Good, good. Well, anyway, I just got off the phone with an administrator from Shands hospital in Gainesville. Seems they got a radio distress call from your crew yesterday. Something about an accident?"

Barry nodded and gave a thumbs up, mouthing the words "Say 'yes.'"

"Uh, that's right, sir," Melissa said. "We did radio Shands from the mine site yesterday."

Roger put a hand to his forehead. Like calling 911, after he radioed Shands hospital about a possible drowning accident and then never showed up, Shands followed up to see what happened.

"I see." Dean Anderson's voice crackled over the cell phone. "Is everything okay? Nobody hurt, I hope."

She looked at Barry, who shook his head.

"No. Nobody hurt."

Anderson sounded like he was getting a little agitated. "Would it be asking too much for you to tell me what happened?"

"Not at all, sir. It was really nothing. Riff slipped on a hillside and went into the water, the retention pond. Roger called it in as a precaution."

"Precaution! Seems a little extreme, doesn't it? For a slip and fall?"

"Well, yes, in hindsight." Melissa appeared to be getting her balance. "But with the safety protocols and all, we thought it best to call it in. And you know Roger."

"Yes, I see . . ."

It was a good bluff. Since we ultimately checked Riff into University Community Hospital by the campus, it would seem to add up.

"Riff said he felt fine, but after we were halfway home, we could see he'd gotten pretty bruised up, so we took him to University Community. They admitted him."

"Really?"

"Oh, for observation, they said. The doctor thinks Riff is probably fine. Just a little banged up, that's all, and they want to be safe."

"Okay." Anderson cleared his throat. "Well, as you know there is some paperwork we need to fill out for that sort of thing . . ."

She nodded. "Oh, yes sir. In fact, I'm on my way over to see you. I wanted to get you up to speed and fill out the report."

"Don't rush. I did an overnight fundraising junket in Tallahassee and I'm still on my way back. Just be sure to get the reports filed in a day or so. And make sure to check in on Mr. Fellings."

"I will." Melissa hung up and exhaled, rubbing her forehead. "I think he bought it."

Barry raised his eyebrows. "Well played, madam. Maybe there are two politicians in your family."

Melissa bowed. "I was raised by a lawyer, so I know how to lie. Anyway, that solves one problem. Dean Anderson's out of town for a while."

"So he can't swoop in and take the machine," I said. "For a while, anyway. That's good."

Roger leaned forward and peered at me. "He can't swoop in at all if he doesn't know about it."

"Right, right." I nodded. "Sounds like everything's all set. Except . . ."

Scowling, Roger glared at Barry again. "Except for that wild card, Findlay."

"Well," Barry checked the clock on the wall. "That wild card should be here any minute."

CHAPTER EIGHT

"What would you do if you could go back in time, to any place, any era? Where would you go? Who would you see?"

Tempers had run hot. I put my question out there, then got up and put a pot on the stove for tea. It would give us some time to cool down while we waited for Findlay. And we needed to cool down.

They had all taken various seats around the machine.

"A time machine." Melissa gazed up at the ceiling. "It's so crazy."

Barry leaned forward. "Why?"

"Well, prior to yesterday, did you even think time travel was possible?"

"Of course it's possible," said Roger. "How do you think Bill Gates knew to create Microsoft?"

"I think we have to be careful." Barry rubbed his chin. "If you go back in time and cause an interruption of what we know happened, like if you were to kill someone like Napoleon or Hitler, you set in motion a chain of events that causes unpredictability." He glanced at Roger. "You know? Like if you went back in time and accidentally killed your own grandfather before the birth of your father, then you would never have been born."

Roger smiled. "Okay, so we don't kill our grandfathers. I think we can all agree on that."

"You're missing the point." Barry stood. "Killing somebody would be a large event. But the ripple effect might be the same for minor events."

Melissa propped herself up on one elbow. "Meaning?"

"Meaning, we can't interact at all. That's an absolute. Not until we know a lot more." Barry walked around the couch, appearing lost in thought. "We need to be observers. Just because you don't think you changed the outcome of a situation, you can't say for sure. You won't know what turns out to be a major issue later." He chuckled. "If the gun misfires on the guy who assassinated Archduke Ferdinand, you don't get World War I, and therefore you don't get World War II."

Roger leaned back into the couch. "Maybe you get something much worse. The Nazis might have had time to invent the nuclear bomb before they started their conquest of Europe."

"Right." Barry nodded. "Things end up much worse. A world of slavery under Nazi rule."

I sighed. "You guys are always so cheery in the morning."

"So," Barry turned back to the group. "No interaction. Observation only."

"I'd still like to kill Hitler," Roger said.

Barry shifted course. "Okay, but you *can't*. I'm not having my grandfather not meet my grandmother and me not exist all because you have hero issues. I have a date Friday. You're not messing that up."

A chuckle went up from the group.

"It's complicated." Melissa played with her hair, brushing the ends over her lips and chin. "I mean, your big date aside, of course. Why do we have to assume things would turn out badly?"

I threw in my two cents. "It could be like a faulty loop formula on a computer."

"Maybe," Barry nodded. "Only time probably won't just freeze things up until we figure out the correct formula inputs. Instead, we just get a wacky outcome later, something that none of us could have predicted."

Roger folded his arms. "It could be benign."

"Or it could be tragic."

"I gotta tell you, that seems a little dramatic, Barry." Roger stretched his large frame before going into the kitchen. "Why does everything have to turn to crap just because we make a simple mistake like bumping into our mother?"

"Or accidentally bumping off our own grandfather?" I didn't want tempers flaring back up.

Barry looked at Roger. "It doesn't. It might be completely benign and safe." He rubbed his chin again. "But, since we can't predict that with any certainty, it makes more sense to proceed with caution and not interact."

"Okay, okay, I get it." Roger opened the fridge and pulled out a soda. "Hitler gets to live."

"And Barry gets his big date on Friday," I said. "Everybody's happy."

An air of unresolved questions hung in the air. "So, what would you do?" I moved back to the living room and observed my teammates as they stared at the large metal oval.

"What do you mean?" Melissa sat up and tucked a leg under herself.

I shrugged. "Money, right? With a time machine you could go back in time and buy a bunch of stocks and bonds. Ones that you know would do well. You could make millions."

"I don't know . . ." Melissa took a deep breath. "If this thing can do what Barry thinks it can do, it could be really important." She glanced around at the rest of us. "What about doing something significant with it? Something that might be meaningful to the whole world, like witnessing the birth of Christ? The beginning of a religion . . ."

"That's not bad." Roger moved to a chair. "For Christianity, you'd have to go at the end, though, you know? At the crucifixion. To see the religion begin."

Melissa spoke quietly, apparently taken by what she'd just said. "You could meet Jesus. Ask Him why God let something terrible happen..."

"The main element of Christian religions is the resurrection of Christ a couple of days after the crucifixion." Barry paced around the room. "The crucifixion is mostly just how they killed him."

Melissa pushed a stray lock of hair behind her ear, coming back to the larger conversation. "I don't think I'd want to see anything so brutal."

"That's for sure." Barry circled the machine. "The Romans, they didn't mess around. That's some ugly stuff, the way they treated people. But it might be the only way to know. That, or one of the miracles."

"Caesar." Roger took a sip of his soda. He leaned against the counter and eyed the machine. "What about the death of Julius Caesar? That was pretty historically significant."

"You could go play detective and see who really killed him," I said.

Roger chuckled. "Although, that was a pretty brutal ending, too."

"What about the start of time?" Barry squatted in front of the machine and glanced up at us. "Go back to day one, minute one, second one."

"What would the date of that be?" Roger asked. "Zero, zero, zero?"

"Although, you'd have to be quick." Barry chuckled as he ran his fingers along the bronze frame. "Or kaboom - *you'd* be a zero zero zero." He grinned, not taking his eyes off the machine. "There's something to be said for Tomàs' idea. Figure out the best stocks, buy them, and make some money. But we can't interact."

Roger took another gulp of his soda. "Well . . . you get some money, go back and buy a bunch of cheap stocks that you know become valuable, come

THE NAVIGATORS

back and sell them for a pile of cash, and then go back and do it all over again. It wouldn't take more than a couple of trips to be rolling in it."

"Where would you," Barry peered up at him, "get the money for the original investment?"

Roger shrugged. "Dude, to make millions? I'd sell everything I own."

"It's gonna take more than a couple of trips to get rich, then." Barry chuckled. "If you sell everything you own, you'll only be going back in time with, like, thirty bucks."

We all laughed, even Roger. It was a good sign. Tempers had cooled.

"Okay, so maybe I'd have to make a few more trips than you, Barry. That's fine. I'll make a trip a day for a month, okay? Even if I only start with thirty bucks, if I double it every trip, within three weeks I'd be a millionaire."

Barry sighed. "I guess you would at that. Seems kind of easy." He knocked a few remaining pieces of dried mud off the machine. "I wonder how many trips you can take before it runs out of gas?"

"Easy? I don't think so," I said. "You have to take some currency that they used back then. You can't show up in 1929 with dollar bills from now!"

"Yeah, good point." Barry glanced at Roger. "Freaking counterfeiter."

Roger shrugged. "Guess I'll be investing in gold, then. Like one of those guys on TV."

"Gold bullion." Barry sat back down at his desk. "Can't use gold coins that are stamped with a modern year, either."

"Well, whatever they said on them, gold is gold. It could have Mickey Mouse on it or the playmate of the month, anybody who knows it's real gold would take it, hands down."

"It's tricky." I went back to check the teapot. "There's a lot to think about."

"What about you, Peeky?" Melissa asked. "Where would you go?"

"Oh, I don't know . . ."

"Oh, come on." She twisted around to face me and put her arm over the back of the couch, resting her chin on it. Her big eyes looked up at me. "Don't tell me you haven't thought about it. It's almost all I've thought about since Barry told us what it was."

Sliding my hands into my pockets, I emerged from the kitchen to lean against one of the bar stools. I studied the floor for a moment. "I think it might be nice to go back in time, and . . ." I was surprised at how hard the words were to say out loud. "If my four-year-old daughter could meet her grandmother, back when she was alive. Back when she was young and healthy and full of life. Before the illnesses started dragging her down . . ." With each word, my voice became more strained. I glanced around at the others, reading their faces. All eyes were glued on me. "I have a picture of her on the boardwalk at the seaside. Back home, you know? It would be nice to see her like that again, so young and beautiful . . ." I swallowed hard. "That would be nice. I'd like my daughter to have met her then. To have had the chance to know her."

The group was silent. The clock steadily ticked on the wall, making the only noise in the room.

"Oh, Peeky." Melissa blinked back a tear.

"It's okay." I shrugged. "Life just . . . had other plans."

Barry pursed his lips. "Sounds like it would be a nice trip, Peeky."

I took a deep breath and glanced out the window at a moving truck that ambled along in front of apartment buildings and their green landscaping, so lush and perfect. Sometimes nothing here felt like home.

"Who's first?" Roger asked.

Melissa eyed him. "Hmm?"

"Which one of us would get to take the first ride in our little time machine here?"

Barry sat up. "Me."

"You?" Roger asked. "Why you?"

"Why not me?"

"Oh, I can think of a lot of reasons 'why not you.' For one thing, you let Findlay in on it. That alone probably rules you out just on general principle."

Barry leaned back in his desk chair and folded his hands in his lap. "I'm sure you had someone else in mind. Huh? Like yourself, maybe?"

"Well, if you insist." Roger stretched, patting his belly. "Besides, with my plan, we could at least finally have some funding for the department."

"After you socked away a million or two for yourself first." Melissa leaned forward. "Right, Roger?"

"Oh, of course."

"Yeah, well, I think the person with the best idea should go first," she said.

Barry drummed his thighs with his hands. "I wonder who you think has the best idea."

"Hey," Melissa laughed. "My idea was better than anything you guys came up with." Then, realizing what she had just said, she peered at me. "Peeky, I didn't mean . . ."

I waved her off. "I know."

"She meant us, Peeky," Roger said.

"We'll draw straws."

Barry rocked forward in his chair. "What?"

"To see who goes first," I said. "We just draw straws. It's more fair."

The others probably liked the idea of using persuasive arguments to plead their cases. They also knew better than to think that anyone would be talked out of a chance at taking the first trip.

The teapot whistled.

"That's the end of round one." Barry joined me as I headed into the kitchen.

"It *is* more fair," I whispered, reaching for some soda straws he had in a jar. They had accumulated just like the dozen or so ketchup packets in the fridge: too many late nights at the lab with a fast food dinner on the way home. I arranged the straws on the counter. "Why do you even have these? You never use straws."

"They throw them in the bag." Barry shrugged. "Seems wasteful to just throw them out. So I throw 'em in that jar."

"Where nobody uses them."

"*You're* about to use them."

I pulled a pair of scissors from the drawer and picked a few straws up, trimming one enough to make sure it was shorter than the others – and letting Barry see which color it was: red. Couldn't hurt to give an advantage to the right person.

"At least it will appear more fair," I whispered. "Go on back out there."

Barry nodded and went to join the others in the middle of the living room. After a moment, I collected the straws and put down the scissors. "Time to draw."

Melissa turned. "What about Riff?"

I walked to the couch. "You all draw for yourselves." I held up a fist of straws, the ends hidden. "Then, Melissa, you draw for Riff. Whatever straw is left will go to me."

"Okay." She and the others gathered around.

We stared at each other, wondering who should pick first.

"Uh, go ahead." Barry nudged Roger with an elbow. It was a bold move to let anyone else go first, since Barry wanted to choose red.

Roger let his hand hover over the cluster of plastic straws, deciding which one was the right one.

Green, red, blue, yellow, orange. He appeared to study them, searching for some kind of advantage.

Barry bit his nail, waiting for Roger to make his selection.

In a quick move, Roger dropped his hand onto the pile and plucked out a straw.

Blue.

I had to contain myself, so as not to give up the game. Roger did not yet know if he had won or lost.

"Melissa, you're next," I said. Barry flashed me a look of panic, then recovered. He wasn't the only one with a bold move up his sleeve.

She stared at the remaining straws, a world of possibility waiting on the selection. Following Roger's example, she let her hand hover over the straws, then dropped it like a hawk after a pond fish and scooped out her choice.

Green.

Barry inhaled, more to express relief, but the others probably took it as a sign of getting ready for his turn.

Melissa looked at me. "Now, for Riff?"

Barry had to hold his breath. "Sure."

"Riffy's favorite color is . . ."

Not red.

" . . .blue. So, since that's gone -"

She plucked a straw.

Orange.

Another masked sigh of relief from Barry. There were two left. Red and yellow.

He decided to appear magnanimous. "Peeky, go ahead."

"No," I said. "I already know which one is the short one. You go."

"Okay." Barry took a deep breath.

He reached out and drew a straw – the red one.

"And that leaves me with yellow," I said. "Everybody show your straws so we can all see which is the short one."

I held mine up with two fingers to reveal a full-length straw.

Everybody else showed theirs.

THE NAVIGATORS

"Booyah!" Roger held up the short straw.

Barry shot me a wide-eyed glance as Melissa gave Roger a high five. I went into the kitchen while Roger mused out loud about what he would do on his trip. Barry followed me. "I said it should *appear* more fair," I whispered, dropping the straws in the trash can where the original short straw rested. "You didn't watch me closely enough."

"I won't make that mistake again."

I came out of the kitchen. "Yes, you will."

Always the smartest person in the room, Barry could actually appreciate it when, once in a while, somebody got the better of him. It was like for a moment they understood the game he'd quietly been playing with the world his whole life.

It was hard to sneak one by Barry. He watched as I showed him a red straw, but didn't keep watching as I turned my back, swapped it out, and cut the blue one. Which made it all seem fair.

Besides, if anything bad happened the first time around, in the test run, it probably shouldn't happen to my future roommate.

Or me, for that matter. Or Melissa. Roger, on the other hand, was . . . most expendable.

Just then, the short, thin frame of Chris Findlay burst through the apartment door. "Hey, everybody, do I have some news for you!"

He stopped and put his hands on his boney hips.

"It's a viewer."

CHAPTER NINE

"What's a viewer?" Roger demanded.

"This is. The machine." Findlay walked over and put a hand on the metal frame.

"I thought it was a time machine." Melissa sounded confused.

"It is. Kind of." Findlay puffed his thin chest out and grinned. "It's a viewer!" He seemed very proud of this statement. The rest of us were still a little confused.

He ran a hand through his red hair and pointed to the panel in front of the machine's metal seat. "All these dials and knobs are settings to allow you to see where the reflected light is from a specific moment and view it."

Melissa held her hand up. "You are totally over my head, Findlay."

"Okay, okay. Think of it like this." He took a deep breath and held his hands out. "When you close your eyes and touch that table, or that lamp,

THE NAVIGATORS

your senses feel it and transmit that sensation to your brain. There is actual physical contact between you and the object." He glanced at a few faces to make sure we were all with him. "But when you *see* something, you are just receiving the reflected light from the object. It may or may not be there, but it doesn't matter. You're only *seeing* it, so it only needs to be reflected light to exist in your visual sense."

Melissa's mouth hung open. "Uh, okay . . . so . . ."

"So the machine isn't really going to take you through time, but it will take you to the point where the reflected light of what you want to see now exists, and you will be seeing it like a transportable 3D movie or something." He turned and smiled at the machine. "It's a viewer. Really, it's rather ingenious."

Roger folded his arms and leaned up against the counter. It was quite a departure from what had been said earlier. "That sounds even more insane than it being a time machine. You came up with this all by yourself?"

Findlay's grinning face froze. "Well . . ."

Roger pounced. "Findlay! You didn't tell anybody about it, did you?"

"I was stuck." Findlay backed a few steps away from Roger. "During that exam I was proctoring, I couldn't get past this one thing. It was stumping me. I checked over the notes Barry and I had put together, and I couldn't get it to add up . . ."

The tension in Roger's arms and neck showed how hard he resisted the urge to throttle Findlay. He spoke through clenched teeth. "So what did you *do*?"

"It, uh, seemed like a numbers problem." Findlay squirmed. "You know, like solving for three or more unknowns in an equation."

I grabbed my stomach. This was bad. Really bad.

Roger pressed. "So you . . ."

"I . . . asked a mathematician."

"Findlay!" Roger grabbed his head with both hands. "You idiot! You're giving everything away before we even know what we have!"

Barry held up a hand. "Hold on, hold on. Who did you talk to? One of your MIT buddies?"

"MIT!" Roger shook his head. "Oh, there it goes!"

"Roger, calm down." Barry turned back to Findlay. "Who?"

Findlay shrugged. "Yeah, one of my buddies at MIT."

"What!"

"A pirate, okay? An illegal hacker guy. He won't go above ground with it."

"How much does he know?" Melissa asked.

"I put it to him theoretically."

Roger pointed a finger. "Don't play games with us, twerp."

"Look." Findlay threw his hands up. "I said I had a theory problem, and he approached it like that. For all he knows it's for a book."

"Except it's not for a book, you moron." Roger rubbed his forehead. "Barry, this is why I didn't want any outside help. The minute you let these hackers in, they start messing everything up and telling the whole world."

Findlay bristled, pointing back at Roger. "You guys were up against it, loser. I solved your problem."

Barry cocked his head. "What do you mean?"

"You had the machine, and you had some ideas of what it was, okay? But that's all you had. Ideas." He softened his tone and leaned into Barry's line of sight. "You guys are diggers, man. Math guys, and physics guys, they bring ideas to life. Sometimes they can reverse engineer a whole concept into something that works." He looked around at the rest of us, then back at Barry. "But here, you didn't know what you had. You figured out some of the concepts, but you didn't know how to make them *live*."

Excitement crept into Findlay's voice now. His small, wiry frame stood taller and he spoke with more force. "Check out all of these dials and knobs." He put a hand on the machine and pointed at its panel of dials. "Barry asked *how* you'd make them or *who* could make them, okay? Was it ancient Mayans or some futuristic descendant of the human race? It's a good question, but it's the wrong question."

Findlay pulled his head from the machine to address us, wrapping his hands around the piping. "The real question is *why* did they make the number of dials they made? And when you approach it as a math problem, the answer jumps right out at you. Watch."

He strode to Barry's desk and picked up a pencil and a pad of paper. "Melissa, here. Write down a date. Any date."

She scribbled on the pad.

"Aha, okay." Findlay picked up the pad and showing it to us. "12/25/2014. Month, day, year, separated by slashes. This date works for us as we stand here in Tampa, Florida, United States . . . We're eastern standard time, too. But what does the military use? They put the day first, not the month, and they utilize a 24-hour clock so there's no AM or PM. That makes it more universal. More *mathematical*. Okay? The language of math knows no limits."

Melissa pushed her hair behind her ear. "Okay."

"Okay. Now . . . " Findlay tapped the pad with a finger. "If you need to be more precise about your selected date, you'd need to know the time, too. Hours, minutes." He laid the notepad on the coffee table and grinned at Melissa, holding up his hand. "So, count with me." With each word, he touched a finger of the open hand with the index finger of the other. "Year, month, day, hour, minute . . . Five variables."

Then he pointed at the dials on the machine's panel. There were five big dials.

Findlay had cracked the first code.

"Oh, wow." Melissa gasped. "Findlay, you figured it out!"

Findlay beamed. "That's just one of the unknowns we were able to solve. And check out the little raised bumps around the dials. Like, this one has twelve."

"Months?"

"Right. And this one has thirty-one."

"Days." Her mouth hung open. "So they used our dating system?"

"Or they knew we would be using it." Findlay shrugged. "But check out the subdials here for the years." The panel had an inset space there for a dial like the other ones, where it contained a set of smaller dials. Like wheels within a wheel.

"This is for the years," he said, sounding slightly amazed. "Look how it counts."

I added up the smaller wheels that sat in the space for the year dial. There were eight.

"A nice round number," Findlay said quietly, only half joking.

"Eight . . ." Melissa was thinking out loud. "If seven digits is a million, and eight is ten million . . ."

"Eight digits could get you to ninety-nine million," I whispered. "If you maxed the first two out at nine."

"If you maxed all eight out, you'd be at almost a hundred million. Think about that." Findlay smiled. "A hundred million years."

"I wonder why only eight?" I asked. "Why not ten? Or twelve?"

Barry leaned forward. "I imagine it takes a lot of power to go back in time at all. A hundred million years might be the most a machine this size can do. Maybe less."

"Maybe more, though." Roger put his hand on the bronze frame.

"Yeah." Barry bit his fingernail. "Maybe."

"Anyway," Findlay pulled himself back from his daydream, "once you program in the date using the universal system, it's just a matter of throwing a switch and the show starts!" Plopping into the chair at the desk, he lifted aside Barry's computer and made space for his feet. He gestured to the long rods positioned along each side of the machine's seat. "Probably one of those big levers, there."

We stared at the machine. The possibilities were amazing.

Roger cleared his throat and clapped his hands together. "Well, thanks for dropping by, Findlay. Time to go."

"What!" Findlay's jaw dropped. Roger walked over and grabbed him by the back of the collar.

Melissa stood up and put her hands out. "Roger, don't."

"Time to go." Roger stood Findlay up. "You're out."

"Out? No way!" Findlay shook off Roger's grip. "Like I said, you guys were up against it. I solved your problem. This whole thing was going nowhere without me!"

"But it did." Barry held onto the machine's bronze frame and eased himself onto the metal seat.

"Huh?"

"It did go somewhere without you. You said so yourself." Barry's eyes scanned the dials and knobs. "It's a math problem, not a computer problem. The math guys solved it, not you." He glanced at Findlay. "You dealt yourself out."

"I'm not out! Nobody's out!" Red-faced, Findlay glanced around the room. "Not now. Not since I know what you have. You can't deal me out."

"I can knock you out." Roger grabbed Findlay's collar again. "That would be pretty 'out,' as far as I'm concerned."

"You can't deal me out!"

"Why not?" Roger growled.

"Because!"

"Because why?"

"Because he hasn't told us how he figured out how to power it," I said. "You must have gotten that answer, too, Findlay, or you wouldn't be here."

"Geez." Roger gritted his teeth. "Who did you tell to get *that* information, Findlay?"

"Am I right?" I asked.

Findlay held silent. He studied each of us, like he no longer knew if he stood in a room full of friends or enemies.

"Yes." He swallowed. "I figured out how it's powered."

"No, you didn't." Barry sounded impatient. "Your big brain isn't mechanical. You got help. From who?"

Findlay sighed. "Coopersmith."

"The engineering professor?"

"Findlay!" Roger turned and put his hands over his face. "Barry, we have lost all control now."

Barry bit his nail. Findlay's answers were unsettling.

Barry stood and went over to a nervous Findlay, patting him on the back. Barry may have been looking at Findlay, but he was addressing all of us.

"It's okay. Findlay here, like most hackers, is a lot of talk and little action. Nobody worth a dime will take him seriously. However . . ."

Barry moved away. He glanced at Roger and nodded.

Roger immediately strode up to the computer geek and punched him in the gut, dropping him.

Melissa shrieked, putting her hands over her mouth. Findlay lay on the floor, gasping.

"I think we can all agree that Findlay won't be talking to anybody else about our little project again. Will you Findlay?"

He couldn't talk yet, but he could move his head. And from the floor, Findlay bobbed his coconut up and down eagerly.

"So we go ahead as planned," Barry said. "Findlay, once he can breathe again, will tell us how the thing is powered, and then he will quietly walk away, forgetting he ever heard of our little project. Right Findlay?"

Findlay's gaze drifted up, eyes agape.

"Otherwise, Roger here is going to stop being so nice about all these transgressions you've been making. They trusted me. I trusted you. Get it? Didn't we agree to keep this thing quiet?"

"Barry," Melissa began. He ignored her, staring down at Findlay. Too much was at stake.

"Mmmmph," was all Findlay could muster.

Roger growled. "That sounds like a 'yes.' Is it a 'yes,' Findlay?"

Findlay nodded.

"Okay," Roger said. "Then there's just one more thing. How is it powered?"

Findlay gasped long enough to get out a few words. "Self-contained system."

"Try it again in non-computer speak, Findlay."

"It's self-contained." He rose to his knees. "Coopersmith . . . thinks it's a magnetic system in a vacuum, with storage cells, but I disagree." He took a deep breath, pausing to rub his belly. "Whoever built it took into consideration that it might use a lot of energy getting to where it's going, but that there might not be an abundance of fuel available for it when it was time to return home."

Roger narrowed his eyes. "So-"

"So it was made with a self-contained, self-limiting system, like the way they reuse oxygen and water on the space shuttle or the space station."

"So it re-uses its fuel?" Roger asked. "How?"

"No fuel is consumed with 100% efficiency. Like on the space station, you drink water, but it's recaptured, so you'd drink reclaimed urine if they could filter it back down to just H2O. So they do. They filter it and remove the contaminants. Am I going slow enough, you cro-magnon?"

"Don't start with me, nerd."

"They burn the fuel and refilter it, cleaning out the unusable particles and retaining what can be salvaged. If you start with an efficient system, you're halfway home. The rest is mechanical engineering."

Melissa observed the framework of the machine. "But how do they know when to . . . fill up the tank?"

Findlay gestured to the metal piping that gave the machine it's oval shape. "Reserve tanks. They're probably distributed throughout the frame, like Lindbergh did with The Spirit of St. Louis. He hollowed out the wings and made them fuel tanks. His whole plane was a big flying gas tank."

Barry nodded. "As long as you have to have the space for a support frame, fill it with something you need anyway. Brilliant."

"And economical," I said. "If you use existing space in a new way, you could allow for more than enough fuel for what you need."

"Still," Melissa placed her hands on her hips. "When do you know you have enough to get back home before you leave?"

"Self-contained or self-governing systems would have that measured." Findlay swallowed, holding his gut. "When you set the trip up, it calculates the energy needed. If there isn't enough, it won't start."

"I love it." Roger laughed. "GM should've thought of that. I've run out of gas twice in my car!"

Barry shook his head. "Gotta turn the motor off while you're with your date in the back seat."

Roger smiled and flipped him the bird.

Sitting back down in the machine, Barry gazed at the dials and knobs. The rest of us gathered around. He let his hands drift over the dials, then looked up. "Roger, please show our guest out, would you?"

THE NAVIGATORS

"With pleasure." Roger grabbed Findlay's arm and forced him toward the door. "So long, butt face."

"You guys are making a big mistake!"

Roger opened the front door and pushed Findlay out. "Sue me."

When the door slammed shut, Roger turned to us. After a long pause, he spoke. "Okay, gang. When do we go for a ride in our new toy?"

"Go for a ride?" Melissa shook her head. "We can't just hop in and try it out! We don't know what this thing is capable of. We're not going anywhere."

"We need to test it." Barry rubbed his chin, his eyes glued to the dials and knobs. He looked at me. "Well?"

"You're right. We need a test."

"Who?" Roger asked.

"Not who. What."

"What do you mean?" Melissa asked.

"We need to conduct a simple test," I said, "to see what the machine does, to see if we even understand how to control it. We have to do that before we try it ourselves."

Barry raised his eyes to meet mine. "What did you have in mind?"

CHAPTER TEN

"A video camera?"

"Sure!" I said. "Think about it. This old video camera goes into the time machine, then it goes back in time five minutes and records what happens. We'll just have to watch the video to see if it's safe."

"I don't know." Barry frowned. "That doesn't seem like it would work. Electronics don't- "

"What would it record?" Roger sat down on a bar stool. "Us, staring at a machine that didn't have the recorder in it yet?"

Barry shrugged. "Einstein believed the separation between past, present, and future is only an illusion."

"Although," I wagged a finger, "he admitted it was a very convincing one."

Barry rubbed his forehead. "Let's think about this. If you are sitting on a moving train, are you moving or sitting still? It's relative. You're doing both. Now-"

"I have something to say."

Melissa had been sitting there, silent, ever since the incident between Roger and Findlay. Her face was drawn and serious, with a distant look in her eyes.

She folded her hands in her lap, gazing downward. "I won't sit by and see this descend into animalistic behavior. I won't watch you guys treat our friends like crap." She took a deep breath and let it out quickly. "I'll walk."

Roger blinked. "You're serious?" He wasn't a rough guy, but Roger viewed things like punching Findlay similar to a body check on the basketball court—enough to get Findlay's attention and send a message without seriously hurting him.

Tears formed in Melissa's eyes. She stared right at Roger. "I'm completely serious. I swear, if anything like that happens again, I'm done."

The words hung in the air, frozen. Her gaze moved to Barry and then to me. We had crossed a line.

Roger leaned back and rested an elbow on the counter. "So walk, then. More trips for the rest of us."

A quiet sigh escaped Melissa's lips as her shoulders slumped. She slowly got up and moved to the window.

"Oh, come on, Missy." Roger bounded off the bar stool. "I wasn't serious."

She stared out the window, placing a hand on the frame, wiping at the base of her eyes with her finger.

Barry cleared his throat. "Listen, Melissa. Findlay has a role in this thing, but . . ."

"Don't." Her voice was a whisper. "Don't try to justify what you did."

"What *I* did?"

She sniffled, raising her voice and waving her hand. "You were just as bad, directing Roger to hit Findlay. He helped us. And you acted like some . . . some thug." She ran a finger under her nose. "Just as bad."

Barry remained quiet. This wasn't grade school playground stuff to her.

She turned to face the room. "Promise me. Promise you will keep this . . . where it's supposed to be."

Barry's face turned red. The team was just getting off the ground and already there were fractures. It was time to reassess and reset.

He nodded. "Okay. I promise."

She asked no such thing from Roger.

"Put a clock in it," I said.

Everybody looked at me.

"To test the machine." I went over and placed a hand on it. "We don't use a video camera. We put a clock in it. That's what the original tests used. The ones with the astronauts. They put an atomic clock in the space capsule that orbited Earth, and when they compared it to a twin clock that had stayed behind, it was off by a few seconds."

THE NAVIGATORS

"Atomic clocks." Barry slapped at his pockets. "Sorry. I seem to have left all my atomic clocks in my other pants."

I shook my head. "The original tests in the 1960's needed atomic clocks and rockets to show that the astronauts were going back in time *a little bit* when they circled the Earth. We can use a regular clock if we're going for five minutes. That's enough of a difference to notice without an atomic clock."

Roger spoke up. "So what do we use instead of an atomic clock?"

"A wind up clock," Barry said. "Nothing with an electrical signal, just in case."

"What, like an egg timer?" Roger folded his arms.

Melissa finally came back to the conversation. "A train conductor's watch. One of the old, antique ones, with the twisty spindle on top to wind it. They're super accurate."

"Good idea." I said. "But, where do we go find an antique train conductor's watch?"

Barry hooked his thumb at the living room wall. "Next door."

"Jonesy has one," Melissa sighed. "I saw it at a party once and asked her about it. It was a beautiful piece. It belonged to her great-grandfather. That's why I thought of it."

It was obvious Melissa was still mad. Her eyes were red from crying and her shoulders were still slumped down. Like the rest of us, she had been bouncing all over the place today. Ecstatic one moment, raging the next. Although she probably wasn't ready to jump back in without agreement from everyone on how to proceed, the train was leaving the station. Like a politician, she got the agreements she could get for now and would try to get the rest later.

"She keeps it on that table thing in the hall." Barry stood up. "In, like, a display case."

Roger rocked back and forth on his feet, frowning. "I'm not getting this. If the test worked, how would we know?"

I shrugged. "The time will be different, plain and simple."

"How long would it take?"

"Well," I thought about it. "We are not really going to see it. The clock can go back in time, say, five minutes, but it should be moving at the speed of light—so we won't see it happening. All we'll see is the machine. Instantly, five minutes will have gone by for it, and we'll just be watching the clock—and it will be five minutes slow."

"Fast," Barry said. "It'll be five minutes fast."

"No, slow."

"Fast, Peeky."

Roger folded his arms. "I'm confused."

Melissa was on her cell phone, calling next door. "Jonesy's not home. I can pick the lock if you want. I know how."

"You can pick a lock?" My jaw dropped. That's the kind of thing I'd have never expected to come out of the mouth of a girl like Melissa. "For real?"

"When I was a kid, one of my dad's clients showed him. He showed me. I can still do it. Wanna see? It's really kind of neat."

"What kind of lawyer learns to pick locks?"

"We don't need to pick the lock," Barry said. "I have a key"

Melissa wrinkled an eyebrow. "Why do *you* have a key to Jonesy's apartment?"

Barry reached into the cookie jar on the counter and produced the key. "Because she is my *friend*."

"Mm-hmm." Melissa eyed him with a slight smile. Her humor seemed to be returning. That was a relief. "Okay. Let's go get the watch." She grabbed at the key in Barry's hand.

"Wait." He pulled it away, holding it over his shoulder. "So, punching a geek is wrong, but breaking and entering is okay?"

"Well, it's not really breaking and entering . . ." Reaching across him again, Melissa's long brown hair brushed across Barry's chin. She slid Jonesy's key from his fingers and held it up. "Because we have this."

"Better take her word for it, Barry." I jumped up to follow them. "Her dad's a lawyer."

"Good thing." Barry got up. "We may need one before this is all over."

* * * * *

The apartment of Denise Jones—"Jonesy"—was meticulous, a rare thing for a sociology major. A beautiful place for a college kid, it had decent furniture and nice paintings on the walls. I had a hard time believing students could afford such luxury–but then I remembered. Students couldn't. Parents could.

Roger scanned the room. "Wow. My mom's house isn't this clean."

The four of us crept into the doorway. I still felt a little like a burglar. Holding my breath, I tiptoed toward the living room.

"Denise!" Barry yelled. I almost jumped out of my skin.

"Geez!" Melissa frowned at him as she placed her hand on her chest. "Will you quiet down!"

"What?" Barry shrugged and walked in. "We aren't doing anything wrong, remember? We have a key."

I stayed by the door, peering around the corner. "Where does she keep the watch?"

"Over here." Melissa strolled to the hallway. A portrait of Martin Luther King adorned the space over a short cabinet. Between some African-style clay pots, a glass case held Jonesy's great-grandfather's pocket watch.

"I remember when she showed it to me." Melissa picked it up. "She said it's still extremely accurate."

"Just put it back when we're done with the test," Roger said.

We piled out the door, back to Barry's.

Melissa twisted the stem of the watch, winding it as she observed the big bronze time machine in Barry's living room. "So now it's like Findlay said? We just set the dials and let it rip?"

Roger took the watch from her. "I guess we'll have to find out."

"First, let's set the dials," Barry said.

We all gathered around the machine. Melissa slid past the rest of us to sit on the metal seat. "Don't anybody accidentally turn this on and send me back to the Flintstones."

Carefully, we reached in and started turning the knobs to where we thought they should be.

"This is 'days.'" Melissa twisted the bronze dial. "So let's turn it to today . . ."

"Years." I said. "Wow. They're hard to turn."

Melissa's forehead wrinkled. "Mine wasn't."

"It's mechanical." Barry stood up. "Think about it. It makes sense that turning a gear for 31 options is easier than turning one for a thousand."

"Ninety-nine million," I grunted. "It doesn't want to even budge."

Roger reached in and helped me turn the dial.

"These must be for location." Melissa pointed to a second set of dials.

I counted the dials. "Latitude and longitude. Does anybody have a GPS?"

"My phone does." Roger nodded. "But I don't know how to work it."

"My car has a removable one!" Melissa jumped up. "I'll go get it. And check the seat. It's loose." Then she scampered off.

Roger bent down and wiggled the seat. "It's got a spring attachment. Maybe it's a 'dead man' switch. So it won't work unless there's the weight of a driver on it."

"Like a riding lawn mower, right?" I asked.

Barry shrugged. "Makes sense."

The dials for latitude and longitude were pretty self-explanatory after Findlay's lecture. Within a few minutes, things were all set. A stack of text books added enough weight to engage the spring contact in the seat, and the old railroad conductor's watch sat on top of them.

I could only think of one last adjustment. "What time should we set it for?"

"It's almost 5:00 PM." Roger checked the wall clock. "How about setting it for five o'clock, and launch at five after?"

"Launch?" Barry winced. "It's not a rocket."

Roger smiled. "You better hope not. You'll lose your security deposit if we burn this place down."

"Over a test with a pocket watch as the pilot." Melissa chuckled.

Barry stopped for a moment. "I hate to break the news to all of you, but you're thinking about this thing in the wrong way. It isn't a rocket. We aren't piloting it anywhere. You don't hop in and go for a drive." He paused to consider what would likely happen. "You set the dials and then sit back . . . I think it does the rest. At best, you just get to decide where you're going."

"So, we're the navigators?" Melissa asked.

"Navigators," Barry repeated, giving it some thought. "Yeah, I guess so. That sounds a little passive, doesn't it? Scary."

Roger glanced at the massive turbine wheel behind the seat. "How do we know if this thing is fueled up and ready to go?"

THE NAVIGATORS

"Good question," I said. "If you were an advanced civilization, how would you let ancient people know the machine you sent them was ready to use?"

"A green light?" Roger tapped the top of the frame. "Right up here."

"Well, maybe not a light," I said, "but *something*. Some sort of indicator. Like a flag."

"Or a color, like litmus paper." Melissa scanned the machine. "Or those little things you press on the battery in the package, to see that it's good."

We all stared at her.

"What?" she said. "It changes color."

Barry rubbed his chin. "Think mechanical."

"How about a float?" Roger leaned on the frame and peered at the dials. "That's mechanical."

I looked at Roger. "What's a float?"

"Like in a lawnmower's gas tank, Peeky." He stood up. "The gas gauge is a floating mechanical indicator. You can just check it and see if it's full or not, or how much it has in the tank."

"Or a thermometer." Barry brushed aside some dirt from one of the frame pipes. The heavy rains during our drive back from the mine had washed so much mud off the machine, we hadn't bothered to continue cleaning it.

The rest of us joined in, rubbing off the remaining dirt with our bare hands. After a few moments, we had our answer.

"Check it out."

Barry inspected a small section of the rear frame. It was clear. Inside was a triangular bar, wider at the top, and thinner at the bottom. It glowed with iridescence: the top was green, the bottom was red. The fuel gauge. Barry ran his finger over it. "I'd guess we have about half a tank."

The rest of us moved to look at it.

"Just like the battery pack thingy!" Melissa threw her hands in the air. She did a little victory dance, singing and swinging her hips. "Ooh, ooh, I was r-ight. I was ri-ight. Barry was wro-ong. Mm, mm, mmm!"

Barry smiled at the show. "Okay, smarty. What's next?"

Roger waved a hand in front of Barry's face. "Uh, how to actually turn the thing *on*?"

"Yeah." Barry returned his focus to the machine. "What about that . . ."

"Ooh, ooh, I was r-ight. Ooh, ooh!"

"Hey, *Beyonce*." Roger glared. "If you were gonna turn this thing on, how would you do it?"

"Flip my hair and smile. That always worked on you, Roger! Ooh, ooh!" She continued dancing.

"It's gotta be one of these big levers, right?" I asked. "I mean, it's the most important thing. You'd make it big and important looking."

"So, the biggest gear shifter, then?" Barry scanned the four rods.

Roger bent over to inspect them. "Which one has the biggest rod?"

"Not you, Roger! Ooh, ooh!" Melissa laughed.

"No," he sighed. "I just *am* the biggest rod, right? Okay. I get it."

"Dance with me, Peeky!" Melissa grabbed me.

"Uh, I don't really dance . . ."

"Oh, come on. Everybody can dance. Go like this." She started hip bumping me. "Come on. Ooh, ooh. Just like that. Ooh, ooh."

Barry folded his arms on the metal frame and grinned at her. "What's with you?"

"I'm exhausted." Melissa stopped dancing and collapsed onto the couch. "I'm beat. It's been a long, stressful day after a long stressful night." She leaned her head back and closed her eyes.

"Preceded by another long stressful day." Barry rested his chin on his folded arms. "Yeah. I guess I can understand that."

Melissa sighed. "Not everybody's brain goes a hundred miles an hour all the time like yours, Barry."

"No, no. You're right." Barry tapped his thighs. "Maybe we should take a break."

"Break if you want." Roger tugged on one of the levers. "I'm figuring this thing out. If Findlay's friends are as good at keeping a secret as he is, we may not have a lot of time."

A jolt of electricity went through me. I hadn't thought of that. "Roger's right. Findlay already told his buddies at MIT, Coopersmith . . . we don't have any time to waste. They'll be demanding we hand this thing over."

"Let's at least try to test it, then." Roger stood up. "With the conductor's clock. What have we got to lose?"

"Okay." Barry nodded. "We need to see which lever activates it. Which one do we push?"

We stared at the machine, hoping it would again provide an answer.

"All of them." Melissa sat up. "We each take one and push at the same time. One of them will activate it."

"Or, we could take turns pushing them," I said. "You know, so it doesn't explode or something."

Roger tapped the frame. "They would have thought of that. Whoever built it thought of a way to engage it so you can't do it wrong. It's gotta be something like putting your car into 'drive.' You can't put it into forward and reverse at the same time."

Melissa crept toward the egg-shaped contraption. "You definitely want to be sure about forward and reverse on a time machine."

"That got handled by putting in the date." Roger walked, sliding his hand along the frame. "Findlay said it had a self-contained system for the fuel. It would make sense to have a self-contained system for the drive, too. So you can't mess it up."

"Why four, then?" Melissa eyed Roger. "I mean, I could see two—one for forward and one for reverse. Why four?"

"Four dimensions?" I asked.

Barry rubbed his chin. "Not enough dials to account for that." He looked at Roger. "I think you're right. Maybe they made it so we couldn't mess it up." He turned his eyes back to the machine. "Maybe they made it safe."

"A safety switch?" Roger asked.

"I think so. Big electrical panels have them, where you can't throw a main switch without pulling a safety switch first. So you can't accidentally do it."

THE NAVIGATORS

Melissa swept her hair out of her eyes. "Jet pilots have them on their ejector seat switches."

"And if form follows function, you'd put the safety farther away when you're sitting in it." I pointed. "So you could have firm control over the real lever when you went to engage it."

"So the rear ones are the safeties." Melissa placed a hand on the big lever. "And the front ones are the main drives."

Barry rubbed his chin. "Probably. And the only ones that will work are determined by what date we use."

We gathered around the big bronze machine, staring at it.

Melissa dug her phone out of her pocket. "A phone is pretty user friendly, right? To get it to work, I don't need to know the process of turning a voice into electronic impulses that get bounced digitally across the country. The people who built it had to know all that. I just push a few buttons and talk, but it only works if I do the steps in the right order."

She looked at the machine and smiled.

"Let's do this."

CHAPTER ELEVEN

"Have we thought of everything?"

Like the rest of us, Barry knew we couldn't actually think of all the things that could go wrong testing out a time machine for the first time, but it was a way to let us vent any remaining concerns.

I looked at him. "I can't think of anything else we need to do. Not for a test."

"Me, neither." Roger patted the bronze frame of the machine.

Melissa smiled. "I think we're a go."

"Okay, then." Barry went to the coffee table. "Missy, is the clock wound up?"

She checked the winding spindle. "All set. Pocket watch says five PM, wall clock says five PM. Time machine set for 4:55 PM."

Barry bit his fingernail. "Do it."

She held the frame and leaned in, placing the watch on top of the stack of books.

"Maharaja." Barry pointed at me. "Go ahead and release the safety."

I leaned into the long rod. It moved into place with considerable ease and stopped with a solid click.

All eyes turned to Roger. "Okay, man," Barry took a deep breath. "Your turn."

"Aye, aye, captain." Roger put his hand on the large lever. "Engaging the main drive."

"Wait!" I shouted. "My role is done for now, right? Should I video the test?"

"Good idea." Barry pointed. "Use my video camera. It'll get a better picture than our cell phones would. It's over on the desk."

I grabbed it and faced my team as they stood around the machine. Their expressions were a mixture of fear and excitement.

I held up the camera. "Rolling!" Then I moved to the other side of Barry's couch.

"What are you doing?" Barry asked. "Peeky, where are you going?"

From behind the couch, I replied. "In case that thing blows up when Roger moves the lever, I'm going to be over here."

"Like the couch is going to protect you?" Roger scowled.

I chuckled. "It's better than nothing!"

They laughed, too. Then Missy glanced around. "Hold on a sec." She trotted over to join me at my sofa bunker.

Roger glared at her.

"What? My part is done, too."

He shook his head. "I guess it's just me and you, Barry."

"Just you, buddy." Barry joined us behind the couch. He squatted low. "Count it down, Rog!"

Roger huffed in disgust. "Cowards. They wouldn't build a machine that would kill the user. Ready?"

"Three. . ."

Melissa and I ducked. I held the camera up over the back of the couch, pointing in the general direction of the test.

"Two. . . "

Roger gripped the lever and took a breath.

"One!"

He moved the lever, sliding it into place with a click.

We hunched down, awaiting . . . *something*. Roger just stood there and stared at it.

Melissa peeked over the couch. "Misfire?"

"I don't know." Roger checked around.

Barry stood up. "I wonder if we got the levers wrong."

Suddenly, the room hummed with a faint whirring noise. It almost sounded like it came from next door, or out on the street, because it was so unfamiliar, but it quickly grew louder.

The whir turned into a whine, like a siren. It grew louder and louder, until it was deafening.

We all covered our ears. Barry yelled something at Roger and waved for him to move away from the machine. The screeching intensified.

I had to close my eyes and drop the camera to protect my ears. I thought about running outside.

THE NAVIGATORS

Roger took a step in our direction, wildly gesturing at the levers like he was wondering if he should disengage them or not. Aside from the loud noise, the machine gave no indication that anything was happening. The turbine was still. The levers didn't even appear to be vibrating.

The screeching intensified, becoming physically painful inside my ears. I couldn't stand it. Roger stood tall between the couch and us, wincing as he held his ears and watched the machine. Melissa curled up on the floor. Barry crouched next to her, holding his ears, eyes squeezed shut. I pressed my hands against my head as hard as I could to keep the piercing whine from exploding my eardrums.

Then there was a brilliant flash.

I was knocked down, not by any force or explosion, but by sensory disorientation. My ears were ringing from the sound, and my eyes were overwhelmed by the light. Like when we'd stare at the sun as kids, afterwards everything looks green and red instead of regular colors.

I simply lost my ability to balance and fell down.

It took a moment for the ringing in my ears to begin to subside. The machine's deafening screech had stopped. By then my eyes were clearing up a little. I squinted into the living room. I could see Barry standing next to Roger, and the two of them were slowly creeping to the machine.

Melissa was still on the floor.

"Melissa!" I could barely hear my own voice over the residual din. I sounded fuzzy to myself, like I had pillows over my ears. I placed my hand on her back.

She lifted her head up, a look of shock on her face. Her mouth moved, but I could not hear her.

I glanced over at Barry and Roger. They were leaning over, peering into the machine.

Then they jumped up and down—carefully, as they had obviously not yet fully regained their sight and hearing either.

I picked up the camera to capture the moment.

Barry held the clock up and grinned. His mouth moved. Roger came over for a high five.

I obliged. My head was *pounding*. A wave of pain gripped the back of my skull.

"Peeky!" Melissa shouted, standing right next to me. I could barely hear her.

But I could read Barry's lips enough to understand.

"It worked!"

Roger jumped onto the couch and reached over, gripping me on the shoulders. "Success, Peeky! The test was a success!"

"Good golly, if that is a success, I don't want to see a failure!" I closed my eyes in pain. Tiny sledgehammers attacked my skull. "They wouldn't build a machine that would kill the user, huh? Just make us all deaf and blind. Where is the aspirin?"

"I think there's some in the kitchen pantry." Barry took the camera.

"Ugh," Melissa groaned. "Now I know how those sailors that watched the nuclear bomb tests felt!" She pressed her eyes shut. "I think I got a concussion."

"Oh, I'm sure you did." Barry rubbed his forehead. "I think we all did."

She groaned again, plopping down on the couch. "And you don't care? Maybe you're a super genius, but some of us need all the brain cells we can get."

"Oh, I care alright. But we had a successful test. See?" Barry held up the pocket watch. It was five minutes slow.

"I'll be darned." Melissa sighed. "Well, I'm glad I could sacrifice my eyesight and hearing in the name of science to break your neighbor's family heirloom."

Barry checked the watch and then back at Melissa, smiling. "It's not broken. It's perfectly fine."

She leaned closer. It was ticking right along.

She peered up at Barry. "What happened, then?"

Barry shrugged, eyeing the machine. "Beats me. Some sort of pulse."

"Like an electromagnetic pulse from a nuclear bomb." Roger stared at the machine.

"Can't be. The electronic stuff would be out." Barry looked around at his computer, the microwave, the wall clock. "Everything's still working."

"A bioelectric pulse," I said, shaking some aspirins from the large bottle. I popped them into my mouth and reached into the refrigerator for a soda. "It knocked us around but didn't harm the toys."

"Well, that's a kick." Barry pursed his lips. "What do you think caused that?"

"What caused that deafening *noise*?" Melissa put her hands on her head. "Man, I was dying!"

Roger slowly shook his head, continuing to stare at the machine. "Who knows? Rust? Maybe we did the levers in the wrong order?"

Melissa rolled her eyes. "Maybe we left the emergency brake on." She grabbed the aspirin bottle from me.

"In order for an object to move through time, it has to approach the speed of light." I sat down on the couch. "Maybe that's what we saw. And heard."

"Well, whatever it was," Melissa dumped a couple of aspirins out of the bottle. "We need to wear protective equipment next time!" She placed the tablets in her mouth. "I'm hoo young hor a hearing aid." Then she disappeared into the kitchen for some water to swallow them.

"That's no joke." Roger rubbed an ear. "That was brutal."

"Yeah." I shifted on the couch, chasing some more aspirin with a sip of soda. Roger reached for the aspirin bottle.

Barry finally joined us, sinking into the cushions and leaning his head back. "We have *got* to figure out what to do about that noise and bright light." He swigged from the aspirin bottle like they were hard liquor and grabbed my soda to wash the pills down.

Footsteps clamored up the outside stairs of the apartment. Probably neighbors wanting to complain about the noise. Barry rolled off the couch and went

THE NAVIGATORS

to the front door. "Well, at least we have a good story to tell Riff."

As he opened the door, Riff grinned at him. "Tell me what?"

"Riffer! You're back!"

Barry went to give him a hug, but Riff recoiled. "Take it easy! Bruised ribs!"

"Good to see you." Roger walked over. "I'm glad you got released so fast."

Melissa blinked, tucking her hair behind her ear. "Why'd they let you out early?"

"I only cracked a few ribs."

"An early release?" Roger folded his arms. "That guy last night seemed pretty adamant."

"Oh, they wanted to keep me longer. But, you know, I was able to get out anyway because of being such a good physical specimen." He puffed out his chest.

Barry went with him back to the living room. "What does that mean?"

"Well, the freaking vampires came by to get blood, and then these other guys were sticking me with all these needles and crap. It was hacking me off."

Melissa sat on the arm of the chair. "Riff, they have to do tests. You might have had internal injuries."

"Yeah, that's what they said." Riff moved over to the couch. "Then the head honcho guy shows up and now he wants to start poking me with needles again. So I frigging poked him a little. I can tell when doctors are messing with me."

"Oh, no." Melissa shook her head.

"And then he brings in an extra security person. Can you believe it? So I threw my bed pan right in their fat faces!"

Melissa's hands flew to her mouth. "You threw a bed pan at the doctor?"

"Well, he moved. It was a security person."

"A cop?" Roger leaned forward. "You threw your pee on a cop?"

"Not a cop, some bozo in a pink apron. With stripes."

"A candy striper!" Melissa gasped. "You assaulted a candy striper!"

"After that, they released me—because I'm in such good shape and they knew there was nothing really wrong with me."

"Oh, Riff!"

"I was kinda in a hurry to get out of there anyway, so I caught a cab and came on over."

"You fled the scene."

"Tomato – potahto, you know?" He stretched out, crossing his legs on the coffee table and pointing to the time machine. "So what's up? What did you find out about this big brown egg from the mine?"

"Is it safe to have this conversation?" Barry asked. "Are the cops about to break down our door?"

Melissa checked the time on her cell phone. "I have to go. Will you guys get psycho boy here up to speed while I run out?"

"Where are you going?" Roger frowned. "I'm missing classes to figure this thing out."

"I have to go do an interview. For Dad's campaign."

"Oh."

"It shouldn't take long. I'll be right back." She slipped her purse strap over her shoulder. "Peeky, can you come along?"

"What?" I blinked. "Uh, sure."

Flipping her hair, she glanced at the others. "Can I trust the rest of you not to do anything stupid while we're gone?"

Barry had been leaning on the machine and pointing things out to Riff. He stopped us before we made it out the door. "Hey, how about getting us some supplies? Ear plugs, for sure, and something to protect our eyes. Like maybe some welder's glasses."

Riff furrowed his brow. "What do we need that stuff for?"

"The machine's a little hard to work with." Barry waved a hand at the turbine section. "It puts out a crazy loud noise and a big flash. We need something to guard us against that if we're going to try another test."

"Another test? You tested it without me?" His shoulders slumped.

Melissa sighed. "Okay. Like I said, get him up to speed and I'll be right back. Barry, where can I find that stuff?"

"Hard to say . . ."

"Try Radio Shack," Roger said. "The one up by K-Mart."

Barry rubbed his chin. "Radio Shack won't have welder's glasses. Maybe try BuyMart. They have everything."

Melissa hung her head. "Ugh, I hate BuyMart."

"Seriously." Roger twisted around to eye her. "Try Radio Shack. That place will surprise you with some of the oddball junk they carry. It could be a front for a covert military operation, with the things they bring out of the back room."

Riff laughed. "They'd have to be. They sure never have any customers. How much money can you make selling batteries to kids?"

"I bet they have 'em." Roger leaned in to inspect the machine. "Hey, what do you guys think about some kind of head protection, too? Like maybe a football helmet?"

"We're half a mile from the varsity practice fields." Riff hooked a thumb over his shoulder. "I can get you some football helmets."

"Don't." Barry waved his hand. "Let's not steal anything else if we don't have to."

Riff glanced at Barry. "Anything else?"

Nodding, Barry patted the bronze frame of the time machine. "Technically, this thing's stolen. When we didn't turn it in on day one. So let's keep our less-than-legal activities to a minimum."

"Well, then." Riff smiled. "In for a penny, in for a pound."

"Let's get some helmets." Roger reiterated.

Barry smirked. "I don't think that's necessary . . ."

Melissa headed to the door. "Okay. Got it. Ear plugs and welding goggles. Peeky?"

THE NAVIGATORS

I jumped up and followed her, not really sure why. She'd done plenty of interviews before. What was different about this one? As we left, I heard Riff whining. "I can't believe you guys figured out it was a time machine and then tried it without me . . ."

"Trust me," Barry said. "You didn't want to be here."

"I sure didn't want to be where I was!"

CHAPTER TWELVE

"Missy, I'm happy to tag along, but why me? What kind of interview is this?"

She stopped at her car. "It's been a long day, Peeky. I don't want to say anything stupid to this reporter." She leaned onto the car roof, resting her head on her arm. "Will you just watch me? Nudge me under the table if I start to say something out of line?"

I straightened myself. "Of course."

A thin smile crept across her lips. "Thanks."

Melissa needed no advice on politics, though. She was sharp as a tack and had been a great asset in her dad's mayoral campaign. We got into her car and I slipped my seat belt into the buckle. "Who's the interview with?"

She started the car and pulled away from the curb. "Janice Peterson, a reporter from the Tampa Tribute. I've met her a few times at some of Dad's business functions and at campaign stuff. She seems okay. But you never know with reporters."

Melissa leaned over suddenly and blew into my face. "How's my breath?"

"I don't know! Is that important?"

"I don't know. I'm nervous!"

"Well calm down. Good grief, what's with you?" Then I chuckled. "Do I nudge you now? That was pretty stupid."

After a short drive, Melissa made a call on her cell phone. I felt around in my pockets for mine. I didn't have it. In my haste, I had left it at Barry's apartment. *Crap*.

We were to meet the reporter for coffee at the university commons, a large open area in the center of campus. Melissa parked at the bookstore and we covered the short distance to the coffee shop.

It was easy to see which one was the reporter. A strikingly beautiful middle aged lady in a well-tailored business suit, surrounded by a sea of twenty-year-olds in tank tops and shorts.

"Ms. Peterson." Melissa strolled in, flashing her million dollar smile.

The lady stood and extended her hand. Another million dollar smile. "Please, call me Janice."

"Janice, this is my friend Tomàs. I'm his ride home. Is it okay if he joins us?"

"Of course. Tomàs, very nice to meet you."

"And you, ma'am."

She gestured for us to sit. "Can I get you two something?"

I held up my hands. "Please, allow me. You two need to chat. I shall serve as Melissa's manservant this evening. What may I get you?"

"A mocha latte, please, Peeky." Melissa reached into her purse. "With Splenda."

"Let me get this." The reporter handed me a $20 bill. "I'll have the same, a latte. And please get yourself something – 'Peeky' is it? What an interesting name."

"I'll let Melissa explain it to you. Be right back."

The cash register was right behind Janice, about three feet from our table. She pulled out a small notepad. "He's charming. Boyfriend?"

"No, no. Peeky—Tomàs—is in my paleontology study group. He's just a friend."

"I see. I like the accent."

"He's from India. Tomàs Pequant. Peeky, for short." Melissa winked at me.

"'Pequant' doesn't sound Indian."

"It's French. His great-grandfather, I think."

"How fascinating." Janice smiled and leaned back, crossing her legs. "You have a lot of interesting people in your life, don't you?"

Melissa smiled back. "I can think of a few."

"Well, the one I'm interested in is running for mayor. Shall we talk about him?"

"Absolutely." Melissa straightened in her chair.

"Do you help with his campaign much?"

"I try."

Melissa had most of her political answers well-rehearsed. I'd seen her do this before: a big grin, a short, upbeat answer, and end with a statement about her dad being the best thing for Tampa. Tonight she seemed a little off. Slow to answer. Hesitant.

Her eyes returned to the reporter. "You've seen me at a campaign event here and there, but I'm pretty busy with school, you know?

"Paleontology." Janice acknowledged, opening her notepad to a fresh page.

"That's right. It keeps my schedule full."

"I can imagine."

"But I help out when I can. Weekends, mostly, doing miscellaneous things for the campaign." I could see Melissa's hand in her lap, folding and unfolding a napkin. Why was she so nervous?

Janice lifted her eyes to Melissa. "Like doing interviews for the family aspect of a campaign."

"That's right."

"Well, I appreciate it." Janice set her pen down. "Your dad and I have been friends for a long time." There was a warmth in her voice, as if she was trying to put Melissa at ease.

"Yes, I've seen you at some office Christmas parties, I think."

Janice nodded at Melissa and changed to a more inquisitive tone. "How did you decide to come to USF to study paleontology?"

I set the lattes in front of them and sat down, handing the reporter her change. Melissa absently toyed with the green plastic cover on the tall cardboard cup, slowly turning it as she spoke.

"When I was a little girl, we were on vacation at the beach making a sand castle—my mom, dad, and me. I wanted to decorate the towers by putting little seashells on top of them. My mom pointed out that one of them wasn't a shell. It was a piece of coral." Melissa glanced up at Janice, who was listening intently. So was I.

"She was a tax attorney, you know? At Dad's firm. But she had a lot of interests." A faint smile appeared on her lips as she stared at the latte. "Dad always said Mom had a million interests, and she was good at every one of them.

"Anyway, she looked around and plucked a little rock from the sand and said, 'See, Missy? This is a fossilized camel's tooth.' I couldn't believe it. A camel in Florida. I'd never heard of that before."

Melissa's eyes never left the coffee. "She and I spent the rest of the vacation combing through the sand. We found tiny whale bone fossils, shark's teeth . . .. I was amazed. It was like the whole beach was a giant crazy jigsaw puzzle. My mom said that any little rock or grain of sand might have a million-year-old story to tell. That was it for me. I never looked at the ground the same way after that."

Melissa paused for a moment. The smile faded from her lips.

"She died two weeks later." Her voice fell to a whisper. "She was killed by a drunk driver while she was out jogging. Rocks and things . . . just kind of became a way for me to stay connected with her."

Janice and I were silent. I had no idea what to say.

Finally, Janice broke the silence. "That's a powerful story." She spoke softly, leaning in and resting her folded arms on the table. "But, I meant

THE NAVIGATORS

how did you decide to come to USF? Your dad is pretty well off. Surely with his connections, you could have gone anywhere."

"Oh." Melissa studied her latte, her cheeks reddening. "I guess so. I had the grades, but Tampa's home. I couldn't bear to think of leaving . . ."

"Your father?"

Melissa raised her eyes. "That's right."

Janice nodded. "How old were you in that story? The one about the beach."

"I was twelve."

"That must have been tough for you."

"It was. For both of us." Melissa placed her hands back in her lap. "I lost my mom, and Dad lost the love of his life."

"That's when he threw himself into philanthropy."

"That's right." Melissa stared down at her hands. "Ms. Peterson, please – don't print any of that."

It was a request, but the look on her face said she was pleading.

"Of course, dear."

Melissa continued her downward gaze. "I'm sorry. I don't know why I told you all that just now." She shifted in her seat and glanced out the window. "It's probably very boring."

I had never witnessed a political candidate's family being interviewed like this before. These didn't seem to be typical questions. Or answers.

Janice's eyes never left Melissa's face. "Not boring at all. I completely understand. I lost my mother at an early age too. Much younger than you were."

Melissa blinked, her jaw dropping.

"My father tried to hide his pain by drinking a lot," Janice continued. "So when I got older, I tried to drown my problems in alcohol. It cost me my marriage."

She tapped her pen on the blank pad. "The way you and your dad dealt with it was much healthier." Then she smiled. "And don't worry. Part of my job is to help make stories interesting, but a political story doesn't need so much deeply personal information."

Melissa took a deep breath and sat back. "Thank you."

Then she glanced at me. "You know, you could have kicked me under the table or something. That's why you're here."

"Sorry. It's my first time doing an interview. Shall I kick you now?"

"Let's change subjects." Janice picked up her coffee. "Tell me about your dad's campaign. How do you think he's doing?"

Melissa brightened. This was her area, the well rehearsed, pitch-perfect answer. "Well, Uncle Troy – that's Troy Morgan, the campaign manager – says Dad's doing great, he's ten points up in the polls and everybody loves him. Unless there's an October surprise, Dad should be our next mayor."

"Do you call all of your dad's partners 'uncle'?"

"Not the women partners." Melissa laughed.

"Aunts?" Janice smiled over the latte.

"That's right."

"One big happy family."

"Just about." Melissa sipped her coffee. "I probably ate a thousand carryout Chinese dinners at my dad's desk with those people. More than I ate at our house, that's for sure. Dad and I never ate at home. I'm not sure he's ever turned on our stove."

Janice shook her head and smiled. "How funny. Could there be an October surprise? Something that happens before the election to derail everything?"

Melissa tucked a stray lock of hair behind her ear. "I don't see how. Dad's pretty thorough. His team has all the bases covered."

"They're a smart bunch. I've met a lot of them at various galas over the last few years."

"Galas." Melissa rolled her eyes. "I used to get dragged to a ton of those."

"With your father?"

Melissa nodded. "Oh, yeah. He would never ask anybody like a date, and he hated going alone. In high school, I spent more Friday nights with him at charity functions than on real dates with boys."

"Maybe that was his plan all along." Janice raised her eyebrows and cocked her head.

"Maybe, but the events stopped when I went to college. There wasn't time. Can't say I miss it." Melissa took another sip of her coffee. "When's your article coming out?"

I shifted on my seat. It sounded to me like she wanted to end the interview.

"Probably Tuesday." Janice closed her notepad. "After I add some background."

"I'm sorry I wasn't much help. I'm kind of tired."

"Exams?"

Melissa glanced at me. "We're, uh, working on a special project at school." Then she turned back to Janice. "I just don't think I gave you much you could use for your story."

"You were more than helpful." Janice slipped the notepad into her bag. "I can write all about Michael Mills' beautiful and charming daughter and how she holds down the fort while studying paleontology at our favorite up-and-coming university. How's that?"

Melissa returned the smile. "That sounds great. You're pretty charming yourself. I don't usually let my guard down like that."

That was true. Melissa usually played things very close to the vest. Some genuine affection seemed to have developed between these two.

"Well," Janice stirred her coffee. "You were tired. Don't worry. There are a lot of snakes that masquerade as reporters. I'm not one of them. You can ask around about me."

"I did. Uncle Troy said you were okay." Melissa's tone was different. Friendly, but direct.

Janice laughed, seeming a little caught off guard. "He did, did he? Well, I've known your uncle Troy a long time. He's a good guy."

"He said you and Dad had gone out a few times."

There it was. Now the strange interview made a lot more sense. I looked at Melissa in shock. Was I supposed to kick her now?

THE NAVIGATORS

I swung my foot and hit the table leg.

Janice's mouth hung open as she desperately appeared to search for words.

CHAPTER THIRTEEN

Roger bolted from the couch and ran a hand through his hair. "What's taking them so long?"

Peeky and Melissa had been gone for over an hour. Meanwhile, as Barry scrubbed the machine, it called to Roger, begging for another test.

He looked over at Riff. "Hey, did you want to be here for the first test? I feel bad that you missed it."

Barry was not amused. He bunched up his cleaning cloth. "What's up, Roger?"

"Nothing's up. I'm just asking Riff here if he'd like to see a test of the machine. After all, the rest of us got to . . ."

Riff sat up. "Heck, yeah, I'd like to see a test."

Barry stood, shoving the rag into his pocket. "Hold on, you two."

"Hold on what, Barry? You're not in charge." Roger walked over to the machine. "We're all part of this thing. Riff only missed out because he was in the hospital, and he was only in the hospital because he was the one who dug the time machine out of the side of the hill."

"What's your point?"

Roger stared at the machine. "The point is, he deserves to see a test."

"Definitely!" Riff jumped up.

"Come on. You're thinking about it, too. Aren't you just a little curious?"

"Okay, I am." Barry said. "But we nearly got concussions the first time. We have to be smart about how we move forward."

Roger folded his arms. "Right. Findlay said it was a viewer, right? So whoever rides in it will get to see something spectacular but not really be there. Like watching a movie, I think you said."

"Yeah. Something like that . . ."

Roger put his hand on the bronze metal frame. "So why don't we fire it up and catch a flick?"

"How's it work?" Riff asked.

Smiling, Roger turned his eyes to Riff. "I'll show you."

* * * * *

"Melissa, I-"

Melissa held up a hand. "It's okay . . . Janice." Melissa spoke in calm, measured tones, like a mix of relief and reassurance. "I love my dad. I want him to be happy. Uncle Troy said . . . you make Dad happy. That you're good for him."

Janice blinked a few times. Now *her* cheeks reddened. "I don't know what to say – and that's a rarity for somebody who works with words for a living."

"Troy's a good judge of character." Melissa drew a breath. "He likes you, so I like you." A smile spread across her lips. "I guess my dad does, too."

Janice arranged her paper napkin on the table, giving a thin smile back. "I'm not so sure . . ."

"Well, just . . . hang in there. He'll come around."

I wiped my sweaty palms on my pants. The tables had definitely turned.

"It's fair to say he has a lot on his mind." Janice cleared her throat. "Considering the election and all."

Melissa sighed, staring at her coffee. "Dad's always watched after me. For a long time, it was just the two of us." She looked up at Janice. "And I tried to watch after him, too."

A smile tugged at Janice's lips. "Am I getting your endorsement for the job?"

"Janice," Melissa leaned forward in her chair. "You've been dating my dad for a while now. If I don't give you an endorsement, you'll never get to first base with him."

"Ha!" I blurted. "Uh, excuse me. I need to, um . . . nothing."

"Sorry." Melissa laughed, appearing to realize what she'd said. "You know what I mean. Give him a chance. Just don't . . ."

"Hurt him?"

Melissa pushed her hair from her face. "That's right."

"I promise."

"I'm trusting you with a lot more than a story here."

Janice dropped her notepad into her bag. "I feel that way, too." Then she added, "I think I ought to have a little chat with your sneaky uncle Troy, though."

"Go easy on him." Melissa sipped her coffee. "He's a tax attorney, not a trial lawyer like Dad. He won't hold up under strong interrogation."

Janice laughed.

The conversation went on that way, laughing and joking like two old friends. It was as if they had discovered a kindred spirit. In a way, I guess that's what they were.

* * * * *

From the back seat of Roger's car, Barry quietly slipped his cell phone out of his pocket and flipped the volume to "vibrate." Then he dialed Melissa.

No answer.

He sent a quick text. *Call me.*

Maybe if she interrupted the test with a phone call, Roger could be persuaded to wait.

Maybe.

Roger drove, glancing at Barry in the rear view mirror. "Quit sulking. You know I'll eventually test the time machine anyway, with or without you. You have to sleep sometime."

"I want to test it. I just want to be safe. There are still too many things we don't know."

"We've been thinking about them ever since we figured out what the thing is. We're taking the precautions we can think of. Now, it's time to test it again."

Roger pulled his car into the parking lot at Radio Shack.

* * * * *

As we walked across the USF commons, Melissa apologized. "I kept you so long! I had no idea, Peeky. Time just flew by."

"Like the way it does when you're on a date and you find the other person so interesting, you don't want it to end."

"I guess so."

I looked at her, the street lights illuminating her face. She seemed satisfied. Happy, even. Her smile hadn't faded since we left the coffee shop.

"That's a good sign for you." I put my hands in my pockets as we walked. "And for your father. After you, who else knows him better? If you like Janice this much after tonight, he must, too. He's known her much longer."

"It's sure something to think about." She glanced at me. "You know a lot about relationships, don't you?"

I chuckled. "Don't take this the wrong way, but compared to you, just about everyone in the world does."

"What?" her jaw dropped. "Just because Roger and I- "

"Bah, Roger. I know there's nothing between you and Roger. Not really. I've seen what's been going on over the past year or so. You two are just – pardon my French – friends with benefits."

She chuckled. "That's not very French, Peeky."

"I'm not talking about that stuff, the superficial things. I'm talking about something real, with

THE NAVIGATORS

someone who actually cares about you. Like Barry."

Her mouth dropped open.

* * * * *

"Where to?" Roger asked, adjusting the dark green welder's goggles. Orange foam earplugs hung out of his ears.

Riff snorted. "You look ridiculous, man."

"Almost as bad as you two, eh Barry?"

"Where are we sending you, Roger?"

"To Julius freaking Caesar, man. Ancient Rome."

Riff plopped down onto Barry's couch. "What's so special about Rome that you need to go there?"

"Nothing." Roger shook his head. "That's the point. It's a viewer. I go check in on Julius Caesar around the time he's about to get whacked." He put his hands on his hips. "We pretty much know the date. We definitely know the location. I can pop in and see everything, and come back, no muss no fuss."

"Cool." Riff nodded. "Will that work?"

"I'm not sure." Barry chewed on one of his fingernails. "Something's bugging me about this."

Roger rolled his eyes. "Hey, it's a viewer. If I see anything, I come back and report. From that, we'll improve our safety protocols and we're on our way." He grabbed the frame and swung into the seat, scanning the panel. "The Big Bang, the birth of Christ, you name it. Any significant event in history that we have a time and place for, we can see it happen."

"Yeah, I know. I know." Barry patted his thigh. "I just can't put my finger on it, but something's . . . not right."

Roger sighed. "What's the problem?"

"When it comes to time travel, there are a lot of variables." Barry paced around the machine. "You get these paradoxes, so what do you do about them? I apply the Theory of Definitions."

Riff sat up. "Like what kind of paradoxes?"

"Like, you want to go back in time and kill Hitler so that no Holocaust occurs. So you do. You're successful. But then we get to today, and there is no reason for you back in time to kill Hitler because there was no Holocaust. See? So you wouldn't go, and if you don't go the holocaust happens. There's the paradox."

"Okay. Paradox. Got it."

"The Theory of Definitions simply asks: how can everything in that situation be true?" Barry circled the machine, staring at it.

"So you start out with, you know, World War II happened. The Holocaust happened. Your parents get together and *you* happen. And now here comes the time machine." He dropped into the couch next to Riff. "In order for all the variables to remain true, you either can't go back in time, or you go back in time but the changes you cause didn't change the outcomes we know happened—you were inconsequential, or you go back in time and you're *unable* to cause changes."

Riff cocked his head, narrowing his eyes. "Okay . . ."

"That last one," Barry tapped the arm of the couch with his finger. "That's the Viewer Conclusion. You're just an impartial observer looking at the reflected light that existed at the time of the events, coming off the objects as they move, but you're unable to interact with them. You can't make a difference, just like a person watching a movie sees the actors on the screen but can't change what is happening."

Riff chuckled. "Dude, I am so lost."

It didn't matter.

"And realistically, if you go back in time and are not a viewer, time is relative." He got up and paced again. "So maybe you go back and you see all these things that might take place over hours or days for *you*, but to them you might only appear for 1/16th of the second—a little blip—and you may witness wondrous things, but to them it's just a flash—they think they see something out of the corner of their eye, and when they look, there's nothing there." He turned and smiled at Riff. "That's Blip Theory. That's really the most plausible . . ."

Roger climbed out of the machine and went over to the computer.

Barry glanced at him. "What are you doing?"

"Finding out where all this Theory of Definitions and Blip Theory stuff came from." Roger typed for a moment. Riff watched from over his shoulder.

Rubbing the back of his neck, Barry walked into the kitchen to grab another Diet Coke. He glanced at his cell phone. Nothing from Melissa.

After an unsuccessful two minutes, Roger turned to look at his friend. "There's nothing on either of those topics. What, did you come up with that stuff yourself?"

"Um...yeah. It's the most plausible, based on . . . you know, the science."

Roger climbed back into the time machine. "Barry, sometimes you scare me."

"Yeah, well." Barry took a sip of his soda. "You scare me all the time."

"You're stalling. You just want Missy here." Riff stared at Barry. "Are you afraid she'll be steamed when she gets back and sees we took a trip without her?"

"No." Barry sighed, slumping back into his chair. "Well, maybe."

"Dude." Roger checked the grip on the side levers. "She and Peeky aren't here, big deal. Riff missed a test, too. We'll all miss a test sooner or later, myself included. But we have to test. We're scientists. It's in our DNA."

Barry rubbed his chin. "I feel like we're rushing. Like I'm forgetting something."

Roger leaned forward on the metal seat and started adjusting the panel dials. "Riff, hand me the coordinates we got from the GPS."

"Roger's right, Barry. Melissa being here wouldn't make a difference." Riff picked up some notes from the table and handed them to Roger. "What would she add right now? Except to make you want to show off for her or something."

Pushing himself up straighter on the cushion, Barry sighed. "Yeah, maybe you're right. I don't know, do you think a girl like her and a guy like me could ever . . ."

"No." Roger shot from the cockpit. "No chance. Melissa's dad's about to become mayor. From there, it's just a short step to Governor. And if that goes well, he'll run for president." Roger sat back, shaking his head. "President of the United States. He'd run, and he'd probably win. And you think during all that careful planning, he'll have his precious daughter dating a rock duster like you? Making no money and spending all your time out in the middle of nowhere for months at a time?" He turned his attention back to the dials. "It's not in the cards, bro. Missy's a chip off the old block. She'll pair up with a south Tampa lawyer that her dad approves of. Somebody with money and a future that meets the expectations of Mr. Mills."

* * * * *

"Don't tell me you've never noticed the way he looks at you."

My tiredness was getting the better of me. It let my mouth say the things my eyes had observed for months. "The way Barry goes out of his way to be around you. The way – just the other day, when you agreed to go on the trip to the mine, he picked you up and twirled you around."

"Peeky-"

"I could go on and on. Why are you wasting your time with Roger?"

Melissa tapped the steering wheel. "Roger and I . . . we aren't serious. We haven't been for a long time."

"Does Roger know that?"

"Oh, I don't know . . ." She was quiet for a moment. "He *should*. No, he *does*. Deep down, he does." She scanned the ceiling as she threw her hands out from her sides. "He's just like, I don't know. It's just . . ."

"Convenient?"

"No. Maybe."

"Familiar? *Easy*?"

"Stop it. We're broken up. We've broken up a half dozen times. It's just sometimes . . . I mean, I get lonely, and . . . sometimes I'm weak."

"You *settle*. An occasional side fling with a guy you thought had a girlfriend."

She let the words resonate and took a deep breath. Then she shot me a glance. "But you're wrong about that other stuff. Barry doesn't think of me that way."

I stared out the window at the passing street lights. "I'm not wrong. Open your eyes."

"Stop, already. This is too much for one evening. I was nervous enough meeting Janice for the first real time, now this. It's too much."

"Fine. It's none of my business." I kept my gaze focused outside. "But don't try to pretend."

* * * * *

"You hid behind the couch?" Riff was incredulous.

"Trust me, that's where you want to be." Barry bit his fingernail.

"I think I'm all set here." Roger looked over at them. "Let's light this candle!"

Barry ignored him and continued explaining the makeshift procedures to Riff. "The bright flash

THE NAVIGATORS

and the loud noise – that's why we got the ear plugs and the welder's goggles."

"Engaging gears," Roger announced.

Riff watched carefully as Roger moved the levers into place. "And it was-"

The whining of the machine overwhelmed Riff's words. He raised his voice. "And it was enough protection?"

The screeching got louder. Barry shouted. "We didn't have any protection the first time. We just videoed the clock, that's all."

Then it dawned on him. He knew what he'd forgotten. "Oh, no."

"What's wrong?"

Barry waved at Roger. The noise quickly grew deafening, even with the earplugs. "Roger! Stop!"

Roger glanced over, a blank look on his face. He gave a thumbs up. Barry waved his arms wildly.

Then there was a brilliant, blinding flash.

And Roger spilled out of the machine, covered in blood.

* * * * *

The rest of the ride was quiet. We'd inadvertently talked with Janice right through dinner without even eating. Maybe our exhaustion had caught up with us. Maybe we'd experienced enough emotions for one day. When we stopped at Radio Shack for the earplugs and welder goggles, Melissa just said "I'll be right back" and went in without me.

The ride to Barry's felt even more awkward after that, but maybe I deserved it.

I followed her up the stairs and through the door into the dark apartment. Melissa placed the plastic shopping bag on the table and flipped on the light. I spotted a note in Barry's handwriting.

"Took Roger to the ER. It's serious. Call, don't come."

Melissa balled her fists. "'Call me?' If it's so serious, why didn't *he* call *me*?"

I glanced at the note. The words "don't come" were underlined twice.

She pulled out her cell phone and her face went flush. "Oh, no. I turned my phone off for the interview."

"You still would have noticed something if it was on vibrate."

"No, I turned it *off* off! So we wouldn't be interrupted." She pressed the power button. The phone began to glow as it powered up.

It pinged with missed calls. "Call me" and "Barry 911" texts illuminated the screen.

Then the voicemail icon lit up. Three messages.

She pressed "play."

Barry's voice shouted over some static. "Melissa! It's Barry. Call me as soon as you get this."

The next message was the same. He was almost yelling, probably driving while he spoke.

"Melissa! It's Barry. We're taking Roger to the hospital. To the ER. He's hurt pretty bad, but *don't* come to the hospital! Somebody has to stay with the machine, and you and Peeky can move it if you have to. It's not heavy."

In the next message, he was nearly whispering, but just as intense.

"Melissa where are you? We're at the hospital. Roger's in intensive care and I can't take a cell phone in there. My battery's almost dead anyway. If you get this in time, *stay with the machine*. You and Peeky can move it if you have to. If anything happens, just take it next door to Jonesy's. She's out of town and won't mind, okay? I have to stay here with Roger because they won't let Riff back in. I'll update you when I can. *Stay with the machine!*"

Melissa looked at me. "What do you think happened?"

"Barry said Riff wasn't allowed in. Call Riff, then."

She dialed quickly. "It's going straight to voicemail. What's with these guys?"

"Leave a message."

"Riff, it's Melissa. Peeky and I are at the apartment with the machine. Call me."

She hung up.

What was going on?

* * * * *

"Are you a mass murderer or something?"

Barry sat up, snapped out of his haze by a loud, authoritative voice in the ER.

"How many friends of yours are you going to bring into my hospital all bloodied up?"

Holy crap. Dr. Harper. Again.

Barry stood and collected himself. "Good evening, doctor."

Dr. Harper ignored the greeting and glanced around. "Where's that young lady and your other friend? You probably buried them in a ditch somewhere."

"No, sir, I – uh, we-"

Harper folded his arms. "Yes, yes, go ahead. I'll wait. Make it something more interesting than rock climbing, this time, though."

If you only knew, doctor.

"What's that?"

Barry shook his head. "Uh, I was asking how's Roger?"

"He's in rough shape but I think he'll survive—no thanks to you." Dr. Harper opened his clipboard, interrupting himself to glare at Barry over his reading glasses. "I'm starting to worry about that little group you're running around with. We get those cases in here from time to time. Thrill seekers. People who like to wreck cars – with themselves in it. All for some kind of sick rush."

"Can I see him?"

"So you can finish the job?"

"Doctor, please."

Harper huffed. "The only reason I'm going to let you see him is because he asked for you specifically. Otherwise, I'd be calling the cops. Do you understand?"

"Yes." Barry exhaled, weary of the give and take. "Thank you."

"Right through there." Dr. Harper grumbled as he watched Barry walk toward Roger's room. He folded his arms over his clipboard, muttering. "Bunch of sick mothers, I'll tell you."

Catching a glimpse of Roger through the doorway, Barry halted and put his hands out to balance himself. The sight made his breath catch in his throat. Even with the room lights dimmed, Barry could see that Roger was all bruised and purple and bloody. His eyes were swollen shut. Tubes ran out of him to various machines.

Roger slowly turned his head to the door. His hand, barely able to lift off the bed, motioned Barry inside.

Each breath Roger took was assisted by a machine. It hissed and clicked with every labored rise and fall of his chest.

Barry stepped to the bedside and placed his hands on the rails. "Tell me what happened."

The breathing machine hissed again as Roger tried to speak. He could only manage a small groan.

Hiss, click.

Roger tried again, straining to raise his head. Barry leaned in.

Hiss, click.

Roger's voice was a weak, raspy whisper.

"It's not a viewer."

CHAPTER FOURTEEN

My cell phone rang with an incoming call. Riff's name appeared on the screen.

"Who is it?" Melissa asked, grabbing my phone.

"It's . . . Riff."

She swiped her finger across the screen and mashed the speaker icon. "Hello?"

"Melissa? What the—did I misdial? Where's Peeky?"

"He's right here. Tell me what's going on."

"We've been trying to call you guys for, like, two hours. I thought you got arrested or something."

"I turned my phone off."

"Why did you do that? You were supposed to be getting supplies! Everybody wondered what happened to you two."

"Riff, calm down. Tell me what happened."

THE NAVIGATORS

"Oh, man," Riff continued. "Roger got messed up, big time. That time machine is a beast. It beat the crap out of him."

"What? How did that happen? Did they try to test it again?"

"Yeah. It was messed up, too. Roger was burning to try the thing out. It's supposed to be a viewer, you know? So you can just go see the reflected light from a prior event, like watching a movie or something? Barry tried to talk him out of it..."

"What did he do?"

"He waited until you were gone and then he said he wanted to try it."

"And Barry let him? Are they crazy? The first test nearly gave us all concussions."

"There was no stopping him. That's why Barry made him wear earplugs and welder goggles."

"Where did he get those?"

"Radio Shack. We tried to call you."

She frowned. "Then what happened?"

"It was loud, like you said. And the big flash. It was intense. I think we still might have gotten concussions. That thing is definitely a self-limiting use vehicle." Static crackled over the line. "Listen, I'm on my way to get some of Roger's stuff and take it to him at the hospital. I'll head back over to the apartment afterwards and meet you guys, okay? Just stay put."

"Riff, what did the doctors say? Is Roger hurt bad?"

He wasn't there. The call had dropped.

* * * * *

"Roger, can you talk? Can you tell me what happened?"

He had bruises everywhere. Temporary air casts held his broken legs in place. Bandages closed wounds. His ribs were taped; his arms and head were wrapped in gauze. Swollen and lame, he was barely recognizable as the cocky athlete he had been just a few hours ago.

Roger pushed himself up in the hospital bed, shooting a sharp wince across his face and spraying saliva onto his chin. His breath came in short, painful bites. "I made it."

"Take it easy." Barry reached behind Roger and adjusted the pillows. "What do you mean?"

A grin tugged at the corner of Roger's swollen mouth, but his answer was a spoken groan. "Rome. I was there."

Barry's jaw dropped. "Get out! What did you see?"

"Everything." He whispered. "We nailed it. I was right there. Big columns, all painted in bright colors. A big room, with banners."

Barry was amazed. Roger had seen ancient Rome. "Go on! Did you see Caesar?"

Roger closed his eyes and barely moved his head back and forth. "It was hot. Smelly. They saw me right away."

"Who's 'they'?"

Roger grimaced. "Roman guard. Soldiers. Palace centurion or something."

He wheezed a little and licked his lips. Barry grabbed a cup from the bedside tray and held the straw up to Roger's mouth.

"They were on me in a minute. A ton of them." Roger groaned. "I never had a chance."

He took a sip.

"I screwed up. I was completely out of place. Jeans. T-shirt. Not speaking Latin." He managed a slight chuckle, immediately followed by a wince.

"That's amazing, Rog," Barry said. "Amazing. You're a pioneer, now. A hero, or something."

Roger groaned. "I'm a screw up. Look at me."

Purple welts rose from every spot on his bruised, swollen body. The visible skin that wasn't covered in bruises was covered in blood.

"Roger, I . . . I'm so sorry, man." Barry swallowed, the words catching in his throat. "This, what happened to you—it's my fault. We should have known it wasn't a viewer. The time on the clock changed during the test. That wouldn't have happened if it was just a viewer. I should have known that." He lowered his head. "I should have stopped you."

Roger closed his eyes. "You tried."

A nurse appeared at the door. "Sir, I'm afraid he's had enough for one night. You should go. Your friend needs his rest."

"Okay." Barry stepped away, unable to take his eyes from his bloody, beaten friend.

She slipped a syringe into the IV. "This is for the pain. He won't be awake much longer."

Roger uttered something. He was weak and fading fast.

Barry leaned in again. "What is it, Roger?"

"Learn," he rasped. "Learn from this."

* * * * *

Melissa paced around the living room. "We should get over there."

"No, they said to stay here. If Roger were at death's door, they'd have said that. In the messages, Barry said stay with the machine."

She plopped down on Barry's couch, frustrated. "Ugh! A week ago, my life seemed perfect! Now, everything's all messed up! School, the project . . . *men!*"

I took a deep breath and let it out slowly. "You need some sleep."

"I'm too wound up to sleep."

"A drink, then."

"What do you have? Or, what does Barry have around here?"

"I am from India, my friend. We shall consume the only thing that a truly civilized person *should* drink at this late hour."

"Rum and Coke?" Melissa asked.

I frowned at her.

"Rum and Pepsi?"

"Tea." I wagged a finger at her and moved to the kitchen, opening a cupboard. "In India, we drink more tea per capita than any other country."

A frown flashed across her face. "Um, I don't think that's true . . ."

"Well, if it isn't true, it should be. Here." I handed her a cup and returned to the kitchen. "Don't try to solve all your problems at once. It doesn't work."

"Yeah . . ."

"Now, regarding your problems with men . . ." I took out the teapot. "Dating men is like shopping for a convertible car."

"Don't I know it." Melissa sighed. "They're always trying to take the top down."

I smiled. "I mean, it's like that commercial for the Auto Trader. The announcer says, 'Show me all the green cars' and a thousand green cars show up. Then he narrows it to cars with two doors, and there are still two hundred green cars with two doors, you know? You keep narrowing it down until you find the right one for you. The sports car may look good, but you can't put kids and groceries in it."

She chuckled. "It's a fun ride, though."

"For a while, sure. In time, your needs change and so do your interests . . . so you must be selective—but open minded. Of course, you can try several before deciding on the one that is right for you. Isn't that what you are doing now?"

"You make it sound so easy." She slouched further down into Barry's couch. Slipping off her shoes and perching her feet on the edge of the coffee table, Melissa stared absently at the oval bronze machine across the room.

I shook my head. "Matters of love can be far from easy, but they are a worthwhile pursuit—and a necessary one—if you can be clear-eyed and honest enough to truly pursue the right thing."

"That can be scary. If you blow it, you've lost *the one*."

"Hmm. You don't strike me as a girl who's afraid of very many things."

"I hide it pretty well." She shifted on the couch to focus directly on me. "What would you do if you were me?"

"About men? That's difficult. But anyone can see Roger is not the best choice for you. Not for the long term."

"No . . ." she whispered, looking away. "I know."

"Do you want to know what my father said to me when I was a young man and I asked him how to pick the right wife?"

"What did he say?"

"He said, 'Ask your mother.'"

Melissa laughed.

"But he was serious," I said. "After all, who better to find a woman for her son?"

It was working. Melissa's face brightened and her smile returned. "What did your mom say?"

"She said, 'Ask your dad.' I think they wanted to avoid the conversation."

Melissa chuckled.

"No, my mother said physical beauty is a sign of good health, and for thousands of years it was what caused a young man's fancy to turn to thoughts of love. Or lust. I forget which."

"Stop it." Melissa put her hand on my knee and shoved. "I'm trying to be serious here."

"She cautioned me, though. She told me physical beauty does not last, and *should* not last. 'A beautiful woman's curves will eventually sag and her hair will turn gray. What will you be married to then? If you choose wisely, you will be married to a beautiful personality and a curious

THE NAVIGATORS

mind that loves your children and who would do anything for you.' That is true beauty."

"Hmmm." Melissa closed her eyes, appearing to postulate on the idea.

"I know. Where's the fun in that, right?"

"Well . . ."

"Relax," I said. "It isn't easy. You are a beautiful young woman who's had men throwing themselves at you all your life. That makes it hard to know who cares about you for *you*, and who just wants to be seen dating an important lawyer's daughter . . ."

She nestled her head into the back cushion. "You're quite a good girlfriend, Peeky."

"Thank you. I grew up with three sisters. I learned a few things."

The teapot whistled from the kitchen. I rose to tend to it. "Now, think of all the men you know."

"What, guys I could date?"

"Well, yes. Let's not get all gross and Oedipal here. Break it down. Whose intellect at school do you respect the most? And who would put your needs above their own? And do not say Roger or I'm leaving."

She laughed. "No, definitely not Roger. He is totally out for himself."

A long moment passed. Melissa cradled her cup in her lap, letting the wheels turn.

When it seemed like she had arrived at an answer, I still had to pull it out of her. "So? When you think of all the men you know, and trust, and who enjoy your company, who among them would put their own needs aside? Who would do anything for you?"

"Barry," she whispered. "Barry would do anything for me." She peered up at me. There were tears forming in her eyes. "But he doesn't think of me like that."

"Doesn't he, Baloo? Are you sure?"

My reply surprised her. She let it sink in. "No, I'm not sure."

I smiled. "Then I'd say maybe it's time for a test drive."

"What if kissing Barry is like that phrase, 'like kissing my brother'?"

"You don't *have* a brother, and I don't think you have to worry about that. I kiss my sister every time I see her when I return home. Barry won't kiss you like that. I've seen the way you look at him, too, you know. When you think nobody's noticing. But saying things like that keeps it all safe, doesn't it?"

She nodded.

"It's like this infernal machine." I waved my hand at the bronze metal egg. "We never built one, because we didn't think along those lines. But somebody else did, and now here it is."

She smiled and blinked back her tears. "Peeky, I don't think I've had a conversation like that ever, with anybody."

"But you had a conversation with yourself." I rose, taking a blanket from the closet. "I just asked some questions."

"Your wife is really lucky to have you. Your daughter, too." She started to drift off. "You're a good dad, Peeky. I can tell."

I draped the blanket over her. Then we sat there, the two of us, exhausted and sleepy, staring over at the time machine, daydreaming about it until our real dreams crept in and put us both to sleep.

CHAPTER FIFTEEN

The apartment door flew open with a loud bang. I jumped off the couch to see Barry barging in, a complete mess from head to foot. Dried blood covered his shirt and neck.

"Peeky. Good, you're here. Call Melissa and tell her to come over right away."

Melissa's head popped up from the couch as she pushed the blanket to the floor.

"Oh." Barry hesitated for a moment. Melissa's wrinkled clothes and disheveled hair obviously indicated we'd spent the night together. "Um, okay," He mumbled. Glancing down, Barry fumbled with a sports gear bag.

"Barry—" Melissa sat up. "This isn't . . . I mean, we—Peeky and I, we didn't. Nothing . . ."

I shifted on my feet. He couldn't think anything happened. Could he?

"Never mind." He waved a hand. "We have a problem."

She blinked. "What kind of problem?"

"Who is 'we'?" I asked.

"All of us. And it's a *big* problem." Barry set the bag on the table. "Findlay went crazy and told everybody about the time machine."

"When you say everybody . . ."

"I mean *everybody*, Missy. The local news, the college brass, everybody. The whole campus is buzzing about it." He came over and grabbed the remote off the coffee table, turning on the TV. "News trucks have been rolling in all morning. They're everywhere. Findlay's getting ready to hold a freaking press conference right in the middle of the campus commons in about fifteen minutes."

Melissa watched the live feed on TV. "Holy cow."

"What do we do?" I asked.

Barry ran his hand through his hair. "We don't have a lot of time. Maybe you guys can go stall them. Cause a ruckus, some sort of distraction. I can't go like this, all covered in blood and crap. I'll be down in a minute."

"Go stall Findlay, cause a ruckus, keep it from happening. Got it."

Melissa held her hands out from her sides. "What's that going to accomplish?"

"I think it's me he wants to confront," Barry said, "so he can take our discovery away from us in front of everyone. So I'll confront him."

"How are we going to stop him?"

"Just buy me some time. Cause a distraction." Barry motioned to the hall closet. "Heck, Missy, grab a pair of sunglasses and one of my hats if you want. The crazier, the better. Throw water balloons, whatever you can think of, just don't let that thing happen until I get there!"

"Okay, Barry. We're on it." Melissa jumped up and grabbed her car keys. "Come with me, Peeky. I have an idea."

Everybody knew what to do but me.

As we headed out the door, she shouted, "Barry! Don't take too long!"

The commons was nearly full when we drove up. The normally half-empty summer session parking lots were jammed. Barry was right. All the local news crews were here, and with one glimpse of that machine from the locals, national news networks would start covering the story—and chaos would break loose.

Melissa wheeled through the parking lot. "There are no spots. Do you see any?"

"No."

"Screw it. This will have to do." She drove the car over the curb and into the grass by the dumpster.

"Can you do that?" I asked, getting out.

"Looks like I just did." Melissa jumped out and ran toward the gathering crowd. "We'll be out of here before they have a chance to tow it!"

In the middle of the open grass of the commons, Findlay sat perched upon a stage that had been erected for an upcoming concert. Chairs had been arranged for the audience, and some of the deans of the college were gathering on stage. University workers rushed out a huge projection TV screen along with some stage lights. Findlay plucked at the ridiculous pompadour on his over-

THE NAVIGATORS

moussed head, makeup powder covering his pasty white face.

Melissa stopped and observed the scene from a distance.

"What should we do?" I asked. "Go tackle him?"

"Wait here." Melissa sprinted toward the campus bookstore. "If Findlay starts to talk before I get back, *then* go tackle him."

"What! I never played American football! I don't know how to tackle!"

"Keep your eyes open!" She yelled over her shoulder. "This will only take a minute!"

"Don't be long! The extent of my extracurricular activities was chess club!"

"Then crown him." She flung open the bookstore doors.

"That doesn't mean what you think it means!"

I faced the gathering crowd. Holding my breath and kneading my hands, I crept closer to the stage and pulled Barry's baseball cap down over my face. I slinked up behind a fat guy buying cheese Danishes from one of the commons' vendor carts.

More students collected in front of the chairs. Then, Findlay appeared. He strutted to a table microphone behind a small sign with his name on it, and sat down.

"Testing, one two three," the idiot Findlay said with a grin, enjoying his voice over the loudspeakers. He put a hand over the mic so it wouldn't pick up his voice. I could just overhear him tell somebody in the crowd that they would begin in just a few minutes. "We are waiting for

Jonas Brown," Findlay said with a smile. Brown was a popular local news anchorman.

I spun around, taking it all in. There were satellite news vans everywhere. Chanel 8 was probably going to beam their egomaniacal morning news anchor, Jonas Brown—Tampa's self-appointed Most Trusted Name In News—in on a live feed from downtown. I glanced back at Findlay. He grinned from ear to ear, bouncing his legs like pogo sticks.

"Test, one, two. Test."

I glanced back at the bookstore. Still no sign of Melissa.

Moving closer to the stage, I kept my head pointed down, using the ball cap to hide my face. Findlay would spot me if I got too close. Several campus security guards stood nearby. Maybe he expected a confrontation.

Clearing his throat, Findlay adjusted his mic a second and third time. Any minute now, this event would start. *Where is Melissa? What am I supposed to do if she doesn't get back in time?*

The TV feed came on. Jonas Brown appeared on the giant screen, talking about a local housing project, and hinting at a special report live from the USF campus moments away. Then they went to a commercial.

What to do?

Tackle . . . tackle. Jump up on stage and grab Findlay? I twisted my fingers together. He was a little shorter than me, but he might be wiry. And what if some of the other people on stage joined in

THE NAVIGATORS

to help him? Things could get embarrassing quickly.

But, it *would* be a distraction . . .

I moved closer, still hiding behind the fat guy. He wanted a good spot for the show.

The commercial ended. Jonas Brown was back on TV. I could feel my heart in my throat, making me want to vomit.

The lights got suddenly brighter up on the stage. Findlay beamed from ear to ear.

The USF logo came up behind Jonas Brown. The caption said "Major scientific Breakthrough at USF?" Good grief, what did Findlay tell these people?

As I watched him, his eyes met mine. Findlay bolted out of his chair and pointed right at me. "There's one of them! That's one of the thieves!"

My heart stopped. Thief? Me?

The security guards scowled, moving toward me. I clutched my stomach and glanced around. Should I run onto the stage? Or just run away?

And where is Melissa?

I glimpsed the platform holding Findlay and the others. It stood almost five feet high. There was no way I'd be able to jump up there. Should I run away?

The guards pushed through the crowd toward me. I turned to run and smashed right into the fat guy with the cheese Danishes, losing my balance and falling backwards. Before I could even hit the ground, something grabbed me under the arms.

More campus security—coming from the other direction. I never even saw them.

They yanked me up, lifting me off the ground.

On the projection TV, Jonas Brown said, "Hello." Findlay jumped up and down like a monkey, seeing me being apprehended.

He quickly regained his composure and addressed Jonas Brown. Narrowing his eyes, Findlay opened his mouth to reply.

Whack!

Findlay's head rocked as something splattered against the side of his face. With one eye shut and one big pasty mouth hanging open, he put a hand to his cheek. The offending object was a clear liquid, delivered in . . . a water balloon? The gathered crowd "Ooh"ed in disbelief.

Splat! A water balloon hit Dean Anderson.

"Findlay!" Someone yelled from the crowd. "You jerk!"

Wearing a baseball cap, sunglasses, and a huge green USF baseball jersey, Melissa pulled a water-filled condom from a plastic shopping bag and threw it.

"Findlay!" She called again, preparing to lob another bomb. He squinted into the crowd.

Then, from the mob of students, came: "Eat it, loser!"

Another missile sailed.

Findlay took another direct hit.

The TV cameramen zoomed in on Melissa. When they did, she spun around and dropped her pants.

"Kiss my butt, Findlay!" she yelled, slapping her bare behind for the cameras.

THE NAVIGATORS

That, the cameramen didn't want to miss. But the offstage director shouted that it couldn't go on the air, and he dumped out of the live feed. The big screen went blank.

Mission accomplished.

The campus cops dropped me to go get Melissa, who was obviously the bigger threat. She moved into the crowd, stripping off the glasses and hat. She undid her pony tail and shook out her long brown hair, then peeled off the jersey and dropped it to the ground.

Then, she calmly—but quickly—mingled into the chaotic crowd and disappeared.

Which was my cue to disappear, too.

In the distance, the beep-beep-beep of a backing truck was barely audible as a tow truck locked on to Melissa's car.

While Findlay wiped the water off his over-moussed head, I slipped away with a group of cheerleaders who had been assembled for the live shot. After the commotion started, they bailed, and I bailed with them.

Halfway across the commons, and far enough from Findlay to avoid scrutiny, I made a break for the bookstore. From there, I could sneak through the parking lots and work my way back to my dorm room.

When I was almost there, my cell phone rang. *Melissa.*

I didn't know if I should answer it. What if she has been caught and they were now tracking us all down?

I swallowed hard and pushed the green button.

"Peeky! It's me!" Melissa was out of breath.

I walked along the sidewalk as fast as I could without drawing attention. "Are you okay?"

"I'm fine. I got away. But don't go back to your room. There was a ton of security at the commons. Findlay was expecting us. They probably have somebody waiting at my apartment and at your dorm room, too."

I stopped in my tracks. "What am I supposed to do?"

"Don't go to your dorm. Don't go anywhere you'd normally go."

"Should I stay off the phone?" Her answers were scaring me a little.

She chuckled. "Peeky, don't be a schmuck. They're campus cops, not the FBI. Get to a safe place like a bar, or someplace else you don't usually go. Then, lay low. Call me when you get there and I'll come get you."

"How are you going to come get me? Your car got towed."

"Oh, no. Really? I'll have to borrow a friend's car, then."

I frowned. "I told you not to park there!"

"I'll get a car, don't worry. Then we can check on Barry."

"Barry," I grumbled. "That jerk never showed."

"There wasn't time. But now he isn't answering his phone."

I thought for a moment. "I'll make my way to the Pancake House on 56th street. Come get me there."

"What!" Melissa was huffing and puffing. "That's like a five mile hike. Just, you know, go to the Chick-Fil-A across the street from school or something."

"I can't! I *live* at that Chick-Fil-A! You said to go where I *don't* usually go. I never eat pancakes."

"Geez, okay, fine. The Pancake House. Or wherever. Call me when you get there, but I'll need at least an hour."

"Okay." I ended the call. Drenched in sweat, partly from running but mostly from fear, I started walking again. It felt like every person on the street knew what I was up to.

* * * * *

Findlay clenched his fists. Now angrier than ever, he wanted his revenge and he knew just how to counterattack. He bellowed into the microphone on the table. "Jonas! Jonas! Are you there?"

The live broadcast feed had stopped, but the cameras and microphones were still connected to the studio. The unflappable Jonas Brown came over the wires. "Mr. Findlay, are you okay?"

Findlay adjusted his ear piece to hear the anchorman better. "Oh, I'm fine. And I still have news for you today. Will you cover it?"

"Well, Mr. Findlay . . ." Jonas cleared his throat. "Based on what I'm seeing and hearing, do you think that would be a good idea?"

"I don't know. Do you think a grad student hiding a stolen time machine in their apartment is a good idea?"

"What? What are you talking about?"

"I *saw* it, Jonas." Findlay held the microphone close to his mouth. "A time machine. It exists, and they have it. I think that's a heckuva story."

Brown paused. "I'm listening."

"Think about it. I was called in to analyze a device that Barry Helm and his nutjob crew of pseudo paleontology students stole from central Florida mine number 31. They found a time machine, Jonas, *and I can prove it!*"

Findlay held his cell phone up to the stationery TV camera at the front of the stage.

"I took pictures of it!"

Findlay continued waving his cell phone at the camera, working hard to get the interest in the story reignited. Jonas Brown, for his part, appeared ready to dump the whole thing and call it a day.

"Jonas, when Barry asked me to come see his discovery from the mine, I took pictures. Later, when I verified my data with Dr. Anderson, we agreed on what Barry had found."

"And you're saying that is . . ."

"It's a time machine. A bona fide, true to life, machine built to bridge time. That's what our major scientific breakthrough announcement was supposed to be today, not the acceptance of another big grant. We had to dupe you guys a little bit, but now you get to do the *really* big story."

"That's pretty incredible, Mr. Findlay." Frowning, he folded his arms over his chest.

"That's right, it sure is." Findlay maneuvered his way around the stage to get close to Dr. Anderson. "And I can show it to you."

"Dr. Anderson, is this true?"

Findlay's hook was baited. Anderson's jaw flapped in the wind as the blood drained from his face. "Well, actually, Jonas, I, uh . . ."

Findlay leaned in close. "C'mon, Herb! Don't be a wimp! It's too late for that now."

The crowd hushed. The loudspeakers were still on. Everyone looked at Dr. Anderson. Had he seen the time machine?

Anderson cleared his throat.

"Well, Jonas . . ."

The distant hum of a lawn mower was the only sound on the commons.

"Yes." Dr. Anderson sat up straight and adjusted his tie. "Yes, I did meet with Mr. Findlay here, and together we verified the data he presented."

Anderson puffed out his chest and took the microphone away from Findlay, walking around the stage and gesturing grandly. "And it *is* a time machine! *We* have acquired a working time machine. *Our* numbers bear it out."

The crowd went wild.

"That's . . . incredible!" Jonas' eyes widened.

Findlay beamed. "It's incredible, all right."

"Quiet, Mr. Findlay." Dr. Anderson covered the mic. "This isn't just your big moment anymore. You got me into this mess, so I'm gonna cash in, too." He lowered his voice. "We're all gonna cash in." A phony grin stretched across Anderson's face. "There will be a lot of big time corporate interest in this now. So smile and wave, Findlay. Smile and wave. You little turd."

Findlay smiled and waved.

Jonas Brown smiled, too. "Let's get our news crew over there for the big reveal, fellas."

"You got it, Jonas." Dr. Anderson smiled, waving at the crowd.

"I'll be there in thirty minutes." Jonas stood and unclipped his mic from his suitcoat, holding it to his face. "Have some coffee and donuts ready, okay?"

Anderson's head pumped up and down. "Okay, Jonas."

The screen went dark. The crowd roared at the news. In thirty minutes, Chris Findlay, Dr. Anderson, and Jonas Brown would put USF on the map by showing the world a time machine hidden in Barry's apartment.

CHAPTER SIXTEEN

Findlay turned to the nearest producer, a tall black woman. "So, we have thirty minutes, then?"

"Oh, no, honey." She coiled up the microphone cable. "We need to move *now*. It takes time to set up a news feed from a remote. How far away is this apartment we're going to?"

"Like a mile or so."

"Yeah, we need to get rolling asap, sugar. Give me the address." She turned to her crew and shouted. "Pack up, everybody! I want two cameras for a live shot at the new location! We're on again in thirty!"

Findlay stood, still wet from the water bombs. "Do I have time to get cleaned up?"

She looked him over, frowning. "I don't think it's gonna do much. You pasty white boys tend to wash out under the camera lights."

* * * * *

Across campus, my escape had slowed from a run to a jog. I hadn't seen anybody following me. That didn't mean they wouldn't be on me soon, though.

I finally allowed myself to walk. I was gassed. What a morning.

There was no way I could wait until I got all the way to the Pancake House. It was easily another thirty minute hike, maybe more. I had to find out what had happened. And I needed to pee. The local news would probably soon be replaying whatever they'd videoed at the commons, so the internet might have it now. I glanced around to see where I could take refuge.

I had almost made it to Chick-Fil-A.

After entering the restaurant, I used the restroom, ordered a soda, and sat. They had a big TV on in the lobby, replaying the melee on campus. Then they went back to a live feed.

"We are now just moments away," the announcer said. "Channel 8 news crews are arriving at the apartment where USF computer science graduate student Chris Findlay has witnessed a working time machine hidden in his friend's apartment."

What! Findlay was taking them to Barry's!

The loud buzz of an engine came over the roof. A news helicopter soared by. Onscreen, the TV announcer continued. "Findlay claims the machine was stolen from a central Florida mine and stashed in the apartment of two USF graduate paleontology students, who are also mentioned by authorities as being 'persons of interest' in the theft. We are

THE NAVIGATORS

coming to you *live* from near the USF campus, where the time machine will be revealed to us—and to all of you—next. Stay tuned."

They went to commercial, but they did a split screen to show the live shot from the news helicopter as it showed a parade of cars descending on Barry's apartment complex. They would be at his door in no time.

* * * * *

As the helicopter circled overhead, swarms of students cascaded into the apartment complex, not knowing which building or apartment was Barry's.

For that, they needed Findlay. He had shrewdly withheld Barry's apartment number. He wasn't about to get dealt out again.

The producer walked up to him and put a hand on her hip. "Any chance you're gonna tell us which door, sugar?"

"No way." Findlay folded his arms over his chest.

"I wouldn't either." She winked at him. "Okay then, you're on in a sec." She motioned to the cameras. "Camera one, be ready to go in close and get any action. Camera two, stay on your tripod and get set shots and wide views." As they nodded, she sipped a coffee. "Okay. Light it up."

A bright set of camera lights beamed into Findlay's pasty white face. He squinted.

"Findlay, you're on in thirty seconds," the producer said. "Be ready. I will count you down from five. Watch for my hand." She waved. "Over here."

He blinked, wiping his hands on his shirt.

She grinned at him. "Don't worry, you'll do fine."

The impeccably dressed Jonas Brown popped out of a nearby van. He marched to Findlay, scowling. "This is supposed to be my shot, kid."

Findlay gulped.

"On in ten, Jonas."

"Okay." Jonas straightened his jacket and turned toward the camera, then glanced at Findlay. "Don't mess this up."

"Five . . . four . . . three . . . "

The producer's hand wagged two fingers, then one, then she pointed at Jonas Brown and Findlay. They were now live, beaming out to millions of viewers.

* * * * *

I watched it all unfold from Chick-Fil-A. The ghost-faced Findlay looked like he was going to wet his pants. Then the perfectly coiffed anchorman began to speak.

"Jonas Brown, here, coming to you *live* from the campus of the University of South Florida, where a fantastic discovery has been made." The shot widened to include Findlay. "With us this morning is Chris Findlay, a student in computer science here at USF." Jonas put the microphone in front of Findlay's mouth "Mr. Findlay, what can you tell us about what we're going to see this morning?"

Findlay froze. The bright lights and all the excitement seemed to have finally gotten to him. He slowly opened his mouth.

Nothing came out.

THE NAVIGATORS

* * * * *

"Mr. Findlay?" Jonas Brown prompted.

The stage director caught Findlay's eye. He managed to look at her. She nodded and mouthed some words. *You're okay. Breathe.*

He breathed.

She smiled. *Go on*, she mouthed.

Findlay's thoughts started returning to him. "Jonas," he said. "Jonas Brown."

He flipped the switch and lit up. "Jonas Brown!" Findlay took a deep breath. "Whew! Buddy, just wait 'til you see what I have for you behind door number one!"

He was back. Findlay had recovered and was now on his game, embracing what would be his big moment. "As incredible as it may seem to your viewers, I witnessed a time machine–an actual, working time travel device–right here in this apartment behind us. It was recovered from a central Florida mine, and *stolen* from the University. And it's just up those stairs."

"You say it was stolen, Mr. Findlay?"

"That's right. Paleontology student Barry Helm stole the property off the USF campus after delivering it to Dean Anderson in the paleontology lab." Findlay grinned at the camera. "The thieves asked me to help identify what it was, but of course I had no idea it was stolen. And then, once they knew what they had, they removed the device from the campus and hid it here in this apartment."

"They *stole* it?" Jonas' baritone voice dramatized the moment. "That's quite a charge."

"They did. They stole it. I have the documents right here, all signed by Dr. Anderson, the Dean of Paleontology." He held a log sheet up to the camera. "These papers say that Barry Helm and the other suspects checked the machine into the USF paleontology lab."

* * * * *

I jumped out of my chair and screeched at the TV. "That's a lie!" Then I lowered myself back down and hunched my shoulders, checking to see if anybody in the Chick-Fil-A had called the cops. A few employees stared at me before returning to their duties.

"The documents are right here, Jonas," Findlay said. Then, he went Hollywood "These log sheets prove that they stole the machine! And the stolen time machine is right up these steps! Follow me!"

Findlay turned and stormed up the steps to Barry's apartment. The news cameras followed.

My heart was in my throat. *Holy cow! They've got Barry dead to rights! It's all over.*

Findlay paused in front of Barry's front door. Next to him, Jonas Brown straightened his jacket again. As the cameras moved into position, he whispered to Findlay. "We really should cut to a commercial and go in after the break for maximum viewer tease and a big draw on the reveal."

Findlay stared back with a blank face.

The camera lights went on again. Jonas stood rigid as ever. "We are here, live, ready to go into the purported suspect's apartment, where - "

Findlay tried the doorknob. It was unlocked.

Jonas Brown interrupted himself. "Mr. Findlay, do we have permission - "

Findlay ignored him. "Barry! Its Chris Findlay and Jonas Brown from channel 8! We're coming in!"

He pushed open the door.

The TV camera refocused and zoomed in on Barry's apartment, scanning the living room. We all looked around with it as it beamed the contents into houses all around the Tampa Bay area.

There stood Barry's couch. His coffee table. And directly across from it was . . .

Nothing. The machine was gone.

Jonas was visibly dismayed. "What's going on here Mr. Findlay?"

Undaunted, Findlay waved Jonas off. "Stay with me, JB. I know it's in here." He began to run around Barry's apartment like a maniac, checking behind counters and in closets. "Barry!" Findlay yelled. "I know you're in here! What did you do with the machine!"

Shaking his head, Jonas made the "cut" signal by waving his hand across his throat.

Just then, a thump came from the bathroom.

Findlay's eyes widened. "He's in the bathroom with it!" He charged ahead. "Come on!"

An ambitious cameraman knocked Jonas aside, sprinting across the apartment.

"You can't go in there," Jonas shouted. "It's trespassing."

The cameraman scurried after Findlay. "If I win a Pulitzer, I won't care!"

Reaching the bathroom at the far side of the living room, Findlay stood ready, shrewdly waiting for the camera to catch up. "Barry!" he called with added dramatic flair. "Come on out. It's all over!"

Findlay put his hand on the door knob and glanced at the cameraman. "Be sure to get this, camera one."

He slowly turned the knob.

"Ready . . .

"Set . . .

"GO!"

Findlay threw open the door to reveal . . . Nothing. *Again*.

From Chick-Fil-A, I saw the toilet, the sink... and the shower curtain.

Findlay stared at it and hesitated for a moment.

The curtain flew back. Riff smiled as the cameras zoomed in. He pulled back his fist and punched Findlay right in the head.

Findlay fell to the floor in a heap.

Riff scowled at the cameraman. "Did you get that, camera one?"

"That's the money shot, baby!" The cameraman backpedalled away from Riff and scampered out of the apartment.

Jonas Brown was not amused. "I need to apologize to our viewers at home." He took a deep breath and adjusted his jacket. "I'm sorry. This appears to have all been an elaborate hoax." Findlay groaned in the background. Jonas ignored it.

"I'm Jonas Brown for news channel 8. Back to you in the studio."

* * * * *

"Aaand we're done," The producer lowered her headset microphone. "That's it people, let's go. Nothing to see here."

"Except a breaking and entering charge for Chris Findlay!" Riff slammed the front door shut.

"Except for that." The producer retreated down the stairs.

CHAPTER SEVENTEEN

Findlay stayed motionless, pretending to be unconscious until he was sure Riff had left. He'd been seeing stars anyway, so it wasn't hard to pretend, and there was no rush.

Despite the blood that had collected on his nose and cheeks and the pounding headache, he started right to work. He dug out his cell phone from his pocket.

The voice on the other end answered before it logged one full ring. "Findlay? How'd it go?"

"It went well enough. I'm in the apartment and we're on to Plan B."

"Ooh, plan B, huh? How bad was it?"

Findlay inspected himself in the mirror, watching a deep shade of purple form on his cheek. He laid a finger on the rising welt and winced. The lump at the back of his head—a result of where he'd met the floor—sent waves of pain through his throbbing skull. "Guess I'll live. Now, walk me through this. Where do we start, at Barry's computer?"

"Yeah. I'll get you into that and then we'll start encoding and downloading. Let me know when you're ready."

Findlay giggled a little as he strolled out to the living room and stared at Barry's desk. "I'm ready now. The cocky jerk left his laptop right here for me."

"Did you bring your stuff?"

"It's in the car. I'll go get it and call you right back."

* * * * *

"Dean Anderson, it's Ashby White, president of Florida Electric Company. How are you?"

Burt Anderson had been driving back to his office, wondering what to do about the mess that was unfolding before him. He considered not answering his phone, but whatever bad news it might be, he knew he'd feel worse if he didn't know.

"Mr. White. Hello."

What did a major donor want? Anderson didn't want to talk, not even to a cash cow like Ashby White, but faculty members can't exactly turn down a call like that.

"Please, call me Ashby. Dean, I've just heard some amazing things on the radio about USF and some sort of discovery. It might be just the sort of thing Florida Electric would be interested in. Very interested."

"How so?" Anderson tried not to sound anxious.

"Well, you know, every once in a while some farmer builds a car that runs on pig manure or something, right? It's kind of like that. A time machine probably uses some creative ways to get around, so to speak. Methods of powering itself that are useful for a power company to know about."

Anderson felt a kind of calm settle his stomach. "Funny, I never hear about pig poop cars driving all over the place."

"No, you don't, do you? And with the proper legal paperwork, you never will. Lots of rich folks in the world like to keep things just the way they are – with themselves in control. Oil companies, kings in oil producing nations. Lots of folks. But that doesn't mean the farmer went away empty handed. If this thing turns out to be what you think it is, I can foresee some very lucrative contracts coming your way. To the university, and maybe some consulting contracts for you and your young friend, Mr. Findlay."

"Mr. White, with all due respect, I have a reputation to consider."

"Oh, I know all about your reputation, dean. Why do you think I called you myself? I've heard that you're a man of vision. One who can see down the road – if he is properly compensated. Now, this machine could be worth a lot of money. The finder's fee alone could be millions – if the discovery is legit. Is it?"

Millions. No more shipping the big fossil finds off to the more prestigious schools. Anderson's hands had been sweaty before from nerves; now they gripped the steering wheel with anticipation.

The dean cleared his throat. "Can I assume there would be other interested parties?"

"Yes, you could assume that, Dr. Anderson." Ashby White chuckled. "You could also assume that other governments would be interested in such a machine and its power source, its technology. Think about it. A hostile foreign government using a time machine against the United States in a war. They'd know our every move in advance. The results could be devastating. Such a thing could never be allowed to fall into the wrong hands. It would ruin our American way of life. Why, it's practically your patriotic duty to sell it to us. And to let us protect you."

"Protect me? From what?"

"Well, I'm not the only person who watches TV. That news feed went out locally, but soon all sorts of people in other countries will be watching it on the internet. People who might wish to do the U.S. harm. How fast could they board a plane and get to Tampa to take it from you? A day? Two? And do you think they'd be nice enough to call you up and ask you about it like I'm doing, or do you think they'd just saw through your neck with a machete and take it? I'm sorry to be blunt, but there are bad people in the world. It took less than five minutes for my people to connect me to your cell phone. If we can track you down that fast, so can others."

Anderson swallowed hard. "I hadn't thought about all that."

"And why should you? You're a man of science. It's your job to be scientific. It's my job as the head of a big bad energy corporation to be aware of the uglier side of life. You sell the machine to us and we take care of everything. Then you can be safe. You and any of your partners."

Images of beheadings had been in the news lately. Thoughts of himself being one were unsettling. "I'll have to think about it," Dean Anderson said, trying to sound confident.

"Of course. This is my direct line I'm calling you from. Call me back when you've made a decision. And, doctor . . ."

"Yes?"

"Don't take too long."

* * * * *

Sitting down at Barry's computer, Findlay dialed his cell phone again. "Okay, I'm back with my little bag of tricks."

"Okay. First, we want to install spyware. While that's getting configured, we can do the other stuff. The most important one was the tracker, which is on your computer. How long do you think you have before these guys come back?"

Findlay glanced around. "If I were Barry, I wouldn't come back at all. Riff, either. They probably talked, so . . ."

"Well, we'll know in a few minutes. Find the skim recorder you planted the other night."

"That's right here." Findlay pulled a band aid sized device off the bottom of Barry's computer. The one he had attached the other morning while the others ate donuts and clucked over their discovery.

"Place the skim recorder onto the downloader and it will automatically replay any key strokes entered on that computer between now and when you put it on. If Barry accessed his computer, it will have recorded the username and password, plus maybe a little more. It'll sift through and search for login information."

Findlay pulled a rectangular device out of his duffel bag. He laid the skim recorder on it and waited. "Do I need to press a button or anything?"

"Nope. Give it a minute. When it finds the skimmer it will-"

The downloader beeped. A short list of words and letters appeared on the screen.

"Sounds like we got it. What's it say?"

"It says the computer registration number and Barry's login information. Unbelievable." Findlay giggled as he typed it into Barry's computer. The home screen appeared.

"Easy as that," Findlay said. "You guys have the coolest gear."

"What did you expect? We're MIT, baby. We kicked Vegas' butt in card counting, for Pete's sake. This kind of stuff is what we do."

Findlay inserted a thumb drive and downloaded the spyware. The progress bar indicated that it was downloading quickly. "Righteous props to Barry. His machine's a beast. It's blazing through this stuff."

"All speed and no security, huh? That's pretty cocky."

"You have no idea." Findlay tapped the desk, staring at the machine as it worked.

"Of course, who would think some rock digger has anything worth stealing off his computer anyway?"

Findlay nodded. "He didn't. Not until he discovered a time machine."

"Well, then his lack of security was his second mistake."

"What do you mean?"

"Trusting you was his first. You stuck a tracker onto the time machine, right?"

"Yeah." Findlay leaned forward in the chair. "Hey, and I was completely trustworthy until he tried to deal me out."

"Really? I seem to recall an urgent phone call about the need to steal passwords and hack cell phones and track movements of objects—and that was a few hours *before* you went back for your breakfast visit."

"There's a word for that."

"Paranoid?"

"Smart." Findlay rocked in the chair. "I figured those clowns might cut and run as soon as they got what they needed from me, and I was right. I think they even concocted a little fight just to make it look good." The spyware download concluded. Findlay pulled the thumb drive out of the computer. "Now those dirt diggers won't be able to sneeze electronically without me knowing about it."

"Fin, you're positively evil."

"I prefer to think of myself as innovative." He slid the thumb drive back into his bag. "How else do you think I was able to spend two years not showing up for a college class or exam and still get straight A's?"

"Nice. So what happens now?"

Findlay leaned on the desk, arms folded, watching the computer screen. "Now, I see where they go, what they do, who they talk to. When the time is right, I'll swoop down and scoop them up, one at a time. They'll never know what hit them. But first, I'm getting into each of their computers and doing a little recon."

"Why do I think you'll also be looking for bikini selfies on the girl's computer?"

Findlay smiled. "Well, if I find that, so much the better."

"Don't be a perv, Fin. Keep it business."

"Hey, this *is* business. That doesn't mean I can't enjoy it."

"How's that tie into crashing their credit cards?"

"Shutting off their cell phones and credit cards will force them into the open. Going through all their computers and records is the best way to find the time machine so I can get it back. Then I'll be running things. It's all strictly business." He chuckled. "The fact that it messes with them immensely is just a nice side benefit."

* * * * *

At his desk, Dean Anderson typed a few words into his computer.

Curiosity nagged at him. He searched on Florida Electric quarterly earnings, OPEC annual revenues, oil prices. It was impressive. Billions and billions of dollars traded hands annually in power companies. It was something he always knew but didn't really *know*. Now he could be a part of it. The money, anyway. And there was a lot of it in the power and energy business. Enough to make Ashby White's opening offer seem very realistic.

While he pondered his next move, he did an image search on the French Riviera and private jets.

He resisted the urge to watch the latest beheading video.

* * * * *

Findlay stared in amazement at his iPad. The screen was displaying the movements of cell phones, laid out over a simple map.

They haven't gone anywhere.

It appeared as though everybody had hunkered down in different locations. Maybe they were asleep. But the blip he was most interested in hadn't come yet. It would, soon enough. It should be pinging away from the location of the other object he tagged during the donut meeting. The time machine.

In a simple motion, he'd stuck a small radio emitter onto the underside of it. As soon as it synched up with the receiver, it would let him know exactly where it was. The cell phone trackers and credit card trolls used different software, but his MIT buddy had assured him that the transmitter would eventually sync up and ping him with its location. So far, it hadn't.

But while we wait . . . let's have a look at some phone records. Who've you been calling on your cell phone, Barry?

With a few keystrokes, he had the phone bill open on the computer. Barry had only called a few different numbers in the last few hours. Findlay clicked open a search engine and dropped the phone numbers into a reverse lookup to see who they belonged to. The first one was Melissa. Scanning the record, he could see that quite a few calls went to her, in a brief time span, but they were all pretty short in duration. Voicemails, probably.

He hadn't reached her.

The second number showed as Tandy Corporation.

Radio Shack. What was he doing calling them? It might be worth a visit to find out.

He typed the last number into the reverse lookup.

Howard Jones subaccount. Somebody's family plan, and not a cell phone, either. A land line.

Another quick search showed the main area code located in New York, but the sub account's area code was 813.

Tampa.

Findlay scratched his chin. He hadn't wanted to be in Barry's apartment this long, but it was hard to walk away from this much information. Relaying it all to his own computer would slow things down.

Barry had the time machine last; Melissa probably doesn't have it because he never reached her. Could Barry have passed it off to this Howard Jones guy? Maybe.

Who's Howard Jones, Barry? Let's find out.

He pulled out his cell phone and dialed.

Findlay heard the purring of the phone in his ear. He also heard a land line phone ringing somewhere else. He pulled the cell phone away and listened. The phone next door was ringing. Jones; Jonesy. Howard Jones must be Denise Jones's father. He walked a few feet to the wall separating the two apartments and leaned into it.

A voice came through Findlay's cell phone. "Hi, this is Denise . . ."

He held his breath and leaned against the wall. The ringing had stopped. He thought he could hear a woman's recorded voice asking him to leave a message at the beep.

And through the wall, he heard a faint beep.

I called the apartment next door. The machine – and Barry – might be right on the other side of this wall.

Careful Findlay. Think about your next move. Don't scare them. Do they know I'm over here? Maybe. Do they know I'm calling next door? They might, if they have caller ID.

Holy cow, what do I do?

Flush them out. Get them to leave that apartment. They'll either leave with the time machine or leave without it.

How do I make them do that?

He quietly paced Barry's living room and stopped at the sliding door, gazing out to the building across the lawn. It was the same layout as this one. One staircase up, small windows, a balcony.

Then his eyes rested on the grill on Barry's balcony.

And the charcoal. And the lighter fluid.

They'll definitely leave if they think the building is on fire.

He went to the front door. Outside, mounted on the wall between the apartments, was the red pull handle box for the fire alarm.

Findlay nearly jumped up and down at the sight. He tiptoed back to the desk and gathered his things to retreat to his car.

I need some backup. I don't need to confront Barry by myself. Couldn't hurt to have the cops take him into custody for stealing the university's property, though.

He pulled out his cell phone again.

"Herb, it's Findlay. I'm at Barry's apartment." He walked over to the pull station by the downstairs apartment doors. "You'll want to get over here, and bring some campus security with you—some big guys Barry won't want to mess with."

"Is the time machine there?" Dean Anderson asked.

"We're about to find out. What's the penalty for pulling one of these fire alarm things when there's not a fire?"

"$25,000 and expulsion if you get caught."

Findlay glanced at the apartment building. "Then I'd better not get caught. You'll need to cover me for that."

Then he yanked the little box open and pulled down the handle, causing the fire alarm siren to blare.

It was louder than he expected. He rubbed his fingers together. They were covered in a sticky yellow goo that would show the fire fighters whoever had pulled the alarm. The handle had been painted with fluorescent grease on the back side to not tip off drunken partygoers. Findlay calmly walked back to his car for a napkin.

One by one, the apartment doors opened. Curious student residents meandered out, checking to see if anything was really on fire. They were used to false alarms—pranks, usually, by partying residents.

Findlay watched. Nobody came out of Jones' unit.

Crap.

He hadn't thought about false alarms. Maybe they'd just sit inside and ride it out. But if they weren't there, surely the machine still would be. He wiped off the paint he could remove, seeing his fingers stained bright yellow. A quick hand check of the crowd would identify him as the culprit. He shoved his hand in his pocket.

A few other doors opened. Residents gathered near Findlay and stared at the building.

Findlay trained his eyes on Jones' door. In a few minutes, fire trucks would be showing up. He began to get nervous. They were off campus. If the firefighters arrived before Dean Anderson, Findlay might get arrested by Tampa police, not university cops. Anderson might not have the clout to help him then.

On the other hand, if it wasn't a false alarm, anybody holed up in there would come out.

The whine of distant fire truck sirens grew louder as they approached. The apartment alarm continued to blare.

"Findlay!"

He turned. Dean Anderson ran up to him. "What's going on? Where's the time machine?"

"It's still inside. They're not coming out with it."

"Are you sure it's in there?"

"Pretty sure."

"*Pretty* sure?"

Findlay nodded. "Herb, I need a favor."

"Haven't I done enough? This is getting serious now."

"Oh, Herb—we're just getting started." Findlay put his hand on Anderson's shoulder. "When the fire department gets here in a minute, tell them that a brave hero named Chris Findlay went into the burning building to rescue people from the flames."

Dean Anderson eyed the building. "I don't see any flames."

Findlay smiled. "Give me a minute."

He ran up the steps to Barry's apartment, walked to the balcony, and inspected the charcoal and lighter fluid for the grill. "Simple grill fire gone wrong," he said. "Happens all the time." Then he opened the sliding door.

The fire trucks rolled up, honking at students to clear a path. As they surveyed the scene, they couldn't help but notice a lack of smoke and flames.

"Where's the fire?" A firefighter asked the gathered students. He was met by a lot of shrugs.

Findlay grabbed the lighter fluid and stepped inside, squirting it everywhere. On the grill, on the carpet, and on Barry's computer. He casually knocked over the bag of charcoal and doused it with lighter fluid, too. The chemical solvent smell hit his nostrils and woke him up to the reality of what he was doing. He glanced around for a match.

* * * * *

"Professor, do you know what's going on?"

Dean Anderson turned to address the fire captain. "I don't know that I do, no."

"Have you seen any flames or smoke, sir?"

"Give it a minute."

"Excuse me?"

The Dean caught himself. "I think one of these upstairs units had something coming out of it. That's why they pulled the alarm."

"You saw who pulled the alarm?"

"Ah, no. He called me."

The fire captain leaned in to Dean Anderson. "Sir, are you saying that somebody went back inside a burning unit?"

Anderson watched the building. "I think so, yes."

Aggravated, the captain placed his hand on his hips. "Would you mind telling me which unit that was?"

* * * * *

Upstairs, Findlay stared at the long nose of the grill lighter. With a snap, a blue butane flame appeared out the end. He squatted and lowered it to the fuel-soaked carpet. With a loud whoosh, bright yellow flames leaped from the floor, forcing him to close his eyes and back away. The fire raced from the sliding door to the desk, engulfing everything in its path: the grill, the charcoal, and the computer.

He blinked in the sudden heat, squinting as he admired his handiwork. The apartment was burning nicely. Not at all like on TV. No smoke, really; just nice clean flames.

That changed soon enough. The plastic in the carpet melted as the lighter fluid burned off. Thick reams of black smoke surged into the air. The burning curtains sent flames sprawling across the ceiling where they danced. Smoke worked its way from the walls to the center and then downward.

I guess I should be going.

He crouched, glancing at the front door. Smoke poured out of it. *That should be enough for the fire department to see it wasn't a false alarm.* He was excited, not scared. A small line of burning carpet barred his way to the door. He stepped over it and turned to survey the room. Patches of carpet burned. The two side walls were completely engulfed and the ceiling was smoking nicely. The couch was starting to smolder.

Mission accomplished. The adjoining apartment should be filling with smoke soon, and then he'd have the time machine.

Dean Anderson pointed over the Fire Captain's shoulder. "There's our hero now." Findlay emerged from the smoking apartment and came down the stairs. The fire fighters had arranged their equipment, spraying the building with water.

Anderson beamed. "Mr. Findlay, thank goodness you're safe." Then under his breath he whispered, "Arson? Have you lost your mind?"

Findlay ignored the comment. "Do you have a hanky?"

Anderson pulled his handkerchief from his pocket. Findlay held it to his nose and blew, leaving two black snot smudges in it. He stared at it for a moment. "Herb, this machine is worth millions. Keep your eyes on the prize." He handed back the handkerchief. "Thanks."

Then he walked to the steps and waited.

Steam rose from the places the firemen sprayed, but black smoke still poured from the apartment. Next door, nothing was happening. Maybe it hadn't worked. Still, anybody inside wouldn't know that. They'd smell the smoke and maybe see the fire trucks. They wouldn't likely risk their lives.

On the other hand, a little prompting couldn't hurt.

"Barry!" Findlay stepped toward the building. "It's all over! The place is on fire! Come on out."

Some smoke began to seep from the roof over Jonesy's apartment. Things had to be heating up inside.

"Barry, I know you can hear me! Open the door and come out. It's getting dangerous."

Findlay watched as the door opened. A small cloud of smoke was sucked inside. Then a stream of smoke poured out the top of the door. There was coughing. One person ran out, then another. They were met on the stairs by fire fighters.

THE NAVIGATORS

Neither looked like Barry.

"Findlay, you idiot!" Anderson hissed. "He's not even in there."

"He's in there." Findlay was resilient. He stared at the door, willing Barry to emerge.

A small yellow pickup truck pulled up and stopped behind the trees just past the apartment building.

"It's now or never, Barry. Give up or lose everything."

There was more coughing from inside the apartment.

Here we go.

After a few thumps, the time machine slid into the doorway. Then the sliding door opened onto the side balcony. A stream of smoke billowed out.

Barry walked out onto the balcony. His face was marred with soot and his hair was disheveled. "Findlay! You can have me or the machine. Not both." He gestured to the front door. "It's right there. Don't let it burn."

As Findlay and Dean Anderson sprinted up the staircase after the time machine, Barry put one leg over the balcony then the other. He squatted a little, then he jumped.

He landed with an awkward thud. Glancing around, Barry limped off toward the nearby tree line.

In Jonesy's doorway, Findlay and Anderson looked at the machine. Smoke was coming out fast. "Grab a rail and pull," Findlay said.

With one or two tugs, they had it out. "Just slide it down the stairs, Herb. On its rails." Findlay walked in front, guiding the machine backwards as Dean Anderson lowered it from behind.

"We're on you," called a fireman. He turned a cooling spray onto the steps.

At the bottom of the staircase, Findlay checked around. Barry was gone.

CHAPTER EIGHTEEN

Melissa turned the yellow pickup sharply around a corner, squealing its wheels and sending up a spray of dust. "Sheila, meet Barry. Barry, this is my friend Sheila."

The two occupants acknowledged each other while holding on for dear life. The three of them were crowded into the front seat.

"Can you tell me why I'm not driving my own car?" Sheila asked, grabbing the dashboard. Barry fumbled for a seat belt.

Melissa smiled. "Simple, hon. If we get caught, you can say you were kidnapped. No federal charges."

"Oh, boy. That sounds serious."

Barry coughed. "I'd say it is."

Sheila glanced at him. "You know, you're cute but you stink."

He nodded. "I need to quit smoking."

"You can say that again."

"No, I mean literally. I just escaped a burning building. I may be on fire. Can you check?"

"The boy *is* on fire." She slapped at some of the smoking parts of Barry's shirt. "What have you gotten me into, Melissa?"

"That's a good point." Melissa hit the brakes. "Get out."

"What!" Sheila's jaw dropped as she glared at her friend. "You're gonna throw me out of my own car? I don't even know where we are."

Melissa pointed to a nearby street sign. "This is an access road that runs near the interstate. It'll dump you onto Fowler Avenue by the pancake house. By the new hotel they built."

"So? I'm not getting out! You borrowed my car, you can't throw me out."

"Sheila, we've been friends since sophomore year. You know you can trust me. Barry and I are in big trouble. You'll be happy later if you aren't seen with us."

"Fine. Then take me back to my apartment. I'm not walking."

Melissa reached over and hugged her. "Oh, sweetie, I would. I hate to do this to you. But the less you know, the better. It's not safe. Our lives may be in danger."

Sheila returned the hug. "Melissa, you're scaring me. What kind of trouble are you in?"

"The kind where they burn down your apartment to get you out," Barry said. "That kind."

"So I'm supposed to just stroll on home? In this heat?"

A moment later Melissa had pushed Sheila over Barry's lap and out the door.

"This isn't right!" She stomped her foot on the hot pavement. "You can't throw somebody out of their own car after you ask to borrow it!" As the pickup sped away, Sheila placed her hands on her hips. "And you better leave me some gas money!"

Barry glanced at Melissa. "Will she turn us in?"

"No. Besides, she doesn't know where we're going."

He grimaced as he adjusted his weight in the seat. "Where *are* we going?"

"Well, I was going to pick up Peeky until you called me. He and I were gonna go somewhere and lay low until we hatched a plan—but now, what's up with your foot?"

"I hurt it pretty good when I jumped off the balcony." Barry took a deep breath and lifted his leg with his hands. "It may be broken."

"Broken?" Melissa glanced in the rear view mirror. "Well, that changes things. How bad is it? Can you put any weight on it?"

He winced again. "No. In fact, it's getting pretty sore just sitting here. It's like somebody's stabbing me with a knife, right above my ankle."

"You broke a shin bone."

"It's the back side. The tibia."

"The tibia's the shin bone. You mean the fibula."

"Whatever, Missy! It's broken."

"Okay, okay. You need to rest it, ice it, elevate it. And get something for the pain until we can get to a doctor." She patted the seat. "Can you put it up here? Would that get the weight off it?"

He lifted his foot slightly. "Oh, crap, that hurts. That's not gonna work. There's not enough room, anyway."

"What about the other way? You need to elevate it. What if you put your head down here and your foot . . ." She pointed to the passenger window. "Up there?"

"That . . . that sounds terrible just thinking about it."

"Well, we have to do something. Should we go to UC?"

"University Community hospital? I'm starting to become a little too well known over there. I don't know if we can risk that." He thought for a moment. "Look, I can probably get around on it with some crutches if we can knock the freaking pain down a few bars."

Melissa stopped at a light and tapped the steering wheel. "Let's think. The cops don't know where we are yet, and if they pick Sheila up she can only tell them we dropped her off near the interstate. They'll probably think we high tailed it north or south on I-75. They won't be looking at hospitals. Nobody knows you're hurt – do they?"

"I wasn't watching the crowd that had gathered. I was preoccupied with jumping out of the burning apartment building."

"Well, if they don't know you're hurt, they won't be looking for us at hospitals. Not right away. We have at least a few hours. We can probably get you in and out before they think of it."

Barry sighed. "I hope you're right. Somehow Findlay managed to put together resources that made him able to burn down my apartment and get away with it. That's pretty formidable. He should be in jail right now. And Dean Anderson stood right there while it happened. That's not by chance."

"Somebody's helping them?"

"Somebody has to be. Things have gone to a new level. There's no way they'd do all this on their own."

"Well, it can't just be the university." Melissa's fingers drummed the steering wheel. "It's gotta be someone else, someone big enough to have the cops on their side—and to call off the fire department. That's a big deal by itself. I don't know who we trust at this point, so I think we lay low.

"Then what?"

The light turned green.

"I don't know." She stepped on the accelerator. "I'm working on it." She made her way down Fowler Avenue. "Besides, what was your big plan, smart guy? Holing up in Jonesy's apartment?"

"For a while, until I could come up with a better idea. I needed to buy some time. I just didn't buy enough."

"Yeah, well, that little stunt Peeky and I pulled at Findlay's news conference didn't do much except hack everybody off. Now we have a whole hive of bees after us."

"I saw that on the news." Barry chuckled. "Pretty funny. Let me ask you something. What was your plan if dropping your pants didn't work?"

She blushed a little. "I don't know." She made the next turn toward the hospital.

Barry smiled. "Man, what a couple of criminals we make. Where's the rest of the gang?"

"Peeky's supposed to be waiting for me at the pancake house. I don't know where Riff is."

"The pancake house we just passed? Why don't we get him?"

"Priorities. I can go back and get him in a few minutes. Your leg gets attention first so we know how bad it is. Hopefully we get that taken care of before anybody thinks to start sniffing around the hospitals. I'll get Peeky after I drop you off. Meanwhile, what about Riff?"

"Riff helped me move the time machine to Jonesy's. He's probably hiding now, too."

"He wasn't in Jonesy's apartment with you? Who was, then?"

"Freaking Jonesy." Barry laughed. "She came home this morning and brought her sister to tour the campus. I asked if we could park the machine at her place for a few hours until I could get a truck to move it."

"What did she say?"

"What *could* she say? Riff and I had already stuck it in her living room. Then we got her apartment burned down around them."

"Oh, no!"

"'Welcome to USF, sis.'"

"Oh, that poor thing."

"She asked for her key back. It seemed reasonable, since I almost got them killed. I'm guessing she and I aren't friends anymore."

"I'm guessing she doesn't need a key anymore. That place was burning pretty good when we left." Melissa glanced over her shoulder to change lanes. "You know, on the news Findlay was saying he had pictures." She eyed Barry. "What do you think? Could he?"

Barry rubbed his chin. "Maybe. I left him alone with the time machine a couple of times for a few minutes. Took a shower, made coffee." He peered out the window, hiding his embarrassment. "There were opportunities for him to take pictures, I guess. Maybe to do more than that."

"Okay, well don't beat yourself up over it. We've all trusted people we shouldn't."

"It's not just that. Getting Findlay involved was a mistake. Roger's in the hospital because I let him try the machine. Riff nearly got killed at the mine because I got distracted."

"Why, Barry Helm. It's not like you to second guess yourself."

He brushed at the soot covering his lap. "Yeah. I've been second guessing myself a lot the last day or two. About a lot of things." Barry studied her face for a moment. He noticed a slight smile, and enjoyed the restful silence.

Sensing his gaze, Melissa nervously fiddled with her hair. "What, uh, what distracted you at the mine?"

He shook his head. "It doesn't matter now."

Melissa stopped the truck in front of University Community Hospital. Barry looked out the window to the Emergency Room doors. "Do you think our favorite ER doctor will be on duty?"

"Dr. Harper?" Melissa sighed. "Geez, probably. That would just be our luck, wouldn't it?" She glanced at the emergency room doors and then back to Barry. "You want me to help you go in?"

"We can't risk it. Harper's probably gonna call the cops the minute he sees me. He thinks we're hurting ourselves on purpose or something."

"What?"

"He's starting to think we're a group of psychosexual thrill seekers who get banged up for the rush. He probably thinks we check somebody in and then come out and grope each other in the parking lot."

She turned to the window, blushing. "Grope? I . . . *here*? It's . . ."

Barry placed his hand on her shoulder. "It's crazy stuff, I know."

"Ha. Yeah, that's . . . crazy. Right?"

"Don't worry about it. I'll deal with Harper. There is one thing, though." He took a breath and looked down. "When I go in there, things could get a little intense." His eyes came up to meet hers. "It might be a while before we see each other again, you know?" A crooked smile tugged at his lips. "The place might be full of cops."

His hand still lingered on her shoulder.

"Yes?" she said, placing her hand on his.

Her warm fingers and soft skin took him away from the current situation. He gazed at her face, taking in her delicate features. The high cheek bones and big eyes. He swallowed and took her hand in his. It was all wrong, the timing, the setting, everything. Wrong to try to say something—

anything—of substance. But he couldn't stop smiling, and he didn't want to put her hand down. It might be a long time before he'd get another chance to say anything to her.

A car horn honked. Somebody had pulled up behind them and gotten tired of waiting.

The moment was gone – if it had ever existed.

He turned back to Melissa. "Uh, go . . . go get Peeky, then see about Riff. My phone's dead and I couldn't charge it at Jonesy's. Riff's phone is probably dead now, too, but we'll hear from him eventually." He popped open the truck door. "As soon as I'm finished here, I'll call you."

"Okay."

"You better take off before I go in so you aren't followed if they identify me."

Her gaze lingered on him. Even with a broken foot and people hunting for him, he still put her safety above his own.

"What?" His face broke into another grin. "What are you smiling at?"

"Nothing," Melissa turned away, putting her hand to her cheek. "Get going."

He slid out, careful not to place too much weight onto the injured leg, and shut the truck door. Balancing on one foot, he hopped toward the ER. As he neared the automatic doors, he glanced back.

The yellow truck was already gone.

* * * * *

"Captain Ferguson, it's Dean Anderson. How are you this afternoon?"

"I was kind of expecting your call, Herb. Saw you and that Findlay kid there on the news earlier. How's everything holding up?"

Nervous, Anderson tried his best not to sound that way. "Well, captain, as you probably saw, things are getting messy. A little bit of trouble that gets into the news becomes a lot of trouble." He fiddled with a pen on his desk. "I hope our campus police might be able to help out."

"What would you like us to do?"

Anderson cleared his throat. "You know, we want to avoid any further embarrassment to the University."

"Of course."

"What I'd like to do—if it's legal and *possible*—is to get a handful of your campus police and hire them as, shall we say, private security for a day or two." He leaned forward in his chair. "Just while we get this mess wrapped up."

"That's certainly possible. We help out with local events all the time in that capacity."

"Well, this would be a little different."

"I bet. What all would you want?"

Anderson knew what he wanted; he just didn't know how to ask. "I probably want maybe five or six officers, two or three squad cars . . ." He cleared his throat again. "We're looking for a handful of students with a big machine, that they've, you know—it belongs to the university—and they stole it. And, well, we . . . we'd like to find them as quickly as possible. And to keep a lid on this as much as possible."

"Avoid any further embarrassment."

Anderson sighed with relief. "Exactly."

"You can hire my guys. Basically, they go for $50 per hour plus vehicles and overtime. It's going to run about twelve hundred dollars a day."

Wow.

"Good grief, captain. Twelve hundred dollars a day *plus* cars?"

"And overtime. Then there will need to be shifts coordinated – a single cop can't work 24 hours straight for two or three days. That's a hundred bucks an hour. So . . . you're staring right at $16,800 a day for however many days. Gratuity not included. Dean, this is usually the place where I ask if your problem is worth spending more than $50,000 over three days to solve."

Remember: millions of dollars in finder's fees and consulting contracts.

Anderson swallowed hard. "That's not a problem." He took a moment to calm himself, trying to balance the millions of possible dollars against a very real bill he wouldn't normally be able to pay. "Now, they're going to be working for me directly, right? So there's not a direct link to the university?"

"No link."

"Privately, so I can kind of protect the department—you know, everybody's looking at me now, about embarrassing us."

"That's not a problem."

"Will they still be able to carry their guns and everything?"

"Absolutely. That's why you hire us and not security guards. But you're not planning on having us kill anybody, are you?"

"No, no, no! But the students we're looking for, I don't want them to know that." He gripped the pen, his hand shaking as he squeezed. "I want them to be scared, big time. I want them to feel like the foot of God Almighty is coming down to crush them like a grape. But don't actually harm them." Anderson set the broken pen down. "Unless it's absolutely necessary."

"Got it. Scared big time, foot of God. Check."

"Captain, I'll trust your discretion to tell your officers whatever you need to tell them, but rest assured there's going to be a nice bonus coming your way for making this happen quickly and quietly." Anderson rubbed his sweaty brow. He hadn't expected that. "Once we get the machine back and get everything under control, well, it's worth a lot of money to the university. And containing the embarrassment is worth a lot to me personally."

"Not a problem. I'm on it. What all can you tell me about these students, so we can get started?"

"I'm going to have my associate, Chris Findlay, call you with that. He'll be able to give you all the information you need."

"Okay. I'll expect his call."

"Uh, there's just one more thing." Anderson lowered his voice to a whisper. "If everything hits the fan, I don't want the University connected too directly. But let's face it, captain, I don't really want

THE NAVIGATORS

to be connected directly myself, either. If we can avoid that . . ."

"That's gonna cost extra, Herb. But I can make it happen. You just sit back and relax. Prepare to watch the foot of the Almighty quietly and quickly start kicking some pesky grad student rears."

* * * * *

"I don't believe it. You're back."

The voice of Dr. Harper rang out like a gunshot over the din of the emergency room lobby. He folded his arms over his metal clipboard and smiled.

Barry closed his eyes. *Of all the stinking luck.* "Hello, sir."

"It's Barry, right?" Harper wagged his finger. "What is it this time? A dead body?" He approached, smiling. "Here to finish off your friend upstairs? Because you're too late."

Barry's jaw dropped. *Roger's dead?*

"We already moved him to Tampa General."

The panic went away and the relief and the leg pain returned. Barry groaned and sat down.

"And what happened to you?" Harper squatted down to inspect.

Barry sucked in and winced. "I think I broke it. I have a constant stabbing pain right here." He pointed.

The doctor placed his hands gently around it. "I'd ask how you did it, but I'm sure I don't want to know."

Barry decided to set Harper straight when he realized the doctor was right. Barry didn't want Harper to know, either. Not the real truth about what was happening. That would get the cops called.

Harper tested the leg. "Does this hurt?"

"Yep."

"And this?"

Barry flinched. "Yes! Are you enjoying yourself?"

Harper grinned. "A little." He stood up. "Okay, hot shot. Looks like you cracked your leg bone. How about we schedule for an x-ray and see how bad it is?" He pointed his pen at a candy bowl on the admitting desk. "Then we'll get you a cast and a lollipop and get you out of here before you hurt anybody else." He scanned the lobby. "By the way, where's that girlfriend of yours?"

"She's not -"

"Hold on, there's my training intern. Gina!" The doctor waved to a young Asian woman across the lobby. "Gina. Over here, please."

"– she's not my girlfriend."

"No?" Harper squatted down again. "Why not?"

"Can you just fix my leg, please?"

The intern appeared.

"Gina, this young man has some lower leg pain concentrated around the upper ankle. Sharp pain when he applies pressure. And no girlfriend."

Barry's mouth hung open. The intern just smiled and shook her head, making notes on her clipboard.

"Note the swelling and bruising." Harper stood up. "Let's get him into x-ray." He handed her a note and walked off.

That was quick.

Gina retrieved a nearby wheelchair as Dr. Harper headed down the hallway. A nurse came over to start Barry's paperwork.

"Here we go." Gina pushed the wheelchair toward Barry. "Do you need help getting in?"

"No, I can do it." Barry lifted himself and glanced at the intern's clipboard.

Isolation, now. Dangerous.

Barry looked up to see that Dr. Harper was gone.

I'm not getting an x-ray, they're putting me in some sort of holding area until Harper can call the cops.

Crap.

He took a deep breath and lowered himself into the wheelchair. The intern began pushing him.

"Which way is x-ray?" Barry asked, spying the overhead signs. It was to the right.

"Just down this hallway straight ahead," Gina replied. "We'll get you in right away. Do you need assistance with your paperwork?"

"Pretty smooth."

"Excuse me?"

As the intern wheeled Barry down the hallway, he noticed Dr. Harper in a side office dialing a phone.

Barry jumped up, hopping on his good leg.

"Sir, you need to sit down, please!"

Barry made his way to the office door. "Dr. Harper, stop!"

Harper looked up, shocked. Barry hobbled his way into the office.

"Sir, please get back in the wheelchair," Gina said.

Barry pushed the office door shut behind him, his eyes never leaving Harper's. He leaned on the back of a chair and eased his leg.

Harper held the phone in his hand, frozen. "I think you should listen to my intern. Get back in that wheelchair. You need an x-ray."

Barry nodded. "I know."

"But?"

"But I need you to put that phone down, sir. Please."

Harper remained still.

"I can't do anything to hurt you. I need your help. Please. Put the phone down."

Harper lowered the phone into its cradle.

"You're in a lot of trouble, son."

"I know."

"You're all over the news." Harper moved slowly, positioning the desk between himself and Barry. "Look at you. You're hurt, you're tired. How did you think this was going to play out?"

Barry leaned on the chair for support. "I thought I could get my leg in a cast and disappear."

"You know I can't let you do that."

"Why not?"

"That's not how it works." Harper looked Barry over. "Sit down."

"I think it's better if I stand."

Gina talked through the door. "Dr. Harper, is everything okay?"

THE NAVIGATORS

"Suit yourself." The doctor spoke to the closed door. "Everything's okay, Gina. We're just going to talk for a minute. Go get some coffee."

Barry bristled. "Do you guys have a code word that you say when there's a hostile situation going on but you don't want people to know what's up?"

"Yes," Harper said. "But that's not it."

Gina spoke through the door. "Dr. Harper?"

"Yes, Gina?"

"Should I leave the wheelchair?"

Harper glared at Barry.

"Leave the wheelchair, Gina," Barry shouted.

Harper smiled. "May I sit?"

"I'm not holding you hostage, sir. I'm asking for your help."

"May I sit?"

"Sure." Barry nodded. "Please."

Harper lowered himself into the chair and arranged the papers on the desk. Clasping his hands, he looked at Barry. "Well, what shall we talk about?"

* * * * *

Officer Bolton was driving his cruiser when he got the update. Captain Ferguson was looking for some volunteers to pull some special security duty for a few days. The hours would be good and the pay would be great.

"What do I have to do, captain?" Bolton asked.

"Not much, Jim. Round up a few stray cats and knock heads a little so they learn how to stay home from now on."

"Heck, I can do that." Bolton rounded a corner and sped up.

203

"Welcome to the team. I'll send the information over to the cruiser's computer."

"How many cats are we looking at, sir?"

"There were four, but one's in Tampa General Hospital now. That leaves three strays, a female and two males, all with brown hair. One of the guys is an exchange student from India."

"Got it, chief. Any descriptions of clothes or anything? Vehicles?"

"They'll be tired from lack of sleep. I'll send over what they were last seen wearing, but they may have changed clothes by now. And you'll get their student ID pictures with the other stuff I'm sending."

"These are the ones on the news, right?"

"That's right."

"Then they're probably still in what they were wearing when they attacked the news conference. We have those images already."

"Then you're good to go, Jim. You can start right after lunch."

"Sounds good. Thanks, captain."

As the on board computer started pinging with incoming messages, Officer Bolton pulled his cruiser into the Chick-Fil-A for an early lunch.

CHAPTER NINETEEN

"Son of a gun."

Officer Bolton was completely surprised. And delighted.

No sooner had he received the descriptions of the so-called campus felons than he spotted the first one right in front of him.

He put his hand on the butt of his gun and chuckled. "Everybody loves Chick-Fil-A." Squaring himself, the big man pressed the button on his shoulder mic. "Bolton to base. I'm about to acquire Tomàs Pequant."

* * * * *

Barry rubbed his sweaty hands on his thighs. Things needed to get resolved with Dr. Harper in a hurry. Right now he might be able to pass himself off as an overly excited college kid, but in a few minutes, he'd seem like a hostage taker. Then there wouldn't be any options left.

Maybe I should just bolt. The throbbing from Barry's ankle increased. When he moved, pain shot up his leg. Leaving without medical attention was out of the question. "Uh, any chance I can just get a cast on my leg and sneak on out of here? Maybe with a few pain killers?"

Harper snorted, folding his arms over his belly.

"You're stalling." Barry narrowed his eyes. "You're buying time while the cops come, right? That's what the phone call was."

Dr. Harper drummed his fingers on the desk. "It definitely seems like you're running out of time, son. Looks like you're running out of choices, too." He leaned back in the chair. "Why are you here?"

Barry shifted his weight and pointed at his foot, wincing. "Broken leg, remember?"

"No, why are you *here*, in this office? Why aren't you sitting over at x-ray?"

"Your intern was sticking me in a holding tank while you called the cops. That's why."

"And now that's probably what I *will* do. Come on." Harper motioned to the chair. "Sit down."

Barry lowered himself onto a chair, keeping his leg stretched out. A bead of sweat trickled down the side of his face.

"The pain is making you sweat. That's your body's reaction to the stress." Harper tapped the desk again. "So, like I asked you, what do you want to try to accomplish here today?"

Barry sighed. "I don't know anymore. I need to get my leg fixed. Then we figure out something from there."

"Not much of a plan."

"None of this was planned." He waved his hand, searching the floor for answers. "It just all kind of exploded on us."

"Hmm. Welcome to my world." Harper grinned. "That's what I do here in the ER. Seven or eight hours of complete boredom followed by three or four hours of sheer panic and terror." He wagged a finger. "But during that time we might save some lives."

"Well, you can save one right now."

"How's that?"

Keeping the leg stretched, Barry adjusted on his seat. Nothing helped alleviate the pressure building in his ankle. He glanced at the doctor. "How about 'First do no harm'?"

Harper frowned. "Don't play games with me, son. I take my job seriously."

"I know you do, sir. Anybody can see that. I just need some help. I need my leg fixed so I can get out of here."

"You need a little more than that. You might need a lawyer."

"I shouldn't. We didn't really do anything wrong."

"That's not what the news reports are saying." Harper dropped his hands onto the leather armrests. "With each update they're making you and your classmates out to be a psychotic band of thieves and arsonists."

Barry slouched, biting his fingernail. "I bet they are."

"I was going let you get your leg fixed. Then the police would have taken you into custody. That's how we do that."

"That's the whole problem, sir."

"Why? If you didn't do anything wrong, what do you have to fear from the police?"

"To be honest with you, it's not the police I'm worried about. It's whoever is pulling the strings behind the police."

Harper narrowed his eyes. "What do you mean?"

Barry pushed himself up straight in the chair, glancing around. "Are the police on the way?"

"You need to calm down."

"Are they? Were you calling them when I came in here?"

Harper raised his hands, spreading his fingers. "I ordered some lunch. Chinese food from the carryout across the street, okay? You need to relax. Trust somebody for a minute. Tell me what happened."

Barry sighed, shaking his head. "All we did was find this machine on the mining site. You saw us that night—when we brought Riff in. That's it. That's all we did. We wanted to try it out, and then suddenly there's a press conference and the police are after us and buildings are being burned down." He rubbed the back of his neck, staring down at his outstretched leg.

"That's . . . not entirely true."

Barry thought about it. Rules were broken. Big rules. "I'd say, in the grand scheme of things, we-"

THE NAVIGATORS

"In the grand scheme of things you feel like you did the least wrong of everyone? Is that about right?"

"Yeah, I suppose so."

"The grand scheme of things, indeed. Funny how that scheme looks a little less grand, depending on who's doing the looking. So what would you like from me?"

"Some help."

"And why would I do that?"

"Because . . ." Barry looked Dr. Harper in the eyes. "Because even when I first met you, I knew you were a little different from the average bear. A cut above. Because you didn't call the police on us even when you said we were psychos. You knew better." Gambling, Barry went all in on a long shot. "It's your training. Your time being an ER doctor told you there was a ring of truth to my story. And if you were going to call the police on me, you'd have done it by now. Or given the code word to the nurse. You didn't."

Barry watched Dr. Harper. Harper watched him right back.

"You know I'm telling you the truth." Barry swallowed. "Help me, please."

Observing the dirty, tired young man in front of him, Dr. Harper drew a deep breath and let it out slowly. "Okay. What do you need?"

Barry smiled. "How about a cast for my ankle and a three-hour head start before you call the cops?"

* * * * *

"Peeky, Peeky, Peeky, you have been just as busy as a beaver, haven't you?"

The holding cell at the campus police station was hardly like a jail. It was mostly used for drunken college students that overdid it at a basketball game. It was meant to let kids sleep it off or get a dose of reality before turning them loose or handing them over to the City of Tampa police. There were no iron bars, just the thick wire screen over the windows and doors like the kind on an indoor high school gymnasium. That, and the presence of a lot of uniformed cops was usually enough to sober up a rowdy college kid. Nobody wants to go to real jail.

Findlay sat at the duty desk and chuckled at his good luck. "Peeky, it's so good to see you. I can't believe we found you first."

"What's going on, Findlay? You can't just keep me here." I was scared, but I didn't expect to see him here. That was unnerving.

"Oh, but I can!" He cackled. "All these nice police officers work for me. Well, Dean Anderson hired them, but I get to call the shots. Can you believe it?"

I had no idea what to say to that. Sitting on the metal cot in the holding cell, Findlay and I could talk, but he was definitely holding all the cards.

"Wanna know what I've been up to since you saw me last?" He couldn't contain himself. "You'll love this. I hacked Barry's computer."

"So? That's hardly a challenge for a computer science graduate student."

THE NAVIGATORS

"I know, right? And he was dumb enough to show me this really cool machine you guys found, and then try to cut me out of the deal. What crap. You don't think that was right, do you?"

I was too scared and confused to answer, but it didn't matter. Findlay wasn't listening.

"I really outdid myself this time. Even a bunch of rock busters like you guys can appreciate that." He bounced up and down in the chair. "I got pictures of course, that first night, when Barry went to take a shower. The guys at MIT loved those." He raised his eyebrows and nodded. "Oh, yeah. Then, on my next visit – when all of you dust busters were there patting yourselves on the back—I planted a tracker on the machine and a recorder on Barry's computer. Right under your noses."

I tried to appear brave. "So you broke your word right from the get-go, then, didn't you? Before we figured it out the next day."

"So what?" Findlay stood up. "I was going to get pushed aside all along. You knew that." He wagged a finger at me, walking up to the door. "Don't tell me you wanted me as a partner. I know you guys too well." His tone changed to anger. "I was in that room, Peeky! Getting punched in the gut."

He leaned in and sneered, a little saliva hanging from his mouth as he yelled. "Remember? While you sat by and did *nothing*?"

The door held him at bay. I tried not to show my fear, but my hands were shaking. Findlay was getting out of control and the officers had guns.

Bolton stepped in. "Hey, back it down a couple of notches." He put his hands on Findlay's shoulder and guided him away from the holding room door.

Findlay took a breath and collected himself, wiping his chin. "Actually, you didn't exactly do nothing, did you, Tomàs? Busy little beaver?"

He sat back down at the desk. Officer Bolton positioned himself behind Findlay, maybe as much to be imposing as to intervene again if necessary.

"He dreamed about getting rich." Findlay sneered. "Didn't you, Peeky?"

I felt a hollowness shoot through my stomach, like a bolt of fear and lightning.

What did he know?

"I hacked Barry's computer—that was easy using the recorder. But from there I was able to access all of your computers. Roger's, Riff's, Melissa's and yours. There was almost no security."

My stomach ached.

"Wanna know what I found?" He chuckled. "Well, a lot of porn on Roger's computer. No surprise there. Not much of anything on Riff's." He turned to me. "You know, I'm not sure that boy's completely right in the head. He plays a lot of video games and not much else." Findlay laughed. "I'd say it's a waste, but is it really? With a bozo like him?"

He stood up and started to pace. "Let's see. Oh, and Melissa's computer. That was nice. Hey, did you know a lot of girls take pictures of themselves to see how they look in a new outfit they're trying on at the store?"

I stared at the floor. Poor Melissa.

THE NAVIGATORS

"A whole folder of her trying on dresses and jeans. That Missy, she's a knockout." He looked at me. "Oh, don't worry. Nothing explicit. The girl's too smart for that. She kept it strictly rated G, even when she was trying on bathing suits." Then he laughed. "Except for the pictures she took with Roger last summer!"

He fell down behind the desk, delirious with laughter. He was drunk on his own power and handling it badly. The wrong person was in the holding cell.

"Hey, I sent some of them to my cell phone. Wanna see?" He stood up, pulling his phone from his pocket. "Check it out."

The first image was a scantily-clad Melissa in her dorm room. Her hands covered her—but just barely.

I averted my eyes.

"Aw, what's the matter? I thought you had a thing for her." He shoved the phone at me through a slot in the door. It fell on the cot.

"You're an animal, Findlay," I said, pressing a button to take Melissa off the screen.

"Oh, Peeky, you have no idea."

* * * * *

Melissa drove past the Chick-Fil-A. There was nobody in sight. The pre-arranged pickup spot at the pancake house proved fruitless—it was almost empty—so she doubled back to the last place Peeky had mentioned. This was nearly empty, too; unusual for a fast food restaurant near campus.

She drove into the parking lot and glanced around. On the far side was a City of Tampa police cruiser and an officer talking to somebody who appeared to be a manager. Inside, she could see employees but no customers.

Strange.

Melissa slipped on a pair of sunglasses from the truck's glove box and proceeded to the parking lot of the bank next door. Her cell phone screen brought her the latest news update.

Missing USF Mystery Machine Found.

She already knew that. Did the story have any new information? She scrolled through, reading. The new stories still weren't publicly naming the suspects.

Charges were now to include arson.

She glanced over her shoulder. The police cruiser was still at Chick-Fil-A.

Near the end of the news story, a mention that the machine would be taken into custody of the U.S. Military. Representatives from MacDill Air Force Base in south Tampa were being scheduled to take the machine into federal custody and move it to the base until further notice.

The air force base? We'll never get it back once it goes there.

Military officials had not yet determined whether to store it at the old Tampa armory or on site at the base. It would be transferred to the USF Sun Dome for safekeeping and kept under armed guard until morning.

The basketball stadium? Why there?

Why indeed. The Sun Dome was one of the few solid concrete buildings on campus, but since it was a stadium, it had been built to allow trucks to drive in and set up for concerts or monster truck rallies. It had solid walls eighty feet high and a parking lot a quarter mile long in every direction.

It looked like a big fortress, and that's exactly what the USF officials wanted to portray.

Invulnerability.

Melissa set her phone down and pondered the possible options. If they hadn't already moved the machine to the Sun Dome, maybe Barry could help her steal it back. Once it got to the Sun Dome, all bets were off.

She glanced over her shoulder. The police cruiser was gone.

There was a rap on her window. Melissa jumped, whipping around to see who was there.

A uniformed police officer stood outside her door, peering in.

* * * * *

"So it turns out, Peeky, that each of your computers was of varying usefulness."

Findlay began to pace again, a sinister look on his face.

"I don't think you can just hold me like this," I said. "You should let me out."

Findlay grinned like a circus clown. "And we will. You can get out right now if you want." He turned to Officer Bolton. "Right, Jim?"

"You're not under arrest, sir." Officer Bolton motioned to the exit door. "You're free to leave at any time."

Nervous energy shot through me again. "I am?" I stood up. "I can go?"

"Peeky, you can go whenever you want. But . . . don't you wanna know what I found on the other computers?"

Findlay grinned from ear to ear, pacing. My knees quivered.

"Yeah, it turns out that Barry had a lot of boring stuff on his computer. Well, nothing I cared about anyway. You wanna know where the really interesting stuff was?" He leaned on the edge of the desk like a vulture waiting for a dying animal to stop moving.

I sat back down.

"There was one folder named 'Paleontology Team.' I thought that was pretty interesting." He turned to the officer. "Wanna know whose computer that folder was on, Jim?"

Sweat formed on the palms of my hands.

His sinister gaze returned to me. "At first I thought it was just some run of the mill garbage about collecting rocks—and the other bits of junk these goofballs dig for. But it was a pretty fat file! And the scanning software was specifically looking for references to the time machine." He waved a hand. "I figured, what the heck. Maybe you wrote down a few notes after talking with Barry. Right? Innocent enough. So I checked. And you know what I found?" He curled his lip into a sneer. "There was a sub folder in there called 'Time Machine'."

He walked up to the holding room door. "The thing is, that sub file was dated *before* your trip to the mine, Peeky. Before Barry ever told you about a time machine."

I shifted on the cot.

THE NAVIGATORS

"Now, Tomàs, I had to ask myself a question. How does a guy know to make a file about a time machine before he even knows there *is* a time machine?"

* * * * *

"Yes, officer?" Her heart in her throat, Melissa cracked the window enough to address the officer without giving him enough space to put his hand through and turn off the engine. The truck was still running so she could speed away if she needed to.

She flashed a brilliant grin and moved her hand to the gear shift.

"Ma'am, are you here for bank business?"

Melissa swallowed, forcing her smile to stay intact. "Excuse me?"

"The lot's pretty full and the bank manager has asked me to only allow vehicles here on bank business to park today."

She glanced at his uniform. Campus police, not a security guard. She squinted, pretending the sky was too bright, and slipped the sunglasses back on. "No, I'm just checking my messages. I can move." She dropped the truck into gear. "What's all the ruckus about, anyway?"

The officer backed up and pointed. "Oh, they're moving that machine they recovered over to the Sun Dome in a few minutes, and I guess the bank manager thought everybody'd want to try to see it."

He didn't seem to know who she was—a good sign. Maybe he knew something, though. "Is it coming by here?"

"I really don't know, ma'am. Doesn't seem like it."

She glanced left and right. "No, it doesn't, does it?"

"The manager's a little ramped up if you ask me, but he's always calling us because people park here when they go eat at Chick-Fil-A and the bank customers can't get a spot. Just about anything gets a call these days."

"Okay, well thanks, I'll be on my way." Melissa backed the truck up a few feet, then stopped, making it appear as though she had just thought of something.

"You know, officer," she said, smiling. "It does sound kind of fun to get a look at the big mysterious machine. Can you check to see if it's been taken to the Sun Dome yet?"

CHAPTER TWENTY

"One hour," Dr. Harper said. "After we put a cast on your leg."

Barry kneaded his hands in his lap. "I need at least three."

"One. And I should remind you, this isn't a negotiation. You don't have anything to bargain with."

Eyeing his swollen ankle, Barry again shifted his weight. The pain was growing worse. "Does the cast dry pretty fast?"

"It's almost instantaneous. They're fiberglass. Dry to the touch as soon as we're done wrapping it and completely hard in a few hours."

"What about meds?"

Harper opened the office door. "Standard pain killers for a minor fracture. You'll leave here with some. And a pair of crutches."

The noise from the ER filled the hallway: phones, conversations, equipment carts being rolled to their destinations. No signs of panic, no sirens, no cops, just business as usual for the bustling hospital.

Barry wiped his forehead with his sleeve, leaving a watery stain on his dirty t-shirt. "Can you wait two hours?"

"I'm not sure why I'm giving you anything."

"Because you want to see the truth prevail, maybe?"

Harper rolled his eyes and plopped down in his chair. "Geez, the nonsense around this place never stops." His hand came down on the desk like an auctioneer's gavel. "Fine. Two hours—but the clock starts right now."

"What?" Barry sat up. "No way. I could spend two hours waiting for the x-ray."

"You're right. It's a really bad deal compared to me calling the cops right now, isn't it? What a jerk I'm being." Harper stood up. "Come on. The clock's running. I'll take you down to x-ray myself. You'll have a cast and a pair of crutches and be on your way in under an hour. Deal?"

Dr. Harper held out his hand, then yanked it back. "What am I offering a deal for? I'm not the one in trouble." He grabbed the wheelchair from the hall "Let's go. I want you out of my hospital."

As the doctor lowered Barry into the wheelchair, Barry smiled. "I know you don't mean that, Doc. You're one of the good guys."

"Pipe down. I have a reputation to protect." Harper pushed the wheelchair down the hallway. "Gina! Call x-ray and tell them to open a spot. I'm on my way down."

* * * * *

THE NAVIGATORS

Findlay slithered his way around the campus police duty desk, addressing Officer Bolton. "Jim, how do you think it is that Peeky here knew enough to create a folder in his computer called 'Time Machine' long before his friend Barry ever told him there even *was* a time machine?"

The big man chuckled. "He must be a pretty good guesser."

"Yes! Good point. Maybe Peeky is a good guesser." He turned to me and extended his nasty grin. "Is that it, Peeky? Are you a good guesser?"

I squirmed on the cot.

"Hmm, cat got your tongue, huh? Do they have that saying in India, Mr. Pequant?"

Findlay's teasing was too much. My heart was pounding, ready to explode. I swallowed, trying to remember to breathe.

He sat on a corner of the desk, a sick grin plastered on his pasty white face. "So, Jim, let me tell you about our little friend from India—by way of France. Do I have that right, Tomàs? It was your great-grandfather who moved the family to India from *le grand Paree*?" He rubbed his hands together. "There was a lot of personal stuff on those computers. For example, Roger weighs himself every day. How vain is that? Barry has a big date Friday. Melissa – oh, Melissa. She's the one I showed you those pictures of. Missy had last Tuesday circled on her calendar in red and then +1, +2, +3 each day since. Do you think she's late for something, Peeky?"

His finger tapped the desk and he grinned. "But what's really interesting is a file Peeky had, or several files, I should say. There was one called Barry, one called Roger, and one called Melissa. I guess his friend Riff didn't make the cut. Interesting stuff in those." He turned to Officer Bolton and wagged a finger. "You learn a lot about people when you can see inside their computers, Jim. Peeky here Skypes a lot. Or he used to. There's some guys named Anil, and Dhaval, and Ankit. Some girls, too – but oddly no wife or child – you'd expect a shared account for that, like he has with his sister. But no, I didn't see that kind of account. There were some other folks he Skyped with, but never with a wife or child." Findlay turned to Officer Bolton. "Wouldn't you say that's odd? A married guy never Skyping with his wife? I mean, if she lives halfway around the world?"

"That does sound strange."

I swallowed hard and stared at the floor.

"Yeah, I thought so, too." Findlay's eyes returned to me. "Oh, and there were notes about a certain local politician's wife being killed by a drunk driver when their daughter was young. You could almost see the ideas about fabricating a story coming together, about pretending to be married and having a child who would never know her grandmother—indicating the writer had lost his own mother. That must have been useful. I couldn't figure out why that would be important until I read about Melissa. See, Jim, they'd kind of have that in common, Peeky and Melissa, so he could manipulate her with it when the time came." Findlay chuckled. "But your mom's fine, isn't she Peeky? I saw her in your Skype history. On your *shared* account. You should really call her. It's been more than a week. What kind of son are you?"

My chest grew tight. The room closed in on me as Findlay continued his interrogation.

"I also saw the file you made on your great-grandfather. Hey, Jim, guess what? Peeky's ol' grandpa was a disgraced scientist. You know, family name means a lot in some cultures. I checked, and I was right. That's why you came here in the first place, to steal a bunch of money and restore the family name. It's all in your notes. Buy your way back into high society. How noble. Virtue by way of theft. You know, my roots are Irish, not French or Indian, but I'm pretty sure that's not how it works."

I squeezed my eyes shut. "I never stole anything."

"Oh, he speaks!" Findlay threw his head back, laughing. "My goodness, of all the things to protest, *that's* the one you choose? Don't be stupid. It worked." He shook his head, smiling. "You must have been very proud, your whole scheme worked out just fine. You got buddy-buddy with Melissa, which got you in good with Roger and Barry, and that put you on the rock digger team with the best paleontology students. You already had a good idea where to look for your great-grandfather's discovery, from all his notes. They just needed a little prodding. 'Let's go dig up a mine site, guys. That's where the good stuff is.'" Findlay scratched the side of his head. "It was probably that easy, wasn't it? You came here with a plan to recruit and network until you were part of a group that could find it – and they did! In just a few semesters, great grand-dad's machine was in your hot little hands."

He leaned in, sneering, his voice a whisper. "But you didn't have it all to yourself. And when you guys did try to work it, bad things happened. So you laid low and waited for your chance to make your money. But time ran out on you." Findlay smiled. "How odd, for a guy with a time machine. That's pretty poetic, don't you think?"

I couldn't move. I was too ashamed. I just stared at the floor.

"Jim, his plan was beautiful in its simplicity. Peeky's big plan was to go back to – well, do you want to tell him or should I?"

I stared at him, red faced, a lump in my throat.

"Okay, I'll tell him. Coca-Cola. That's it. Do you love it?"

"I'm a Pepsi man, myself," Officer Bolton said.

"No, no, not as a drink. As an investment. Check it out. A single share of Coca-Cola stock when it was originally issued in the early 1900s was about forty-five dollars. Wanna know what it's worth today?"

Bolton nodded.

"Nine million dollars, Jim. Peeky had one heck of a payday up his sleeve." He smiled at me. "Honestly, Peeky, my hat's off to you. It was a beautiful plan."

Bolton sat down at the desk. "Heck, I'd screw all my friends over too, for that kind of money." He grabbed the keyboard and punched the keys. "Hey, this says Coke stock's trading around forty bucks right now. What gives?"

"A hundred years' worth of dividends and stock splits and all sorts of financial stuff. Today it's worth nine million big ones. And he had it all set to go, didn't you, Peeky?"

Findlay wasn't finished. "So, how exactly did great grand-dad get so disgraced, anyway? That part wasn't in your notes."

I stared at my hands, beaten. Whether I said anything now or not, it was only a matter of time before the rest of the story came out. I wanted out of the holding cell and away from Findlay. "The family history was always well known to me, even as a child. He was recruited to lead a mapping expedition through parts of Florida in the early 1900s. They found a machine."

Findlay was practically drooling. "Go on."

"There were . . . some accidents. When they went to use it. Some of his men were killed."

"They were all killed, weren't they? All but great grand-dad?"

My cheeks burned and my eyes never left the floor. "There was a trial. Nobody believed any of what came out of the madman's mouth. The sole survivor out of forty men, they . . . they said he was crazy, rambling on about a strange machine, how it killed his men, and how the rest of his crew killed each other fighting over it. When it all ended, he was the only one left."

"I know. I looked him up on the internet." Findlay chuckled. "I just wanted to hear you say it."

I glared at him. "You're a real piece of work, Findlay."

"Am I?" He sat up, putting a finger to his chest. "Well, I have news for you, pal. You are twice the snake I ever dreamed of being. You lied to everybody, all your friends, from day one. You knew the time machine was dangerous, but you let them test it out anyway. I notice you didn't get in and go for a ride, did you, Peeky? You needed to try it out on a few Guinea pigs first to figure out how the thing worked so you didn't end up like one of great-grandpappy's men." He narrowed his eyes and pointed his finger at me. "You set them up. All of them, even Melissa. Heck, you're worse than me by a long shot. And . . ."

Findlay danced. "And, and, and . . ." He stopped and looked at me. "And I'm going to tell all of them what you did."

It was like a gunshot to my belly. My heart sank. Such . . . *humiliation*. I couldn't bear it.

"It's all over, pal. No more time machine, no more Barry or Melissa – although they aren't ever going to want to talk to you again after they hear all this. No more Roger – that's no loss, except he'll probably beat the snot out of you when he finds out what you did, so there's that. No more USF–you're sure to be expelled. Dean Anderson has that at the top of his list for all of you."

I clenched my fists and glared at him. Fear and rage loomed inside me.

"Oh, yes, all of your so-called friends—expelled. All because they trusted you. Then there's Melissa's dad. His campaign goes up in flames."

"What?" My rage vanished. "How?"

THE NAVIGATORS

"Are you kidding me? Maybe India's politics are full of corruption, pal, but here in the good ol' U S of A, we like to pretend our politicians are squeaky clean–and that goes for their families, too. Why, when word gets out about the mayor's daughter stealing university property and getting expelled, not to mention those pictures of her going out all over the internet -"

"Stop!" I jumped up and put my hands on the door. "Why do you have to do this?"

He cocked his head. "Peekeeey . . . you poor stupid schmuck. You don't get it, do you? I don't have to do any of this."

"What?"

"I don't *want* to do any of it. I don't have to ruin your friends' lives or your life, or get you expelled—and let's face it, you're a felon. You'll probably get deported. But none of that has to happen. Don't you see?"

"I . . . I guess I don't."

"You're the golden ticket, buddy. The other rock busters, they still trust you. They don't know about all this yet. You're still part of the team."

My head was buzzing. Findlay folded his hands in his lap and waited, watching me.

"I know Barry. He's not gonna let that machine sit over there at the Sun Dome without trying to go steal it back. I'd even help them do it if I could, but when it's over I don't need my fingerprints on it, so to speak. Instead, you do it. Help them steal it back. Then you give the machine to *me*, and I disappear. *I'll* go back in time. *I'll* go buy the Coke stock." He chuckled. "How far did you think a brown-skinned man was going to get in New York City—in the most elite club in the world, the stock exchange—in early 1920's anyway, buddy? Come on. But me, I'm Irish. My people practically ran that town in the 1900s." Holding his hands out at his sides, he shrugged. "Me, I look the part. I can *talk* the part. But with your funny Middle Eastern accent and strange black hair? No way. It's simple. You just help me. We'll split the cash."

He looked me in the eye. "Four and a half million dollars each, just to get started. I figure you already have your seed money, too. If it was in a bank account somewhere, I'd already have it by now. I'm thinking precious metals. I'm thinking, maybe an ounce of gold. That, anybody would trade. Even with a foreigner."

I nodded. I had saved for many years, borrowed from everyone I knew, to amass $1500—enough to buy one ounce of gold. That would be roughly the equivalent of $45 in the 1900s, and that would be enough.

"You give me your gold, I put it with some of the cash from Jim and his friends, and I go back and buy a few shares of the Coca-Cola stock. I come back and we cash out in a private exchange. Everybody wins, Peeky. Think about it. You return to India as the conquering hero. I get to spend the rest of my life getting with fashion models on South Beach in the back of my Porsche. Everybody's happy."

I glared at him. "Except my friends."

He shrugged. "They were gonna lose anyway, right? Your plan didn't include cutting them in on your nine million, did it? At least, that wasn't in your notes – a curious oversight. You were planning on screwing them over anyway. Let me in as a partner. I can help."

It was overwhelming, what he was suggesting.

"Besides, if you don't take me as a partner . . . I'll tell them anyway. Do you think they'll trust you when they know about all this?"

He let the words hang on me like the death sentence they were.

"It's over, Peeky."

I dropped to the cot, the air going out of me. I had worked too long, spent too many years fixing bicycles for pennies and doing odd jobs, borrowing from everyone I knew, including members of my family who couldn't afford to loan me anything. I couldn't allow it all to go to waste.

It was crushing me just thinking about it. There were no other options. Not now.

I looked up at Findlay. "Will you wait until I can take at least one trip for myself?"

"Yes! All I want is the machine," he said. "I'll make my cash run, then I give the machine to the school. They're going to turn it over to the highest bidder and I'll ride off into the sunset with a huge finder's fee. You, too, maybe. The thing is worth billions to the electric companies and the oil consortiums, and I can cut you in for a piece. I should clear $2 million on the handover deal alone, plus consulting fees worth about $2 million a year over the next ten years. I'm sure I can get you a similar deal if you help me."

He got up and went around to the chair, plopping down. A big smile stretched across his face as he crossed his feet on a corner of the desk and folded his hands in his lap. If he'd had a cigar, he'd have been smoking it.

"It's everything you came here for, Peeky."

CHAPTER TWENTY-ONE

"This is for the swelling."

Gina handed Barry a small bottle of pills. "Your ankle pain will only get worse if you move around a lot, so stay off it. Which I know you won't."

He balanced on his new crutches and shoved the pills into a pocket. "Thanks."

"Hold them like this." She repositioned his hands on the crutch handles. "Try to put more weight on your hands, and not let the top of the crutch rest in your armpits—you'll get chafed in no time, and then you'll start bleeding. You don't want that. Armpits are tender. Sore ones are worse."

Barry tried to rebalance as she'd instructed him. She shook her head. "Just do your best." His attempt at movement was labored at best. Hopping, basically. She scrawled a few notes on her clipboard. "Do you know where you're headed?"

"I'm . . . not sure." He smiled. "But I probably shouldn't tell you anyway."

"No, that's true." She nodded, pointing at the lobby TV. Another update on the movement of the time machine crawled across the bottom of the screen, with images of the morning's melee. "The police might figure out you were here and start asking me things. I'd hate to tell them the wrong information and send them off on a wild goose chase."

Barry stopped trying to maneuver on the crutches and looked at her.

"I can only tell them what I know, or what I heard you say." Gina lowered her voice. "Even if it's not true. How would I know?"

"You'd help me? Why would you do that?"

She shrugged. "Dr. Harper's not the only one you convinced back there."

"You were listening at the door?"

"I wouldn't have heard anything good if I had listened at the water cooler."

He balanced again, finding his new center on the crutches. "Gina, you're all right."

"Look," she said. "The news says they're moving the machine to the Sun Dome, right? That's right here on campus. But the prior update said they were thinking about taking it to the armory – that's close to downtown."

"So if I was, say, hitting on a pretty intern, she might get me to admit that I only knew about taking it to the armory."

"She might."

THE NAVIGATORS

Barry grinned. "Would she lend me her cell phone, too?"

* * * * *

"Can I drop you somewhere?"

Officer Bolton had a squad car and a sudden burst of generosity. I can't say I had the same for him—but it was a long walk to the pancake house.

I didn't know where else to go.

It was where I told Melissa I'd meet her, before all my worst paranoid fantasies started coming true. Now, with all of Findlay's accusations and wild theories, my head was humming. I couldn't figure out if it was safe for me to go back to my apartment or not. The campus cops had already grabbed me, and now they were letting me go. Maybe somebody else was looking for me, too.

Bolton must have sensed my detachment.

"Come on, buddy, it's not so bad. You're gonna make a fortune. In a few days, none of that other stuff will matter. You'll see."

I sat alongside him as we drove to the pancake house, but I just stared out the window. "Have you never been shamed?"

"Sure. Everybody has. You know what they say, though. It's not how many times you get knocked down, but how many times you get back up again."

Folk wisdom. Not what I needed right now.

We pulled into the parking lot of the pancake house. Bolton glanced over at me. "You gonna be okay?"

"Are you worried about a suicide?" I opened the cruiser door. "We're not on campus. It's not your jurisdiction." I got out and slammed the door.

Bolton bristled. "You could be a little nicer, you know."

Funny, I was just thinking the same thing about you.

* * * * *

Melissa had already rolled past the pancake house once. Seeing none of her friends in the parking lot or visible through the large windows, she kept right on going. She circled back to the Sun Dome. Nobody knew the yellow truck as something she'd be driving. It was safe enough to do some reconnaissance.

But nothing seemed to be happening in that parking lot, either—not that she knew what she should be seeing. In fall or spring, there would be at least intramural sports going on inside; people coming or going from sorority volleyball or a pickup game of basketball, things like that. Not to mention actual NCAA basketball games during the season. In summer, however, if there wasn't a concert in town, there wasn't much happening at the big dome.

And that's how it looked now: not much happening. Nothing, really.

Did I miss it, or am I early?

She tapped the steering wheel.

If they moved the time machine into the Sun Dome, there was still a chance to steal it back. The building might seem like a concrete fortress, but it was just a college basketball stadium. Once the

THE NAVIGATORS

machine left the campus for the armory or the air force base, it was unlikely they'd ever see it again. Campus cops were one thing; armed military personnel were another.

No, their best chance would be to steal it back, right from here, after it was moved and after everybody settled down and relaxed a little. When everybody might lower their defenses.

But when would that be?

* * * * *

Barry made his way along Fowler Avenue, USF's south border, with the use of his crutches. Even with the borrowed cell phone, he wasn't getting through to anybody.

The number you have dialed is not in service at this time . . .

It was slow going, just as Gina had mentioned. Walking on one foot was awkward. The palms of his hands were already hurting, so he let the crutch slide up into his armpit, which made him chafe.

He paused to try Melissa's cell phone again.

Nothing.

Why is everybody's cell phone out today?

He huffed and puffed, half stepping, half hopping, along the hot sidewalk.

Or is it maybe that this borrowed cell phone can't call them for some reason?

He dialed his parents' home in Miami. After a few rings, it went to the answering machine.

So it works, but it can't call Melissa or Peeky. What about my own phone?

The battery was dead, sure, but the service was still on, and he knew he'd paid his bill. He dialed, sweating in the sun as he waited for the call to connect.

Again, the tones. *"The number you have dialed . . ."*

Then it hit him. Somebody had purposely shut off their cell phones.

It was almost a relief to discover.

But now what? I can't call my ride.

He scanned the grassy areas of the empty campus.

If somebody cut off the phone, what else might they have shut down?

A bus stop bench under a nearby tree offered some relief from the sun and the painful crutches. He pulled out his wallet and dialed one of his credit card companies. Within a few minutes, he'd confirmed what was nagging at the back of his head all along. Somebody had accessed his accounts and shut them down on purpose.

The cops? Could somebody in the police force do this, to draw us out, maybe? Or at least make life difficult for us while we try to hide?

If so, it was working. They didn't feel safe going back to their apartments. Without cell phones or credit cards, they couldn't go too many other places. Most hotels chains were out. And since he didn't see this coming, he didn't pull any cash out of an ATM. Barry flipped through the bills in his wallet. About fifty bucks.

The paperwork at the hospital had been processed with no problems, so somebody could track his movements to there. Then to Dr. Harper and Gina. Then to, well, the south Tampa armory. He chuckled.

Or if they happen to drive by, they might spot me on this bus bench. Better get moving.

Barry didn't know all of Melissa's friends' phone numbers, but he knew a few. He could look some up on the phone's browser. Maybe if he spoke with them, they could somehow network a message to Melissa if she called one of them to check in. It was a long shot. Where might she go?

If I were Melissa, where would I go?

* * * * *

"Can I help you, sweetie?"

The waitress at the pancake house was a friendly, plump middle-aged woman. Such cheerfulness would usually be reciprocated by me. Today, I couldn't.

"Do you need a little more time with the menu?"

I sighed. "Do you have anything that's not pancakes? I don't care for pancakes."

"Then a pancake house makes an odd choice for you to eat at, doesn't it? But we have hamburgers, great milkshakes. It's pretty hot out and you look like you've had a bad day. Some folks have a shake with a Belgian waffle. How 'bout that?"

It didn't sound good. Nothing did.

"A glass of water, maybe?" I handed the menu back and put my cheek to the cold table top, wrapping my arms around my head and uttering a low groan.

"Oh, I see. Okay. Um, how about a shake? On the house. Chocolate. Sound okay?"

Without lifting my head, I attempted to nod. "Can you put sprinkles on it?"

"Sure can, sweetie. Whipped cream, too. You just sit there and relax. We'll get your hangover fixed right up."

* * * * *

Why didn't I eat something when I had the chance?

Barry continued his sweat-filled trek across the campus, leaving the hard surface of the sidewalk for the shaded grassy patches underneath USF's many large oak trees. There was even an occasional water fountain along the jogging trail. The water was warm, but it was better than nothing.

Food, on the other hand, was nonexistent on this side of the campus.

Then he remembered. Melissa said she was picking Peeky up at the pancake house.

Even if the two of them had already caught up with each other, Melissa might realize it had been the only rendezvous place they had discussed. She specifically said she'd meet Peeky there. Since their phones had all stopped working, maybe they'd be watching for him.

So how do I make myself visible to my friend and not to my enemies?

Not by hiding under oak trees.

Back to Fowler Avenue and the heat, chafed armpits and all.

* * * * *

There it is.

THE NAVIGATORS

After about an hour of waiting in the Sun Dome parking lot, a small caravan of trucks drove up. Melissa hunched behind the wheel of the pickup truck as they rolled by. On the back of a flatbed sat the time machine, the big bronze egg that had been the source of so much trouble.

They delivered it using one of the university trucks, the way Barry and the rest of them had done a few days earlier. Right in the open for all to see.

Several maintenance workers got out of the first truck and opened a few large overhead doors, allowing the vehicles to enter the floor of the Sun Dome.

Within minutes of arriving, they had disappeared inside.

She sat back, imagining the workers unloading the machine and storing it somewhere in one of the locker rooms or storage areas. Before long, they re-emerged, shut the big door, and drove off.

As simple as that? Maybe I should have tried to sneak in while they had the door open.

From a side door, a figure emerged that she knew well: Dean Anderson. He was accompanied by a uniformed police officer, but from where she parked, Melissa couldn't tell if he was a campus cop or City of Tampa police, or what.

More vehicles approached. She slid down in her seat.

Two campus cruisers sped by. They drove up to Dean Anderson and the other man. They hadn't seemed to notice the yellow truck, but a stray vehicle on a large college campus wasn't unusual. Runners parked in random spots to go for a run.

Students played Frisbee on the large spans of grass. A little yellow pickup on the edge of the Sun Dome lot wasn't cause for alarm.

Four officers went into the stadium. Dean Anderson and the other officer got into one of the squad cars and left.

This will be the security for the machine, at least until the military guys show up. Four guys. Campus cops.

The news report had said the Air Force brass at MacDill were organizing a transfer in the morning.

So our time machine will be spending the night right here. We have one night to get it back.

* * * * *

I was just finishing my second chocolate shake when the waitress returned again.

"Looks like you're feeling better, sugar."

I smiled. "I am."

"Would you like a hamburger to go along with all that ice cream?" She glanced at her notepad. "Or are you gonna go for a third shake?"

"As tempting as a third shake sounds, I think I've reached my limit. Better call it quits before I explode."

"Okay, hon." She set the check down on the table.

"Can I sit here for a minute and . . . digest?"

"You bet. Flag me down if you need anything else."

As she disappeared, the front doors banged open. A figure on crutches was attempting to enter—and doing a bad job. The crutches smacked into the door glass while he worked to keep his balance.

Barry.

I grabbed my credit card out of my wallet and waved it at my waitress before dropping it on the table and rushing to help him. "Barry! What happened to you?"

"Long story." His t-shirt was drenched with sweat. He handed me a crutch. "Help me with these, will ya?"

Between the two of us, Barry's ankle cast, and his crutches, we had more trouble walking through the entry than when he was doing it alone. Everything got tangled up. Finally, a waitress came over to hold the door. Barry hopped through.

"Over here," I said, helping him to my table. "Miss? Some water for my friend, please?"

"Sure thing, hon."

As he lowered himself into a chair, Barry winced.

"What is up with you?" I asked. "You look terrible."

Barry's hands were swollen and red, with some blisters starting to appear. He pulled at his armpits. "Crutches are definitely a cruel joke, I'll tell you what." He clacked them together and leaned them against the table. "My hands are raw and my armpits are fricking bleeding."

"What are you doing here?"

"When Melissa was driving me to the hospital, she said she was supposed to meet you here. I took a chance."

"Where is she now?"

"No idea. I thought she'd be with you."

The waitress returned with some water and my credit card. "Sir, this card's been declined."

I was surprised, but Barry intervened. "Mine have been cancelled, too, Peeky." He eyed the waitress and reached for his wallet, pulling out twenty dollars. He slid it across the table to her. "I'll just pay in cash, ma'am."

Her face turned white. "You're the ones they're talking about on the news, aren't you?"

My heart stopped. She backed away from the table, holding her arms up. "We don't want any trouble!"

I stood, floundering for some words. The waitress bumped into the counter and yelled. "Somebody call 911!"

Just then a yellow pickup truck drove into the pancake house parking lot. Barry recognized it. "Peeky!"

"What!"

He jumped up. "Run for it!"

CHAPTER TWENTY-TWO

The door of the yellow truck opened. "Missy!" Barry yelled, hobbling his way toward the pickup. "We need to get out of here."

Melissa's face appeared, then went back into the truck. As the motor started, Barry opened the passenger door and fell in. I squeezed in next to him.

"What's going on?" Melissa steered the truck through the parking lot.

"The waitress figured out who we are," Barry said.

Melissa pulled onto the street and headed east toward the interstate, squealing the tires as she did. I grabbed the dashboard. "Take it easy, you'll draw more attention to us."

Melissa glanced in the rear view mirror. "That's the point."

* * * * *

Findlay's cell phone rang in his pocket. It was Captain Ferguson.

"What's the good word, *el capitan*?"

"Findlay, what do you think a college football helmet costs?"

"Why would I care about a thing like that?"

"Because one of your little friends was caught trying to steal some this morning from the practice fields. A fella by the name of Richard Franklin Fellings."

Findlay bolted upright. "Riff? Hoo boy, this is my lucky day, isn't it? What a bunch of screw ups I'm dealing with."

Ferguson chuckled. "Turns out these helmets cost the school about $400 apiece."

"Four hundred dollars for a freaking football helmet? What a rip off." He leaned back in the chair. "No wonder tuition costs so much."

"That may be, but seeing as Mr. Fellings was apprehended with four of them, that's $1,600. That kicks him up to grand theft."

"And?"

"And early today he was transferred to the custody of the Tampa Police Department. He's been booked and has been sitting in jail all day."

"That was this morning and they still have him? He didn't bond out?" Findlay scratched his chin.

"Fellings gave them a fake name, so it slowed things down for a while. But when they saw our bulletins on the wire, they ID'd him. The captain there's a buddy of mine, and he wanted to know if we'd like Fellings back or if they should keep him."

THE NAVIGATORS

"Hmm, what's the smart move here, Ferg?"

"Well, if we take him back, we can question him. If they keep him, he sits in jail until he posts bond. As it is right now, he's probably out of commission for overnight or a little longer."

Findlay grinned. "It's probably better if he stays out of the way for now. Riff's pretty useless anyway, except maybe as a bargaining chip if I need one. Is any of this un-doable if I change my mind?"

"Like I said—the captain's a friend. We can do whatever we want as long as we decide in the next 24 hours or so."

Findlay nodded. "Then let him rot in the Tampa PD lockup for a while, getting the crap scared out of him." He chuckled. "Maybe he can become some bubba's girlfriend. Then if we need him for anything, he'll be more cooperative." Using Riff as a bargaining piece might come in handy when it came to do the next step or two. "Ferg, would the same thing apply for Roger?"

"The guy in Tampa General hospital? Sure. He'll stay there while he recovers, but he's up for theft of school property, too. All four of them are. Plus conspiracy to defraud, evading arrest—among other things."

A thin smile crept across Findlay's face. "Then let's go ahead and arrest Roger, too."

"Consider it done." Ferguson hung up.

Findlay took stock of the situation. *Riff is arrested and in police custody, Roger is in intensive care at Tampa General and is about to be arrested, and Peeky has already been flipped to my side. That just leaves two little mice to catch, and without cell phones and credit cards, that won't take very long.*

* * * * *

The Motel 6 on Fowler Avenue stood a few miles west of I-75 and the pancake house, and it had one big advantage besides a swimming pool and cable TVs. Near the university and respectable enough to let parents house their friends there during graduations, a little more than sixty bucks would get a tired traveler a room for the night.

As she pulled the yellow truck into the parking lot, Melissa presented our options.

"We have to assume the people at the restaurant saw you get into this truck. But they also saw me speed east toward the interstate. From there, we could go anywhere. North, south—the cops won't know where to look for us. That'll buy a little time." She glanced at Barry and me, as if to make sure we were following her logic. "By doubling back to here, we should be fine for a while."

"Fair enough," Barry said, "but this is a pretty easy car to spot."

"Yeah." Melissa pursed her lips. "We'll have to ditch it."

Barry checked the truck's cab. "Is there anything in here we can use?"

A backpack rested on the floor. "Grab that," Melissa pointed. "Peeky, see if the glove box has anything."

Barry laid the backpack in his lap. "You gonna call Sheila and tell her what's up?"

"No way. The less she knows the better."

THE NAVIGATORS

I rummaged through the overstuffed glove compartment. "There's a pen and some tampons. CDs. Lipstick. A hair brush. Corkscrew. Several corkscrews, actually." I smiled. "Your friend is a party girl."

"Okay," Melissa said. "Bring that stuff. Bring all of it. Stick it in her backpack."

"What for?" Barry stuffed the items into the backpack.

"It's her stuff, Barry. The least we can do is save it for her."

"Meaning?"

Melissa sat up straight and addressed us. "Meaning, I'm going to take the car and ditch it behind the mall or an office building somewhere." She gripped the steering wheel. "If it ends up getting stolen, at least my friend will have some of her personal things."

Barry peered past her to the motel office. "What's the deal with this place? I'm not sure any of our credit cards are working anymore."

"They aren't," I said. "Findlay made sure of that."

Barry cocked his head. "How do you know?"

Oops.

I collected myself. "I mean, he *probably* did. It makes sense, right? Who else would have a reason to cut all of our credits cards off right now? Or the ability? Findlay's a hacker. He did it, I'm sure."

Melissa glanced at the office. "Doesn't matter. They take cash."

Barry opened his mouth but nothing came out.

"What? We used to come here to party freshman year. After hours stuff." She dug into her pocket. "Everybody ante up. How much money do we have?"

"I have a twenty." Barry shrugged. "I left the rest on the table when we fled the dang pancake house."

I dropped my cash into Melissa's hand. "All I have is two dollars."

Barry chuckled. "What the heck, Peeky? Two dollars?"

"That's it. Rub it in, rich guy."

Melissa stayed focused. "Okay, okay, I've got . . . forty-one dollars. That'll be enough. Give it to me. I'll go get a room."

"Hold on." Barry peered at the office window again. "Do you think they might identify you and call the cops?"

"Good question." She sighed. "How did that waitress know? Do you think they've put our pictures out on the news now?"

"No. I think she just happened to know the descriptions. We're wearing the same clothes. Peeky was fine until I showed up. Then she put it together. The news hasn't even announced our names."

I was curious about that. "Why do you suppose they haven't done that yet?"

"Because they know who we are and where we live." Barry gritted his teeth. "Findlay saw to that. They're trying to keep a lid on things until they find us. After that, who knows?"

I squirmed in my seat at the mention of Findlay's name again, then gritted my teeth and stared out the window.

"Anyway," Melissa said. "We can get a room, get cleaned up a little, and get some rest. And we can stay under the radar as long as I get rid of this big yellow Hey They're Right Here sign that I'm driving." She tapped the steering wheel. "Then we can go get our time machine."

Barry stuffed the last of the glove box contents into the back pack. "You know where it is?"

"The Sun Dome. I saw them dropping it off just before I found you guys." Melissa opened the door.

"Uh . . ." Barry looked at me. "Should one of us come with you?"

She guided a strand of hair away from her face and tucked it behind her ear. "Sure. Which one? The guy with the broken leg or the guy from India, both of whom were just spotted by a waitress as the guys on the news?"

The door shut as Barry opened his mouth to reply.

* * * * *

"Jim, what happened?"

Findlay was angry. Even though the campus cops were working for him, he could only push things so far. He kept his anger in check and leaned in to the speakerphone at the campus police station.

"What can I say?" Officer Bolton squinted at the oncoming traffic as he prepared to make a U-turn across the grassy interstate median. "They got away."

"How is that even possible? You were right there. You dropped Peeky off at the pancake house. All you had to do was sit in the parking lot and wait for somebody to come pick him up."

"And I did. But I didn't know what kind of vehicle to watch for. All of a sudden the kid comes running out and jumps into a yellow truck, and they took off."

"Was he alone?"

"Peeky ran out of the restaurant like his hair was on fire. He was following the other kid, Barry. I'm guessing the girl was driving the truck."

Findlay pounded the desk. "Man, we could have had both of them along with Peeky."

"They peeled out of the parking lot and took off for the interstate," Bolton said. "By the time I got my car turned around and out of the lot . . . they had a big lead. I couldn't see through all the traffic whether they went north or south, so I guessed south. There's nothing much north anyway."

Captain Ferguson walked over to Findlay. "It doesn't matter. With a decent head start, they were sure to get free and clear. There are too many exits around that part of the interstate. They could have lost three of our cars."

Findlay rocked in the chair. "Okay, so we know they're together and we know they're on the run. They're probably scared." He eyed Ferguson. "What do people do in that kind of situation?"

"Head for home, or get out of Dodge," said Bolton.

"Or counterattack." Ferguson rubbed his chin. "Jim, you better stick with Findlay for now."

THE NAVIGATORS

"Why didn't your boy Peeky just drop a dime and let us nab them all in the restaurant? I was sitting right there."

Findlay stared at the speakerphone. "I don't know. Maybe there wasn't time."

"Or maybe he didn't really flip."

"Maybe. I don't know that, either." Findlay stopped rocking and sorted it all out. "This was always about the money for Peeky, so I doubt he'll let that go. He's put in a lot of work to get this far. Remember, he put on a good act, but he's a money grubbing little turd underneath it all. So I don't know what's going on with him, but I do know this—they won't leave town and they won't go to their homes. They're going to come for their machine."

Ferguson sipped his coffee. "The best chance they'll have to reacquire the machine is during the transfer."

"Against armed military people? No way." Findlay sat back in the chair and folded his arms.

"This isn't a piece of weaponry. The transfer team won't be armed. They'll be a couple of regular guys with a truck."

"What the heck, Ferg! I was expecting like an army!"

"Nope." He emptied his coffee cup with a gulp. "Just a couple of guys and a truck. That's what they're sending."

* * * * *

The pimply faced guy sitting behind the registration counter ogled Melissa as she approached. The motel office had a large window, but it was like the drive through at the bank—a glass pane with a small opening and a metal pass-through drawer. After a certain hour, all transactions were done through the thick glass instead of in the lobby so the clerk didn't get robbed. He lowered the volume on his small TV.

Melissa unfolded the bills in her hand. "I need to get a room for a night, please."

"Just you, miss?" The clerk stood, looking her up and down.

"That's right. How much is it, please?"

"Well, have you heard about our USF 'Free for a Flash' program?"

She glared at him. "I have not."

He smiled. "Yeah, well, you know the room is free . . . for a flash."

Frowning, she narrowed her eyes. "I'm not flashing you."

"Hey, then we might be all full for the night." He sat back down. "I'm just sayin'. Sixty bucks is a lot of beer money."

Melissa noticed the office TV switch over to a news update, featuring the three students who were allegedly on the run. She leaned into the window. "You mean, if I show you," she pressed her t-shirt against the glass. "You'll give me my room for free?"

Pimples licked his lips. "Normally I just knock off ten bucks for a flash. But for you, I'd go the whole way." The TV update continued.

Melissa pointed. "And would that be a security camera right there?"

He glanced over his shoulder at the small camera on the office wall. "Uh . . ."

"It is, isn't it? So after I get my little discount," she wiggled against the glass, "I can become an internet sensation. How thoughtful."

Pimples had no reply. The news update finished.

Melissa leaned back and folded her arms. "Does your boss know about your little scam?"

He winked. "Who do you think installed the camera? Hey, a discount's a discount. Most college girls are happy to get it. High schoolers, too."

"You're disgusting."

"I'm employee of the month, momma. The manager likes that I keep the rooms full. He doesn't ask how I do it."

"Terrific. Maybe I can name both of you in my harassment lawsuit. Meanwhile, before you sneak off to the back room to do something even more disgusting, do you think you can tell me the real price of a room?"

"Fifty-five, plus tax."

Barry appeared over Melissa's shoulder. "Is there a problem?"

Pimples straightened up. "No problem, my man. I was just fixing the lady up with a room. Chill. You'll be bumping and grinding in no time, stud." He slid a key under the glass. "You two have a good time tonight."

Melissa counted her change while Barry scowled at the clerk. "What's he talking about?"

"He's just showing me that the employees at cheap motels are just as creepy as ever."

"I see you brought your backpack, stud. Got all your toys? Your video cameras and stuff? Yeehaw, cowboy. Ride that pony."

"You're lucky this is bulletproof glass, *cowboy*, or you'd be wearing your nose on the other side of your face right now."

"I hear that every twenty minutes on a Friday night, pal."

Melissa put a hand on Barry's side. "Stop. We're trying not to draw attention to ourselves, remember?"

"She's got the key, stud." Pimples winked. "Go have fun, you two."

As they headed to the room, I ran to catch up.

Pimples loved that. "One more? Oh, yeah, baby. Sweet thang got a three-way going for her tonight. Booyah!" He pressed his face against the glass as we rounded the corner. "I knew you was a freak baby! Maybe I should come visit on my break."

Once inside the room, Melissa collapsed on the bed. "It's only a matter of time before our pictures appear on those news updates and that creep at the front desk figures out who we are."

I sat on the edge near her feet, but from the expression on his face, the wheels were already going a hundred miles an hour inside Barry's head. He shut the curtains.

"He may figure it out anyway. The waitress did." Barry leaned the crutches against the wall and lowered himself onto the bed, rubbing his eyes. "Let's focus. They have the time machine at the basketball stadium, the Sun Dome. The question is, how do we get it?"

"We're stealing it, right?" I said. "Isn't that the idea? I'm not sure how, though. The cops watching it have guns."

"Yeah, yeah. But let's break down the problem. They've got our machine inside of a big stadium. We need to get it out. The only things preventing us from doing that are really just a few small obstacles . . ."

Melissa raised her head off the pillow. "Those obstacles are called guns."

"Yeah, yeah, guns." Barry bit his fingernail. "That's one challenge, but there are locked doors, too, and locked gates. Then, the actual guards. And they could call for backup over the radio, too." He stared at the window. "The trick is, since we can't afford to confront them, how do we get them to abandon the machine?"

I put my hands on my knees. "I don't think they're going to just walk away from it for a coffee break, if that's what you're hoping."

"We have to make them *want* to leave it. Then we could almost stroll in and take it. Like, if they thought it was radioactive or something."

Melissa groaned. "Come on. Tomorrow that machine goes into military hands and we never see it again. Be realistic. You're talking crazy."

"I know." Barry turned to her. "But that's kind of the same approach Findlay used on me. He got me to give up the machine at my apartment by setting fire to the place. He smoked me out."

Melissa sat up. "We are *not* setting fire to the Sun Dome."

"No, no. We don't have the resources to burn it . . ."

"Besides, it's concrete." I said. "I'm not sure it would even burn."

Barry put his elbows on his knees, rubbing his face and letting out a big sigh. Then his head snapped up. "Hey, did you guys know that the big canvas roof on the Sun Dome collapsed once?"

"No."

He chuckled. "I used to think it was an old wives' tale. Our freshman year, they told us that whopper to keep us from climbing up there. You know—scare us into thinking it could collapse if a bunch of us walked on it. So, of course, we all had to go try it, right?"

Blank stares.

Barry blinked. "Neither one of you ever walked on the Sun Dome roof?" He shook his head. "It's hard to believe we attend the same school."

"Why is that such a thing with everybody?" Melissa shoved Barry. "What about it?"

He shifted on the bed, carefully stretching out his sore leg. "Well, the thing about the Sun Dome is, they put up the big concrete walls, but the roof is just canvas. It's held up by air pressure."

"Right." Melissa pushed up on her elbows. "That's why when you go through the revolving doors you get that big wind rush."

Barry nodded. "That's right. And almost every door into the stadium is a rotating door, so you can't accidentally leave one open. It maintains the pressure."

"I wouldn't know." I folded my arms. "I never went to a basketball game."

A big grin stretched across Barry's face. "Something like twenty years ago, the power went out, and the fans that pump the air in stopped working. There was a cleaning crew inside at the time. They said it was scarier than an earthquake. The big canvas roof started sagging right away and the support frame was *groaning*. All the big stadium lights were breaking off and falling to the ground, exploding like missiles. It scared the crap out of them."

I shrugged. "How does that help us?"

"Would you stay in a building if the roof was collapsing? If all the lights were falling down around you? The scoreboard, the concert speakers?"

"Why is this better than burning it?"

"Honestly, it's simpler." He rubbed his knees. "If we were to stop the fans, or put some big holes in the roof, that's it. It would collapse."

"Wow." The idea of a stadium collapsing while things crashed to the ground inside . . . it amazed me. "And when the fans come back on, it'll just blow itself back up?"

"Oh, no. Last time, it was completely destroyed. That much canvas weighs tons. It caused all kinds of damage."

"How do you know it would even work?" Melissa asked.

"It'll work." Barry stretched his leg out again. "If we cut enough holes."

Melissa frowned. "But still we have to cut the power?"

"No. We don't need the whole roof to collapse. We need it to *start* to collapse. That'll be enough to scare those guys out of the building long enough for us to come in."

I grabbed my head. "All that stuff will fall on us!"

"We'll be inside the truck." Barry waved a hand. "And we'll be coming in quick and leaving even quicker."

Melissa nodded. "After we grab back our time machine."

"Can you imagine?" Barry chuckled. "You're a campus cop who got stuck watching this stupid machine all night, and all of a sudden the stadium roof is collapsing and lights are exploding all over the place?"

I smirked. "That would make me leave."

Barry pointed at me. "And you probably wouldn't stop to pick up a time machine on the way out the door, either, would you?"

"So then . . ." I shrugged. "We just drive in and take it?"

"Well . . ." Barry rubbed his chin. "We'll have to pick a couple of locks along the way. Then we sit in the truck and wait for the chaos to start."

Melissa peered up at Barry. "This seems awfully elaborate, Wile E. Coyote."

"I'd agree, if it hadn't already happened before. And a good plan today is better than a perfect plan tomorrow, right?"

I was nervous. "How long would it take?"

"Doesn't matter." Melissa stood up. "We have all night, no tomorrow, and no plan B." She put her hands on her hips. "Let's go for it."

CHAPTER TWENTY-THREE

" 'A couple of guys and a truck.' That's what they're sending?" Findlay pounded the table. "Why don't we just *give* them the stupid time machine?"

"Well." Ferguson cracked his knuckles, taking care to ensure that each joint popped before flexing his large hands. "Your buddies—they don't know that. They don't know if the Air Force is sending F-16s."

Findlay wasn't listening. He was lost in thought from hearing his own words as he'd said them out loud to the captain.

* * * * *

I took a deep breath. "So those very brave campus police officers with the guns are going to run for their lives? Then we just run in and scoop up our machine?"

"Yep," Barry said. "Besides, they won't have a reason to shoot at us. Who shoots at a collapsing roof?"

I pointed to his cast. "Who's us, gimpy? You aren't running anywhere. Or climbing up a roof to cut any canvas, for that matter."

Melissa gathered her hair into a pony tail and slipped a rubber band around it. "Nope. I guess we'll have to do that part, Peeky."

My stomach knotted. This was a fine line for me to be walking, but what choice did I have except to play along? "Well, you know what they say." I shrugged. "A good plan today is better than a perfect plan tomorrow. Unless it lands you in jail."

"I have news for you, Peeky." Barry looked at the window again. "Getting that time machine back is the only thing keeping us out of jail right now. That puts us back in the driver's seat."

Melissa folded her arms. "What do we need?"

"A knife, for the roof. Something to pick the lock on the generator fence. Flashlights, maybe."

"A getaway vehicle would be nice," I said.

She waved her hand. "We can still use the truck. We were gonna ditch it anyway. We'll just use it to grab the machine back first."

"Peeky's right. It would be better if we had a different vehicle."

"Look," Melissa said. "We go with what we have. I'll drive us over near the Sun Dome, but not so close that anybody will see us. I'll park behind the tree line to the soccer field. Peeky and I will sneak out. Barry, you stay with the truck. When we give you a signal, you bring the truck over and we'll put the time machine in it."

"Meanwhile, you two have to get onto the roof, slash the canvas, and turn off the generators. Gee, no problem."

"Yeah," Melissa frowned. "It would be nice if we had some help. But as it stands, we don't. And the last chance we have to grab back the time machine is tonight." Her face grew firm with resolve. "So unless anybody has any better ideas, this is what we're doing."

"Can't we just smash through the overhead door like they do on TV?" I asked.

Barry shook his head. "It might not work. Those big roll-type doors are made of some kind of thin metal slats, but they might be reinforced with steel bars or something. We want the guards to leave the machine. If they hear a bunch of noise and think they're under attack, they might not leave—and they might fight back. Then those pesky guns might start firing. Besides, if we tried to smash through the gates and didn't make it, game over."

"Okay, okay. We'll do it your way."

"You know," he rubbed his chin. "The only other thing we could really use is a couple of two way radios. Where could we get something like that at this time of night? Radio Shack?"

"Why do we need radios?" Melissa narrowed her eyes.

Barry patted his broken leg. "I can't run around with you, but with communication, I could tell you what to do. And you could give me updates while I keep lookout from the truck."

It made sense to me. There was only one problem. "We don't have any more money."

THE NAVIGATORS

"Yeah, well . . . we're already thieves." Barry glanced at me. "If you can create a distraction inside Radio Shack, I'll grab some walkie talkie radios and run out. They only ever have one guy working. It shouldn't be too hard to distract him. "

"How you gonna run anywhere, gimp boy?"

Melissa held her hand up. "I'll create the distraction. Peeky will grab the radios. Barry, you have to wait in the car."

His mouth curled into a smile. "You gonna distract the Radio Shack guy the way you did with the motel clerk?"

"Maybe. You jealous?"

"Maybe I should just stay here in the hotel."

"Oh, no." Melissa straightened up. "Last time we split up we almost didn't reconnect. Let's stay together. That slime ball at the front desk can't find us if we aren't here."

"Well, we *are* coming back here, aren't we?"

"Kind of." She glanced at the window. "There'll be some high school party going on in his motel somewhere before midnight, I guarantee it. They won't want their parents to know what they're up to, and they sure won't want the front desk guy checking up on them. So they'll be happy to trade rooms with us." She winked. "Happens all the time."

Barry seemed satisfied. He turned to me. "Listen, at the Sun Dome, the two of you should be able to boost each other up onto the rain gutters. I'll point them out to you. They're these big concrete downspouts, like aquifers, but they start out about ten feet off the ground on a column. Melissa can help boost you up like this." He squatted a little, interlocking his fingers and holding them out like a step. "One foot goes here, in her hands, then your other foot goes on her shoulder. Missy, if you lean back against the column, it'll support you and you'll be able to hold his weight." He turned back to me. "Then you reach down and help pull her up. That's all you need to do."

I looked over at Melissa. "Make sure we have enough gas in the getaway car."

"The tank's half full. Anything else?"

"Sure," I said. "Knives. Lock picks. Bullet proof vests."

Melissa grabbed the backpack. "We can't go on a crime spree to put together all the stuff we need. We'll have to improvise." She unzipped the bag and dumped it on the bed. "Let's see what Sheila's got in here." Moving her fingers over the pile, she sorted out useful objects. "Hairpins – that'll help with the locks." They went into her pocket. "A corkscrew. And check it out." With a quick flip, a one-inch blade appeared.

"Why does a bottle opener have a blade attached?" I asked.

"It's a foil cutter, for expensive wines. It's small, but it will have to do."

"Besides," Barry said. "It only has to work for a few minutes."

"I guess that just leaves us needing some radios." Melissa put her hands on her hips, sighing. "Okay, let's go rob the Radio Shack."

* * * * *

THE NAVIGATORS

We sat in the Kmart's enormous parking lot, about a hundred yards away from Radio Shack, staring at it through its big glass windows.

Barry shifted his weight in the passenger seat, trying to keep his broken left ankle as comfortable as possible. "Look, it's a simple smash and grab. You see it on the news all the time. People just run in the door, grab the stuff, and run out again before the clerk even have a chance to figure out what's going on." He eyed Melissa. "The only difference is, we're gonna send Missy in first to cause a distraction."

"Are we sure the distraction's even necessary?" I asked.

"No, but it's a little like adding an extra level of safety."

Melissa shook her head. "Safety during a robbery. What a concept." She rested her hands on the steering wheel. "I'll try to get the guy to go way to the back of the store with me. As soon as that happens, Peeky, you run in and grab the walkie talkies."

"Do we know where they are?"

"They shouldn't be too hard to find. That stuff will be up front with the cell phones." She gazed at Barry. "Stay in the truck with the engine running. You're our getaway driver. When Peeky comes out, you guys take off. Then drive around and meet me in the back a few minutes later. That way they don't think we're together. The key is, remain anonymous."

I took a deep breath. "Okay, I guess we're ready. Let's go."

"Let me drive," Barry said. "I'll drop you off first, a little ways away from Radio Shack. That way, you can walk up and not be seen getting out of the truck."

"Right." She nodded. "Anonymous."

From across the parking lot of the unsuspecting Radio Shack, we made our final adjustments for our assault. Barry slid behind the wheel of the truck.

I got out and peed behind it.

"Come on, Peeky," Barry announced. "Time to go."

* * * * *

At five minutes to closing time, the clerk at RadioShack was in no mood for customers. There was paperwork to do and a cash register to count.

But a pretty girl was always a welcome sight.

So when Melissa passed through the front door, she was not surprised at his smile. What *did* surprise her were the words that came out of his mouth.

"Hey, I know you. You're that politician's daughter—Melissa Mills, right?"

Oops.

* * * * *

Findlay was amazed at the simplicity of the words he'd just spoken.

Maybe I should let them get the machine. Then I can just take it from them. They do the hard part of getting it away from the military guys, and I can pluck it from them afterwards. I can still go take my gold rush ride to buy the Coca-Cola stock and turn the machine over to the school afterwards. Who'd know?

THE NAVIGATORS

Heck, I'd be the hero for getting the stolen machine back, and Peeky can let me know where it is.

* * * * *

Melissa smiled at the Radio Shack clerk as he came over to greet her. "Melissa Mills, right? From the political commercials. Your dad's running for mayor."

She was aghast, but managed to hold her smile in place. "Why, yes. Yes, I am."

"Yeah, I saw you on TV the other day talking about your dad."

We can't rob this place now. "Um, well—make sure you vote for him, okay?" She glanced up and saw a security monitor. Her jaw dropped.

"Oh, sure, I think your dad's a good guy. And he's well-known around these parts. He's done a lot for the community."

Returning her gaze to the clerk, she forced another smile. "You've sure done your election year homework."

"Yeah, yeah. So what can I do for you this evening?"

She thought for a moment. Anonymous was out, but that wasn't really the key. Not being tied to the robber was the key.

Peeky can still come in and grab the radios.

"Ma'am? Miss Mills?"

She regained her thoughts. "Um, well . . . I need one of these things over here." She walked back to the back of the store.

He followed her. "Speaker wire and cable coils, eh? You installing a stereo?"

* * * * *

The bell on the front door of the Radio shack jingled as I pushed it open and stepped inside.

The clerk waved. "I'll be right with you, sir!" Then he turned to Melissa. "So, Miss Mills, what are we rigging up? A sound system?"

As soon as I heard the clerk utter Melissa's name, I froze.

He knows her name!

Fear gripped me. I looked at Melissa.

She looked back at me, her eyes wide.

Should I run out now and scrub the mission?

As the clerk squatted down to explain speaker wire, Melissa waved at me. She mouthed the word, "Go."

Go? I hooked a thumb at the door. *Leave?*

She winced, mouthing again: "Get the radios."

I repeated it back, to be sure. "Get the radios?"

She nodded emphatically, the blood draining from her face. Above her, I spotted the video camera. It had recorded our interaction.

I mouthed. "What about that?"

She glanced up to the monitor, then back at me with a scowl, mouthing, "Do it!"

I scanned the packages on the shelves. Everything suddenly looked the same. Some were toys, some were cell phones, but each plastic package was indiscernible from the next.

My heart was in my throat, convinced we'd get caught. I blinked a few times. I could see colors in the boxes—blue, red, green—but I wasn't sure what I was staring at.

Am I having a panic attack?

THE NAVIGATORS

My hands were sweating. I heard myself huffing and puffing.

Melissa directed the clerk to something on the lower shelf. "What are these over here?"

He grabbed a small box. "These? These are cable junction boxes. What's the project you're doing?"

I tried to examine the boxes of gadgets in front of me. There were all kinds of things; I couldn't figure out which was which. I'd never stolen anything before in my life. I was a nervous wreck.

Every package looked the same. They might have all been walkie talkie radios, but I couldn't figure it out.

Melissa glared at me again, her eyes growing wider.

I was frozen with fear. I couldn't think.

Suddenly the front door burst open again. It was Barry.

He leaned on the open door and supported himself by placing a hand on the frame. "Where do you keep the walkie talkies?"

The clerk looked up. "I'll be with you in just a moment."

Barry hobbled his way over to me. "Where are the walkie talkies?"

The clerk stood up, pointing. "Right there . . ."

Barry glared at the shelf. He grabbed a box and turned for the door.

"What's going on?" the clerk asked.

The bell clanged again as Barry threw open the door and disappeared through it.

"You're robbing us!" The clerk's jaw dropped as he watched Barry disappear. He looked at me. "You're robbing us, too?"

"Uh . . ." I glanced at the door.

"Geez, can't you two follow some simple directions?"

He turned, appearing crestfallen, to Melissa. "Are you robbing me, too, Miss Mills?"

The yellow truck appeared in front of the door. Barry honked the horn.

"Yeah, I kinda am." Melissa shrugged. "I'm sorry."

"Miss Mills! Don't – don't do it."

She ran for the door. "Can you bill me for it or something?"

As it glided closed again, I stood there staring at the clerk. He stared back at me, his mouth open.

I reached for the door. "I . . . should probably go."

The horn honked again. The clerk shook his head. "I have to call the police. You guys are in a lot of trouble."

"Please don't call the police."

"I'll lose my job if I don't."

Barry laid on the horn again. This time, the sound unfroze my feet and I ran.

* * * * *

Barry drove like a madman. "What happened to you guys in there?"

"What!" Melissa threw her hands up. "Why did you come barging in, John Wayne?"

"You guys were taking too long. What happened?"

"I went through the door and the guy knew who I was right away. He called me by name."

"What?"

"Yeah. He said he knew me from my dad's TV commercials and stuff, or from interviews or something."

"Okay, so we had a perfect distraction." Barry turned to me. "What happened to you?"

"I panicked! I never stole anything before! I kept thinking about how mad my parents would be if I got caught. I froze."

"Geez, Peeky."

Melissa pounded the seat. "You know, it was a simple plan. Stroll in and grab a walkie talkie." She glared at Barry. "And you were supposed to stay in the car!"

I shrugged. "There were all these security cameras, too..."

Barry groaned. "Peeky, it's a Radio Shack. They *sell* security cameras. They have them on display." He took a deep breath. "Well, it doesn't matter. We got the radios."

Melissa looked at the box. "Did we?"

"What?"

"These are, like, kid walkie talkies, Barry."

"What! Are you kidding me? I grabbed the wrong box? Crap. Hang on." He hit the brakes and pulled over. "Let me see it."

Barry scanned the box for a moment. It was pink with a castle on it.

Cinderella.

Barry's cheeks turned red. He pored over the box. "Well, it doesn't matter, they'll still work for what we need done. They'll have enough power."

"They're freaking Cinderella walkie talkies, Barry." Melissa said. "I had a set like this when I was a kid. They're lousy."

"I'm sure they have some kind of decent range. They'll work just fine as long as we don't have any interference. Which we shouldn't, in an empty basketball stadium parking lot."

Melissa stomped her foot. "We really are the gang who can't shoot straight. If we can't even pull off a simple robbery of a Radio Shack, how are we gonna shut down the Sun Dome? And that clerk's going to call the cops. This is not good, you guys."

"Nothing has changed." Barry's voice was even. "We don't have any time? We didn't before, either. The cops are gonna get called? They were already after us. What's a few more?" He poked the dashboard with his finger. "This all comes to a head tonight, whether we like it or not. If we can get the machine, we can clear our names. It's that simple. If we get the machine, people will believe us when we tell our story. But *we* have to tell it, not Findlay, and not Dean Anderson."

He smiled, looking resolute in his words. "And believe it or not, I think shutting down the Sun Dome will actually be easier than robbing Radio Shack."

Sandwiched against the truck door, I had only one thought.

It better be.

Melissa flipped the pink box over. "Do these

things need batteries? Should we go back to Radio Shack, or do you wanna knock off a 7-11?"

CHAPTER TWENTY-FOUR

"The burglary gods took pity on us." Barry pulled batteries from the Cinderella walkie talkie box.

Melissa and I stood under the trees at the soccer field, overlooking the Sun Dome parking lot. Barry sat in the truck a few feet away.

"Robbery gods, not burglary gods, Barry." Melissa snapped a battery into one of the pink princess radios. She turned it on and held it up to her mouth. "Burglary is when you take things from a person. Robbery is when you take things from a place. *Over.*"

There was a little static, but otherwise the radio sounded fine. Barry adjusted his volume and answered Melissa. "10-4, good buddy. So we burgled Jonesy when we took her clock? *Over.*"

"I burgled Jonesy?" I laughed. "I don't like the sound of that. Very . . . unwholesome."

Melissa frowned at me. "No, she wasn't there." She put the radio up to her mouth again. "Negatory, negatory. We robbed her."

Barry's staticky voice came over her radio again. "*Negatory?* Is that a word? There was a clerk present at Radio Shack. Did the three of us burgle him?"

I covered my face. "Oh, I hope not."

Melissa chuckled. "I think you burgled him all by yourself, big guy. We just watched."

"10-4. And, yuck."

The parking lot of the Sun Dome was big, empty and dark. On game nights the lights were bright enough to illuminate every square inch of asphalt over the acres of parking, making it bright as daylight. Tonight, only about one in ten of the parking lot lights were on, and the empty lot was beginning to accumulate a nighttime mist. The top of the stadium, however, glowed. The stadium lights inside caused the canvas roof to light up, making an eerie white crescent-bubble against the backdrop of a black sky.

Barry spoke over the radio again. "Okay, you guys. It's zero hour."

We walked over to the truck.

"Just remember, it's all pretty simple." Barry was a stickler for details, despite his demonstrated impulsiveness during the Radio Shack heist. "You boost each other up onto the gutter, climb your way up to the roof. Then you just want to poke a few holes—you know, make some slashes. You'll start to feel the air coming right out."

I observed the stadium in the distance. "That thing's not gonna pop like a balloon when we stick the knife in it, is it?"

"No, it won't be anything like that. Kind of slice at it with the blade from the bottle opener." He made a sawing motion with his hands. "It's an old canvas. There are probably little holes all over it. Find one and open it up."

Melissa eyed the tiny blade on the opener. "And it'll just slice?"

"I'm sure it'll put up some resistance. I mean, it's not thin like a bed sheet. You'll have to put some muscle behind it." He took the bottle opener from her and examined it. "Just don't break the blade and all should be well."

She nodded. "How big of a hole should I cut?"

"I don't really know." Barry sighed. "If I were to guess, I'd say a hole the size of a door." He glanced at the dome. "They're always worried about people leaving a door open. The rumor is an open door will deflate the roof in about fifteen minutes." He rubbed his chin. "That sounds a little fast, but I'd say a door-sized hole would still do the trick."

"A door-sized cut." Melissa took the bottle opener back and shoved it into her pocket. "Okay."

"Just be sure not to fall through the hole while you're cutting it."

She glared at him. "How am I supposed to do that?"

"There's a skeleton frame underneath the roof. You'll see it because the inside lights are on and it'll cast a shadow against the canvas. Now, moving around up there isn't going to be like bouncing on a mattress. It's not a giant bounce house. The whole canvas will be firm and hard, but the supported places will be extra solid. The canvas attaches there. Just sit on the frame area and cut next to it, okay?"

She nodded.

"You don't have to cut one big hole, either. Five or six big slices would probably work. If you can do more, do more." He shifted his weight and lifted his broken foot off the ground, wincing. "Pay attention to the roof, though. If it starts to feel soft at all, get off it. Fast."

I cleared my throat. "Uh, why do we need two of us on the roof?"

"You don't." Barry cocked his head and pointed at the dome. "But it will take two of you to get onto the *gutter*, and at the top there's a buttress. You'll have to boost each other over that to get onto the roof. Besides," he turned to me and smiled, "you don't want Melissa running around up there by herself, do you?"

"I have absolutely no problem with her being Lara Croft all by herself."

"You'll be fine, Peeky." Melissa snickered. "Come on, let's go."

"One more thing." Barry put up a hand. "Come down the same way you went up. Not every gutter goes down to the ground. Some go onto other roofs, like the ticket office. You'd be stuck there."

I looked down. "I'll mark it with one of my socks or something."

"Okay. Once you're down, start picking the lock for the overhead door, so we can drive the truck in when it's time. Do you have the pins?"

"Got 'em." Melissa patted a pocket. "It won't be easy, but they should work . . . eventually."

I shook my head. "That's not funny."

Folding her arms, she eyed Barry's cast. "You make this all sound so easy—considering you're going to be just sitting in the truck."

"Maybe we'll get lucky and one of them smokes." I gestured to the side doors. "He'll come outside for a cigarette and leave the door open."

"Then what?" Barry laughed. "You overpower him and take his gun?" He squinted at the stadium. "How many do you think are in there?

"Three or four," Melissa said. "That's what I saw when they unloaded this afternoon."

Barry climbed out of the truck, leaning on it for support. "Okay, remember. It's a college campus. All kinds of kids go jogging around here at all times of the night. Nobody will think much of two of you running alongside the stadium." He pointed at the far edge of the parking lot nearest the dome. "Run down the sidewalk until you're close to the big downspout, then cut over and hide in the shadows."

He reached through the window and picked the pink princess radio up off the seat. "When you're ready, let me know on this." He clicked the talk button a few times, causing the one in Melissa's hand to crackle. "I'll be waiting for you down here and directing you as best I can."

She laughed. "Cinderella, my hero."

"I'm kinda nervous for you guys." Barry sighed.

"Don't be. We got this. Right, Peeky?"

I took a deep breath. The safety of my friends depended on a solid co-conspirator, and I was anything but that right now, thanks to that turd Findlay. "Actually, can you excuse me for a moment? I need to relieve myself at the back fender of the truck again."

"Geez, Peeky." Barry turned back to Melissa. "Are you okay with all this?"

"I'll be fine." She placed her hands on his arms. "Watch me from down here and keep me safe."

He nodded. "I will."

He took in her face, illuminated under the nearby parking lot light. The bright eyes, the delicate curves of her cheeks. As he opened his mouth to speak, Melissa leaned forward.

A muted trumpet noise rang out from my location at the back of the truck.

"Oh, Peeky!"

"Excuse me. Just a little gas. Sorry, I'm nervous."

Barry shook his head and dropped his arms. "You guys better get going before he explodes."

* * * * *

"Findlay, I think we just caught another break." Captain Ferguson hung up the phone. "That was my buddy over at Tampa PD. Guess what he said."

"That moron Riff hung himself in his cell trying to floss his teeth?"

"Nope. He said that a Radio Shack store just north of the university was just robbed by two fellas matching the description of our guys, and they got a positive ID on the girl with them, Melissa Mills."

Findlay's jaw dropped. "Wait, what? They're robbing Radio Shack stores now?"

"That's right." Ferguson folded his hands behind his head. "All three of them. They're still here in town."

"Seems odd for Melissa to implicate herself in a robbery. I thought she'd be smarter than that." Findlay rubbed the back of his neck. "But, oh well. I'll take my luck where I can find it."

"That store's not ten minutes from here."

"I wonder what they took from it?" He glanced at Ferguson. "Cash?"

"Radios. Specifically, walkie talkies."

Findlay sat back in his chair, his mouth dangling open. *What would they want with those? Would walkie talkies somehow be useful in scrambling a radio signal during the transfer tomorrow? No. What are those bozos up to?*

Ferguson cleared his throat. "My friends at the Tampa PD want to put out an APB. It's pretty much protocol at this point, Fin, but they'll hold off if I ask them to. You should let them. Things are getting too big to control from here on campus."

"We aren't just here on campus, Ferg. Dean Anderson has some powerful friends in the wings helping pull strings."

"They better be big."

"They are. Big enough to make a call to the fire captain and let me walk on an arson charge, and big enough to prevent some police paperwork from ruining my manhunt." He rubbed his hands together, pacing. "Still, we ought to up the ante. Things are taking too long."

THE NAVIGATORS

The captain reached for his coffee cup. "What did you have in mind?"

"Well . . ." Findlay smiled. "We have a prominent local politician whose daughter is out robbing the citizenry. Maybe the press would find that interesting. Let's give 'em a call. See what some outside pressure does to our lab rats. They're out of money and out of time. Soon, they'll be out of options. When they have nowhere else to go, they'll come crawling to me on their hands and knees."

"You sure?" Ferguson sipped his coffee.

"Ferg, it's like this. Melissa Mills, daughter of the likely next mayor, possibly being involved in taking a time machine that has already been recovered? Her lawyer father will have a rational explanation for that before the newscaster finishes reading the announcement." Findlay waved his hands. " 'It's all a big misunderstanding, folks.' It's embarrassing, but it mostly just hurts Melissa. Now, a news story about Melissa robbing a Radio Shack? Maybe getting arrested? Oh, that hurts Daddy. Big shot wants to be mayor but can't control his own daughter." He chuckled. "She won't want that to happen. Trust me, when word of that gets out, she'll fold in an instant." He plopped into a chair, a grin stretching across his face. "And she'll get the rest of them to fold, too."

Invigorated, he rocked forward and pulled the computer keyboard close. "Let's see what the after hours number for the Tampa Tribute is."

* * * * *

As we jogged to the stadium, Melissa in front and I enjoying the view, I considered at what point I might switch sides.

I wasn't at all sure Barry's plan to reacquire the time machine would work, and if it didn't, there was a good chance it would disappear for good. I'd never get my chance for a trip and all my hard work would be wasted. I'd never be able to pay back all the money I'd borrowed. I'd disgrace the family name just like my grandfather did, something I wasn't sure I could live down. It ruined him.

My stomach was a knot. I wasn't sure I could trust a deal with Findlay, either. He might take my money and run off with it, leaving me just as disgraced and even worse off financially.

Worst of all, I was in too deep to bail out.

We neared the Sun Dome sidewalk. I was almost out of breath. Melissa's bouncing booty showed no sign of slowing.

"Peeky, can you keep up?"

I gasped. "I . . . have a rule . . . about talking . . . while I run."

"Oh yeah?" She glanced over her shoulder. "What's that?"

"I . . . can't do it."

"Okay, I'll stop talking. We're almost there."

"Still . . . talking"

We neared the main gutter column. She glanced around. "Get ready."

A shadow from some trees crossed our path and created a dark spot all the way to the stadium dumpsters. When we reached it, Melissa made a hard left turn and ducked behind the trash bins. Seconds later, I was there, too.

I could see her silhouette heaving as she caught her breath. "Let's hold up for a second."

I nodded, my hands on knees as I sucked in air as fast as I could. She peeked around the dumpsters. "Doesn't seem like anything unusual's happening."

Barry's voice came over Melissa's radio. "How are we doing?"

"We're good." She kept the radio to her face for a moment. "We'll catch our second wind and start up the gutter. How is it from your side?"

"Perfect. I don't see anything."

I bristled. "Tell him to move to where he can see, then."

Melissa grinned. "He means he doesn't see anything out of place." Then the smile left her face. She held the radio to her mouth again. "You *do* mean you don't see anything out of place, right Barry?"

"That's right. And let's try not to use our names."

I snapped my fingers. "We should have thought up code names."

Melissa looked at me. "Who do you want to be? Red Dog One?"

I shook my head. "You can be Red Dog One."

"I'm no dog, period."

The radio crackled. "Peeky can be yellow dog."

"What does that mean?"

Melissa put the radio back in her pocket. "I'll tell you later. Ready to climb up a giant gutter?"

"No."

"I'll take that as a yes." She turned to the stadium gutter, looming large before us.

"Melissa, should I climb up you, or should you climb up me?"

She placed her hands on her hips. "You climb up me, then turn around and help me pull myself up."

"Are you sure?"

"I did gymnastics in high school. I can get up that thing with a little help." She hooked a thumb over her shoulder. "Could you pull yourself up that column?"

I shrugged. "Again, chess club fails me."

"Okay. Let's go."

* * * * *

"Tampa Tribute news desk."

Findlay sat up straight in his chair, nearly drooling on the desk with delight. "Hi, I have some interesting information that your political beat reporter might be interested in. Can you patch me through?"

"We have forty-five different political races going on right now, sir. Can you tell me which one this involves?"

"This is for the Tampa mayor's race, regarding candidate Mills."

"Candidate Mills. Got it. Let me see which reporter we have assigned to that race. Just a moment."

"Sure, take your time, darlin'. Like I've got all night." Findlay leaned back and rubbed his nose, snorting. "But this information is a bombshell, and it won't wait. So maybe get me connected *now* or

I'm on the phone to your competitors in three minutes."

* * * * *

Barry stared at the dark spot on the stadium gutter where Melissa and Peeky should have been.

There was a loud knock on the driver's window. He nearly jumped out of his skin.

A uniformed officer.

Barry rolled down the window. "Yes, sir?" It was a bicycle cop. That's why he hadn't seen him approach.

"Sorry, I need you to move the vehicle. You can't park here."

"Oh, okay." He peered over at the Sun Dome. Melissa had finally gotten over to the gutter and was helping Peeky up.

The officer shined a flashlight into the truck. "Everything all right here?"

"Uh, sorry. Just letting off a little steam after a fight with the girlfriend. Thought I'd park and cool off for a while."

The officer clipped his flashlight back into its holder. "Well, you can't cool off here, pal."

"No problem, sir." He started the engine.

* * * * *

"Hello?"

"Hello, are you the reporter covering the mayoral race in Tampa?"

"I am."

"Well, sweetie, I have some news that's gonna blow your socks off." Findlay rubbed his hands together, holding the phone with his shoulder. "Get this. The daughter of the so-called next mayor of

Tampa has been implicated in the theft of university property at USF, so she went on the run. Now, the Tampa Police Department has just reported that Melissa Mills was 100% positively identified as one of three people involved in holding up a Radio Shack just north of the USF campus." He chuckled. "Does that sound like something the Trib would be interested in?"

"It definitely does. I can guarantee you, the Trib would be interested in learning more about your story, Mister—what did you say your name was?"

"Chris Findlay. And you are?"

"My name is Janice Peterson."

CHAPTER TWENTY-FIVE

The climb up the gutter was harder than it looked. It was a continuous concrete shaft over 100 feet long, just wide enough for a person to walk in. The gutter's concrete side walls would hide us as we worked our way up—if we crouched—but it was installed at a steep angle, so it was a difficult climb. Melissa managed to hunch over as she ran up the dirty gray shaft, so I tried to follow suit. She was at the top before I even got half way.

Gasping, I arrived at the buttress where the gutter met the roof. It was as Barry had described, a concrete wall about six feet high, but it had seemed much smaller from the ground.

Melissa was staring at the parking lot.

"What's happening?" I wiped the sweat off my brow and squatted next to her, peering at the empty lot. "I thought I heard a car."

"You did. Barry . . . moved the truck."

A twinge of fear shot through my belly. "He left us?"

"He didn't leave us. Barry wouldn't do that."

"Then where's the truck?"

She took a deep breath. "I don't know. It doesn't matter. We still have a job to do." Standing in front of the concrete buttress, she reached up and ran her fingers along the top.

I pointed at the Cinderella walkie talkie in her pocket. "Call him on the radio."

"I tried. There was no answer."

"Then how do you know he didn't just leave?"

Her head whipped around. "I know that the same way I know you wouldn't leave if you were in the truck." She pointed at the empty lot. "Something's happened, that's all. A temporary glitch." She turned her face to the concrete. "He'll be there when we need him to be, just like you would be."

I swallowed, holding back the guilt. "Okay, you're right. What's next?"

She sniffled. "Help me over this stupid wall." She jumped up and grabbed the top, swinging her leg to catch the lip.

"It's a big buttress, not a wall."

"Who are you saying has a big butt? Because it's a long way down, fella."

"No, no, I mean—forget it." I grabbed a handful of her rear end and shoved.

"Hey! Watch the hands." In an instant, she was laying on the top, a bent leg on each side like the buttress was a concrete horse. She held out her hand. "Grab hold and pull yourself over."

* * * * *

Janice Peterson set down her notebook and leaned forward, pressing her cell phone to her ear. "Mr. Findlay, that is quite an interesting story you have there. How do I know if any of it's true?"

"Oh, it's true all right, lady. I have pictures, videos, cell phone records, you name it. So is this front page material or what?"

"Possibly. As it happens, I'm working very closely with Mr. Mills' campaign for the paper." She looked at the file folder of notes she'd accumulated on the Mills family. "This is the kind of information that can change the course of an election, depending on how it's handled. But I'd need exclusivity. Only The Tampa Tribute gets your story and your information. And I'd need that in writing."

"You got a deal. How soon can we meet?"

"I can send you an exclusivity agreement right now, and you can send me what you have. We can meet tomorrow morning to go over the details. How's 11am?"

"The sooner the better, Janice. This is awesome. I feel like I made a new friend."

"I'll see you tomorrow."

Janice sorted through a large stack of notes on her coffee table.

There was a pile about the mayoral election, a pile about the happy Mills family, a pile about the motherless daughter. She sifted through that last one; that story could be written so many ways. Poor Melissa Mills, the girl who had everything but had no mother; rich girl gone bad; mayor's daughter is newly crowned internet slut. Depending on who was doing the writing, it could win Michael Mills the election or ruin him politically. A mayoral hopeful who can't control his own daughter? With the underwear photos and the robbery, the beautiful young Melissa was sure to be a front page news sensation. That would drive sales, and sales was all any newspaper really cared about. With headlines came exposure; with exposure came power. Enough to secure a better position with the Trib for a long time to come.

She chuckled. *Good thing I got Findlay to agree to exclusivity.*

* * * * *

The canvas roof of the Sun Dome was surprisingly hard.

Even though Barry had said it wouldn't be like a bounce house, for some reason I still expected it to be soft. It wasn't. It was hard as concrete.

Gazing over the oddly lit roof was a bizarre experience in itself.

"Peeky, get up. The roof's safe to walk around on." Melissa was making her way to the top of the dome. "Come on."

I lifted my head a few inches off the canvas surface, where I lay prone in a spread eagle position, not daring to budge. "I'm . . . just inspecting it."

She kept moving. "Don't be afraid. Stand up. You're not going to fall through. I didn't."

I stood, feeling the need to hold my hands out for balance against the wind. The concrete buttress at the top of the gutter was six feet tall, but the rest of the stadium perimeter barely rose a few inches higher than the point where they met the roof. And the canvas sloped away at a dramatic angle. This had not been designed to walk on.

"It's weird, isn't it?" Melissa turned around and held her arms out. "It looks like we're on the moon."

I glanced down. "The surface of the moon would be all full of rocks and dust, and with a lot less gravity. And it wouldn't have a parking lot for me to fall to my death."

"Peeky, every once in a while take a break from being a dork, okay? For ten minutes here and there." She came towards me. "I meant that the roof surface is kinda like those pictures they took on the moon, where it's a big bright white curved surface underneath and when you look up the background is just black."

I crawled toward her, glimpsing the night sky. "Oh, I see what you mean."

Melissa pointed. "Just watch out for those-"

My foot snagged and I fell forward. My face slammed into the hard canvas surface. The next thing I knew, I was sliding and rolling. Black-white-black-white, the Sun Dome roof traded places with the night sky as I rolled towards the edge.

All the while I heard Melissa desperately screaming my name.

* * * * *

"Melissa, can you hear me? Melissa? Peeky?"
Static.

Barry tried the little pink walkie talkie again. "Melissa, Peeky, can you hear me?"

He moved the truck to the street side of the soccer field, but that was just far enough to lose the weak signal the toy radios could muster. He talked; static answered. From his new location, he couldn't see the stadium roof or the gutter.

But parked on the street, the cops wouldn't bother him to move the car again, so it was a good location.

Maybe I can drive past the stadium every five minutes and see what's up. That way, no parking issues – but I'd eventually raise suspicion. After a third pass, somebody might notice.

And then what would I do?

"Melissa, can you hear me? Melissa? Peeky?"

Nothing.

He bit his fingernail. Normally, he'd just move around until he could see something, but with a broken ankle, walking had become more difficult. Each step hurt, even with a cast.

"Melissa, can you hear me?"

He concluded it was best to wait in the truck for a while. If Peeky and Melissa were making progress putting holes in the roof, they wouldn't be finished and needing a pickup just yet.

I wonder how it's going up there.

* * * * *

"Peeky! Hold on! I'm coming for you!" Melissa scurried across the curved roof toward me, being careful not to fall herself. "Don't move!"

I was a little dizzy, and something hard and sharp pressed against my back. My cheeks stung from hitting the canvas as I rolled. I twisted my head just enough to see her spider-crawling to me, a kind of sit and scoot motion that kept both hands and both feet on the surface. Her eyes were huge. "Don't move. I'm almost there."

She lifted herself over a metal spike and rolled onto her stomach. "Grab my hand. Nice and easy."

She flattened herself as much as possible and stretched her hand out to mine. The wind seemed stronger and the dome seemed rounder. Bigger.

I lifted my hand. She stretched even further. "Can you reach me?"

I moved my hand toward hers.

"I'm going to pull you this way, okay? Stay flat on the canvas."

She grabbed my wrist and leaned her body weight back. The wind tugged at her hair, whipping it around her face. She moved her hands and feet back a bit and pulled again. "That's it, Peeky. Nice and slow."

I felt the whole right side of my body ease pressure, like it was being unstuck from a wall.

Melissa's voice was calm but stern. "You're doing good. Push this way a little with your feet if you can."

I pushed.

"A little more, okay? Can you crawl with me?" She tightened her grip on my wrist. "Come on, crawl. A little with your feet, a little with your hands. Like I'm doing."

I pushed a little with my feet, a little with my free hand.

"Okay, good. You're coming." The wind whipped her hair again.

I pushed myself up onto my elbows. "What happened?"

"Don't do that!" Melissa pulled me down. "Keep a low center of gravity." She took a deep breath and lowered her voice. "Just . . . keep looking at me."

"Why? What's-" I turned my head and stared straight down at the parking lot, a hundred feet below. Adrenaline jolted through my belly. I was perched right on the edge of the roof.

It was so far down to the ground. All the air went out of me. I tried to force myself to breathe but nothing would come.

"Peeky. *Peeky*!" Melissa tugged my wrist again. "You're okay. Look at me."

I turned my head to her, blinking.

"You're okay." She pulled again on my wrist. "Come this way."

I tried my best to move in her direction while not allowing any body parts to move in the other direction—off the roof. It was suddenly very cold up there.

"You're doing good." She eased herself backwards. "Just a little more."

I kept myself pressed against the canvas roof as much as possible, inching myself away from the edge.

"Good. Good. Keep coming."

After I had put about ten feet between myself and certain death, I was able to take a breath. "What happened?"

"You tripped."

I closed my eyes and hugged the canvas. *Tripped. Of all things.* "Okay, I think I can crawl on my own now."

She tightened her grip on my wrist. "Go ahead. I'm not letting go."

"I need to try to regain my manhood eventually."

"You can do that later."

"Promise?"

She chuckled. "Right now, just crawl with me."

We inched our way along the canvas to where the angle didn't feel as steep. At the peak the dome was nearly flat. Every ten feet or so, a metal spike would rise up out of nowhere.

I maneuvered myself over to one and inspected it. "Why are these things sticking out of the roof?"

"I think they're lightning rods."

I tapped the rod. "Don't they know people walk around up here?"

Melissa bent her knees and lay back, breathing hard. "I guess they figure that's on a need to know basis. Maintenance guys need to know. Drunken college kids don't."

Her voice sounded funny. I could see her eyes were closed and a tear had run across her face. She hadn't been catching her breath after all.

I pretended I hadn't noticed. "They have that backwards, then. Drunk college kids need to know about trip hazards most of all." I wiggled the rod. "What were they thinking?"

Melissa swiped the back of her hand across each cheek. "They were probably thinking there are a thousand lightning strikes a day in Florida, even on a clear day. So maybe lightning rods would be a good way to keep a canvas roof from getting hit and catching on fire."

"A thousand a day!" I flexed the rod in its pocket.

"Yep. Even at night."

I let go of the rod and moved away.

A gust of wind blew across the canvas and tugged at my shirt. I looked over at Melissa. "You saved my life."

She sat up and shook her head. "I didn't. You stopped all by yourself when you hit the edge there." Leaning on one hand, she pointed at the little concrete rim with the other. "You gave me a pretty good scare, though." A deep breath through her nose helped mask a sniffle as her shoulder came up to wipe her eye. "Don't do that again."

"Deal." I sighed, observing the tiny ridge that spanned the side of the canvas dome. "What a difference a few inches makes, huh?"

"Every girl knows that, sweetie." She smiled. "You ready to do what we came up here for?"

I shook my head. "No. My life flashed before my eyes back there. It wasn't pretty."

"No?"

"Kind of boring, actually."

"Well," Melissa stood up and put her hand out to me. "Let's see if we can add an exciting chapter, then."

* * * * *

"Who is this?" A boy's voice came over the Cinderella walkie talkie.

THE NAVIGATORS

Barry hesitated. He held the little pink radio up to his mouth and thought for a moment. "Uh, this is official police business. We need to keep this line clear."

"That's a load. Who is this?"

"Hey, watch your mouth. I said this is police business. Now let's keep this channel clear."

"Screw you, mister. This isn't police business. You're broadcasting into our baby monitor. You woke my little sister up, you bozo. Now my mom's mad."

Crap.

"Now who are you, buddy? And who's Melissa?"

Barry cleared his throat and sat up in the car. "Okay, kid, I'm warning you."

"Oh yeah? What are you gonna do, tough guy? You're talking on a baby monitor."

Crap!

"Who are you? And who's Melissa?"

* * * * *

Melissa unfolded the little blade from the bottle opener. She tapped her nail against the canvas roof and shrugged. "Well, here goes nothing."

Positioned just as Barry had suggested, with her weight on the support frame, she guided the knife into a tiny hole in the Sun Dome roof.

I took a deep breath. "If this does pop like a balloon, I'm going to be awfully upset."

She held the knife ready. "Barry said it wouldn't do that."

"I notice he isn't up here."

She touched the blade to the hole. "Ready?"

"No."

"One . . .

"Two . . .

"Three." She pushed the blade in. The roof didn't pop.

I drew a deep breath and let it out. Slowly, Melissa moved the tiny knife up and down, sawing away. A slit of about an inch appeared. Lights from inside the dome illuminated it a little brighter than the dull glow of the rest of the roof.

I strained to look, not wanting to get too close. "Can you see anything? Is it working?"

"I definitely feel air coming out." She ran her hand over the opening. "I mean, it's a strong stream, but this isn't going to do the job."

"Well, the canvas is pulled tight. Can you slice across instead of sawing?"

"I don't know, it's pretty thick. Let's see."

She grasped the knife with her fist and put it back into the hole. Leaning back, she pulled the blade toward her.

Whoosh!

A gust of air blew her hair up as she fell backwards to me. The canvas roof hissed its displeasure.

A twelve-inch gash.

"I'd say that's the way to go."

Light beamed out from the cut. She readied the blade again. "Watch out, I'm going to scoot back as I cut – if I can."

I backed up a few feet.

She re-gripped the blade and heaved. The canvas roof sounded like ripping sheets as the

THE NAVIGATORS

escaping air helped rip open the roof. The hiss grew to a roar.

She looked up and said something I couldn't hear over the wind rushing out of the hole.

The support frame ran in big sections, making a kind of shadow grid across the roof. I backed up again as she turned to make another slice.

From over her shoulder, I saw the hole grow. I backed up a little more. "Slow down. Barry said to only make a hole the size of a door!"

She glanced at me, holding up the bottle opener. The blade had broken off. Then she looked back at the hole as it continued to open on its own. The noise from the air was deafening now.

The roof shook as a loud groan emerged from beneath us. Melissa crouched down. The hole widened, its loose end flapping upward like bed sheets in a hurricane. A four-foot hole became ten. Melissa backed away as it chased her, growing wider.

The twenty-foot section of roof seemed to explode upward in pieces.

She scrambled to her feet. "Let's get out of here!"

* * * * *

"What is that?"

A guard inside the Sun Dome turned his eyes to the ceiling. A huge hole had opened in the roof and the whole building seemed to be shaking. His partner crouched in the middle of the basketball court next to the time machine. The quiet stadium was now filled with the noise of air rushing out the roof.

"It's an earthquake!"

The lights attached to the support structure swayed, causing shadows to dance around them.

"What should we do?"

"Our instructions were to protect this thing at all costs."

A light smashed next to them, sending glass in all directions. The hideous groaning of the roof grew louder.

"I'm outta here, Joe." The officer ran for the door.

Joe looked up. Debris swirled up and out through the gaping hole in the roof. The ceiling lights danced crazily in the wind.

Another broke loose and exploded next to him. His co-worker shouted from the door. "Joe! That thing's coming down. Get out of there!"

With his hands covering his head, Joe bolted. Another light crashed to the floor. He paused at the doorway. "What now?"

"What now? We get outside and call this in, that's what now!"

"Ferguson's gonna be mad we left our post."

A rack of concert lights crashed into the stands above them.

"Ferguson ain't here. You can stay. I'm getting out." With that, he ran into the parking lot. As more lights crashed to the ground and the roof began to sag, Joe made the only decision he could.

He got out.

* * * * *

Barry sat silent, thinking that after a few minutes the kid would grow bored and go away.

He was wrong.

"I know you're out there, baby monitor guy." The boy was singing now, taunting. Then, in an artificially high voice, he mocked him. "Where's Melissa. Where's Melissa? Ooh, mommy, I'm going to pee my pants if I don't find Melissa."

There was no stopping this brat.

He sang. "Me-*liss*-a? Where *are* you?"

Stupid little punk.

A second voice came over the radio. "Hello? Who is this, please?"

Oh, great. Now, it's his mother.

Barry put his face in his hands. He calmed his voice. "Yes, ma'am. Uh, this is . . . the USF student volunteer security patrol."

"Why are you talking on our baby monitor?"

"Well, we're picking up, uh, cross talk on our radios in this area. We've had a number of complaints from some of the students—female students ma'am—about a young boy."

The woman sounded irritated. "What are you talking about?"

"It seems a boy in the area has been sneaking over to the campus swimming pool to watch the female students sunbathe. Topless."

"Are you talking about my Jimmy?"

"Jimmy! Yes, that was the name we were given, ma'am. There have been complaints of, well, lewd comments . . ."

"Oh, no."

" . . . and fondling."

"Jimmy!"

"Mom, he's lying! He's full of it!"

"And bad language, ma'am. That sounds like our guy."

"How many times have I told you!" Whacking noises came over the pink walkie talkie. Jimmy wailed in the background.

"I'll be darned." Barry started the truck. "Sorry, Jimmy."

* * * * *

"Oh, no! Oh, no! Oh, no!"

Going down the concrete gutter was a lot faster than going up it—and a lot scarier. The ground was *way* too far down, and it was the only thing to look at. Behind us, the roof was creaking and groaning so loudly it sounded like it might collapse at any moment.

We were down in seconds, and back to our hiding spot at the dumpster.

I crouched in the shadows. "What happens next? Does Barry come get us?"

"Barry? We have to pick the lock first and open the overhead door. Then we'll radio for Barry." She dug in her pocket for the hair pins. "Let's hope these work."

She handed me the radio. "I'll go over to the truck entrance door. You try to call Barry when I wave at you."

"Are the guards gone?"

"Would you still be in there with all that going on? I don't even want to be out here."

"I *definitely* don't want to be here."

"Hey, toughen up." Melissa smiled. "You owe me one, remember?"

"You said you didn't save my life."

She dashed for the overhead door. "I might have lied."

CHAPTER TWENTY-SIX

Melissa had been able to pick locks as a party trick since she was a child, just never while somebody was shooting at her.

Hopefully, that streak would continue.

"It's all tumblers, Missy." Mr. Mills twisted the long wiry lock pick in the keyhole. *"You hold each one up with the pick, and then you can turn the knob. See? Focus on the tumblers."*

It was fun to watch a mini Houdini work her way out of a locked closet or bedroom in front of family and friends. After a while, she got good enough at it to work on other types of locks.

But that was a long time ago, and the stress of performing in front of an office full of her father's employees at a Christmas party was a far cry from opening the security locks for the Sun Dome's truck entrance with a few borrowed hairpins.

As the roof caved in.

And if the armed guards saw her, they'd stop her.

Put that out of your mind, Missy. It's just tumblers. Focus on the tumblers.

She wiped her sweaty hands on her pants. She knew: work each pin, one at a time, slowly. Still, she knew she was rushing. Each time she had a few tumblers in place, the hairpin would slip or bend.

She glanced at the massive door. There was no way to drive right through it the way they do on TV. She took a deep breath and started again.

* * * * *

From behind the dumpster, I could see Missy squatting as she worked the lock.

I didn't know how long it took to pick a lock—only what I'd seen on TV—but this seemed to be taking too long. From inside the stadium, the noise continued. Crashes. Groaning metal rafters bending under the increasing weight of the sagging canvas. If we didn't get in there soon, the way to the machine might be blocked completely.

I thought about trying Barry on the radio. She said to wait, but at some point he needed to be called whether we got in or not.

My heart pounded. I checked around for the guards. Maybe they had left. Maybe they were watching the destruction from the other side of the stadium.

Maybe they would be waiting for us when we got inside.

* * * * *

"Crap!"

The hairpins slipped again. The lock simply would not comply. Missy pounded the big steel door. "Open up, you stupid . . ."

She blinked back a tear. "Everybody's counting on me now. I am *not* going to let them down."

Focus on the tumblers, Missy.

She glared at the cold steel lock. "Okay, lock, here's what's gonna happen." She held up a hair pin. "I'm gonna do this one more time." She took a deep breath. "I'm going to go slow, okay? I'm going to hold the pins in place firmly." She slid the pin into the keyhole. "And you're *going* to open up. Do you hear me?"

She inserted the second pin, holding the first one tightly in place. The wire bent a little, so she applied even more force, causing the pins to dig into her fingers. Then the third pin, holding the other two, squeezing her eyes closed against the pain. She slowly turned them.

Click.

The lock popped open.

Melissa exhaled. "About time." She licked the blood off her finger and placed her forehead against the big door. "Thank you."

* * * * *

Melissa waved her arms at me. Time to cue Barry. I stood up and lifted the little pink radio to my mouth.

Headlights appeared on me, bouncing their way toward us. I dropped back behind the dumpster, motioning at Missy. "Get down!"

The truck drove right at me, screeching to a halt in front of the dumpster.

"Did somebody call for a taxi?"

It was Barry. I stood and shielded my eyes from the glare of the headlights. "Good timing."

He smiled. "Tell that to Jimmy. Where's Melissa?"

"Barry!" She lifted the gate a few inches. "Peeky! Come help me. The gate's stuck."

I ran over to her as Barry hopped along behind me. He checked the door. "These overhead doors work on a chain system inside, like a pulley." He looked at Melissa. "Slide under. It should be on one side of the door."

He knelt down. The wind from inside blew his hair back. "Peeky, help me lift."

Barry balanced on one foot so his broken ankle wouldn't bear any weight. We put our hands under the big steel gate and lifted.

"Okay. I can get under that." Melissa dropped to her back and disappeared under the door.

I bent over and called into the opening. "Be careful. There's still a lot of stuff coming down."

Barry grinned at me. "Told you."

The gate began to rise with a noisy metal rumble. Melissa appeared. "Break time's over. Let's go get our time machine." With that, she turned and ran towards the stadium floor.

Barry stood up, watching her go. "She's kinda Lara Croft all of a sudden, isn't she?"

I nodded. "Yeah."

"Kinda hot, isn't it?"

"Yeah."

We watched for another moment. "Okay." Barry opened the truck door. "Get in."

He drove down the ramp to the basketball court. There, in the middle of the massing debris, stood the time machine, resting on a simple wood palate. The stadium fans pumped wildly, creating a howling wind that escaped through the gaping hole in the roof and any other openings. Aside from a lot of noise and broken lights, not much else had happened yet, but above us the sagging roof was collapsing under its own weight.

Melissa waved at us from beside the machine. Barry pulled up next to it. "Peeky, you two should be able to lift it right onto the truck bed."

I jumped out. Melissa was already lowering the tail gate. "Help me pull it over."

I grabbed the machine and pulled. It moved easily.

Melissa shouted over the wind noise. "On the count of three, lift this end up." She patted the machine. "Put it on the tailgate. Then we can just slide it in. Ready?"

I nodded.

A flash came off the roof of the truck, sending little sparks in all directions. A little round hole appeared in the truck bed. I looked at Melissa.

She pointed over my shoulder. "They're shooting at us!"

I ducked down, holding the machine. "Let's get out of here!"

Melissa shook her head. "We're taking this with us!"

"Hey, you guys!" Barry leaned out the truck door, shouting. "I think somebody's shooting at us!"

"They're missing on purpose." Melissa crouched behind the time machine. "They won't risk hitting the machine."

Following her gaze to the source of the gunfire, Barry frowned. "Are you sure?"

"Pretty sure."

I cringed. *"Pretty* sure?"

There was another thump as a shot hit the truck bed.

Barry grabbed the machine. "Let's get it onto the truck and get out of here. Lift!"

We shoved the time machine into the back of the truck and Melissa slammed the tailgate shut. "Peeky, get in the back."

"That's where the bullets keep hitting!"

"Get in. You'll get shot if you try to go around."

Barry climbed behind the wheel. Melissa slid in behind him. "Move over. I'll drive."

She dropped the truck into gear and stomped the gas pedal. The pickup's wheels squealed as she spun the truck around.

The two guards appeared in front of the vehicle exit, guns pointed.

"Get down!" Melissa hit the accelerator.

We sped toward them. The men fired a few shots, shattering the windshield. Then we were past them and out into the parking lot.

She punched the gas again and we raced away from the stadium

* * * * *

It must have appeared odd to see three people carrying a large bronze egg up the stairs and down the hallway to our motel room. That's probably what got the young girl's attention in the first place.

"That looks like a party." She sipped a beer as we hustled by. "Some kind of bong?"

Melissa eyed the girl. "It's a time machine."

"Awesome."

"Yeah." Melissa smiled. "Hey, any chance you and your friends would want to trade rooms? I'm sure the manager was as cordial to you as he was to me."

"Ugh. That guy gives me the creeps."

"All the more reason to switch rooms. Then he can't find you when he goes on break."

The girl nodded. "Okay."

"Thanks. We're just over here, okay?"

The switch went smoothly. The party girl and her friends were happy to regain some anonymity from the pimply front desk clerk.

"You really have done this before, haven't you?" Barry sat down on the bed. I found a place to sit on the floor.

Melissa patted the time machine as it rested in its new home. "Hey, I hung out with some party girls in high school. They just wanna drink, have a little quality time with their boyfriends . . ."

"Underage drinking." Barry lifted his cast onto the bed. "I can't believe my ears."

"Hey, I didn't say I did it."

"No? What were you, the designated driver?"

She looked down. "Somebody had to be."

Barry chuckled. "I think you just went up a notch in my book and simultaneously down a notch, too."

I shifted on the floor, letting my back rest against the wall and closing my eyes. "I think it's nice you watched out for your friends."

"Speaking of which, we need to take stock of our situation and see what's what." Melissa peered out the window at the parking lot. "We have our time machine back. Now, we need to dump the truck before they track it down and find us here." She glanced at Barry's leg where it had become swollen above the cast. "Looks like you could use some medical attention, too."

"No doubt." Barry winced. "I'm sore, but we can't risk that right now."

I opened my eyes. "There's a pharmacy a few blocks from here. I could go get you something."

"With what money?" He shook his head. "Or are we holding up drug stores now, too?"

Melissa put her hands on her hips. "Peeky, you could get to the free clinic over off Nebraska Avenue. It's a pretty far walk but they'll have something for the pain. I'll ditch the truck and get another car for us."

I rubbed my neck. "How will you do that?"

"Same way I got this one. I'll just ask a friend to borrow theirs."

"At this hour?"

"Well, I'm sure I know somebody who won't mind, even if it's late." She glanced out the window again. "Either way, that truck outside's gotta go. It is way too easy to spot."

I visualized the truck bed. "Especially now that it has bullet holes in it."

"Yeah," Barry said. "That's got to be priority number one."

Melissa grabbed the keys off the dresser. "So we're agreed. Peeky will go to the free clinic and I'll find another car for us."

Barry shifted his broken ankle on the bed. "What am I supposed to do?"

"Stay here and guard the time machine." She went over to him. "Get some rest. You need it. That ankle looks bad. You have little blood stains on your armpits, too."

Barry pulled at his shirt. "That's from the crutches. Turns out they're Medieval torture devices."

Melissa put her hand on Barry's shoulder and slid a pillow behind his back. "If I can borrow a credit card or some gas money, I will. I'll see about getting us some food and a change of clothes, too."

"Pretty generous friends." I rested my head on the wall.

"Yeah, they are." She smiled. "We take care of each other."

I opened an eye. "Even in the middle of the night?"

She nodded. "Especially in the middle of the night. I've held back hair for plenty of girlfriends as they yawned at the porcelain god to stave off alcohol poisoning. They'll open the door for me."

"We can move faster if we go together." I stood up.

Melissa shook her head. "Can't risk it. That truck is a big yellow Here They Are flag and none of us can afford to be seen together right now.

They'd ID us in a second. I'll ditch the truck behind the mall and then hike across campus to a friend's apartment. On foot, on the grass, in the shadows. It'll take a lot longer but we won't get spotted." She pointed a finger at me. "You do the same thing. Walk to the clinic, but try to stay off the main streets. Use the alleys that run behind the stores, and keep to the shadows. Get whatever you can for pain and swelling, then come back."

She set the backpack next to Barry. "Meanwhile, you stay here and rest. Hang onto this in case there's anything you can use in it."

He rummaged through the bag. "There's another bottle opener. Maybe I can cut off this cast and let my ankle breathe."

"Don't even joke about that." She snatched the backpack out of his hand, dropping it to the floor. "There's a snack machine downstairs. We have enough money for a few packs of peanut butter crackers. I'll get you something to eat until we get back. Okay?

Barry sighed. "Okay."

Melissa turned and disappeared out the door. Barry watched as it clicked shut. "She's a real piece of work, isn't she? Bossing everybody around?"

"Yes, she is."

He looked over at me and smiled. "Kinda hot, isn't it?"

"Yeah."

Barry shifted on the bed again, stretching out. "Man, I need some sleep, but somehow I don't think I'll be able to."

His leg looked rough. The swelling was getting worse. I needed to get going. Turning on the TV, I flipped through the few channels Motel 6 provided. "Here. The USF baseball team is playing." I handed Barry the remote. "You can watch the big game. It's just starting."

"Baseball." He groaned. "If anything would put me to sleep, it would be that."

I went to the sink. "I'm going to wash up before I head out."

"Have at it."

When Melissa returned, she had some crackers and Cheetos. I got Barry a cup of water from the bathroom.

Melissa fluffed up his pillows again. "Get some rest, okay?"

Barry took a deep breath. "I can't make any promises. Getting shot at has the effect of waking me up pretty good."

She moved a wisp of hair from his forehead. "Try."

He rubbed his neck, peering up at her. "How long do you think you'll be gone?"

"A few hours at least, maybe more. Will you be all right?"

He nodded.

"Okay, well . . ." She glanced at me. "The sooner I get rid of that truck, the better, so let's go. Peeky?"

I headed to the door.

Barry pushed himself up in the bed. "Be careful, you guys."

CHAPTER TWENTY-SEVEN

Barry stared at the time machine and recalled Peeky's words from a few days ago.

If you had a time machine, where would you go? Who would you visit?

It might as well have been years ago that he'd uttered them.

How much has changed since then.

His eyes drifted over the dials and knobs. They called to him.

What would you do if you had a time machine?

Time was short. It may have already run out. The police were after them, the news was broadcasting about them . . . in his heart, Barry knew the last grains of sand were slipping out of the hour glass. He and his friends had fought the good fight, but it would soon be over – and there were no indications they'd emerge on the victorious side.

How long could they last at the motel? How long before the clerk saw the news and put two and two together?

They were being hunted by friends, too—people who knew their homes and families, who would put road blocks on the interstate highways and surveillance on their houses. Their phones and credit cards had been shut off. The hunters were probably networking through their classmates and friends, finding out who'd been contacted. Eventually Melissa, Peeky or Barry would have to surface for air, and when they did the game would end. Even the idea of going public seemed dashed, since Melissa had been seen robbing the Radio Shack. The store surveillance video would implicate them all, and any credibility would be lost.

What would you do if you had a time machine?

He stared at the big bronze oval.

Well, I have a time machine. Maybe not for much longer, but I have it right now.

Peeky's words taunted him.

Where would you go? Who would you visit?

"I would . . ." He took a deep breath. "I'd pack a lunch and go see some dinosaurs."

Looking over the control panel, he chuckled. "Go back about a million years, maybe drop in at Badlands, Montana. Say 'Hi' to T-Rex." He pulled himself out of the machine and checked the fuel gauge. It had dropped considerably.

"Wow." He slid back into the seat and inspected the metal frame. "You aren't built for economy, are you, old girl? A five-minute trip with a clock and a quick visit to Rome, and half of your gas is gone?" He ran his hand up and down the bronze oval. "We don't even know how to refuel you. Probably never will." Slouching, Barry shook his head. "Not enough time. How's that for irony? I don't have enough time to figure out how to refuel my time machine."

The dials and levers provided no answer. "I'd be willing to bet, though, that you use a lot of power getting up and running. Like a jet airplane. They burn a lot getting off the ground. Then a trip of two thousand years or ten thousand years hardly makes a difference . . ." He turned a few knobs. "And a self-regulating system won't let me launch for a trip I can't return from, will it?"

He glanced around for the borrowed cell phone. "Minnie?" Barry eyed the time machine. "You don't mind if I call you 'Minnie' do you? 'Time Machine' just sounds too formal at this point." A few taps on the phone screen brought up the mapping app. Barry located Vero Beach, Florida.

"Minnie, it seems around 10,000 years ago, the lovely seaside town of Vero Beach was literally inundated with mastodons. Yep, they were crazy for the place—what, with three underground springs and all, it was an easy place to graze and water. Mastodon heaven."

He cranked the machine's latitude knobs. "It still might be, too, if they hadn't all died off. Now it's geriatric heaven. But that's a whole other thing. It's a relatively short trip, so we should be able to go and get back on the fuel we have left, and we'll only be gone a few minutes . . . What's that? Peeky and Melissa?" He rested a hand on the frame. "Good point, old girl. They'll miss out again."

"Well." He patted his broken leg. "We all have to make sacrifices."

Barry glanced at the phone and made the last few adjustments to the knobs. "What do you say, darling? Are you up for a late night stroll?"

Placing his hands on the levers, he pursed his lips. "Hold your ears and close your eyes tight, Minnie, there's going to be a heck of a racket in a minute. But you already know that, don't you?" He leaned over to toss the phone onto the bed–no cell service 10,000 years ago–and stopped himself.

The tiny dot of the phone's camera stared at him. "Pictures. Minnie, what a good idea. Thank you." Glancing around at the room one last time, his eyes fell on the packets of crackers. "And there's lunch." He reached over and grabbed them, stuffing them into the backpack with the phone.

"I think that's about it, Minnie. Ready?"

Dropping his hands onto the levers, he shifted them into place one after the other.

Here we go. Sorry about the noise, neighbors.

The whirring started. He let the backpack balance on his knees while he covered his ears with his hands. "I remember this as being pretty bad, Min!"

The whirring grew louder. "Yep," Barry shouted. "This is what I remember."

The noise grew to a deafening pitch. He scrunched down, pressing his hands to his head as hard as he could. "This sucks!" He squeezed his eyes shut. "Wow! Owwwww!"

THE NAVIGATORS

Then there was a brilliant flash.

* * * * *

It had already been a long day and still a lot needed to be done. Melissa leaned against the truck and inspected her feet. The lone security light from behind the mall shoe store was enough to see what she already knew.

Blisters.

She sighed, shutting the truck door. The keys dangled from the ignition.

If we can pull this off and somehow save ourselves, these sore feet won't matter. If we don't, all the blisters in the world won't make a difference in what happens.

Basically, the blisters don't matter.

So let's get ready for a nice long jog across campus, because nobody cares about your sore feet, Missy.

* * * * *

Barry's head throbbed. He uncoiled himself from the backpack and looked around. A lush tropical forest stretched out in all directions, bright green and sunny.

This definitely isn't the motel.

The ringing in his ears wasn't as bad as he expected, and his eyes didn't seem to have the afterburn problem he'd had as an observer. Humid air washed over him, bringing the noise of birds and the scent of pine trees.

He eased himself off the metal seat, holding the machine by one hand, taking in his surroundings with a silent reverence as though he were in a church. The awesomeness of what he'd just done came to him in a wave. Roger hadn't explained it. The raw forces of physics coming together to take him to another place in time. It was overwhelming. His knees wobbled, causing him to grab the oval frame.

He swallowed, blinking back a tear, his voice a whisper. "Minnie . . . I think we did it."

Massive palm trees stretched toward the sky and huge ferns hugged every available inch of ground. The heat rose up from the tall, wet grass like a sauna. Flights of small birds cut through the clear sky.

Barry stood there, mouth open. "It's . . . it's so beautiful." In the distance, a light mist hovered over patches of the long grass.

I guess it just rained.

Stepping out and holding the frame for balance, he inhaled and tasted the ancient air. "It's . . . paradise. Hard to believe that in just ten thousand years, none of this will be here." He chuckled, drawing his eyes over the tree line. "I sound like my grandpa, not a scientist. 'All of this used to be palmettos'—that's what he was always saying. 'Now it's condos. Darned shame.'"

He breathed deep. *Now I know what he meant.*

"Minnie." He patted the machine. "I hate to leave you, old girl. But if we did what I think we did, I have to go see about some mastodons." He glanced up at the sky. "Looks to be mid-morning. Maybe there are a few around getting some water. What are your thoughts? Go check? Don't mind if I do. I don't think anybody's going to come snatch you away, so . . ."

Easing his foot into the wet grass, he winced and prepared for a jolt of pain. The broken ankle was still swollen and steps were becoming more difficult. "A crutch, eh Minnie? I guess I'll have to. My armpits are still bloody from the last ones, but beggars can't be choosers."

Tall, wide laurel oaks stood on the other side of a small clearing, rising above the palms. "What I need is one of those camels that used to live around here. I could sure use a ride."

He gritted his teeth and put his weight on the foot again. "Well, if I don't bang the cast around too much and hop gently, I might get to those trees and find a suitable branch for a crutch. Maybe I'll cross paths with a mastodon along the way."

He eyed the backpack. "In which case, I'll be needing the camera." Slinging the bag over his shoulder, he sighed. "It's just as hot as modern times. No wonder people didn't move here in volume until there was air conditioning." He turned to the machine. "Don't look at me like that. You were buried in a nice cool mine."

Balancing, he turned to the trees and took a few tentative steps. "I'll be back in time for dinner. Don't wait up."

Cicadas buzzed the tops of the grasses as birds and small animals announced Barry's approach to the forest. A stream meandered through the clearing, winding its way around large chunks of lime rock and an occasional tree root. The thick mass of grass made walking difficult. It softened his steps but it tangled around his legs, slowing his progress.

A sharp sting pierced his neck "Holy crap!" Barry slapped at it, whipping his head upright. Blood came away on his hand. "Mosquito. Figures."

A cloud of insects hummed around him—then came the bites, like mini daggers. The mosquitos engulfed him, flying onto his arms and his legs, up his shorts, down his neck. He was dressed for heat, not insect defense. The tiny vampires buzzed his ears and flew into his mouth.

"Ow! Ow! Ow!" He swatted in all directions. The mosquitos attacked every inch of unprotected skin. "Ow!"

The stream. He made a mad one-legged dash for it, batting at the attacking swarm as he ran for the water.

In seconds, he was upon it, splashing in at full speed. He pushed his way in a few steps and fell forward into the current. Rolling over, he threw water onto his face then resubmerged, rubbing his burning arms and legs as fast as possible. Another breath. The bugs were waiting. He fanned them with his hand long enough to grab a breath, then plunged his face under the cool surface again.

The stream's bottom was muddy. Breaking the surface again, Barry smeared handfuls of mud across his cheeks and neck, pushing it over his nose and ears, slapping it onto his forehead and chin. "This is how the old guys did it, you little blood suckers." He reached down and grabbed more mud and plastered it over his mouth. "If this worked for them, it'll work for me. Try to bite through this."

THE NAVIGATORS

He raised himself up to chest level as a few mosquitoes hovered near his face. None landed on his muddy skin.

"Yeah, that's what I thought."

His body heat and warm breath kept the interest of the mosquitoes for a while, but with nothing to eat they would eventually move on. The mud would work well enough as a barrier; it was simply too thick to bite through and the risk of getting stuck in it was a death sentence for a predatory insect.

Barry sat by the side of the stream, slathering mud everywhere. Behind his ears, up his shorts, everywhere. Any forgotten surface would be remembered quickly with the next mosquito bite, and he already had over a hundred. He pushed a thick swath of mud through his hair.

The stream was pretty, and it was cool. As he neared completion of his paint job, Barry noticed the steamy humidity again.

Not too many animals would be out in this heat. Certainly not big ones like mastodons. Where would one go to avoid the sun and to graze? The forest seemed likely. It contained thick trees and thin ones, a variety of leafy plants for mastodons to eat, and shade—important relief from the incessant, broiling sun. Although modern elephants used mud for that, too, tossing dirt onto their wet backs to make a sun shield. He didn't know if mastodons did.

They were cousins, though, the mastodon and the elephant. Aside from a haircut, they looked alike. Maybe they acted alike, too. How much could change in ten thousand years, anyway? After all, the long trunk remained, and so did the big ears.

They were known to have a keen sense of smell but only mediocre eyesight. Their hearing was top notch, though.

I guess if you're the biggest beast in the jungle, you don't have to worry too much about seeing what's-

Out of the corner of his eye, something moved. It glided through the tall grass, a large shadow on a path parallel to the stream. Barry held his breath and lowered himself back into the water.

What is it? An animal of some sort. A predator, from the way it moves.

The shadow was only about twenty feet away, but the wind was in Barry's favor. He held the backpack on his chest and submerged up to his nose.

All animals can be dangerous, and a surprised animal is the most dangerous. Whatever this was, it was inadvertently coming near him, but hadn't seen him yet. His heart pounded as he watched the shadow creep closer.

A shock went through Barry as he realized what had happened. The fragrances used in shampoos and deodorants—so common in his time—would be intriguing scents here. Getting wet in the stream had revived the aromas, but as he piled on the mud, he dampened the modern human smell.

Dampened, but not eliminated. He slid down another inch. The mud on his head helped hide him visually as well as aromatically, but he needed air—and he needed to see.

This would be a game of wait and watch. If Barry didn't move and the animal didn't see him, he could stay put until it passed. Maybe it wasn't even stalking him at all. Every animal needed water, so the streams were a natural watering place—and a natural hunting ground.

Maybe whatever it is just needs a drink.

He remained rigid, not daring to blink as the shadow slinked through the ferns and grass, moving slowly as though it had lost sight of whatever it had been tracking. It moved steadily alongside the stream, closer and closer, obscured by a few feet of tall grass.

He clenched the backpack tighter, not daring to breathe.

It stopped and raised its head to sniff the air. Its nose and ears became visible. It was one of the big cats, a relative of the saber-toothed tiger, and just as dangerous. It looked to be five or six feet long, not counting its long tail. Normally it might hunt a baby mammoth.

It lowered its head and took a few more steps, gliding effortlessly through the underbrush. The long grass made no noise as it passed over the animal's long body. Barely a twig snapped under its tremendous weight.

Barry remained frozen in the water. His only hope was if the predator didn't see him. He squeezed the backpack to his chest. It wouldn't make much of a weapon. Fighting a bear or any large predator, the idea is to make yourself "big," to present yourself as a threat and hope to avoid a conflict.

If an attack were to occur, the goal was to fight back as hard as possible. The animal wants a meal, not an injury. Even the smallest wounds got infected in the jungle, and infection is death—even for a tiger.

He wrapped one strap of the backpack around his hand. Maybe throwing it at the tiger would be enough of a scare to chase it off.

If not, I've lost my only weapon.

He drew another slow breath.

The tiger moved again, lifting its snout to the sky. It smelled something, and it seemed to want to explore that smell. What could intrigue a big cat that much?

Then he understood.

Blood.

Barry pulled at his shirt. His armpits had been stained with blood from the crutches, and the scent was now in the water. Sitting by the stream while he piled mud onto himself had put the blood scent into the air.

The tiger would eventually figure it out, and then find its source.

That's why he's hunting in daytime.

The big cat moved again, this time drawing a line in Barry's direction. No longer walking parallel to the stream, the cat now looked to actively enter it. In a moment, it would spot Barry, too.

Do tigers swim? I know gorillas can't. I'm pretty sure tigers can. What do I do? I can't outrun it. I have to stand my ground and fight. Is that better done in the water? I can get up a tree—but so can it. Better than me, especially with a cast on.

A heavy, soaking wet cast.

Barry could see the whole outline of the tiger as it moved, glimpsing its long, extended fangs. It was less than ten feet from him now. He froze as the big cat pushed effortlessly through the tall grass toward him.

CHAPTER TWENTY-EIGHT

I had stayed mostly to side streets and alleys as I made the long hike to the free clinic. There weren't many cars on the street at this hour, and the few that passed were mostly late night party goers—nobody interested in a dirty, disheveled young man walking alone.

The dark store windows and the street lights overhead created a mirror every twenty feet. I didn't dare look. I wasn't sure about that person anymore.

I shoved my hands into my pockets and continued onward. The time would come when a decision had to be made.

Does the possibility of running away even exist anymore? Probably not. Not for an exchange student with a student visa.

Less so for a fleeing felon.

On the corner stood a shoe repair shop with a pay phone on the wall. A relic from another time. A sign from the gods that fate is the result of choices.

I could call Findlay and tell him the location of the machine, then just walk away. I could save myself and maybe restore my family.

As I stared at the phone, I thought of my father and grandfather.

How will you be remembered?

I knew the ancient answer to the riddle. I had been raised on it. We are remembered for the difficult choices we make, never for the easy ones.

And this was no easy choice.

* * * * *

The tiger had a fix on Barry's scent. It was crouching, sniffing the air for him, but so far the wind wouldn't comply. It was close enough for Barry to hear the big cat's breathing—a low, menacing rumble.

He tightened his grip on the backpack.

The big cat turned and stopped, raising its head. It glanced back toward the tree line, perking its ears.

Then Barry heard it, too. The familiar whirring of the time machine as it revved up to make its return trip.

Minnie was announcing it was time to go.

* * * * *

Melissa had run the campus par course many times. Rarely at night, and usually in running shoes, but tonight the dirt surface and periodic water fountains between the outdoor exercise stations gave relief like they never had before.

She was soaked in sweat and her feet were bruised.

A few miles remained between the mall and her friends' apartments; even the closest ones lived on the far side of campus. The shortest, safest route was this one—a dark, slender running path.

She paused for a moment by the fountain, getting a second wind.

A difficult day had turned into a difficult night. As long as she appeared at least a *little* like a jogger, nobody would give her a second thought, but the threat of campus security loomed as word had certainly gotten out about the Sun Dome by now.

The cops weren't likely to let that slide, and since I'm still wearing the same clothes . . .

It wasn't worth thinking about.

Move quickly, move quietly, and stay in the shadows.

It's going to be a long night and it's still just getting started.

* * * * *

The noise from the time machine grew louder, beckoning its imminent departure. Barry sat still in the water, afraid to move and afraid to stay. The saber-toothed tiger seemed intrigued by the sound but hesitant to explore it.

The whirring grew more intense. Barry thought to cover his ears, but couldn't risk catching the eye of the big cat.

Minnie's wailing reached a deafening peak. Barry closed his eyes for what was about to happen next. The cat crouched, its ears obviously hurting from the noise.

It was dizzying. Barry wasn't sure what was taking so long. Usually the machine had let out with its blast of light by now. Instead, the incessant siren continued.

The cat was feeling it, too. It flinched and shrugged against the noise, backing away.

A huge blast shot out like lightning. The cat leaped back and ran for the trees. The echo of the whirring faded through the forest, and only a ringing in Barry's ears remained.

Minnie had saved him.

And maybe she had killed him, too.

If the machine had left without him, he was now trapped 10,000 years in the past, and dead to all his friends and family; anyone he had ever loved. But he had survived becoming dinner for a saber-toothed tiger – for now.

Barry inched his head out of the water, straining to ensure the tiger had departed. There was no sign. The big cat had enough.

He sat on the side of the stream, breathing hard. After his pulse returned from the stratosphere, he decided to go see what had happened to Minnie— but he walked a long circle from the tree line where the tiger had disappeared.

The grass was just as tangling as before. It tugged on his cast and stuck to it, covering his legs with briers and stickers from local flora. Gratefully, no sand spurs had appeared yet, but it was probably only a matter of time.

He made his way to the place where he'd left the time machine, craning his neck to see over the large ferns and palmettos.

It was still there.

The grass was matted down under it, like a steam valve had opened and flattened everything in a ten-foot diameter.

"Minnie!" Barry hopped to the big bronze egg and hugged it. "You didn't leave without me!"

He stepped back, admiring his luck – but only for a moment.

"*Why* didn't you leave without me?"

He inspected the flattened grass all around the machine. "You build up all that energy for a trip, and when none happened, you had to let it go, didn't you? Must be a venting system underneath."

Scanning the dials, nothing appeared to be out of place. Then he checked the fuel gauge: empty. His heart sank. He placed his forearms onto the frame and dropped his forehead against them. "Why didn't I learn how to refuel you when I had the chance!"

He slung the backpack into the machine. It bounced a little from the spring in the seat.

Barry felt a shock go through him. "The dead man switch." He smiled, wiping the sweat from his brow. "Minnie, you little devil, you have a safety switch in the seat. You never fly solo, do you? No driver, no trip."

He pushed the backpack aside and sat in front of the control panel, feeling the springiness of the seat. He nodded. "Yeah, brilliant. You can't get stranded."

Barry sat back and exhaled. "Except, I got stranded." His fingers drifted over the console. "Minnie, you have my apology for ever doubting you. You've had us covered from the get go." Leaning forward, Barry rested his cheek on the control panel. "Now tell me, dear. How do I fuel you back up so I can go home?"

Easing himself outside the machine, he stood and inspected it. For every time they had needed an answer, the designer of the machine had provided one.

There was always going to be a need to refuel; now I just need to figure out what it is.

He rubbed his chin and stared at Minnie. "Actually, I don't need to figure it out, do I? Your designers have already done that. I just need to find what it is they set up."

Everything's been pretty simple so far. Why not this?

Simple, he reminded himself, was a relative term. He leaned on the frame and checked over the hardware. The machine wasn't obviously a time machine at first; he needed Findlay to figure that out. And Findlay needed some of the deans from other disciplines. Math, specifically, and experts in physics and mechanical engineering. There was an underlying mechanical side to everything about this strange contraption; the levers, the dials.

What haven't we used yet?

When he stood up, the answer was staring him in the face.

The large turbine just behind the passenger seat was the last remaining mystery. So far, it hadn't done anything. First, it didn't move because it was caked with mud from the mine. Later, when they had cleaned it up, it moved freely, but seemingly without purpose.

He put his hand on the little handle.

It slipped forward an inch, then engaged with a gear, becoming very hard to move. It wasn't weight. It was resistance.

Barry inspected the turbine. It was moving. A slight scraping noise came from inside.

He walked around to the fuel gauge. There, the slight glow of the iridescent paint pulsed in rhythm with the scraping noise.

I'll be darned.

He went back to the flywheel and grabbed the handle, cranking it faster. The scraping noise increased its rhythm. He turned the wheel several times, hoping that cranking it would start an engine somehow, like a model T Ford or an old lawnmower, but the scraping sound remained consistent.

Let's rev this thing up and see what happens.

He grabbed the turbine handle again and spun it hard, hoping to really get the wheel moving fast.

Instead, halfway around the first strong push, it stopped. The wheel seized up, jamming his hand and sending a shock wave up his arm.

Barry stepped back, rubbing his hand and inspecting the machine. The rhythm was consistent. It hadn't sped up or slowed down. He checked the fuel gauge. It was pulsing rhythmically with the turbine.

Speed isn't the important factor here, for this part of the machine. Whatever it's doing, it's doing it the way it was built to do it.

At this speed; no faster, no slower.

He massaged his wrist. *Okay, Minnie; we'll do it your way.*

THE NAVIGATORS

Checking the gauge every few minutes, Barry hoped to see the bar rise. There was no discernible movement. The scraping inside the machine continued at its pace, however, and despite several attempts, the handle would not be moved again—so whatever was happening, it seemed like it was happening correctly.

Minnie just needs a little time.

He gave it to her. He cleaned the briers off his clothes and inventoried the scant contents of the back pack. The cell phone was waterlogged—a dip in the stream had seen to that—and the peanut butter crackers had become soggy. The rest of the items, a bottle opener and some miscellaneous pens, tampons, and CDs, had gotten soaked to varying degrees.

He toyed with the pen, debating on writing a note in case he was unable to return to the present day, but decided that was too bleak a decision for this early in the journey. He also kept an eye out for saber-toothed tigers. After killing time for an hour or so, he checked the gauge.

His hopes evaporated as a twinge of fear rippled through him. The gauge had moved, but it had moved insignificantly. An hour's time had barely budged it. To fully charge it would take weeks; to get enough fuel for a return trip would probably take a day or more.

He did the math. A quarter of a tank had been enough to allow him to take a trip of 10,000 years, so about an eighth of a tank might be enough to return him. The rough estimation of how far the gauge had increased in an hour, divided into the amount needed was . . . about a day and a half. Maybe two.

Two days. Barry glanced around, biting a fingernail.

That's a long time to spend in saber-toothed tiger land.

* * * * *

Resting in the time machine, Barry listened as the turbine continued its rhythmic scraping noise behind him.

Why does it scrape? What's happening in there?

He didn't know if the machine had been damaged from all the activity over the past few days. It hadn't been shot—he checked—but it might have been broken somehow when it went into the mine way back when. In any case, he wasn't sure it was actually refueling itself, either. The fuel for all the trips so far had been there when they found it; they had only used what was in the tank.

It might not refuel at all.

A sad thing to consider. He envisioned Melissa, returning to the motel room and not finding him there, the machine gone and him with it. Would she think he'd taken it for himself?

Hadn't I?

His gaze drifted to the stream. Eventually, animals would make their way down game trails to the water. At dusk, he might see the mammoths. At night, different species would come to drink.

At night.

He bolted upright.

THE NAVIGATORS

Mosquitoes are one thing. I need a fire to ward off anything bigger. That tiger's going to return eventually.

He pulled at his shirt again.

I'm almost as bloody as I was before, and I haven't started a shelter or a fire or even found a good stick for a crutch! Time to get busy.

He glanced at the sky and mentally noted the position of the sun. Several hours would pass before nightfall, but there wasn't a moment to spare. First things first; a weapon, and a fire. The smoke would help keep the mosquitoes away, and the fire would keep any animals away—no matter how hungry they were.

Then, if there was time, a shelter.

He got up, looking around for the nearest tree. A hundred yards away, a thick pine tree stood.

Throwing the backpack over his shoulder, he started toward it.

Two hours later, Barry had a small fire going. The TV show *Survivor* had taught him how—rub two sticks together, pushing one into the other, and don't give up. A flint works better, but flint wasn't available. He knew from TV that getting fire from two sticks and no matches required an inordinate amount of time, patience and effort. By the time the wood finally began to smolder, he had a new layer of blisters.

The pine cones and evergreen needles burned nicely once they got going. Pine sticks burn fast and hot, but pine bark smolders. Laying grasses onto the fire dried them out enough to make smoke without allowing the fire to burn too quickly.

With his fire and a fallen limb for a makeshift crutch, he was ready to start a shelter, but by then the sun was setting.

It would be a long night of huddling close to a small fire by the time machine.

And hoping that nothing came along to eat him.

CHAPTER TWENTY-NINE

Barry leaned against the machine and faced the fire, feeding sticks to the flames while listening to odd animal noises as they echoed across the forest. It was a scary and unnerving way to spend the night. The fire would keep animals away, but that didn't let him relax enough to really sleep. Each snap of a twig was a saber-toothed tiger. Each gust of wind was the breath of a hungry bear. As scared as he was, though, he still drifted off here and there. Exhaustion simply overruled any other plans.

When the sun finally rose, he took it in with a throbbing ankle and sore, red eyes.

He was stiff. His neck hurt, his back hurt—everything hurt. The humid night air made him cold and sore, giving him an indication of what his elder years might be like if he lived to see them. He grabbed a handful of mud and slathered it on for more protection against the next round of mosquitoes.

With a grunt, he stood and checked the fuel gauge. The amount of charging that had taken place overnight was barely half what he thought he'd need for the return trip. But the rhythmic scratching of the turbine continued, and the handle would not allow additional cranking, so he let it do its thing.

He put his hands on his back and stretched. "Minnie, it looks like we'll be spending another -"

The sound of breaking branches cut through the air, coming from the forest. Snorts and loud huffs. Barry crouched behind the machine and strained to see.

The nearby stream widened out as it moved along, becoming shallow and slow. In the orange glow of the dawn, a mass of gray-brown shapes emerged from a distant tree line.

The herd of mastodons ambled toward the water as sunrise washed in over the meadow. They were majestic, walking slow and sure. Leading the pack, a huge male with long tusks took to the water's edge, lazily dropping his trunk into the water and then holding it to his open mouth. He sprayed, swallowed, smacked his lips and tossed the trunk in for another round.

Behind him, mothers and babies drew their turn. They lined the side of the shallow stream and drank.

Though he picked this location because it was a well-known site for mastodons, Barry watched, mouth agape, at actually seeing them in the flesh.

He smiled. "I should have taken a poetry class, Minnie. These animals are too beautiful to be described in my poor, flat words."

THE NAVIGATORS

There were about a dozen that he could plainly see; some large, some small. Behind the first herd, farther away and harder to see in the morning mist, a second group emerged. He saw a few Key deer and dozens of large cranes flying in from the distance. He admired the view, letting the sun burn off the light fog and expose more animals further downstream.

If the water is safe enough for the mastodons to bring their babies to, the big cat probably isn't around.

It would be safe for him to get a closer look. He stood up, getting his bearings. Everything ached, but this was the chance of a lifetime. He wouldn't miss it.

"Minnie, we've hit the jackpot. I need to go check this out. Be back soon." He took a few steps, then turned back to the machine. "Gather some firewood while I'm gone, would you?"

Picking up his makeshift wooden crutch, Barry tucked it under his arm and grabbed the backpack. Leaving the bag was only an invitation for a raccoon or bird to make off with it. He stuffed its random collection of items back into it. The phone probably wouldn't work, but if it had dried out enough to take a picture . . . he didn't let the thoughts run away with him. There was a long walk ahead.

Wet and tired, hungry and sore, Barry limped off for a closer view of the mastodons.

It was a difficult trek. The grass was wet once again from the overnight dew. Before long, the skies would cloud up, turn gray, and dump torrents of rain everywhere, the same as they did every afternoon in summertime.

Some things never change.

He slogged his way along, using his crutch as best he could, trying not to re-blister too many of the same spots on his hands.

When he was about a hundred yards away from the herd, he slowed his pace. Moving through the grass allowed Barry to be relatively quiet. Its long strands made for good grazing for the mastodons, who pulled it up in clumps with their long trunks and tossed it into their ready mouths.

Just like elephants.

The tall grass helped hide him as he crouched, but it also meant that he could easily get snagged in it and fall, potentially exposing himself to the herd.

The humid morning air was almost absent of any breeze, but what there was blew directly into his face, bringing the musky stench of the large beasts to him.

It was a combination of hay and . . . poop.

The animals grunted as they stuffed their mouths, snorted as they drank. There was no need to be quiet, and they didn't seem to try. Limbs snapped as they walked by a tree; the ground turned to mud under their massive feet.

They were beautiful, though. They had always been sketches, artists' renderings and stuffed mockups with bad hair—until now. What a difference flesh and blood made. There was purpose in their movements. Dirt stuck to their toes; leaves clung to their coats. Two females grappled at the same berry bush. Their long tusks were yellowed and scratched, with chips missing here and there from a long life of rough grazing. A large male kept the members of the herd in line with a nudge or a look, but he was massive enough to enforce the rules at any time.

From his new vantage point, Barry could observe mothers watching over their babies. Large adults on the perimeter of the herd were on the lookout to keep them all safe from any would-be predators.

It would not be unusual for a pack of female saber-toothed tigers to attack a baby Mastodon, or an elderly one, or any smaller animal that was too sick or too slow to keep up with the pack. Key deer, sand hill cranes; anything would do for the big hungry cats.

Barry watched as the herd managed itself. After a while, some of the bigger ones began splitting themselves off, disappearing back to the tree line to take advantage of the leaves, a favorite of elephants and probably a favorite of mastodons, too. They reached up with their powerful trunks and grabbed whole limbs, shoving them into their massive mouths and crushing them into pulp. Their dung reflected their eating habits—it was a mass of grass fibers and undigested wood fragments. Elephant dung made for good kindling once it dried out—if the smell could be tolerated.

The stream was shallow enough to cross. Barry moved quickly, waiting until the wind was in his face so the noisy mastodons would not pick up his scent, and found a place near a lone oak tree. He checked the wind again. The mastodons' large noses made them even better at detecting a foreign presence than the tiger.

Entering the tree line a hundred or so yards west of the herd, he could weave his way through the trees and get a better view.

It was not fast or easy to move through the forest. There were few game trails, and it was better for him to stay off them until he was more familiar with the inhabitants of the area. Easy walking could mean easy pickings for a predator. The patches of thick brush required him to constantly push them aside with his makeshift crutch just to see where to place his next footstep. Stray tree limbs snagged the backpack; one nearly yanked him backward. The mastodons, meanwhile, simply pushed their way through. The humid forest was a dank combination of slender trees fighting for sunlight around a few larger trees. Occasionally, a large limestone boulder rose up between them. There was a smattering of sugar maples on the higher ground, and a wall of cypress trees closer to the low, swampy area. Mostly it was pines and oaks that dominated this part of the woods, with palmettos and ferns below.

The mastodons ate all of it. They reached and pulled at anything green, grabbing masses of leaves with their trunks and defoliating everything in their path. A herd of twenty or thirty adults could easily wipe out a small forest in a few days, but they fed on enough lush grasses that it wasn't necessary.

It was, however, always obvious when they had made their way through an area. The trees were broken and stripped bare to a height of about twenty feet—the maximum reach of the adults' trunks—

and the ground was trampled into slop. Barry would have no problem following them if he wanted to visit them again.

He moved a little closer, about 75 yards away from the nearest adult mastodon. She thrashed about, pulling on limb after limb of a eucalyptus. The minty aroma filled the air as the subtle breeze carried it to him, along with the musky scent of the animal's backside, and maybe a hint of bad breath.

He held back a cough.

Better have another bite of eucalyptus, big girl.

Squatting behind a big tree, Barry set his crutch down and rummaged through the backpack. He pulled out the cell phone and looked it over. A stone's throw away, the mastodon noisily continued her breakfast, breaking branches and snorting.

The phone had drained and dried out after yesterday's swimming adventure. It seemed good to go. That didn't mean it would work, but it was worth a try. Fresh water was much more forgiving on modern cell phones than salt water was. When he dropped his old phone in the live bait tank while deep sea fishing, it was ruined almost instantly. The one he dropped in his mother's pool fared much better. After a quick rinse and a lot of time in the sun, it lasted almost six more months.

He held down the button on the phone and waited.

The newer cell phones did an even better job of resisting water than the old ones, but the key was still to get the water out of it as quickly as possible. Once dry, they had a fair shot at returning to normal.

The little phone showed a glimmer of light. Maybe it would work.

There was a crash above Barry's head. He ducked, turning to see a giant female mastodon towering over him, pulling at the leaves on the tree he sat beneath.

He fought the impulse to run.

Don't move. She might not see you if you don't move.

He held his breath, watching her reach for another bunch of leaves.

Barry stayed frozen. Stray sections of broken tree fell around him as the female pulled at the more desirable limbs.

Easy. She'll move to the next tree in a moment. If you scare her, she might trample you to death.

It was a rare combination of fear and humility, to be so close to such a massive animal. Heart pounding, Barry watched.

She ripped at a leafy branch, causing some others to drop. He closed his eyes and winced as they fell near him.

The female paused, scanning the foliage for her next bite, and moved to a young oak.

Barry took a slow, deep breath, watching her inch closer to the main herd. For whatever reason, she hadn't noticed him; she was only interested in the next tasty tree. A trick of the wind. She had come up behind him, but the wind had shifted just enough to not let her catch his scent; her focus was on leaves above, not objects below. Pausing at the base of a tree to dig through the backpack may have saved his life.

He breathed a sigh of relief.

He had not thought to take a picture while she was so close, but now that she was farther away he felt safer.

Let's give it a try.

He raised the phone. The screen had come on, but there was no telling if any of the features would actually work. Barry pointed the lens at the female as the crunch and crackle of the feeding herd filled the forest.

Hold on. What will her reaction be to the noise it makes? He peered over his shoulder. *What's my escape route if this goes badly?*

A few big trees had branches low enough for him to reach. He could definitely climb them, but the cast would slow him down, and the reach of the mastodon would require him to climb high as well. Like modern elephants, they could knock down a decent sized tree anyway, or shake him out of it by pushing and ramming it.

Beyond the trees was another tall outcrop of lime rock. That could work as a safe spot. High enough to be out of reach, and not anything they could knock over.

Besides, they don't want to fight; they want to eat.

He heaved the backpack over his arm and turned to snap a picture of the grazing female.

Instead he was staring right at the massive male.

It was an enormous beast. Not twenty feet away, the mastodon's head still looked to be five feet across, maybe more. His muscular trunk swayed back and forth across the tops of the grasses. His long tusks were even longer and more threatening close up.

He was not eating. He raised his trunk and sniffed the air, huffing loudly.

Barry's breath caught in his throat. He clutched the tree and glanced around. Suddenly the lime rock outcropping seemed very far away.

The mastodon sniffed the air again. Flapping his ears and pawing at the ground, he looked over at the female. She had wandered another thirty feet or so. Beyond her, the other members of the herd continued breaking apart trees as they ate.

The male let out a low growl, fanning his ears again, but holding them out now. The breeze carried his stench to Barry, musky and thick like stale urine. The trunk went up again, sniffing loudly.

Barry held the tree, careful not to move. The tops of the distant trees swayed as the wind shifted.

The male's massive head immediately swung around. Barry was staring right into the enormous eyes.

The mastodon pounded the ground with its front feet, letting out a deafening trumpet. Barry stood, frozen. It was a warning shot. The animal fanned its ears wildly. A massive foot pawed at the dirt, sending debris everywhere. It raised its thick trunk and blasted the air with a second, ear-piercing screech.

He's defending his territory. He wants you to go.

Barry swallowed. *So let's go.*

THE NAVIGATORS

He released his grip on the tree and took a careful step backwards.

Nice and slow. Back away. Show no aggression.

The mastodon charged. His massive steps shook the ground as he ran a few steps. Barry jumped back, losing his balance. The grasses had snagged his cast. He fell to the ground. The mastodon stopped, rearing its head and screeching again.

Barry scrambled to his feet, not taking his eyes off the huge beast. The mastodon pawed the ground and snorted. Again, the ears fanned out, a sign of aggression. The next charge might not be a scare tactic.

Barry stared at the huge eyes. The mastodon huffed, emitting a low, guttural growl.

It charged again. A tree splintered as the mastodon's massive head pushed it aside. As Barry turned to run, he was immediately jerked backwards. The backpack had snagged on a tree limb. The mastodon closed in, crashing through the brush and shaking the ground. Barry wiggled free as the tusks reached the tree. He sprinted for the lime rock, each step shooting lightning up his leg from the broken ankle. As he neared it, the mastodon roared.

The backpack dangled on the tree limb for an instant before the mastodon's enormous trunk snatched it up, throwing it to the ground and tearing it to pieces. The contents flew everywhere. Barry made his way up the rocks. The mastodon heaved and screeched, ripping apart the backpack. Bits of white fluff—the padding in the shoulder straps—drifted upwards into the trees. The massive animal thrashed his tusks and pounded his feet, obliterating the bag and its contents.

Barry watched in amazement as the mastodon finished its work. The stuffing fragments floated out from the edge of the forest. The winds had shifted again, carrying Barry's scent in the other direction. With a few final snorts, the mastodon swung his massive head around and walked back to his herd.

Catching his breath, Barry sat. The mastodon moved through the forest like nothing had happened. The encounter was an amazing and deadly experience he'd never forget. He took a moment to calm himself, wiping the sweat from his brow and feeling his heart ease back into his chest.

The faint rumble of distant thunder rolled through the forest.

Barry sighed. It would rain soon. He needed to build up the embers from his fire or there would *be* no fire tonight. The heavy summer rains would make everything too wet to burn. With a strong fire going first, there was a chance to keep the flames alive until nighttime. Fire was the only defense from predators at this point.

He wiped the sweat from his forehead and massaged his throbbing leg.

There might be some kind of painkiller plant around here, but I sure don't know what it is.

His gaze returned to the mastodon herd. They had made their way downstream. Barry slid down from the rocks and walked to the backpack.

THE NAVIGATORS

Almost nothing remained of it. The debris from its contents had been pummeled. Whether the mastodon had been distracted by it because it smelled of food or humans, the backpack had saved Barry's life. Anything with the scent of a human had been destroyed. He bent down, picking up a piece of the cell phone. It was scattered everywhere. Whether it had taken a picture or not, there would be no evidence now.

Barry sighed. His crutch had been demolished, too. A large limb had been knocked from the tree in the encounter. He bent over and picked it up. It was heavy, but it would make a decent replacement. He leaned his sore armpit onto it and hobbled back to the campsite.

The embers from last night's fire were still hot. With a little effort, they would start a new fire. Shelter might now move up in priority. The stream would provide plenty of fresh water, and he didn't plan on searching for food sources because he hoped the time machine would charge up fast enough to not require it.

He poked at the embers. Time for more firewood.

A cool gust of wind whipped across the grassy meadow, tugging at his muddy clothes. It was refreshing, but a clap of thunder followed it. Barry squinted up at the sky. "It's gonna rain soon, Min. You should have collected that firewood like I asked."

He tucked the new crutch under his arm and headed out to the trees.

CHAPTER THIRTY

The storm front would move in quickly, as they always did in central Florida. The brutal afternoon air temperature dropped ten degrees or so and the wind picked up—a nice change from the stale humidity—but it was deceptive. It signaled a fast-moving thunderstorm that would soon drop torrents of rain like they'd sprung from a giant fire hose. The pounding downpour might last twenty minutes or it might last all day and into the night.

Barry mumbled to himself as he moved along. "No telling how much rain we're in for. I'd check the weather radar on the cell phone if that big hairy elephant hadn't destroyed it." He chuckled. "That intern—Gina, she'll appreciate *that*. 'Thanks for letting me borrow your phone, but I'm sorry—a mastodon ate it.'"

He neared the trees. "Think that's covered under her cell phone insurance plan?"

THE NAVIGATORS

Barry gathered some pine cones and a handful of pine needles for kindling. They burned quickly, but they would work well to help turn the embers back into a flame. Then the thicker sticks and limbs would catch fire. With a little luck, he'd have enough wood for the night in just a few trips.

He pulled at his t-shirt. The makeshift crutch had worn his armpit raw again. Red stains grew on the white cotton.

Barry sighed. Maybe some Spanish moss could work as padding. The early Conquistadors had used it as bedding. It was usually full of bugs, though, and he had enough bites from the mosquitoes. It also burned well, compared to other things that got wet every day in the summer rains. Spanish moss dried out quickly, burned slowly, and smoked a lot, but it would keep the fire going and keep the mosquitoes away.

He scanned the trees. There was plenty of moss hanging from the oak branches. It swayed in the wind like tattered sails on a shipwreck, making the tree appear haunted and inviting all at the same time. A well-groomed lawn with an oak tree full of Spanish moss was a southern tradition and a welcome sight. That same tree in a dark forest would look like something straight out of Grimm's fairy tales.

Barry lifted his crutch, trying to reach some of the lower hanging bunches. A few heavy drops of water splattered on his outstretched forearm. He peered out over the meadow. The first wave of rain had begun to fall.

The wind gusted up again, making the hanging moss move and dance.

This is no use. I can't grab any from here.

He stared up at the tree. There was plenty bunched up around the trunk.

I can reach that.

Leaning on his crutch, he worked his way over to the tree. He grabbed a thin vine and stripped off its leaves, fashioning it into a simple loop for the crutch, and tied it on.

Now I can climb with you.

Slinging the crutch over his shoulder, he put a foot on the tree trunk.

As long as I don't put too much direct weight on my ankle, I should be able to use my arms and good leg to help lift.

He hugged the tree, working his way up a few feet.

I think this will work.

Even where branches had broken off, enough of a nub remained for a foothold or handhold. The climbing was almost easy as long as he clung to the tree hard enough to keep pressure off the bad foot.

He stood, balancing, and looked for the moss. Some was near the trunk, so he grabbed that first.

Dropping the batches down by the base of the tree, he glanced around for more. Better to have too much than too little. The next clumps were a little too far to reach. He lowered his shoulder and let the crutch slide down to his hand. Hugging the tree, he propped the makeshift appliance under his forearm and leaned out to snag the swaths of hanging moss.

He checked the balance, eyeing his forearm to make sure the thick crutch didn't get too heavy and make him drop it.

Beyond his eye line, something moved in the grass. A jolt went through him. The big cat had returned.

From the ground, its graceful motion would have been undetectable. From the tree, it was a barge cutting through a sea of grass. Rain glimmered in the light. The slick, shiny grass parted as the tiger slinked toward him.

Barry's breath hung in his throat. There was nowhere to run. He pulled his crutch in and slid it back over his shoulder, staring up at the tree. Lightning had taken the top off, but it was still big. He could climb higher if necessary.

So could the tiger.

The rain fell harder. Barry wiped his eyes and glanced around. He could not climb down and get anywhere safer. There *was* no place safer.

There's no safe place at all.

Rain pelted his face and arms, loosening the mud. It softened and washed off, carrying his scent and traces of blood from his raw armpits down for the big cat to find. His wet shirt clung to him; he clung to the tree.

He watched as the tiger raised its head to sniff the air, looking for him. It was only a matter of time. The cat would smell the blood and come right for him. The tree would barely slow it down; saber-toothed tigers were excellent climbers.

Barry watched as the cat's pink tongue whipped over its face. Lifting its nose into the rain, it smelled for him. Thunder rumbled overhead, but this was a noise the cat knew well. No flash of light would scare it this time. Hunger drove this pursuit, and a bleeding animal was a wounded animal—slow to run, easy to kill. The storm was not a deterrent.

Lightning rippled through the clouds, illuminating the meadow. Its tall grass waved in the wind; its limestone boulders stood like sentinels. They would watch this kill but not interfere.

The cat followed its instincts. Its huge teeth gleamed as it licked its lips and opened its mouth to embrace the aroma of him falling down around it.

There was nothing to do but watch. Barry stood, unmoving, in the tree, seeing the big cat inch toward him, wishing it away.

But kitty being kitty, it wouldn't take no for an answer—stupid cat. In the distance, Barry saw a thin trail of smoke rise up as the rain doused the embers of his campfire.

Lightning cracked again. Something nearby had been hit. Probably another tree; half of the oaks in his mother's yard had lightning damage.

Maybe staying in this tree wasn't the smartest idea after all.

Water ran down Barry's face and dripped off his nose. The tiger raised its head again. This time, their eyes met. Fear shot through his body as Barry saw the method of his death.

The big cat growled, creeping up to the tree. Streaks of rain fell down around it as it looked up at him. The huge canine teeth seemed even more massive.

The cat slapped a paw onto the tree trunk. The vibration shivered its way up to Barry. Such power in one fist.

It shook the rain from its head, staring at him.

The paw hit the tree again. This time, the claws extended. They were huge. Barry hugged the tree a little tighter.

The cat jumped. It was a smooth, effortless motion, landing it halfway up the tree. It growled, baring its giant teeth. The enormous claws ripped into the tree trunk, holding its massive body weight right in place.

The cat moved another paw, driving its claws into the bark. Muscles rippled under its wet fur. It pulled itself closer.

Barry readied himself. He firmed up his footholds and hugged the tree, reaching back with his free hand for his crutch.

The cat raised up its hind legs, pushing forward. It swiped at Barry's broken foot.

The heavy cast took most of the blow, but the pain from the impact shot through him. Barry cried out, hugging the tree harder. He gritted his teeth and raised the crutch up.

He swung. The cat reared back, letting the crutch pass, then opened its mouth wide and growled at him.

Barry was unbalanced by the momentum of swinging the crutch without making contact. He regripped the tree and raised the crutch again. Lightning flashed. The eyes of the cat grew wide as it pawed at his cast again.

Barry swung the crutch down, striking the big cat's paw. It recoiled with a growl. He gripped the crutch tighter and swung again, missing.

Keep swinging, keep swinging. It's staying away.

The tiger swiped at Barry's foot again, working to knock him from the tree. Barry glanced upward, trying to find another branch to climb to.

The cat snarled, raising its paw. Barry plunged the crutch downward. The tiger flinched but remained undeterred. Barry grabbed the nearest branch and raised himself, pulling his cast away from the tiger's reach.

It followed. The big cat stuck two paws into the tree trunk and pushed upward at him. The tree shuddered with the heavy cat's motion, nearly shaking Barry loose. He turned again and swatted at it, then glanced upwards for the next branch

The cat climbed just as fast, pausing only long enough to get a firm grip and stay out of Barry's reach.

The big drops pelted them. The tree swayed with the strong winds. Barry blinked the rain out of his eyes. There was nowhere left to climb. The tiger growled again, working its way up for the kill.

Barry pulled the crutch toward himself, grabbing the vine he had tied onto it. He quickly wrapped it around his wrist, then lifted his heavy cast. He stood there, poised and ready, waiting for the cat to make its move.

The tiger complied. It pushed forward again, and when it did, Barry dangled the heavy cast in its face. As it raised a paw to swipe at him again, Barry

THE NAVIGATORS

lowered himself and kicked with all his might. He struck the cat in the face. It recoiled. Barry raised his foot again, a shock wave of pain coursing through his body. The cat shook its head and Barry plunged his cast into its face again. He gritted his teeth and swung the crutch with full force, landing it on the side of the big cat's head.

Barry screamed at the tiger. "I'm not giving up without a fight! Do you hear me? I will fight back!"

The big cat squinted up at him in the rain. It growled again, louder and more menacing, its muscles flexing for a pounce.

Barry launched the crutch down straight into its eyes. The cat recoiled. Blood appeared on its face. Barry thrust the cast at it again, striking a blow on top of its head. He batted its ears and poked at its nose, raining blow after blow at the big cat's head.

As it hesitated, he saw his opportunity. He grabbed the branch at his waist and dropped, slamming the full force of his body weight into the tiger's face, cast first.

The tiger fell backwards from the tree, landing on the forest floor with an awkward thud.

That was all he needed. Barry slid down the tree, its rough bark scraping up his arms and belly. He dropped down next to the stunned cat. Gripping the crutch with both hands, he raised it high over his head. Barry gritted his teeth and slammed the crutch down onto the tiger's head. A loud crack filled the air as the crutch shattered against its thick skull. The impact jarred Barry's fingers, sending a jolt up his arms.

He limped across the meadow carrying what was left of his crutch, rain streaming down his face. The time machine sat in the distance. Ready or not, it was time to go.

Jumping into the seat, Barry rested his crutch on the control panel. He scanned the dials. Everything was still set from before; he only needed to engage the levers.

In the distance, he heard the big cat howling in pain.

His heart pounded. He placed a hand on the first lever, hoping it would slide into place. If the machine had not recharged itself enough for the trip, the lever would not move.

Taking a deep breath, he pushed.

The lever glided into place with a clunk.

Barry laughed. "We're going home, Minnie!" He grabbed at the other gears. One by one, they moved into place.

Panting, he checked around. The meadow grasses whipped in the wind as sheets of rain swept over them. He held his breath and leaned back in the seat, bracing himself. The familiar whirring began.

He wiped the rain from his face as the noise grew louder. Gazing out over the stream, he gripped the frame and readied himself, watching the place where the mastodons had grazed.

Suddenly the grasses parted. The face of the tiger emerged. It raced toward Barry.

He grabbed the crutch and batted at the cat, holding it at bay as the time machine's whirring neared its deafening peak.

The tiger pounced, landing a claw on Barry's cast. He cried out in pain, swinging the crutch again at the big cat's paw. It sunk its claws in, tugging at him, trying to pull him from the machine.

He bashed at it with the crutch, holding the frame so he wouldn't be dragged outside. The cat heaved again, unseating him. He braced his foot against the frame and hit at the cat with the crutch.

The eyes of the tiger flashed as it seized its prize.

Then a brilliant flash of blinding white light burst forth from the machine.

* * * * *

The ringing in his ears made the voice sound like it was underwater.

It was a man, droning on about something. Barry took a breath to clear his head.

It was the TV.

"There you have it sports fans, going fourteen hard-fought innings, the USF Bulls men's baseball team delivers a stunning defeat to the would-be NCAA champs . . ."

Barry looked around. He was back in the motel room.

What has happened?

He went to stand. Pain shot through his leg. The TV announcer was still talking. "A record game, logging in at a whopping four and a half hours. You know, Chuck, you almost hate to see either team lose a game like this."

Barry glanced at the bed, the nightstand. There were the cracker wrappers from the vending machine. The cup of water Peeky had given him.

He placed a hand on the machine and hoisted himself up.

"Yeah, both teams really deserved to win this game, Tom . . ."

He turned the volume all the way down on the TV. The room was so . . . quiet. And calm

And safe.

He limped to the window. The girls they had traded rooms with were outside, drinking in the hallway. Friends had apparently joined them.

Relief washed over him. He sat down on the bed.

I'm back.

Soaking wet and exhausted, Barry felt like he'd won a million dollars. The baseball game had just finished; the party was still going on next door. He was back where he'd been when he left.

A trip through time. A few days had passed in the span of a few hours.

Incredible.

Barry peered at Minnie. "I guess I'm a time traveler now, eh old girl?"

He carefully pushed himself onto the bed, favoring his leg. Leaning back into the pillows, he let his heavy eyes close. He sighed deeply to reclaim his heartbeat, unable to avoid the call of the pillows. Drawing deeper and slower breaths, Barry folded his hands over his belly and let sleep finally overtake him.

* * * * *

When I returned to the room, it stunk to high heaven. The cheap window shade let just enough illumination in from the parking lot for me to find my way around. Barry was asleep on the bed—sprawled on his back, and snoring like a buzz saw. The old air conditioner must have gotten musty and, mixed with the body sweat, created a foul odor in the room. But since he was asleep, the generic Tylenol I'd gotten from the free clinic would wait. I set them on top of the TV and plopped down in the corner.

I worried that Melissa hadn't returned, but she had proven to be more resourceful than me, and if Findlay had run into her she wouldn't give us up.

That was my job.

I leaned my back against the wall and fell right to sleep, only to wake up about an hour later when Melissa finally tiptoed in. She fumbled around in the near-dark for a minute, making sure a sheet covered Barry as he slept, then rolled up the bedspread for a pillow and laid down on the floor by the bed.

"Peeky?"

"What?"

"Do you want to share this bedspread?"

"No, I'm okay. Did you get another truck?"

"Yeah. My friend Mandy let me borrow hers."

"Wow, that's great. You have generous friends."

She yawned, nuzzling the bedspread. "Yeah, well . . . friends take care of each other."

I sighed. It was not a concept I wanted bouncing around in my head before I went back to sleep.

"You boys get showered in the morning. It's getting kind of ripe in here."

"Will do."

"Okay. Goodnight, Peeky."

A moment later, she was out. I could see her belly gently rising and falling as she slept. I shook my head. Even when snoring, she was still cute.

I closed my tired eyes and leaned my head against the wall. It had been a rough time for everyone, but it wasn't over.

CHAPTER THIRTY-ONE

I bolted awake to the sound of a phone ringing. I hadn't heard one in days, and wasn't expecting one now. Nobody knew to call us on the motel room's land line, and our cell phones hadn't worked in a while.

Still curled up around the bedspread, Melissa dug into her pocket.

She has a working cell phone?

Barry sat up. As the first rays of dawn came through the motel window—all three of us, lacking for sleep as we were—now found ourselves pretty much completely awake. Adrenaline and paranoia will do that.

The phone rang again. Melissa stared at the screen. "Oh, boy." She buried her head in the bedspread.

Barry and I leaned over to listen in. When she lifted her head back up to answer, her eyes were squeezed shut, bracing for impact. "Hello?"

The man's voice was very clear even without the speaker being on. "Melissa, honey? It's me. Are you okay?"

She swallowed. "Hi, Daddy."

Barry eyed me and mouthed the words, "Oh, boy."

"Missy, thank goodness. I've been trying to reach you for days. What's going on? Your cell phone isn't working, you're not answering the phone at your apartment . . ."

"I'm okay. I just got caught up in . . . a project."

"Project?" Her father sounded concerned, but he still spoke in measured tones. "Honey, I got a call from Bill Dinger a little while ago—Mandy Dinger's dad. Bill said she was very concerned for you, that she thought you might be in danger. Are you okay?"

"Yes."

"Yes? Good. Uh, okay, where are you? I'll send a car to pick you up."

"What?" She sat up. "No, don't do that."

"Excuse me, have you seen the news? I got a call saying my daughter might be involved in a few robberies and thefts around town, and you're not going to come talk to me?"

Melissa pushed her hair back from her face. "No, of course I'll talk to you. But don't send a car. I can drive myself in."

"I think it's best if we don't drag Bill's family into this any further by continuing to use Mandy's car. I got a call yesterday saying *your* car was towed. Did you get it out of the impound lot yet?"

She stared at the ceiling. "No . . ."

"No, of course not. I guess I get to spend three hundred bucks for that privilege."

Melissa squeezed her eyes shut.

"Now, sweetie, let me send a cab for you. Come down to my office and let's talk this out. You and your friends, whoever's involved."

She hesitated for a moment, looking at Barry and then at me. "Okay." She closed her eyes and dropped her hands into her lap, ending the call.

"So?" Barry propped himself up on the bed. "What's the deal? What do we do?"

She stared at the phone. "We go see my dad."

"Really?" I kneaded my hands. "Is that our best move?"

Melissa shook her head. "It's our only move. He knows everything. Mandy ratted us out."

Barry sighed. "Well, don't be too hard on her. She was probably scared. I can't say I blame her."

She turned to reply but stopped, her mouth falling open. "What happened to you? You're all muddy." She made a face. "And you stink. Is that what I've been smelling all night? I thought the air conditioner was pumping moldy air or something."

Barry checked himself over, picking at some dirt clumps. "I had a rough night. Not you, though. What gives?"

Melissa peeled off the bedspread. She had on clean jeans, a clean shirt, freshly washed hair... *makeup*. She looked like a million bucks—and smelled nice, too. Leaning over, she grabbed two plastic grocery bags. "I took a shower at Mandy's. I couldn't resist. She lent me some clothes, and I borrowed a few things from her boyfriend for you guys."

Tossing a bag to me, Melissa stood up, smiling. "She gave me some cash, too, so I paid for another night in these luxurious accommodations and got some bagels. From Einstein Brothers."

I pulled out a pair of white socks. "Do we need that?"

"Are you kidding? Their bagels rock."

"No, I mean another night here."

"Well, we can't risk traipsing around town with the world's most wanted machine. This will be a good hideout for it."

"Makes sense." Barry rolled out of bed. Bits of mud dropped everywhere. "Dibs on the shower."

"What did you *do* last night?" I eyed the bed sheets. "Was there a mud wrestling contest in the parking lot?"

Barry limped to the bathroom. "I'll tell you all about it in the cab. Missy, what time do we have to be at your dad's?"

"When he says come in, he means right now. Shower fast." She picked up a bagel and took a bite. "And there's a razor in the bag."

"In case I want to slit my wrists instead? Good idea." He shut the bathroom door.

I wrinkled my nose up at the muddy bed. There was mud on the floor, on the wall; a little path of mud flakes trailed off to the bathroom. "You're going to get a big bill for cleaning this place up."

Melissa smiled. "Not me. That high school girl who booked the room."

I reached for a bagel. "How much trouble are we going to be in?"

She sighed. "A lot, probably. He knows everything."

"He didn't say that on the phone."

"He's a lawyer. They always know more than they let on."

* * * * *

The first half of the cab ride to the law offices of Michael Mills was animated. Barry told us about the mastodon, the tiger, and his near death escape. It was a fantastic story, and we listened like children at bedtime hearing adventure tales at our grandfather's knee. We spoke in hushed tones so the cab driver wouldn't think we were crazy—he did regular work for Mr. Mills' law firm, taking clients to the airport or to meetings—but even so, the story was too far gone for anyone who hadn't lived our lives for the past few days.

Melissa and I were intrigued, peppering Barry with all sorts of questions. We were jealous of him stealing a trip, but excited about the possibilities of the machine.

Melissa laughed. "'Minnie,' huh? Like Minnie Mouse?"

"My trip was over the top, completely insane." Barry placed his hands on his head. "You guys have got to try it."

As soon as the words left his mouth, though, he must have realized the irony. We were probably on our way to face the end of our time with the machine.

Traffic was light for a Friday morning, so we traveled quickly, but nobody spoke much. It was as though we had all suddenly realized the same thing. The game was over. There was no way we were going to be able to keep the machine. There would be no more trips. With each passing mile that took us closer to the law office, that thought became more and more of a reality. The heavy feeling in my stomach was a sadness like I'd never felt before. Melissa stared out the window. I'm sure she felt it too. As much as Barry gushed to us about his trip, he probably felt guilty about going without us, and sad that we would never get to go ourselves.

It was a tricky bag of emotions to share in the back seat of the cab. No words could adequately express it, so we didn't try.

The firm was located in one of those grand, ornate old houses that attorneys liked to buy and renovate into law offices. This one was a giant yellow antebellum place with white columns and bright white trim, and a thick green lawn that said they ignored the summertime watering restrictions. We got there at about nine o'clock, parking in front of a tiny sign with the words "law office."

The cab driver walked up the steps with us to receive his payment inside. He glanced over at Melissa. "You Mister Mills' daughter?"

"Yes." Even in her doldrums, she managed a polite smile.

"I thought so when I picked you folks up." He opened the large front door and stepped back to let us pass through first. "Maybe you can tell me something. I've been here lots of times. Dropping clients off, taking folks to the airport. I always wondered why this place has such a small sign."

Melissa walked with him to the receptionist desk. I had never been here before. I stood in the doorway, admiring the place. It was all wood floors and high ceilings. A large, expensive-looking couch adorned the lobby, but I felt too underdressed to sit on it.

"Good morning, Miss Mills." The receptionist smiled. She was certainly dressed nice enough to sit on the couch.

"Good morning, Terry. This gentleman needs some money for bringing us over in his cab."

"Of course. How are you this morning, Johnny?"

"Fine, Miss Terry, just fine." He handed her a slip of paper.

Melissa turned to him. "It's a lawyer thing. The sign. The more powerful the lawyer, the smaller the sign needs to be."

The cabbie raised his eyebrows, nodding. "Your dad's sign is the smallest I've ever seen."

Melissa peered at the massive front door. "Yes, it is."

The receptionist handed Johnny a small envelope and turned her eyes to Melissa. "Miss Mills, your father will see you and your friends now."

Melissa started down the large hallway. Before we could follow, the receptionist called after her. "The conference room, dear."

Melissa appeared surprised. "Oh." She eyed the two massive wood panel doors on her right, and stepped up to them slowly. "Thank you, Terry."

Her hand touched the door like she didn't want to go in. By osmosis, neither did I.

Lowering her head, Melissa took a deep breath and pushed the door open.

* * * * *

"Missy!"

It could have been Christmas, judging by his enthusiasm.

Michael Mills was an average size man. He was handsome, with a simple haircut and a winning smile. When he flashed it, his dimples showed, wooing juries from Miami to Tallahassee. He had a real boy-next-door appeal to him, even as a man in his fifties, with no gray hair and few if any wrinkles.

He was one of the most powerful men in Florida, and probably the most powerful man in Tampa, but he greeted his daughter with unbridled joy. Bounding out of his leather chair, he engulfed Melissa in a bear hug, picking her up off her feet and swinging her like he hadn't seen her for years.

He buried his face in her cheek and gave her a kiss, then set her down, standing back and admiring her. "You look great. Did you eat? We have bagels."

She stared at her shoes, blushing. "No, no, dad, we ate."

He nodded, smiling from ear to ear at his pride and joy. "Okay, well, come in. I think you know just about everyone."

My stomach sank. Around the conference table sat Dean Anderson and Dean Coopersmith, officers Ferguson and Bolton from the university police, and some other men in suits, probably the university's lawyers.

Just about everybody who'd been making our lives miserable for the past few days.

Mr. Mills gestured to us. "Melissa, boys. Please, sit down."

Officers Ferguson and Bolton glared at me as I neared the chairs. So did everybody else. I picked the seat farthest from them.

Mr. Mills sat in the chair at the head of the table, in front of a large stack of papers and two telephones. A businesslike demeanor came over his face. He went around the room and introduced the rest of us. "Also, on the phone I have conferenced in representatives of Florida Electric Company, and students Roger Conrad, who joins us from Tampa General Hospital, and Richard Fellings, who joins us unfortunately from the desk of the duty officer at the Hillsborough County jail." He cleared his throat. "Can all of you hear us okay?"

Voices on the phones acknowledged that they could. I glanced around. It seemed like there should be a court reporter taking notes somewhere, but there wasn't.

Mr. Mills sat back. "Now, we're all aware that some . . . *unusual* things have been happening around the USF campus lately." He glanced at the faces around the table. "Well, let's get right to it, shall we?"

He put on his reading glasses. "I have never seen such a mess as this. My staff has assembled quite a pile of paper in the last few hours, and after just a few interviews." He waved a hand as he picked up a folder from the stack. "We have students stealing things from the school." He glared at Melissa. "Allegedly." He picked up the next folder. "We have university Deans selling university property illegally under the table to bigger universities—also allegedly." Grabbing a few folders, he flipped through them. "We have kids breaking and entering, professors conspiring with power company officials to defraud, wild stories of grand theft, arson, kidnapping—it goes on and on." He set the folders down, shaking his head.

"Just about everybody at this table has some lawsuit or criminal charges that they're ready to level at somebody else here." He took off his glasses, using them to wag at the seated parties. "And most of these allegations have merit. There's enough fighting here to tie all of you up in court for years. It's a young lawyer's dream."

He sighed. "But it's a father's nightmare. And as a resident of this area, it's embarrassing to see so many prominent members of the community acting like children."

Mr. Mills leaned back in the big chair. "Which is why I'd like to propose something. The way this is heading, it's going to end up like one of those ugly divorces you read about in the papers, ruining everybody involved. Instead, I have a suggestion." He rocked forward and placed his hands on the table. "All of you should just kiss and make up."

"What!"

"I ought to be suing those jerks!"

"Well, I ought to be stomping your head."

The room exploded in outrage. Mr. Mills sat back, folding his hands in his lap, letting them vent.

* * * * *

"Did you have any trouble finding the place?"

Findlay sneered. "I sure did! Why don't they have a bigger sign?"

Janice Peterson smiled. "I'll have to ask. Let's go inside, shall we?"

As they climbed up the big steps, Findlay fanned himself. "It's hot. Is this where you have all your meetings?"

"Some." She walked past the big white columns and reached for the ornate front door.

* * * * *

"This is insane!" Barry pointed at Dean Anderson. "These maniacs torched my apartment."

"Don't wag that finger at me." Anderson pounded the table. "You stole university property. Then you wrecked the Sun Dome!"

The accusations flew across the room in all directions. Mr. Mills smiled at Barry. "I heard about your apartment." He shook his head. "It does sound insane. Did you really jump off the balcony?"

"Yeah. I cracked my ankle in the process."

The others continued shouting. Mr. Mills seemed unfazed by it all, possibly enjoying it.

"Excuse me." Roger's voice came over the speaker phone. "Before we go any further, should I get a lawyer or something?"

Riff spoke up. "Yeah, what about that?"

Mr. Mills wagged a finger. "Oh, that's a good question. All of you are free to get a lawyer at any time. This is, shall we say, a simple meeting among friends."

"Friends!" Barry jumped up, holding the table for balance. "Are you kidding me? Mr. Mills, these guys tried to burn me alive!"

I nodded. "They took me hostage."

"You were never a hostage." Bolton bristled. "You were informed that you could leave at any time."

Mr. Mills waved his hands. "Calm down, calm down."

I looked at Melissa. She was strangely quiet.

Mr. Mills pointed at the stack of papers. "It's plain to see that everybody here has a gripe with somebody else here."

"A gripe?" Barry pointed at Dean Anderson. "I ought to sue these jerks. Mr. Mills, you don't know what's been going on."

"Barry, please." Mr. Mills eyed Barry over the reading glasses. "I'm well aware of what's been going on. Between the newspapers and the allegations everyone's been logging since six A.M. to my staff, I've become acutely aware. It's quite a story." He picked up a stack of papers. "This pile of reports here is from a small army of paralegals who detailed almost all of it. Robberies, thefts . . . But I've lived and worked in Tampa for almost thirty years, and I won't stand by and see our beloved city become a laughingstock over a misunderstanding between people who should be friends. Not over some crazy machine that might not even exist."

THE NAVIGATORS

"You keep saying 'friends.'" Barry pounded the table. "What about what they did? Is arson in that stack of reports? I got a broken ankle because of these morons. And where's Findlay, anyway? He's part of this too." He glared at Dean Anderson. "Are they covering for him?"

"Barry . . ."

He stood up again. "No, Mr. Mills, it's not fair."

"*Barry*." Melissa glared at him, then looked at his chair. Barry lowered himself into it.

Mr. Mills rubbed his eyes. "Barry, my billing rate is $750 an hour." He took off his glasses. "When a man who makes $750 an hour wants to give you a piece of advice, you should listen. You know?"

Barry sighed. "Okay."

"Okay." Mr. Mills put his glasses back on. "Now shut up for a moment." He looked out over the table. "Let's all start by thinking of this whole thing as a big family blowup. A squabble."

Riff's voice came over the speakerphone. "Can I say something?"

Mr. Mills shook his head, throwing up his hands. "Go ahead, Mr. Fellings. But first, let me get everyone up to speed on your situation." He grabbed a folder and opened it. "You're currently staring at theft of state property, conspiracy to defraud, plus you assaulted several members of the hospital staff, lied to a police officer, obstruction of justice . . ." He set the folder down and eyed the phone. "Riff, if these charges go through, you're going to be a fat middle aged man when you see

377

your next sunrise. Now, what sort of amazing legal insights would you like to share with us today?"

"Uh, nothing. I'm good. Sorry to interrupt, Mr. Mills."

"Thank you, Riff."

"Well, I have something to say." It was Roger.

"Ah, Mr. Conrad." Mr. Mills picked up another folder. "Two assaults on a Mr. Findlay, breaking and entering, stealing, conspiracy to defraud the state, theft of state property. Do you really want to make legally binding statements right now?"

"Uh . . . I guess not."

Mr. Mills glanced around the table again. "While we're at it, just so you kids don't get the impression that it's a one-sided show, the rest of this group is no better off. For example, Dean Anderson is staring at theft, fraud, conspiracy to commit arson, filing a false police report, aiding and abetting . . ." He smiled over his glasses. "Professor, you might be old enough to spend a year or two of your pension before you die of old age when you get out of prison. Except you'll be fired and there won't be a pension. A word of advice for showering in the state pen: don't drop the soap."

"Are you all getting the idea?" He looked at each of us. "This is a 'no win' situation for each of you. Yes, you can sue and press charges. And while you're doing that, somebody else here will be suing and pressing charges against you. And like I said, each of the charges has merit." He picked up a few folders. "Which means everybody will win, or in this case, since you'll all be bankrupt, humiliated, and in jail, everybody loses."

Barry slumped in his chair. "It's not fair."

Mills beamed. "Finally, something we can all agree on. It isn't fair, is it?" He leaned over to Barry. "Dropping a fifty-year sentence against the stealing, cheating Dean in exchange for dropping only a thirty-year sentence against the brilliant young paleontology student. Seems there's a twenty-year differential to be dealt with, for fairness." He leaned back in his chair. "But you'll still get *your* thirty years. You'll miss out on a lot during that time." Mills laid down the folders. "Life, love, children, a career. Think about it."

He glanced out at the sullen faces at the table. "Which brings me back to this: first, everybody drops all the charges against everybody else. You'd all end up in jail, just for varying lengths of time." He glared at Melissa. "That can't sound good to any of you, I'm sure. That's why Dean Anderson graciously agreed to drop all charges against you, provided everybody else reciprocate."

He folded his hands on the table. "As your friend, that's my recommendation. I personally think it's time we settled things, and I think we can do it in a judicious manner. But first I need to meet somebody." He called to the door. "Terry, would you show our guests in?"

The door opened to reveal Findlay standing with Tribute reporter Janice Peterson.

CHAPTER THIRTY-TWO

Upon spotting Findlay, Barry jumped up. "You! You're a dead man." He limped toward the door.

Mr. Mills turned to Melissa. "Is he always like this?"

She shook her head. "Not until recently."

As Barry neared, Findlay moved behind Janice Peterson. "Hey, cut it out! I'm here for a meeting."

Barry stormed up and reached over Janice, taking Findlay by the collar. Grabbing Barry's hand, Findlay peered over at Melissa and me. "Call off your dog!"

"Christopher Findlay." Mr. Mills' voice was enough to keep Barry from killing Findlay in front of everyone. "I've been waiting to meet you all morning."

Findlay looked past Barry's grip on his collar. "What's the deal here? I'm supposed to be having a meeting with this reporter."

"And you are." Mills smiled. "It's just part of a slightly larger meeting." He gestured to the table. "I think you know everybody. Dean Anderson, the officers."

Findlay turned a whiter shade of pale than his usual pasty look.

"As I was just explaining to the others, you could probably think of this as a last stop before prison and a bunch of lawsuits." Mr. Mills picked up another folder. "You're quite a character, Mr. Findlay, and you've had quite a week. These officers were kind enough to fill me in on your activities. Theft, harassment, arson – oh, that's a biggie, arson. But ironically, not your biggest."

He stood up, going over to where Barry held Findlay. "Do you know much about wire fraud, son?" He tapped Barry's hand. Barry released his grip on Findlay's collar. "I did a case a while back involving a couple of computer hackers who got into other people's computers." He leaned in close. "Did you know that when you send information over the internet, it crosses state lines?"

Mr. Mills made a back and forth motion with his hand. "It goes from one computer to a big server somewhere in Seattle or Atlanta, then travels back. Almost at the speed of light. Did you know that?" He turned away, eyeing the others. "Well, of course you did. You're a computer science guy. Just about everybody knows that."

Walking over to the side table, Mr. Mills poured a glass of water. "But that internet stuff falls under the Federal Penal Code. They consider it mail and wire fraud." He took a sip of water and set the glass down. "Now, here's the interesting part." He went back to Findlay. "It's a twenty-year sentence for each count. But the neat thing is, every stolen picture, every transferred file – each one of those is a separate count carrying its own twenty-year sentence. Why, once a guy has five counts, he can go away for a hundred years."

Findlay swallowed.

Mr. Mills smiled. "Yeah. How many computers did you hack? How many files did you transfer?" He pointed toward the table. "These officers say it was over a dozen. You strike me as a guy who's good at math. Can you tell me what twenty times twelve comes to?"

Findlay opened his mouth but nothing came out.

Mr. Mills cocked his head. "I'm sorry, son. I didn't hear you."

Findlay cleared his throat. "Two hundred and forty."

Mr. Mills leaned back. "I know. I just wanted to hear you say it." He walked back to the table. "A bunch of little ones and zeroes go across interstate phone lines, and the phone company tracks it all. They keep incredible records. Even if we were to get the charges dropped, you can probably forget about computers for a living. Plus you probably will end up getting all your MIT buddies expelled."

Findlay just looked at him, mouth agape.

"Nice job." Mills nodded. "I'm sure they'll be happy." He leaned on the back of his chair, cracking his knuckles. "So now that I have your attention, maybe you'd like to sit down and start playing nice with the other kids."

Findlay managed a smirk. "Oh, I don't have to do that. You wanna talk tough? I have information that you'll want to see, mister big time mayoral candidate."

Mills smiled. "Mr. Findlay, I've learned a lot of lousy things about you in the last few hours. Please, don't live up to my expectations." He picked up another folder. "Besides, you may want to hear the rest of this." Mills sat again. "Even my own daughter is facing thirty years."

Melissa opened her mouth to speak, but stopped herself.

Barry shook his head. "This isn't right."

Mr. Mills stared at the stack of folders. "Basically, you were all gearing up for some serious jail time. And a boat load of lawsuits. But somebody swooped in like a fairy godmother and suggested a different way to go. Want to know who?" He pointed at the phones. "The power company."

The fine folks at Florida Electric had been very quiet this whole time.

"You still there, Ashby?" Mr. Mills said to the speaker phone.

"Yes, Michael. We're here."

"Well," Mr. Mills smiled at the room. "My friend Ashby here may or may not have broken the law. So far, it's not clear what they actually did that was illegal. I think they implied they could do some things that they never actually tried to do, like get an arson investigation called off." He looked at

Dean Anderson and Findlay. "Sorry, fellas. Ashby may have lied to you, but that's not necessarily illegal." He scanned the faces at the table. "Can you believe it? The evil corporation may be the only innocent party here.

"Which brings me back to this." He took off his glasses. "All of you—*all* of you—should just shake hands and walk away from this whole thing."

The group exploded in outrage.

Findlay turned red with rage. "You can't be serious!"

Mills glared at him. "Hey, 240, I'm completely serious. Sit down."

Findlay sat.

Mills made sure to look each one of us in the eye as he spoke. "Let's just bottom line it, shall we?"

The room was silent, all eyes on Mr. Mills. He rubbed his chin. "The university drops the charges and agrees not to sue the students. Findlay drops the assault charges and agrees not to sue." He peered over his glasses at the faces around the table. "Get the idea? Everybody was going to charge and sue everybody, so let's just have all that cancel itself out. And where we end up is, nobody goes to jail. In exchange, the University has demanded expulsion of the students, immediate return of certain missing property from mine site 32 to USF, who will in turn sell the rights to Florida Electric, to be administered by this firm for a big fat management fee."

There was silence as it sank in. Barry leaned back in his chair. "Wait a minute. We're expelled and those guys get to make the money from the machine?"

Mr. Mills nodded. "You stay out of jail, too. Don't forget that part."

"So do they."

"Yeah. It all cancels out."

Barry gritted his teeth. "But they still benefit."

"They do, yes." Mills nodded. "So do you. You're all expelled from USF, but not from the entire state university system. You can all transfer—with relatively clean records, mind you—to another state university, with assistance from Dean Anderson, who will resign shortly thereafter for health reasons. He's also agreed to repay the money he may or may not have received from the other schools."

Mr. Mills glared at Barry and me. "My personal stipulation is that you all go to different colleges afterward, so we don't have any of this stuff boil up on us again. You can all restart your academic careers in the fall."

He cleared his throat. "Melissa, your new alma mater will be Newton State College in Sarasota. Not very prestigious, but it's nice and close. So I can keep an eye on you."

"What!"

"That's right." He looked at me, then at Barry. "So don't any of the rest of you bother applying there. Especially you, Barry. Think about becoming a Florida State University Seminole. Tallahassee is far enough away where I won't run into you, and by the time I'm Governor, if that were to happen, you will be long gone from there, too."

Melissa sighed, staring at the table. "What about Peeky? He's here on a student visa. If he gets expelled, he has to go home to India."

"What, Tomàs Pequant, our foreign exchange student?" Mr. Mills folded his arms. "That's fairly straightforward, unfortunately. The ship has sailed on him and on Mr. Findlay. Those are federal offenses. Not much I can do."

Mr. Mills looked at me. "Peeky, I'm sure you can guess how this is going to go for you. You're expelled. You also violated the provisions of your student visa, so that'll be revoked." He stroked his chin, laying down the folder. "Your admittance to the United States is provisional on you staying out of trouble, which you pretty much didn't."

My stomach sank.

Mills sighed and flipped through a folder. "You're to be deported, Peeky, and since you seem to have committed felonies while in the United States, your deportation is expedited." He looked up at me. "These are Federal rules, Peeky, set in motion by Mr. Findlay over there who apparently was working on sending you home to India after he had you kidnapped by the campus police." He shook his head. "I'm sorry. It's out of my hands. You are to meet me here, tomorrow morning at eight A.M., to be escorted to customs for immediate processing." Mr. Mills sighed. "I can't tell you how sorry I am, son. That's the law."

"Why-" Melissa's voice broke as she tried to speak. She eyed her father. "Why does it have to be so harsh?"

"Well, aside from the other reasons I mentioned, it's an election year. Our politicians in Washington aren't too keen on people committing felonies while they're here as our guests." He hooked a thumb at me. "On top of that, he's a young man with no family here. That makes him a flight risk. He has no compelling hardship argument since he hasn't got a wife or child . . ."

"But he does!" Melissa jumped from her seat. "He has a wife and a child."

Mr. Mills shook his head. "No, he doesn't. I have his visa papers from the school right here." He read from the folder. "Tomàs Pequant, a single man from India . . ."

"It's a mistake." She looked at me. "Tomàs! Tell him! Tell him about Meghu and Rasha."

My stomach tightened into a knot as I looked at Mr. Mills. "Sir, can we speak about this in private?"

"No. Everybody else took their spanking in public. So can you."

"Wait a minute." Findlay's jaw dropped. "You—you didn't tell them." He threw his head back and laughed. "You little Middle Eastern snake. You are amazing."

Barry took a step toward Findlay. "Tell us what?"

Findlay kept his gaze on me. "Even now, you're still working on a way to wiggle out and keep your scam alive." He shook his head. "It's incredible."

Melissa glared at Findlay. "What are you talking about?" She turned to her father. "Peeky has a family."

"No he doesn't." Findlay chuckled. "He made it all up."

"What?' Melissa turned and looked at me. I swallowed, feeling the heat burning my cheeks.

Findlay grinned, his eyes alight. "It was all in Peeky's computer when I hacked into it. How he played each of you, collecting eager beavers to traipse off to a mine to find an old hunk of junk his great-grandfather had lost." He laughed. "He had a file about your dead mother, Melissa. Another one on the brainiac paleontology student, one for all of you. But to get in with you rock dusters, he created a whole fake back story to sucker you in and win you over. He created a wife, a kid—a deceased mother—all designed to gain your trust and help you go find his machine."

"This is crap." Barry walked up to the table. "Tell him, Peeky."

I couldn't speak. I couldn't breathe. I just sat there, squirming.

"Crap? Really?" Findlay laughed again. "Tell me this, big brained Barry. Whose idea was it to go digging for fossils in the mines? Yours? That's what you told me. But Peeky had a file on his computer saying he'd mentioned it to you as a reason he couldn't move in with you and that idiot Riff—he said he had to save his money to work the mines over the summer. You got the idea from him."

"Well, maybe I did. So what?"

"So nothing. Just another lie in a whole web of them. A better story to sucker you all in. The poor immigrant gains favor with the group, working you one after another. Playing you like fools so he could acquire the time machine for himself."

There was silence. Everyone stared at me.

"Did he ever tell you what his goal was?" Findlay looked at Melissa. "You'll love this. Money. That's it, plain and simple. You know, you might think I'm a lousy guy, but I never created anything as elaborate as that. And for all my failings, I never in my wildest dreams lied to you the way he did." He pointed across the table. "That's your friend. Tell them, Peeky. Tell them about how we worked out a deal to split the money. While you dummies were dancing around on the sun Dome, he was figuring out a way to sneak the machine out from under you and give it back to me."

Findlay sat back, folding his hands across his belly and smiling. "He lied about everything from day one. Every word out of his mouth was a lie. Everything he ever told you."

"Peeky, is this true?" Melissa eyed me with pain and disbelief in her eyes. I couldn't speak. I couldn't think of any words at all. I just wanted to sink into the chair and disappear.

She lowered her voice to a whisper. "Peeky." Hands in her lap, her eyes brimmed with tears. "I . . . I understand. You thought you had to say those things." Melissa sniffled, staring at the floor. "I don't care about that. What about when you said you'd like to use the time machine to let your little girl meet her deceased grandmother? Your mother. When we talked at Barry's apartment."

She viewed me with pain in her eyes. I wanted to say something, anything to make the hurt stop. It seemed as though it would crush her beating heart.

Still, I could find no adequate explanation that would release me from the terrible grip of the truth.

I swallowed hard. "I'm sorry."

She slumped, burying her face in her hands.

Mr. Mills reached over and patted his daughter's back. "Tomàs, I think you've done enough. Tomorrow. 8 A.M., here. Do I need to assign a security guard to you or can I trust you to show up?"

I sighed. "I will be here."

"With your bags packed. I think the sooner you get out of here, the better." He looked at Barry. "Maybe for your own safety at this point."

"This whole thing stinks," Findlay sneered, pointing at Mr. Mills. "You're just a corrupt lawyer angling to help your buddy at the power company cover everything up. You just needed a few scapegoats like me and Peeky to hang out to dry. You're just as bad as any of the rest of us. And I'm going to ruin you."

"How's that, exactly? You just admitted to computer fraud in front of a bunch of witnesses. I'm not sure now is the time to start trying to throw your weight around."

Findlay grinned. "Your scheme is so generous. All the problems go away, except we're still expelled and the rest of you make a bunch of money. I don't think the voting public wants to elect a corrupt mayor."

Mills scratched his head. "Findlay, were you dropped on your head as a baby? Let me tell you something about people. They know the truth when they hear it. They'll always respect a man who stands up for other people, especially people who need help. That's what I've done here today, even for you. I'm sorry you don't see it that way."

"It's not about how I see it; it's about what the voting public thinks." He pointed at Janice. "This lady is a reporter with The Tampa Tribute and she has all the details. She knows all about what's really going on."

"I know. She told me."

"What?" Findlay's jaw dropped. "When?"

"Last night, after she hung up with you." Mills smiled. "She was at my place at the time."

Findlay turned to Janice. "You Judas! You're corrupt, too. Hiding the story."

She shook her head. "Findlay, I said the Tribute was interested in the story, and they are. I can't predict which way an editor wants to portray things. I never said they'd tell the story your way."

"Well, I can still do it." Findlay pointed at Mr. Mills. "You have a fundraiser in a few hours. I was planning on watching you squirm in front of whoever showed up to throw tomatoes at the corrupt politician. Instead, I can march right out these doors and announce it to the world." He pounded the table. "When you get to your big fundraiser downtown on the plaza this afternoon, I'll be there with a bullhorn. I'll tell what happened. You'll never be mayor, buddy, that's a guarantee."

"Findlay, for a bright guy, you're pretty stupid," Mr. Mills said. "Didn't your mother and father love you as a child?

Janice glanced at Findlay. "You don't understand, do you?"

"Understand what?"

"When I told Michael what you told me, I knew what he would do."

"Huh?" Findlay blinked. "What's that?"

"He insisted we tell the public immediately." Janice gazed at Mr. Mills. "He's an honest man, and the voters love him for it. He insisted that we run the whole story in The Tribute's online coverage. It's been up for hours, the lead story on the news all morning . . . how he wanted to avoid the embarrassment for you and the other students, help the school, and everything else. He's been above board this entire time."

Findlay's face sank and his shoulders slumped. "So everybody knows all this?"

"Pretty much." Mr. Mills shrugged. "Now we just need to see how the voters take it. I'm guessing we'll know after the fundraiser downtown."

"You have it all figured out, don't you?"

"Don't take it personally, Findlay." Mr. Mills glanced around the table. "Barry, you owe the very kind and understanding manager at Radio Shack thirty dollars. Turns out he's a supporter of mine, so he agreed this was all more or less a rowdy college stunt."

"Yes, sir."

"And Ashby, your company is going to have to pay for the damage to the apartment building and the Sun Dome."

"What!"

"Well, your board of directors can't find out how stupid their CEO has been, running around potentially encouraging people to commit arson. You'll lose your job, Ash." He looked out at the shocked faces around the table. "That goes for the rest of you, too. Go home, get some rest, and come back after you've signed these releases my staff has prepared. It's the best deal you're going to get, trust me. Now scoot."

"Not so fast, counselor." It was one of the university lawyers. "I'm not so sure we should sign anything until we see how this sits with the public."

Mr. Mills eyed them, his face turning red and a vein throbbing on his forehead. He faced Barry and spoke in measured tones. "You're originally from Miami, is that right?"

"Yes, sir."

"I'm not originally from Florida. Ohio was my home. I had to move here to paradise." Mr. Mills stood up, walking behind his chair. "But I met an old boy down in your neck of the woods by the name of Mark Rothman. He's an attorney and we did some business, and then we went fishing on his air boat. Out in the swamps. Saw a fifteen-foot alligator."

"Impressive."

"Indeed. Now, do you know how a fifteen-foot alligator gets to *be* a fifteen-foot alligator?"

Barry shrugged. "No, sir."

"By not letting the world *know* it's a fifteen-foot alligator." He patted the back of the leather chair. "I guess sometimes it's best to not draw attention yourself. On the other hand, do you know how an eighteen-foot alligator gets to be an eighteen-foot alligator?"

"How's that?"

"By killing every filthy, stinking fifteen-foot alligator that crosses its path." He narrowed his eyes and shot a look at the university lawyer. "Did you honestly think that I was going to let *your* professor order *your* campus police officers to shoot at *my* daughter—and just let it go?" There was fire in Mr. Mills eyes. The room was completely still.

"Or you, Findlay, you micro brain little turd, for what you took from her computer? That I'd let you get away with that?"

Findlay shrunk back into his chair. The verbal assault by Mr. Mills seemed to awaken him to a new reality.

Mills turned to the speakerphones. "Ashby, our friend at the power plant. You stirred up this hornet's nest by poking the professor over here—who until then was basically a pretty law-abiding buffoon whose only bad habit was illegally selling artifacts out the back door."

"How dare you-"

Mills leaned on the table. "You all need to stop thinking about whether or not you can win a lawsuit or keep yourself out of jail, and start thinking about *whether I'm fool-crazy enough to risk everything I have to protect my daughter!*" He slammed his fist into the table. "Because about now you should be realizing that I sure *am* crazy enough. Did you think I called this meeting to save all of *your* tails? That's just a happy byproduct for you, but if you give me a reason to change my mind, I will rip each of your stupid heads off. Am I making myself clear?"

Standing straight, Mills gritted his teeth. "Why, I ought to get my shotgun out of my office and shoot every stinking one of you right now. And if I had that stupid time machine, I'd be hard pressed not to go throw it into a swamp. That way, nobody'd have it. It's turned you all into a bunch of lunatics."

He pointed at the door. "Now you take these releases and you show them to your lawyers or to your mama or whoever you want to show them to, but my patience has just about run out and so has my generosity about not taking up my daughter's *numerous* cases and suing every one of you into bankruptcy. And you know I'll do it. I'll bury you in legal motions and complaints. I've taken on bigger fish than any one of you and flat out annihilated them." He stormed to the doors and yanked them open. "Now all of you get out of here. Get your minds right, and get back here by nine o'clock Monday morning with a signed release, or at ten o'clock the legal filings start."

CHAPTER THIRTY-THREE

"Dad?"

Mr. Mills took a deep breath and let it out slowly. He turned to his daughter. "Yes, sweetie?"

"We don't have any way to get back to campus."

He sighed. "Okay, have Terry call some cabs for you and the fellas. But Melissa, I'd appreciate it if you'd go to the house for now."

"Why?"

"I just think it's best, given the circumstances."

I wished I could wait somewhere else, anywhere else. Anyplace but outside, with the friends whose trust in me I had just destroyed. But this was not the time. I slinked out of the room and headed to the front door. Barry and Melissa followed.

Only a shell shocked Findlay stayed behind.

As I walked across the beautiful wood floors and past the ornate couch, I felt the eyes of the world upon me, looking down on me, making me want to crawl into a hole. Worse than that, I felt the glare of my friends burning a hole into my back.

* * * * *

"Am I really going to jail?"

Mr. Mills nodded. "This computer hacking is serious stuff."

Findlay eyed the floor.

"It felt like fun and games until now, huh?" Mr. Mills scratched his chin. "Yeah, that's the problem. Politicians tend to think guys like you will grow up to hack places like Target and steal everybody's credit card information. They're getting tough."

Findlay swallowed. "What should I do?"

"You can start by destroying the pictures. And apologizing."

Findlay glanced up. "I'm sorry, Mr. Mills."

Mills buried his face in his hands. "Not to me, you idiot."

* * * * *

I stood on the sidewalk, searching for a cab. Any cab. A local TV news van was parked across the street. That was probably Findlay's idea, to have a news crew waiting to hear him brag about taking down mayoral hopeful Michael Mills—before he went into the meeting and got his head taken off.

He wasn't the only one.

Barry called to me. "Melissa says the cabs will be here in a minute. They have a place around the corner and they always rush for Mr. Mills."

Melissa stood just beyond him with her back to me.

After a moment, he walked toward me, limping on the sore leg. "The receptionist called one for each of us, so you can go wherever you need to go."

I looked at Barry. "I'll be going to my little dorm room and doing some packing."

He nodded. "Peeky . . ." He shifted his weight, rubbing his neck. "You know you didn't need to do that stuff, not any of it. You didn't have to lie to us. We always liked you and trusted you."

"Because of who I was or what I could do for you?"

He shook his head. "Tomàs, you were my friend. That was enough."

* * * * *

The first cab appeared in the distance. Barry walked to the curb and waved at it. He turned to Melissa. "Why don't you take this one?"

She joined him, watching as the vehicle approached. "Thanks."

"Are you going to your dad's house?"

"Looks like it. You?"

He smiled, patting his leg. "I need to get back to the hospital. I've abused this leg and this cast. It's killing me. They may have to amputate."

As the cab rolled to a stop, he leaned over and opened the door. She stared at the seat for a second before climbing in. Then she looked up at Barry. "I—I'll catch up with you. After the campaign rally or something."

"Is your dad going to let you out of his sight again so soon?"

Melissa pushed a strand of hair away from her face and tucked it behind her ear. "He will. He believes in second chances and not carrying a grudge. It's one of his best qualities." She forced a smile. "It's pretty irritating sometimes."

"No grudges? Could have fooled me. He seemed pretty hot up there."

"Courtroom theatrics." She waved her hand. "Most people aren't used to it. I grew up with it. Sometimes he'd practice with me, like an actor going over his lines."

"Theatrics? Well, if you say so." He shifted his weight and looked down the street. "Do you think those guys will sign the releases?"

"Oh, they'll sign them."

"How can you be so sure?"

She drew a slow breath. "Because dad's got a reputation for not bluffing and everybody knows it. That's what he meant by talk to your mommas. He was saying if they ask around, they'll see he's serious."

"He talks in code, huh?"

"Yeah. It's a lawyer thing." Melissa sat in the cab, gazing up at him, not knowing what else to say, but not wanting the conversation to end with just the drab discussion of legal releases.

Barry said nothing, smiling back at her. It had been a long couple of days. There was still a lot that each of them wanted to say to the other. They had squandered too many opportunities.

"Where will I be taking you today, Miss Mills?"

She answered the cabbie but kept her gaze on Barry. "To my dad's house, please."

"Missy." Barry leaned on the cab door, opening his mouth to speak, searching for the right words. None came. Exhaling, he patted the roof of the cab. "Catch up with me later, okay?" He pointed to his broken ankle. "You know where to find me."

She smiled, nodding. "I will."

He eased the door shut and watched the cab drive out of sight.

* * * * *

A second cab pulled up where the first one had been. Barry started for it, then stopped. He looked up at the big antebellum law office, then looked at me. "Hey, Peeky. Why don't you take this one? I forgot something inside."

Without waiting for my answer, he limped back up the steps and through the office's ornate front door.

I walked up to the cab and let myself in, unable to focus my thoughts on anything but my own embarrassment and shame. The driver spoke to me, breaking my haze.

"I'm sorry, I didn't hear you."

He eyed me in the rear view mirror. "Where to?"

I sighed. "The freshman dorm at USF, please."

"The university, eh? That's quite a drive. You're a long way from home."

"Yes, I am."

* * * * *

Barry rushed into the law office lobby. "Is Mr. Mills still here?"

Terry nodded. "He's in his office right-"

Barry sped past her, hobbling as fast as he could.

"Sir, please wait!"

In his personal office, Mr. Mills was preparing to depart for his campaign rally. He picked up his keys and headed for the door, with Janice walking alongside him.

Barry opened it first.

"Mr. Mills, can I speak to you for a second?"

The lawyer bristled. "Barry, I'm on my way to an event and I'd kind of like to get there. Can we talk later?"

"It will only take a moment, sir." He glanced at Janice. "It's important."

She nudged Mr. Mills. "Go ahead, Michael. We have a few minutes."

He sighed, backing away from the doorway to let Barry enter. Janice slipped through. "I'll be in the lobby." She pulled the door closed behind her.

Mills stepped back to his desk. "What would you like to talk about?"

"Actually, I wanted to tell you something."

"What's that?"

Barry took a deep breath. "It was all me. There's no reason to punish anybody else."

"What do you mean?"

"I mean I did it all. Everything. The stolen time machine, the breaking into the Sun Dome, everything. It was all me. I'll put it in writing right now."

Mills put his hands on his hips. "It was you, eh. You did everything all by yourself?"

"No, I forced Melissa and Peeky to come along. And the others. They had to play ball or I'd throw them off my team."

"That's a big deal?" Mills shrugged. "Getting thrown off your 'team'? What, your study group?"

Barry was practically standing at attention. "It's a big deal. It was a guaranteed 'A' for them. I threatened them with that and with other things if they didn't do exactly what I wanted. They didn't want to. I made them. But I did all the major stuff that you were talking about."

Mills folded his arms. "Like the time machine. You stole that?"

"I did. I made the others help me, but it was all my idea."

"You broke into the Sun Dome?"

"That's right."

"You picked the locks on the Sun Dome gate and climbed up on the roof?"

"Yes sir."

Mr. Mills pointed to Barry's cast. "How'd you climb up that big gutter with a broken ankle?"

Barry looked him in the eye. "I pulled the truck up and stood on the roof. Then I climbed up. The officers guarding it probably told you they saw me driving it."

Mills nodded. "They did. But they said other things, too." He walked out from behind his desk, scratching his chin. "So you picked the locks on the security gate and drove the truck into the stadium?"

"Yes, sir."

"Why would you lie about that?"

THE NAVIGATORS

"It's no lie. You can have them expel me. There's no reason to expel Melissa and no reason to expel the others. Peeky, either."

Mr. Mills went to his desk and opened a drawer, rummaging through it. "Okay, you climbed on top of the Sun Dome with a broken leg, then you climbed back down and picked the lock on the gate, right?" He pointed to a door on the far side of his office. "That's my private bathroom. It has a very sophisticated lock on it. Very difficult to break in to there, that bathroom. Not sure why the contractor put such a high tech lock on a bathroom, but he did. It's always annoyed me, but I've always been too lazy to change it out."

He stood up. "Have a look at this." He dropped several devices onto the desk. "These are the tools of the trade for burglars. Lock picks." He thumbed through them. "Different kinds. I've acquired these from some of my clients over the years. Kind of kept them as souvenirs, you know?"

Mr. Mills pointed to the bathroom. "I'll make you a deal. If you can pick that lock on my bathroom door, I'll have no choice but to believe your story about breaking into USF and the rest of it." He smiled. "What do you say? Take any set of tools you want and go unlock that door."

Barry stared at the odd-looking assortment of devices on the desk.

"If you can get yourself out of that bathroom, I'll convince everybody this whole thing was all your doing. You can take the rap all by yourself. The other students will walk."

Barry reached over and grabbed one of the tools off the desk. He limped to the bathroom.

Mr. Mills followed. "How about a fifteen minute time limit?"

Nodding, Barry stepped into the bathroom. Mr. Mills locked the door and pushed it shut.

From inside the private restroom, Barry stared at the lock. He knelt down and held the tool to the keyhole, sliding it into the opening. It didn't fit. He slumped his shoulders. He jiggled the knob a few times for good measure, sat back on his heels and sighed.

Mr. Mills opened the door. "You didn't even pick up the right tool. *This* is a set of lock picks." He dangled a ring of lock picks on one finger. "*That* is some kind of bizarre Chinese wrench set that came with my treadmill." He pointed at the bathroom door. "And *that* was a cheap seven dollar lock from Home Depot. A rusty nail would have opened it."

Chuckling, Mr. Mills moved back to his desk. "So we know you're not a locksmith. Which means you didn't break into the Sun Dome. But I think I know who did. I just want to know why you're covering for her."

Barry sighed. "I . . . it seems pretty unfair to let everybody get expelled, that's all."

"I can appreciate you feeling that way."

"This whole thing just sort of spun out of control."

"I can see that, too. Doesn't change things." He got up from his desk and went to the office door, opened it, and stood next to it silently.

THE NAVIGATORS

Barry took the hint. He walked out without a word.

Janice passed him in the lobby. She entered Mr. Mills' office. "What was that all about?"

Mr. Mills pulled his car keys from a pocket. "Oh, he was trying to be a hero or something. He volunteered that everything was his fault and offered to take all the blame for everybody."

"Did you let him?"

"Why should I have? He's obviously lying."

"Why? Because he has eyes for your daughter, Michael. He's trying to protect her."

* * * * *

Findlay walked down the stairs at the front of Mills law office.

"It didn't go like you thought, huh?" It was the news producer from the other day.

"Nope." He stared up at the big law office building, then he looked at her. "How'd you guys find out about the meeting?"

"We got a tip. Some cop friend of yours. Officer Bolton?"

"Hah." Findlay's shoulders slumped. "Yeah, that figures."

"He said we'd find a really explosive story here when the big meeting was all over. Guess not, huh?"

"It was explosive all right. But not the way you mean." Findlay kicked at the ground, rubbing his neck. "Hey, would you wanna get a cup of coffee with me?"

"Are you asking me on a date?"

He put his hands in his pockets and shrugged. "I kind of thought we hit it off the other day." He sighed. "I could use a friend right now."

"They say, 'In politics, if you need a friend, get a dog.'"

"I'm not in politics."

"What would you call it? You took a shot at the next mayor of Tampa. If you shoot at the king, you better kill the king—otherwise you're the one who gets killed. It doesn't get much more political than that."

"Yeah, well . . ." Findlay gazed at the ground. "I feel like I got killed pretty good up there just now." He raised his eyes to meet hers. "How about it?"

She put her hands on her hips. "What's a pasty white boy want with a girl like me, huh?"

He shrugged. "I'm of Irish descent. Some of my people were pretty adventurous, you know?"

"Look where that got you."

He nodded. "Yeah, okay."

She winked. "You'll be all right, Findlay. Not today, but maybe when you're feeling better, call me sometime. When you're not licking your wounds. And we'll talk." She climbed into the news van. "You can get me through the TV station."

He managed a smile. "Okay."

She started the engine and drove off.

It might be a few years before I can call, though.

* * * * *

Mr. Mills snorted. "He has eyes for my daughter? So has every other young man in Tampa over the years."

Janice shook her head. "Oh, Michael, how can you be so smart and so dumb at the same time? That Findlay guy must be rubbing off on you." She leaned in front of him to look into his eyes. "Weren't you ever young and stupid?"

"I was, sure. I don't usually like to talk about that in front of my daughter, lest she get the wrong impression of her prim, proper and successful old dad, but once upon a time I was pretty young and foolish." He chuckled. "Me and Carl Baker ran naked through a sorority house and stood on the retention pond wall singing Christmas carols. Nothing like this."

"And why did you do that?"

"Oh, we were drunk, probably. Come on, let's go."

She put her hand on his arm. "Wait a minute. You can be drunk anywhere. Why run through a sorority house or sing a serenade from a pond wall?"

"What, to impress some girl?"

She raised her eyebrows. "Ya think? Michael, that boy has known your daughter for years. He's not trying to be seen at the right restaurants around town with her."

"He can't," Mills huffed. "He doesn't have any money to take her out. His parents are probably still paying his bills."

Janice sighed. "The point is, he's not after your money."

"He's just after my daughter."

"He's being noble."

"He's being stupid."

Janice reached over and adjusted his tie, purring at him. "He's impetuous. Not unlike a certain naked singer I've only recently heard about." She smiled. "He's willing to sacrifice himself just to protect her. That sounds like the kind of guy you'd want dating your daughter. Besides, I think Melissa has eyes for him, too. Now, do you believe in second chances or what?"

Mr. Mills sighed. "Come on, we're going to be late."

CHAPTER THIRTY-FOUR

There is a certain feeling a person's childhood home has when they visit as an adult. It is the same house, but it is different somehow. Smaller. Quieter. It belongs to them less, or they belong somewhere else more.

Melissa walked from room to room, looking at the changes her father had made since her last visit a few weeks ago. Mostly it was campaign stuff. Boxes of posters and buttons. The garage was brimming with signs.

She went to her room to get some of her own clothes to wear—Mandy's had been fine, but there was no reason to stay in them. She had plenty of clothes at home.

Funny, it wasn't that anymore. Home. Her apartment was home now. It had been for some time. This was now her old house. Dad's house. She drifted from room to room. It felt different from

how it used to feel. Just as warm, just as inviting–
but different.

Of course, the house is the same. I'm what's different.

She checked the clock over the fireplace. It was time for the campaign rally to begin.

The remote for the TV was on the coffee table. So was one of the cordless phone handsets. Its little red light flashed.

Messages. Better check it, in case there's an emergency.

"Michael, it's Troy. Listen, I'm begging you, don't make that speech today at the campaign rally. Let's just cancel and run some polls to see how the public is taking the story first."

The second message was the same – Troy, the diligent campaign manager, hoping to persuade the eager politician from career suicide. Melissa shook her head.

Uncle Troy, you still haven't learned after all these years.

There were several more messages, all from Troy, all begging Mr. Mills not to give the speech. She sighed.

I guess I'd better watch it, then.

She clicked on the TV and found the one of the local news channels.

The TV announcer was doing a live shot. "We'll be covering mayoral hopeful Michael Mills' speech today, his first public appearance since the shocking revelations in today's online edition of the Tampa Tribute."

Melissa wandered into the kitchen. The TV had always been visible from there, even though nobody ever cooked. Certainly not her father.

"And here comes candidate Mills to the podium now."

The kitchen was a spectacular array of high-end appliances. The never-used stove, the stainless steel pots and pans in the chef's chandelier. If not for the cleaners, it would all be covered in dust from lack of use.

They were pretty, though.

Polite applause greeted Mr. Mills. "Thank you, my friends."

Grabbing a Diet Coke from the fridge, Melissa settled in at the counter, placing her elbows on the cold granite surface. She leaned in to watch her father's speech.

"You may have been disturbed about some of the things happening on and around the campus of the University of South Florida. I know I have been."

Some ripples of laughter went up from the crowd.

"It's fair to say that the stories I've read have been troubling to me, not only as a political candidate, but also as a father."

Melissa winced, not realizing she'd be addressed so directly in the speech.

"I was supposed to give a political speech today, but I'd like to just talk to you for a moment." He set aside some papers. "I know that many of you would be troubled if you read about a loved one in the paper, or if you got the kind of bad news I've been receiving over the last few days."

The crowd grew quiet.

"And it would strike many of you to use all your power, to reach out with any means necessary, to help those you love. In this regard, I am the same as you." He scanned the forum, taking in the crowd, taking in their faces. The expression on his face was one of pain. "I'm sure I felt the same way any of you would have felt under the circumstances."

The speech didn't have his usual cheeriness. It lacked the warmth he was known for.

Maybe Uncle Troy was right. Maybe this wasn't the time to go out and give a big speech.

"As a parent, we would do anything for our children. We have but one life. We . . . would gladly trade it—to protect our offspring."

He looked out over the crowd again. The camera zoomed in on him. A tear rolled down his face.

"I will never apologize for sacrificing everything to protect my family."

A few people in the crowd called out comments, but they were too far away to be understood.

" . . .and neither would you. We don't have to reach for the stars but we can certainly acknowledge what's right in front of us."

A few more comments were shouted from the crowd. Melissa shifted uncomfortably on her feet.

"My friends, I believe in second chances. Today, I have done what I believe in my heart is good and right and proper, and the best thing for all involved, including my family, and the city I love." He looked down. "But . . . I leave the decision to you. If you read the story, you know the facts."

Then, the brilliant smile. "Can you stand for an honest man to be your next mayor?"

The crowd erupted in applause.

"It would be a nice change in this country, wouldn't it? Because there is only one version of the truth. You know it when you see it."

There was cheering. People rose to their feet.

"We all love our families. You do, and I do."

The applause grew louder.

"And we love our city. We want the best for both."

The television cameras pulled back to show people cheering and applauding. Putting the truth in the paper first had worked. The city still loved her father.

His speech now seemed to be directed at her.

"Life is full of difficult choices and wasted opportunities. Fight for what you believe in. Fight for what you want. Demand it."

There was more, but she was no longer listening. The crowd had seen fit to rally behind her father, and the city would, too. Uncle Troy's polls would show it soon, but she had been around politics long enough to see it in front of her. She knew it instinctively.

And she knew what she needed to do.

* * * * *

About an hour later, the phone rang. It was Troy.

Melissa, fresh from the shower, took a break from picking out her clothes while she toweled off her hair. She picked up the phone.

"Melissa? Where's your father?"

"I don't know. I thought he would be with you at the campaign rally."

"Normally, yeah, but I needed to stay at the campaign headquarters all day to put out fires."

She slid into her jeans with a slight hop, holding the phone to her ear with her shoulder. "And?"

"And the speech was a home run. He's even more popular than he was before. Turns out the people trust him more than I did."

"Really? I didn't think the speech was that good. Why are you calling here, anyway?"

"I can't reach your father on his cell phone. He's been avoiding me all day."

"I bet." She picked over some tops she'd laid out on the bed. "I heard the messages you left."

"Okay, well, we're running a flash poll and it's sailing over the rooftops. It's ninety percent approval. I've never seen anything like it."

"You haven't done any other political campaigns. That could have something to do with it." She quickly set the phone down and put on the shirt.

"Could be, but the guys who've done this for a living say it's pretty remarkable. Your old man really dodged a bullet."

Melissa winced. "You think so?"

"I know so."

"Then now would be a good time to hit him up for a favor?" She sauntered to the living room to check her look in the big mirror. It was a cute outfit.

"It just might be. Have him call me when he gets in. I gotta go. The phones are ringing off the hook here."

As she hung up, the front door opened. Her father, smiling from ear to ear, walked in.

"Did you see that?" He held out his arms. Melissa ran into them, closing her eyes and squeezing him.

"Dad, you were amazing."

"No, it was all you."

"What?" Her cheek still pressed to his chest, her eyes flew open. "What do you mean?"

"I gave a speech to a crowd, but I was thinking of you the whole time."

"Why?"

"I'm not sure. I guess I just wanted the whole world to know how much I love you." He picked her up in a massive bear hug and spun her around, then kissed the top of her head. Setting her down, he strolled into the kitchen.

"Hey, where's Janice?"

"Oh, she's busy doing some reporter stuff. You know how it is. I'll be meeting her at the Hilton in a few hours for a fundraiser dinner." He tossed his wallet and some papers onto the counter. "I booked a suite and a limo, so I'll be staying down there tonight. You'll have the house to yourself."

Melissa shoved her hands in her pockets, eyeing the floor. "Janice is . . . pretty special, isn't she?"

"Oh, she's the best."

"No, I mean she's *special*. You can admit it. It's probably the worst kept secret in Tampa anyway. Even Uncle Troy knows you've been dating her."

Mr. Mills crinkled his nose and scratched the back of his neck. "He does, huh?"

"And it's okay, Dad. Really."

He sighed. "Missy, you know I would never do anything to disrespect your mother."

"I know. And you haven't. Mom . . . would have wanted you to be happy."

"I tell you, kiddo, I look at you, and I see her face, her strength." He smiled broadly, showing the brilliant smile and boyish dimples that had made him famous. "How proud of you she would have been, to see what a beautiful, strong young woman you've become." His smile faded. "That's why this thing with Janice, it really—I wanted to keep it quiet. I just . . . I didn't want to hurt you."

"You didn't. She's nice. I like her. A lot."

"I like her a lot, too, but . . ."

Melissa hugged her father. "Dad, I love Mom and that will never change. Nobody can ever replace her." She gazed up at him. "But I love you, too, and part of that is wanting you to be happy." She buried her face in his chest. "You've done so much for so many, it's okay to do something for yourself. Mom would want that for you, your happiness. Give Janice a chance. It's okay. Really. We have one life, right?"

THE NAVIGATORS

Mr. Mills gently patted his daughter on the back. "Just like your mom. You get right to it, don't you?"

"Maybe she's not the one but it's okay to test the water. You'll never know if you don't at least try. Right?"

"Right."

"So, you booked a suite at the Hilton?"

"Yes."

"For just *yourself*?"

"Well . . ."

She looked up. "It's okay. I'm teasing. Go. Have fun. Do you have protection?"

"Missy!"

"I'm just kidding. But, seriously—do you?"

He stood back. "Okay, I have to shower and change before the next event. May I?"

She made a sweeping gesture in the direction of his bedroom, bowing. "Please do, Mr. Future Mayor."

"Thank you." He breezed past her, disappearing around a corner. "Will you be staying at the house tonight?"

"Actually, I was just thinking I might borrow the BMW."

"What? No. Get your car out of the impound lot."

"Come on. You have a limo and I need a car. I can't get mine until Monday."

He peeked around the corner at her. "It might not be a bad idea for you to stay here until then."

"Please, Daddy?"

He sighed. "Okay. That smile doesn't work on me. I'm just being nice because I'm in a good mood." He disappeared again. "You're not running off to go see that Barry character, are you?"

She smiled. "I thought I might stop by the hospital to see him, yes."

Mr. Mills walked out of the bedroom. "Maybe I'd better tell you a few things about that guy first, then." He sighed. "Sit down."

* * * * *

Mr. Mills' BMW was a sleek machine. Top of the line. Like the ads said, it practically drove itself. Even so, it was illegal for Melissa to be talking on a cell phone while driving it.

"Mandy, we need to make a vehicle trade. My dad's 500 series for your crappy pickup truck, for the whole weekend. What do you say?"

"I don't think my dad will let me."

"Then don't ask him. Come on, I need a favor and you owe me."

"No way I owe you. You got me in some deep trouble with *my* dad. I don't owe you anything."

"Yeah, you're right. Just forget it." Melissa glanced out the window. "Hey, by the way, does your dad know your boyfriend moved in with you?"

* * * * *

Melissa paused outside the door to Barry's hospital room, one hand on the knob and the other poised to knock. She took a deep breath, cracking the door open. "Knock, knock."

Barry glanced up from his magazine, then broke into a big smile. "Hey."

"Hey, yourself. How are you doing?"

He set the magazine on the side table and pointed to the sling holding his broken leg. "They think I'll survive. All that running around made my leg swell up so bad, they had to cut the old cast off and make me another one. I'm supposed to keep it elevated now."

Melissa sauntered to the foot of his bed. "Does it hurt much?" She laid her hand on the cast, noticing the bruised knee, the firm muscles of his tan thigh, the hem of the hospital gown . . . "Oh!" She whipped around to face the wall.

"Sorry about that." Barry stuffed the bottom of the gown between his legs and pushed himself upright in bed. "Missy, what are you doing here? I thought your dad locked you away like Rapunzel in her tower."

She walked to the side of the bed. "Actually, Dad told me what you did. Lying to protect me."

"He did, huh?"

Melissa put her hand on his. "Nobody's ever done anything like that for me before." She looked down, stroking his hand. "I mean, my family, maybe, but nobody else. It meant a lot." She raised her eyes to meet his. "I wanted to say thanks. You know, none of this would have happened if it weren't for you."

"Yeah. Don't remind me."

"You know what I mean."

"Are you laying out your case for my defense here, counselor?"

"No. You don't need anybody to do that for you. Not now. But there is one more thing I wanted to say."

"What's that?"

Melissa leaned over and kissed him, locking her mouth on his, letting the warmth of his lips electrify her. She wasn't sure her heart had ever pounded so fast in her life. She found herself pulling him closer, straining forward to him, aching for him. Her hands glided along the sides of his neck and into his hair, winding her fingers up in his brown locks.

Their eyes met as she pulled away. He gave her a crooked smile. "You're a good talker."

"I was raised by a lawyer." She lingered there, her face inches from his, gazing into his eyes.

Not at all like a brother.

His face was more mature to her, more familiar, more handsome. Even the stubble on his chin looked delicious. More than anything, she wanted to feel his lips on hers again. "Any rebuttal?"

"Oh, yeah." He pulled her close and kissed her deeply, lifting her onto the bed with him. She reached inside the neck of his gown, feeling his muscular shoulders and warm, smooth skin. His heart beat against her hand. Time slowed for her—in that moment it was like the Earth paused to simply allow her to fully find him.

He rested his forehead on hers. "I have wanted to do that for a long time."

"Why didn't you?"

"I don't know." He shook his head. "Whatever my reason was, it sure seems stupid now."

* * * * *

Dr. Harper walked out of his office and over to the desk where his training intern was waiting. "Time to make the rounds, Gina. Who's on the roster today?"

She handed him the clipboard. "You have a recovering appendectomy in 2201, a broken arm in 2203, and a broken ankle in 2207."

"This won't take long then. Is pharmacy preparing their meds?"

"Yes, doctor."

"Then let's have another look at this appendectomy's post-op report. Always double check, Gina – that way there are no surprises."

* * * * *

Melissa kissed Barry on his neck, tugging at the hospital gown. "Hey, what day is it?"

He stroked her cheek. "Um, Friday."

She glanced up. "Aren't you supposed to have your big date tonight?"

"Uh, yeah, I guess so . . ."

Melissa sat up and kissed him again. "Cancel it."

Keeping his eyes on Melissa, Barry grabbed at the phone on the side table.

* * * * *

"Okay, Gina. Pharmacy's getting ready to do their job. Let's do ours. Room 2201. Appendectomy. What are we looking to see with this young man?"

Gina eyed the sheet the nurse had prepared. "We are checking the stitches and making sure there is no sign of infection. Then he can be readied for release."

"Good. Good. This will only take a minute, and then we'll go see about the broken arm. Let's have a look." He knocked on the open door. "How are you, young man?"

* * * * *

"Sophia, I'm sorry to call on such short notice, but I can't make it tonight. I kinda broke my leg."

"Oh no, you poor dear. Are you okay?"

Melissa nuzzled his neck.

"Um, I'll be okay, but I might be laid up for a while."

"Can I get you anything?" Sophia asked.

Melissa closed her eyes and pressed her lips to his cheek.

"No thanks, Sophia. I have everything I need." He aimlessly dropped the phone onto the side table and reached for Melissa.

* * * * *

Dr. Harper walked out of room 2203 where the broken arm resided, sliding the x-rays back into the folder. "Who's next, Gina?"

"Broken ankle, room 2207."

"Oh, yes." Harper took the clipboard from her, scanning the notes. "Barry Helm, broken ankle, cast removal, new cast applied." He turned to Gina. "You remember Barry—he broke the ankle and then did all this crazy running around, to the point where his whole leg was swollen and painful."

Gina smiled. "Yes, I remember."

Harper shook his head. "Quite a character, that one." He gave the clipboard back. "I wonder what kind of story Barry will have for us today."

* * * * *

Melissa stroked Barry's jaw line, her eyes never leaving his.

"Missy, should we slow down a little?"

She gazed up at him. "I'm done with going slow, just floating along like a leaf in a river." She reached up and kissed him again. "It's time to plot a new course."

He slid his hands down her back. She leaned over him, letting her hair brush his face.

The door to Barry's room flew open. Dr. Harper cleared his throat loudly. "Am I interrupting something?"

Melissa shrieked, grabbing the sheet and diving for the floor. Barry bolted upright.

Harper smiled. "Barry, how are you?"

Barry swallowed. "Good, sir."

Harper motioned to the intern. "You remember Gina?"

Barry pulled at the hem of his hospital gown and nodded.

Harper addressed the pile of sheets on the floor. "Miss Mills? Everything okay down there?"

"Just peachy," the sheets replied.

Harper scanned his notes. "Well, it's time for your pain meds." He peered over the clipboard at Barry. "Or is this a bad time?"

"I, uh . . . I—"

"Could you come back in a few minutes?" the pile on the floor asked.

Barry smiled. "Can you come back?"

Harper glanced at his clipboard. "Not a problem. Gina, make a note, please. And watch that ankle, son. If I have to put a third cast on it, I'm breaking the other ankle, too. Understand?"

Barry nodded again.

Gina peered around Dr. Harper. "Should I still give him something for the swelling?"

"Maybe when we come back." Harper winked and shut the door.

As they made their way down the corridor, Harper folded his arms over his clipboard. "Better get used to that, Gina. It's fairly common." He frowned. "There's just something about the white hallways or smell of a hospital. Maybe it's the way the gowns don't close, I don't know. But those college kids get admitted and suddenly it's a frat party orgy in here."

He sighed. "Gina, do you get migraines?"

"No, doctor."

He squeezed his eyes shut and rubbed his brow. "You will."

CHAPTER THIRTY-FIVE

"Will he still be there?"

Melissa sat on the edge of the hospital bed, pulling one of her shoes on. "Probably. Where else is he going to go?"

"I don't know." Barry took a sip of water from the bedside table. "He doesn't have much stuff to pack."

"Packing is not what keeps someone in their room all day." She stood up. "I'll be fine.

"Oh, I'm not worried about you." Barry smiled. "I'm worried about Peeky."

"Just worry about resting that leg and getting out of here."

"Yes, doctor."

She nodded. "We'll play doctor again when I get back. I have to go trade dad's BMW for Mandy's truck."

"And she's going to let you?"

She leaned over and kissed him deeply, letting her lips linger on his. "I can be very persuasive."

"Don't I know it."

* * * * *

My small, unfashionable suitcase stood in the center of the tiny dorm room. It had been humbling to stand in line at the airport to receive a piece of luggage so old and out of style. Other travelers grabbed sleek, expensive bags. Mine looked fifty years old, maybe older; a faded tan color with brown trim. It might have been more than fifty years old. I had not asked Ankit how old it was when he offered to lend it to me.

"You will go to America, Peeky, and you will return rich and famous. And I will be able to say I helped you."

Ankit was a good friend. I wondered if he still would be when I returned disgraced and without the riches I'd promised everyone. And with no way to pay them all back.

It was all I could think about, just a taste of what my great-grandfather had gone through, to be sure. At least there was the mercy of not going through a humiliating trial like he did. Just a quick deportation hearing.

Then this country would be rid of me the same way it had ridden itself of my great-grandfather.

I sat on the bed, staring out the tiny window. The dormitory linen service would come by in a few minutes to pick up sheets and towels, with their exit forms for me to sign. I knew I wouldn't sleep; there was no sense in pretending I needed sheets.

There were so many things I was going to miss. The university had been so different from what I expected. So much newer, and modern, and so much more open and accepting. And beautiful. The grounds were lush with landscape. So many places to eat, or shop, or just hang out.

But try as I might, I couldn't distract myself enough times to erase the memories of the people who had become my friends. The ones who trusted me, who had taken me into their hearts.

I would miss them all. My heart hurt as I bathed in my loneliness, my self-inflicted exile. No amount of deep breaths and busying myself with linen receipts or repacking my suitcase could stop the sadness.

There was a knock. I picked up the forms from the small desk and walked over to open the door.

Of all the people in the world, she was the one I expected least.

I almost couldn't speak.

"Melissa."

It came out as a whisper.

She stood in the hallway staring at me, neither smiling nor looking angry. She seemed to be sizing me up in the dim light, debating about how she wanted to act towards me.

I stepped back, opening the door further. "I'm surprised to see you." I swallowed. "And happy, I think."

She took a few paces into my tiny room, stopping with her back to me.

I couldn't hold back. "Melissa, I'm so sorry." I searched the ceiling for words. "I'm sorry about everything." I tried to get past the lump in my throat and hold my emotions in. "You were all my friends, and I-"

"Stop." She put a hand out, lowering her head. "You sound like you're going to cry." She turned to face me, her eyes full of tears. "And if you start crying, then I'll start crying." A tear rolled down her face, followed by another. "And I don't want to cry for you, Peeky. I hate you right now. So don't you say anything else to me." She folded her arms, sniffling a few times. "I had a friend I could talk to when I felt this way, and that friend is gone now." She turned away, placing her hands on the desk.

I cleared my throat. "Okay."

She wiped her eyes. "I didn't come here to make a scene." When she turned around, her eyes were puffy and red. "I had it all planned out and it didn't include any crying."

I stood silent, ready for whatever admonishments she wanted to throw at me.

She wiped her eyes again, taking a slow, deep breath. "I thought a lot about not coming, but Dad always says people deserve a second chance. I'm not so sure." She sighed, glancing around the room, looking at anything but me. Her eyes brimmed again with tears. "You . . . you were my friend for a long time, before you weren't. You helped me through some tough times. So even though you lied to me like a snake, I'd like to believe that some of that good guy still exists. I'd like to believe I wasn't a complete fool."

"Melissa, I didn't know what to do. I had an ugly, deceptive plan that was born a long time ago for a lot of reasons that seemed good at the time. After I met you guys, you were all so nice to me—I wanted to come clean, but . . ." I stared down. "I just couldn't think of a way to do it without turning you all against me."

"And yet you managed to do that anyway." The tears rolled down her face again.

I nodded. "That's right. So here I am. I'd do anything to regain your friendship."

She stared at me, seeming to size me up, to see which person was the real one. After a long while, she came to her conclusion.

"If you're really still my friend, prove it."

"Tell me what to do."

"Everyone else from our original group is either in the hospital or in jail. Things have gotten pretty far out of control." She looked me in the eye. "But I picked up the machine from the hotel. It's in Mandy's truck outside. She and I were able to get it out of the room and loaded into the truck bed. I'm supposed to turn it in to the University tomorrow morning. Instead, I want to ditch it." She glanced over her shoulder at me, her eyes full of pain. "Tonight. Let's drop the thing in a swamp or back into the mine where we found it. I want to get rid of it."

I couldn't believe what I was hearing. "Why?"

She shook her head. "That thing is evil. Not devil-evil, but evil in its own way, like bad luck. It's bad news. Nothing good happens to anyone who comes near it." She walked back to me. "Think about it. Riff nearly got killed just unburying it.

Roger almost died testing it. Barry was almost killed on his trip."

"To throw away such a valuable-"

"Valuable? What value?" She threw her hands in the air. "It's a tool of destruction. Its mere presence has caused every rational person who gets a whiff if it to drop any moral framework they ever had. The Dean, the police . . ." She glanced back out the window. "*Us*. Maybe its creators had noble intentions but that isn't how it worked out. For Pete's sake, look at what happened to your own family."

Melissa turned to me, drying her eyes. "I've studied enough broken pottery to see that a lot of ancient people thought they had things figured out, and suddenly their whole civilizations vanished. We are not meant to travel through time. We can't handle it." She folded her arms, walking across the little room. "It's like the kid who took the family station wagon for a drive when she was ten years old. It's a disaster waiting to happen, and just . . . a matter of how bad it will be."

She moved back to the desk, arms folded, and sat on the edge. "The original creators probably figured that out and threw the thing in an old well or a deep freshwater spring hoping nobody'd ever find it again. And then by pure accident, the machine was rediscovered—and disaster followed. We're no different." She looked up at me. "We need to get rid of that thing, but I can't do it by myself. Can you help me? Can you be a friend and do that?"

I sighed, nodding. "I can do that."

* * * * *

THE NAVIGATORS

The drive to Florida Mining and Minerals site number 32 was a long one. And of course it had to rain.

Melissa drove while I sat there watching the borrowed truck's GPS tell me how many minutes remained until I threw my dream into a hole. I was only a few feet from the machine I'd sacrificed so much for, over so many years, separated only by the truck's small rear window.

Now I was helping take it to be dumped into a pond, in the middle of a mine, in the middle of nowhere. The workers of the next shift would unknowingly bury it, and it would be lost forever.

I didn't speak much on the ride. Melissa had been emotional in the dorm room, but a two-hour drive will cool most heads.

I kept thinking there might be a chance to persuade her to do something else with the machine.

It was already dark when we arrived, and the incessant downpour caused the watchman to barely stick his head out of the guard shack to check Melissa's credentials. He didn't seem to care that we weren't in a university truck. He just waved us on through and went back to his newspaper.

We bounced along the dirt road for a few minutes, making our way to the center of the massive, muddy work site.

She stopped the truck and leaned forward over the steering wheel. "This looks like it."

I peered out my window. There were no street lights, no work lights, just the high beams of the truck shining up onto a small hill through the rain.

Beyond it was the pond. The pretty blue waters that she and Roger had gone swimming in a few days ago. It had appeared so inviting then. It seemed so foreboding in the dark.

Melissa turned off the engine and pointed at the hill. "We're going to pull the time machine off the truck bed, drag it up that hill to the far edge, and drop it off the cliff. It's straight down into the deep water from there." She looked over at me. "When the miners start working this area again, they'll backfill this whole thing with a few million cubic yards of dirt. The machine will be buried for good."

My heart sank. Her words echoed in my brain, but I couldn't let myself believe them. Surely she'd listen to reason. But time was running out.

She opened her door. "Come on."

The rain finally stopped, allowing the constant humidity to create little clouds of mist around the pond's cooler surface. Between the two of us, we were able to get the time machine off the truck and up the muddy hill.

From there, even in the darkness, we could see the water below. The dump mounds were notoriously unstable, especially in the rain, but this one seemed sturdy enough for our work. Grass had started to grow on it, so it had been around a while. At the top of the peak, the time machine rested, visible from the lights of the truck. I walked around behind it, taking it all in one last time and waiting for an opportunity to talk Melissa out of this madness.

She stood on the edge, hand on her hips, staring into the dark water below. Behind me, the noise of

THE NAVIGATORS

the truck's intermittent windshield wipers was the only sound.

I knew there was no talking her out of it. No way to get her to see things my way. I could imagine the determination on her face.

There were only a few moments before that machine disappeared forever. Only she stood between me and my dreams.

She, who stood on the edge of a cliff right now, in the middle of nowhere.

"Peeky?" She turned to look at me. "You have a strange expression on your face." She smiled. "Having second thoughts?"

I went over to her, my heart pounding. "How far down do you think it is?"

She peered over the edge. "I don't know. Forty feet. Maybe more."

"Four stories of a building." I nodded. "That's pretty high." I could feel my heart thumping in my chest.

"It doesn't really matter how high we are, it matters how deep the water is."

I swallowed. "There's stuff in that water sometimes. Old equipment. Big rocks. Something could land on it and get all smashed up. Maybe not sink at all."

She looked at me. A concerned expression came over her face. "What's with you?"

"I worked too hard, Melissa. I sacrificed too much."

"To what? To give up the machine? Haven't you been paying attention? It has ruined the lives of everyone who's come in contact with it. You, of all people, should know that. It ruined your whole family."

"I have a chance to change that."

"It doesn't work that way. I know that now."

I shook my head. "You don't know that. We hardly know anything about the machine."

"I know enough. What are you thinking? You still want to chase after your fortune? Is that it? And I'm standing in your way?" She glanced around, holding her hands out. "Well, here's your chance. Nobody else is here. We're all alone, Peeky!"

I swallowed hard, staring at her.

It would be easy. A quick push . . . The machine would be mine. I could remove the shame of my family . . .

By doing the unthinkable?

The reality of it hit me like a blow to the gut. I felt my knees weaken.

What am I becoming?

I looked over at Melissa, suddenly sick to my stomach at the things I'd allowed myself to think.

Maybe she was right about the machine.

Pain and humiliation swept through me. "Why did you make me come here?"

"I needed help getting rid of this thing."

"You could have gotten somebody else. Why me? Why did I have to be present for its destruction?"

"So you'd know. So you wouldn't chase around the rest of your life looking for it."

I found myself panting hard, like I had been holding my breath for a long time. "It doesn't have to be evil."

"What?"

"The machine. It doesn't have to be a bad thing. We were too ambitious. We should have taken smaller steps. Or tried to change something bad that happened." I glanced at her. "We should have done something noble."

She stood there, shaking her head.

"I want us to use what we found before we throw it away forever. It's the chance of a lifetime. Maybe we could change things."

"We might be able to do something but that doesn't mean we should. Fate might not be very forgiving if we do."

"Fate? You mean God. And why would we be given the intelligence to find this thing and not use it?"

"We can kill a person with a gun that somebody was intelligent enough to build. That doesn't mean we should do it."

"I just . . . don't think I could live with myself if I didn't at least try."

"Oh, you just want your money! I thought we were past that."

"You're past it!" I pointed at her. "You're not getting deported tomorrow morning. You don't have a life of shame and humiliation waiting for you the way I do." I gasped. "You have money and a respected family name. What if you didn't? I'm not making excuses. I did some bad things and I deserve what's coming to me."

I stared at the ground. "But do I deserve my whole life to be ruined forever? Yours won't be.

Barry's won't be." I sighed, looking up at her. "Friends help each other, don't they?"

She put her hand on my shoulder. "Everything we tried caused something bad to happen, Peeky."

"So we adjust. We don't throw it all away. We're scientists. We make mistakes, but we learn from them. Early doctors had way more failures than they did successes. Leeches and bleeding people—but they built on those failures and created a world where they've saved millions of lives."

I lowered my voice, looking into her eyes. "We have that opportunity. We just start small. Safe." I turned to the machine, putting my hands on the rail frame. "There's enough fuel for a trip like that. Two short trips, maybe." I glanced over my shoulder at her. "One for you, then one for me. We could achieve something great. We could right a wrong."

She folded her arms like she was hugging herself, shaking her head but staring at the machine. "We'd be playing God, changing things that have already happened."

"Or would we be thwarting His will by *not* fixing something that was within our grasp?" Now was my chance. "Isn't there something you'd like to change about the past?"

Melissa glared at me, her eyes filled with fear. "You don't speak for God."

"Neither of us does. What if this was put here for us to use to fix things? To change a terrible situation that had happened to one of us?" I held my breath, assessing her reaction. "What if you could change things—and save her?"

Melissa recoiled in horror. "Don't do that! Don't put me in a position to save my mother's life and not do it!" She fell to her knees. "It's wrong somehow. Haven't the trips showed us that?" She eyed the time machine. "It has brought nothing but bad things into our lives, and you want me to go back and use it on my family?" Tears ran down her face.

"But what if-"

Her words were choked with emotion. "But what if it didn't? What if the drunk driver kills both of them next time? They always jogged together, but Dad stayed behind to take a business call. He would have been with her." She looked up at me. "I could have lost both of them."

Melissa shook her head as tears spilled down her cheeks. "We were all chopping up vegetables, the three of us. To make chili for some big football game. It was our first home cooked meal in the remodeled kitchen." Her voice drifted off. "It had to cook for a long time, like three hours. So they decided to go out for a jog, but the phone rang." She swallowed. "Dad took the call and mom went out jogging by herself. I . . . never saw her again."

I knelt down next to her. "Let me help you see your mother. Then we can talk about maybe helping me. What do you say?" I leaned into her line of sight, making her look at me. "Aren't you curious? Haven't you wanted to try? When we were in Barry's apartment and we were all sitting around talking about time travel, didn't it cross your mind?"

"What if God punishes me for doing something I shouldn't do?"

I sat back. "I think you've been punished enough by losing your mother when you were just a child. Maybe this is a way of getting a second chance. Everybody deserves one."

She burst into tears again. "I'm afraid."

"I know you are."

She stayed there, staring at the mud, unsure of what to do.

"Maybe we could pick someplace safe instead. Just-"

She snorted through her tears. "Safe? Like what? A police station? A meadow full of flowers?"

I smiled. "A place where you don't get beaten up by the Roman guard."

"Or eaten by a T-Rex."

I was relieved at her comment. I was happy to see the raw emotions had passed. My opportunity might present itself yet.

Melissa spoke quietly. "The safest I ever felt in my life was at the beach that day, making sand castles."

"Let's do that. Go there. It's safe." My opportunity was suddenly within reach again. "Give me the location and date. I'll set the coordinates on the time machine by using the truck's GPS."

She shook her head, turning away. "I- I can't. I'd be afraid to . . . ruin it."

I nodded. "Then don't go to the beach. Go to the other place."

CHAPTER THIRTY-SIX

Two papers.
Two destinations.
I sat in the truck looking at what I'd written on pages from a dusty, yellowed notepad. One held the coordinates for Melissa's safe trip, the family outing at the beach.

The other was for the accident that killed her mother.

The happiest and saddest days of her life were separated by two weeks and about twenty miles.

I dropped the pen back into the glove compartment and slammed it shut. As I walked back up the muddy hill, I stuffed the two notes into my pocket—next to a third one, for me. The one I'd written out years ago, for the stock exchange and New York City.

Life is full of difficult choices.

* * * * *

"How about a cold one?"

Carter Garrett glanced up at the clock on the wall. Nearly six o'clock. It would be getting dark soon.

Stupid daylight savings time.

"Thanks, I'll pass."

His brother looked over at him. "You ruined my joke. You're supposed to say 'yes,' and then I'm supposed to say 'grab me one while you're up.'" Bobby craned his neck to see Carter's empty hands. "What, are you not drinking today?"

"I'm drinking." Carter leaned back into the recliner. "I'm just not getting drunk."

"Boys, how are we fixed for beer?" Randy rolled off the couch and went to the refrigerator. Everybody else had been throwing them back pretty hard, but so far Carter had hardly imbibed. It was early, and the big game was coming on, so he was pacing himself. He wanted to stay awake through the whole game even if his friends didn't. Too many of these annual rivalries had come down to a last-minute field goal.

"Carter, we got about twelve beers for the rest of the night. Is that gonna be enough?"

"Twelve?" He sighed. "No, not with the rest of the guys coming over."

Bobby picked up a chicken wing from the foil carry out platter on the coffee table. "Well, why didn't you buy more?"

"Two cases should have been enough." Carter hooked a thumb at Randy "– if you hadn't brought your hollow-leg friend."

Bobby smiled through a mouthful of chicken wing. "You want me to run out and get more?"

"No, I'll do it." Carter got up from the chair. "You've had too much already. I've only had two beers since lunch."

"You sure?"

"I'm sure." He grabbed his keys off the hook. "Be back in a few minutes."

* * * * *

Madison Mills threw the last of the peppers into the big pot and covered it with the lid. She stepped back from the granite counters of her newly remodeled kitchen.

"Okay, Missy." She turned to her daughter, who was engrossed in a teen magazine. "This needs to cook for a while, so don't touch it.'

"Got it." Came the halfhearted reply from the living room sofa.

Maddie bent over, watching the gas flame as she adjusted it. "You're in charge of the kitchen. Keep an eye on that pot." She did a little more fine tuning of the flame, not quite comfortable with it yet.

"Good golly." Her husband reached over and grabbed a handful of her rear end through the shiny black Spandex. He hugged her from behind, whispering. "How am I supposed to go jogging with you looking like that?" He nuzzled her ear.

She grinned. "Like what? This is a t shirt and leggings."

"Yeah, but I know what's underneath—or *not* underneath." He pulled out her waistband. "Oh, boy. Now I really can't run."

She gave him a quick kiss. "There will be plenty of time for that when we get back. Now come on."

"Yeah, yeah."

The phone rang. Melissa jumped on it. Then she voiced her disappointment without looking up. "Dad, it's for you."

He gazed at his wife. "Good thing. I'd get arrested trying to go out like this."

"Okay, well, I'm heading out."

He picked up the extension. "I'll catch up. Which way are you heading?"

"My usual route. Through the S turns."

"Okay." He put the phone to his ear, then cupped his hand over the mouthpiece. "Hey, be careful. That's still under construction and it's getting dark-"

She had already disappeared out the door.

* * * * *

"Carter, you going to Winn Dixie or the 7-11?" Bobby leaned out the door.

"I'm just running up to 7-11." He placed his hand on the roof of his car. "Why?"

"We could use some more wings."

"Winn Dixie doesn't sell wings." Carter opened the door and got inside.

"No, but Hooters is right past it."

He shook his head. "Okay, fine. Call it in." He shut the door and started the engine.

* * * * *

Maddie was an elegant runner. Her long legs took graceful strides as she rounded the driveway and headed into the street. She never liked stretching, preferring instead to just jump right into the run.

Michael, on the other hand, would stretch—which she knew was better—but he took too long. Sometimes she thought he stretched just to postpone the run. But he ran faster than her, so if he didn't goof off too long—and if he didn't talk all day on the phone—he might catch up before she was finished with her two miles.

He fussed too much anyway. Run facing traffic. Wear light colored clothes. Don't wear your Walkman, you can't hear cars coming up behind you. Too many rules. The road was meant to be run on. Cars were always gracious as they passed.

It was her neighborhood. She had been running through it for years. She could do it in her sleep.

The S turns were about halfway through the run. They had been under repair for over a week as contractors redid the sidewalks under some old oak trees. Grand oaks, the city called them, so nobody was allowed to cut them down. Instead, they'd just replace the sidewalks every few years when the trees' roots cracked it all again.

As she weaved her way through the turns, her gray t-shirt began to show signs of sweat. It was still hot out for this time of year. She debated about taking a longer way back. The chili wouldn't be ready for hours, and Michael wouldn't be off the phone for a while if it was business—the only kind of call he ever got. Still, she decided against it, knowing how disappointed he'd be if she went another way and he didn't catch her on his run.

She adjusted her earphones and turned up the volume, bounding off into the setting sun with her favorite tunes blaring.

* * * * *

"Are you ready?"

Melissa looked out at me from the seat of the time machine. "Maybe." She repositioned herself. "Is this going to hurt?"

"Barry said he had to hold his ears, so do that. And when it gets close to going, close your eyes really tight."

She took a deep breath. "Okay. I'm ready."

There were two destinations I had written down for her, but only one had been dialed into the machine. The other went back into my pocket.

"I think you made the right decision." I gave her a thumbs up. "I think if I were you, I'd be doing this trip. It's the right thing to do."

"It better be." She took another deep breath and closed her eyes. "I hope I'm making the right decision."

"Okay, here we go. Lever one."

In the near darkness, I watched as she pushed the first long handle into place with a click.

"Lever two."

I backed up a little, checking around for something I could hide behind. There was nothing.

As she engaged the final gears, the familiar whirring noise began. I covered my ears.

She looked out at me again. She was saying something.

"What?"

"Peeky, I'm scared."

THE NAVIGATORS

"You'll be fine."

The noise grew louder.

"Come with me."

"What?"

"Come with me. Hurry!"

I shook my head. "We've never done that before. And there's no room."

The whirring reached a deafening pitch. Her eyes pleaded with me. She patted her lap. I saw her mouth form the words "Come on."

I only hesitated for a moment. The noise was at its peak. In a second the machine would take its trip.

But my friend needed my help.

So I squeezed into the machine and sat on her lap, grabbing the frame and holding on as tightly as I could.

Then there was a brilliant flash.

* * * * *

The noise of the machine was almost as bad riding in it as it had been when we first tested it. Luckily, being outside, the noise was able to go somewhere instead of bouncing off Barry's apartment walls, so it wasn't as overwhelming.

I lifted myself off of Melissa's lap and climbed out. "Another first. A two person trip." I looked around. "Where are we?"

She stood up. "Oh my gosh, we're right near my house. Look at all this! It's so different. It's all . . . so *new*." She glanced around. "We must have gotten the coordinates wrong a little. My house is a few blocks away. Those are the S turns over there. I forgot they were under construction at the time."

She grabbed my arm. "She should be coming by here any minute. What should I do?"

I patted her hand. "Relax. Just do what we talked about. When you see your mother, call out to her and have her get out of the way of the car. That's all you need to do."

"Okay." Melissa took a deep breath. "Keep your eyes open. She was running in black leggings and a gray t-shirt."

I gazed at the sky. "She better hurry. It's getting dark."

"I'm so nervous. I don't know exactly what time it happened."

"But it happened here? On these turns?"

She pointed. "Right there, under those oak trees. Where they have the flashing construction lights." She inhaled deeply, flinging her hands like she was shaking water from them. "Okay. Okay. I'm ready. I need to go over there."

"Okay. Go. Do you want me to come with you?"

She looked at the S turn. The corners were too sharp to see around in both directions. "No. You stay here and watch for her coming that way."

"Got it."

* * * * *

The smell of spicy wings perfumed the inside of Carter's car in a way that only a hungry man can appreciate. He'd procured more beer and would be back in time for kickoff.

The boys would be happy.

THE NAVIGATORS

Mostly, Carter would be happy. Hooters had been slammed—game day—but Winn Dixie was practically empty. He'd made good time.

Now the excitement of the big game was in the air. He pushed the accelerator a little harder as he neared the S turns.

Accelerate through the turn, baby. Just like on NASCAR.

* * * * *

"Do you see anything?"

Melissa had traveled about a hundred yards toward the S turns. I didn't see anyone, but it was getting dark. People would be harder to see. "Not yet."

"Okay. Keep your eyes open." She walked a little further.

We didn't know if we were early or late, so we didn't know which way to be looking. But we knew a woman would be jogging, and we knew a car would be coming.

The light from the sunset had faded and darkness was approaching. Gray and black would soon be hard to pick out in this light. I squinted past the trees where the yellow construction flashers were. Melissa walked further, peeking around the corner.

I turned back to the other side of the corner. In the distance, an elegant form appeared. It moved in long strides, graceful as a deer.

It was her. Gray t-shirt, black leggings, Walkman. Melissa's mother.

I turned, cupping my hands around my mouth. "Melissa! She's coming."

Melissa's head whipped around. She sprinted toward me.

Melissa's mother moved at a good pace, facing traffic for safety as she ran. I watched her coming from the other side of the road, stepping back into the grass. Melissa would be in time. My heart swelled. A tragedy would be avoided.

Melissa yelled wildly as she ran. She bolted down the middle of road, unable to contain herself.

Lights illuminated the scene behind her. An oncoming car.

Melissa looked down at herself. She was clad in blue jeans and a dark top. She peeked over her shoulder as the car made the turn. She hesitated, slowing as she raised her hands to block the glare of the oncoming headlights.

She was right in the middle of the street.

The headlights jerked suddenly, swerving off the road to avoid her. Melissa threw herself in the other direction, barely avoiding getting hit.

Mrs. Mills moved to get out of the way, but the oncoming vehicle moved faster. The car collided with her, wrapping her body around the grill. Her hands tried to brace her head as it slammed into the hood. Then she bounced away, flying backwards like a toy.

The headlights bounced up and down as Carter Garrett's car hit the base of the grand oak and stopped. He sagged in his seat, unconscious.

Nothing moved for a moment.

Melissa stood up, her hand and knees scraped and bloody from the asphalt. She ran to her mother. "Oh, no, no, no, no!"

THE NAVIGATORS

Mrs. Mills stirred on the tall grass, moaning and writhing in pain.

In the headlights, Melissa gazed into the eyes of her young mother. The oncoming darkness helped hide Melissa's twenty-two-year-old face.

She leaned over Mrs. Mills, not daring to move her. "Mom! Mom. Are you okay? Where are you hurt?"

Her mother tried to look up. "Who . . ." Blood appeared at the corner of her mouth.

Melissa stifled a gasp. "Mom, it's me. Melissa."

Mrs. Mills tried to talk again. "I . . . don't understand." She gasped for air. "My Missy . . . is a little girl. Please . . . Get an ambulance." She whimpered from the pain.

I stood helpless as the tragedy unfolded before me.

Melissa was in tears. "Mom, it's me."

Mrs. Mills blinked. "Why . . . are you calling me that?"

"Mom, please." Melissa took her mother's hand.

Mrs. Mills shook her head, but just barely. She swallowed, holding back the pain. "My husband . . ." She gasped, looking into the sky. "I have a little girl... Please . . . tell my daughter..." She swallowed again. More blood appeared on her mouth.

"Mom, it's me, Melissa. I- I came here to save you. Please, don't go." She glanced around "The ambulance is on the way. Hang on."

I saw a light come on at a nearby house. "Keep talking to her."

Melissa stroked her mother's hand. "Mom, it's me . . . it's Melissa. Try to hold on." She looked into the pained face of her dying mother. "Close your eyes. Just listen. It's Melissa. I'm here, mom."

"Missy?"

"Shh. Close your eyes." She stroked the hand. "I'm so sorry, Mom. I'm so sorry. It's my fault."

Mrs. Mills reached out, touching her daughter's face. "Missy?"

Melissa choked back the tears. "I'm here, Mom."

A faint smile appeared on Mrs. Mills' lips. "Oh, Missy. My Missy girl . . . I love you, baby." She touched her daughter's arms. "A thousand . . ."

Pain consumed her, causing her to twist on the grass. She squeezed her eyes shut, whimpering.

"Mom, you – you've had a shock." Melissa began to sob. She stroked her mother's hair. "There, there, it'll be all right." She swallowed. "Mom, I'm sorry. I know it doesn't make sense to you. I thought I could save you."

"Save . . . me?"

"I was wrong." Melissa leaned over her mother, gently pressing her face to her mother's. "Please, just hang on a little while longer. The ambulance will be here soon. Stay with me. You'll be home soon with me and dad."

Mrs. Mills mustered the strength to shake her head. Her voice was faint. "It's my time. Life had other plans."

"Please mom, stay. Hold on. The ambulance- " She sobbed. "The ambulance will be here soon."

It was no longer convincing. Mrs. Mills summoned her strength to smile as she looked up at her daughter. "Missy. My Missy girl . . ." She reached out and took her daughter's hand, whispering again. "A thousand . . ."

Then the hand released. She was gone.

Melissa buried her head into her mother's hands, sobbing uncontrollably.

In the distance, the machine began to whir.

I stood, afraid to move and afraid to stay. Finally, I ran to the machine, searching desperately for a way to stop it, to give us more time. "Melissa! We have to go!"

The noise grew louder. I knew she would not leave her mother's side.

I sat down at the controls, unsure of what to do. I wanted to push a button and stop the machine from leaving. I wanted to give her more time. "Melissa, you have to come now! There's no way to stop the machine. It will leave without you." I scanned the dials looking for answers. "It's going to leave. You'll be trapped!"

Melissa screamed at me over her shoulder. "It's my fault! I killed her!" Tears streamed down her face.

I twisted the dials frantically as the noise grew louder. "Melissa, we have to leave now!"

Melissa lifted herself and ran toward me. When she reached me, she stopped and put her hands on the machine's frame. She said words I couldn't hear, staring back at the car and the woman in the grass. The tears continued to roll down her face.

I reached up and grabbed her, pulling her limp, sobbing body into the machine.

Then there was a brilliant flash.

I sat there, hugging her, letting her cry, letting her vent her pain. She was inconsolable.

The bright sunlight nearly blinded me as I looked out from the time machine. I closed my eyes, letting my friend bury her face into my shoulder as I rubbed her back. "Shhh. It wasn't your fault. It wasn't your fault."

She finally looked up at me. "Peeky, it was. I caused it all. That car swerved to avoid me. That's why it hit her. She might have survived if I hadn't been there."

I shook my head. "No. You're wrong. Before we ever went, she was . . . she was already gone. She passed away when you were a child. Remember?"

Tears welled in her eyes. "Yes, but . . . Maybe . . ."

"Shh. Don't think that way. It had already happened. You *know* that."

She lowered her head. "I wish I'd never gone. I should have left everything alone. And she wanted to tell me something. 'A thousand.' What did she mean?"

As much as I wanted to help, to ease her pain, I could only shake my head. "I don't know."

She sighed. "I'll never know."

Slowly, the noise of the waves drifted to us. Seagulls squealed in the distance.

Melissa glanced around "What, what is this? Where are we?"

I lifted her off my lap and helped her onto the warm sand. "We wrote down two destinations." I gazed over at a handsome man and his beautiful wife watching their young daughter make a castle in the sand. "This was the other one."

Melissa's hands flew to her mouth. She stood, jaw open, looking at her family on the day she had described as the happiest in her life.

She turned to me. "What did you do?"

"I changed the destination."

She sniffled. "You won't have a trip now."

I shrugged. "I don't need a trip. I need a friend."

She hugged me. "Oh, Peeky."

I wrapped my arms around her, happy to push back the bad memory I'd just help put into her head, temporarily replacing it with this beautiful one. "Hey, you're wasting time. I don't know how long we have here." I looked at her. "Your mother loved you. And right now, just over there, she can show you how much."

Melissa held the frame of the machine with one hand and touched the other to her face. "What should I do?"

"Watch. Enjoy. Remember this moment, not the other one." I nudged her. "Go on, get closer. But not too close."

Melissa smiled, taking a step toward them. Her mother was alive and happy again. I knew it wouldn't quell her pain, but at least for a few minutes it might let her forget. How could it not?

She had been right. Using the machine was a mistake. I understood that now. We weren't able to control things or change them. It was foolish to think we could.

Melissa stood there, watching her young beautiful mother play with her twelve-year-old self. She saw her father, sitting in a beach chair nearby, enjoying his daughter and wife building a sand castle.

The little girl held up a shell.

Her mom leaned over, explaining about how each grain of sand has a story to tell. The twelve-year-old Melissa didn't seem very interested.

Dread shot through me. Had I caused her best memory to be taken from her? Had she remembered it wrong? I looked in horror at Melissa's face.

But she was smiling.

Beaming.

She seemed filled with joy at the sight of her family. They were happy, healthy, young and alive.

Mrs. Mills said something to young Melissa.

Twenty-two-year-old Melissa leaned forward. "What did she say?"

Twelve-year-old Melissa leaned forward. "What did you say?"

Mrs. Mills said it again, louder, grabbing her daughter and squeezing her in a massive bear hug. "If I held you in my arms for a thousand years, it still wouldn't be enough."

The little girl squealed with delight. "How many?"

Her mother rocked her back and forth in her arms. "A thousand!"

Melissa gazed at me. This time, her eyes were filled with tears of joy.

THE NAVIGATORS

A thousand.

"I know this won't make everything right between us, but-"

She put her hand over my mouth. "You did fine."

She sniffled, taking the scene in.

The machine began its whirring again. Melissa slowly moved to sit on my lap. She covered her ears and squinted her eyes, watching as long as she could, savoring the images before they disappeared.

Then she turned to me. The noise was already too loud to hear, but she mouthed the words. "Thank you."

Then there was a brilliant flash.

CHAPTER THIRTY-SEVEN

Florida Mining and Minerals, site number 32 was dark and quiet. The little hill looked out over the pond, waiting in the warm night air.

Melissa and I stood there, our hands on each side of the machine.

It hardly made a splash when it dropped into the water.

Some bubbles made their way to the surface for a few seconds, then the ripples faded from view and the pond was still again.

In some ways, it was as though the machine had never existed.

But it had existed. And its existence had changed things in ways that could never be repaired.

I peered at Melissa as she drove us back to Tampa. "Just like a ten-year-old trying to sneak out with the family station wagon, right?"

"Right. Nothing good could ever come of it."

THE NAVIGATORS

"Can you forgive me? For making you-"

"Peeky, you hurt me a lot this morning and you put me through more tonight. That's going to take a while to get over." She turned to me and smiled. "But you also gave me the greatest gift anyone has ever given me, and that means a lot." She stared at the road. "So let's give everything some time."

I nodded. "I don't have a lot of time left. I have an appointment with your father in a few hours."

"Yeah, I know. I'll drive you." She sniffled. "We'll get donuts."

"Don't start crying again. You'll make me cry."

"I think I'm cried out for one night." She sighed. "How about we listen to some music for a change?"

She turned on the radio. We drove the rest of the way without speaking much, digesting what had happened over the past few hours. We made a few quick stops along the way. One for gas, one for my suitcase.

And one for Barry.

He smiled as we pulled up in front of the hospital. "You didn't think I'd let you leave without saying goodbye, did you?"

The hospital had given him a new pair of crutches to go with his new cast. He balanced uneasily on them.

"You still can't use those things," I said.

"Bah." He chucked them into the truck bed next to my suitcase. "It's easier getting around without them."

"Hey, you use those until you're back to 100%." Melissa frowned. "Doctor's orders."

She climbed into the truck.

Barry nudged me. "She's really getting into that whole bossing people around thing, isn't she?"

"Yeah."

"Kinda hot, huh?"

"Yeah."

We climbed into the truck.

Mr. Mills was waiting outside his office when we walked up. He was smiling, too.

Melissa kissed him. "You're in a good mood this morning." A wry smile crept over her face. "Where's Janice?"

"At the hotel. Get your mind out of the gutter." He straightened his suit jacket. "I got some good overnight polls, that's what I'm smiling about."

She winked. "Uh huh."

"I'd ask how your night went, but I don't think I want to know. You two look a mess." He glanced at Barry. "At least one of you got cleaned up."

A few uniformed officers stepped up to Mr. Mills. "Peeky, these are customs officials. They'll be taking over from here." He stepped back. "If you'd like to take a moment to say your goodbyes, now would be the time."

I looked at my friends. "There isn't enough time to say I'm sorry as many times as I want to, but – I'm sorry. For everything."

Barry nodded. "Peeky, you did some really crappy things. But you did some really great things, too. You helped open my eyes." He gazed at Melissa. "I can't be unhappy about that."

He put his hand out. I shook it.

Melissa looked at me. "I'll never forget what you did."

I stared at my shoes. "Please try."

"You know what I mean." She reached out and hugged me. "You're my friend. I'll miss you."

"There's a saying. 'If you know a man's story, you have heard his confession.'"

She squeezed me tighter. "Okay, then. We know each other's stories pretty good now. That's what makes us friends."

"Peeky, I hate to see this happen to you." Mr. Mills patted me on the shoulder. "It's time to go. But who knows, in six months, maybe a well-placed letter from the new mayor of Tampa will go a long way to helping you come back. Between that and a job waiting for you here, who knows? Chin up, okay?"

"Okay, sir. Thank you."

Melissa looked at her father. "What was that all about? What job?"

"Oh, I've had Troy and some staff members doing some digging. This whole business about requiring people to turn over their fossil finds to the state, it's a bunch of hogwash. It's practically communism." He stroked his chin. "I was thinking it ought to be more like the shipwreck laws, where the person who digs the goodies up gets to keep them, and the state gets a share. That's more fair. It would give people an incentive to go out and spend resources finding these things." A big grin crept over his face. "That could sprout a whole new industry for our fine state. Just the thing a new Governor wants."

Melissa smirked. "You mean mayor."

"Give me time." He straightened his jacket again. "Anyway, Troy made some calls. The legislature would look kindly on revising the state statute. So our office is creating a new wing to create private dig sites around the state." He winked at her. "What do you think? I'll need some smart people to head it up. Any interest?"

Melissa's jaw dropped. "Are you offering me a job running a new department at the law firm? I'm no lawyer."

He waved a hand. "Lawyers, we have. Smart young diggers, we'll need. Will you do it? The person in charge will have to find good people to run dig sites all over the place. I can't do that and be mayor, too."

"I just might be interested." She turned to Barry. "What do you think? Want a job?"

He looked at her. "So, I'd be . . . under you?"

She tilted her head and grinned. "I guess so, yes."

Mr. Mills cleared his throat. "Okay, let's keep this rated G, people."

Barry smiled. "Sounds very interesting. I'll think about it."

"Come on! It would give us a chance to do *what* we love, with *who* we—you know—who we know can do the job."

"I said I'll think about it. Maybe we should have a meeting to discuss it further."

She took his arm. "Maybe we should. My place or yours?"

"Yours. Mine burned down, remember?"

THE NAVIGATORS

Mr. Mills cleared his throat again. "Well if you're going to have a meeting like *that*, I just have one thing to ask. Melissa, do you have a- "

"Daddy!"

"- umbrella? It looks like rain."

"Let's go return Mandy's truck before he changes his mind."

"Mandy's truck? Where's my BMW?"

She slipped her arm into Barry's and started walking. "Goodbye, Daddy. I mean *boss*."

"Okay, sounds like you've accepted the job. Here's a new cell phone." He tossed it to her. "Business calls only." He turned to me. "See that, Peeky? Get things straightened out and come back as soon as you can. Here's my card. You call me and we'll help arrange everything. Maybe you'll be back in less than six months."

"Thank you, sir. I don't know what to say."

"Say the truth." He wagged his finger at me. "From now on. It'll be a job requirement."

"Deal."

* * * * *

In his office, Mr. Mills took out a cell phone and dialed it. Melissa answered on the other end.

"So, Missy, did you dump it?"

"Just like you said to, in the pond."

He bristled. "I said a swamp. Doesn't matter, it's gone now."

"What will you do about the lawsuits?"

"Oh, I'll handle it. It's hard to sue over something that doesn't even exist. For all they know this was all an elaborate hoax by some rowdy graduate students."

"Sounds good to me." She sighed. "Dad, there's something I've been needing to ask you."

"Fire away."

"Well, if you could go back in time and change things, would you?"

"It doesn't really matter, honey. We can't."

"But what if we could? What if I was able to go back in time . . . and save Mom?"

"But sweetheart, you couldn't. As painful as it is for me to say this, the night your mother passed away was the night she was supposed to. I've thought about a million things I could have done differently, blaming myself that I didn't go jogging with her. That's not how it works. It's just the plan of life. A big part of me will always wish it would have turned out some other way, but life . . . had other plans."

Melissa held back her tears. "But I had a time machine. I did go back. What if I went back in time and I caused it—her death?"

"I think you're misunderstanding me. You can't cause it just like you can't uncause it. Things happened a certain way. Going back and trying to interfere with them might add a new variable, but it could never change the outcome." He sat back in his chair. "Sometimes I think you science types get everything backwards. You have to understand that there is something greater than yourself at work in life. Have a little faith."

"Faith." She sighed again. "In God? Sometimes I don't know if God even exists."

"It's the not knowing that requires faith. But I know God exists—because I have you. Nothing will ever convince me that your beautiful face and energetic spirit are some sort of grand accident. I look at you and I see something divine was at work. I just can't explain it."

"I guess I don't understand."

"If it was easy to understand, philosophers wouldn't still be debating the first questions two thousand years later. Did you have to know everything about that machine in order to use it? No, you went on faith. Give yourself some credit."

"Okay, I'll try. Thanks, Daddy."

"Bye bye, sweetie."

* * * * *

Findlay sat alone in his apartment waiting as the phone number he dialed connected.

"Findlay. How's it hanging?"

"Just great. Looks like I'm going to jail."

"Whoa, you broke your cherry? Welcome to the party, pal."

"Yeah, you could have reminded me that all you MIT jerks went to jail after you got busted in your Vegas card counting scheme."

"Hey, caveat emptor, pal. *Buyer* beware. Besides, it was practically common knowledge. So what's up? Why are you calling me now?"

"Well, come to find out, your tracker never really did its thing. I mean, I peeled off the tape and stuck it onto the bottom of the time machine, but my computer never did receive a signal."

"You found the time machine, didn't you?"

"Not because of you. The tracker never transmitted."

"What do you want, a refund? Because there's no refunds on illegal stuff, dummy. Run a diagnostics test. Maybe it'll sync up with the tracker."

"I shut my computer down already. I have to pack everything up. I'm going to jail. My arraignment's in two days."

"Yeah, they move fast on that hacker crap. Hope you have a good lawyer. Wait, you said you peeled off the tape?"

"That's right."

"*One* piece of tape?"

"Right. Peeled it off and stuck the tracker on the underside of the time machine."

"You didn't do it right. There were *two* pieces of tape to remove."

"What do you mean?"

"One to make it stick, and the other to uncover and activate the tracker's transmitter. No wonder it never pinged your computer. You left it covered. It never activated."

"So what happens now?"

"Nothing. It won't transmit while that thing's on there. I mean, it might fall off in a year, or if it got wet enough the tape might come off or something. The paper tape would break down in the elements, but if it gets wet, the device is going to corrode pretty quickly, too. That stuff isn't made to last forever."

"Crap!"

"Calm down. Maybe it'll get wet."

"Yeah, maybe." He hung up the phone. "Jerk."

* * * * *

At the bottom of a pond at Florida Mining and Minerals site number 32, stuck to the underside of the time machine, was a paper-covered tracking device.

The spillway waters were notoriously corrosive. They soaked through the tape and into the device in a few hours.

Before the minerals ruined the sensor completely, they dissolved the paper enough to send a ping out.

To Findlay's computer.

Which he had just shut down.

THE END

Note to Readers

If you have the time, I would deeply appreciate a review on Amazon or Goodreads. I learn a great deal from them, and I'm always grateful for any encouragement. Reviews are a very big deal and help authors like me to sell a few more books. Every review matters, even if it's only a few words.

Thanks,
Dan Alatorre

ABOUT THE AUTHOR

International bestselling author Dan Alatorre has published more than two dozen titles, has been translated into 12 languages, and is read in more than 120 countries around the world.

You'll find edge-of-your-seat action in the murder mystery *Double Blind*, a gripping paranormal roller coaster ride in *An Angel On Her Shoulder*, and heartwarming and humorous anecdotes about parenting in the popular *Savvy Stories* series. Dan's knack for surprising audiences and making you laugh or cry – sometimes on the same page - has been enjoyed by audiences around the world.

And you are guaranteed to get a page turner every time.

"That's my style," Dan says. "Grab you on page one and then send you on a roller coaster ride, regardless of the story or genre."

Readers agree, making his string of #1 bestsellers popular across the globe.

Regardless of genre, his novels always contain unexpected twists and turns, and his endearing nonfiction stories will stay in your heart forever.

He has also written illustrated children's books, as well as stories for young readers, and his dedication to helping authors of any skill level is evident in his wildly popular blog "Dan Alatorre - AUTHOR" at DanAlatorre.com

In addition to being a bestselling author, Dan achieved President's Circle with two different Fortune 500 companies. He mentors grade school children in his Young Authors Club and adults in his Private Critique Group, helping struggling authors find their voice and get published.

Dan resides in the Tampa, Florida area with his wife and daughter.

Made in the USA
Columbia, SC
16 October 2024